A Game of Deception

THE SCOTTISH BILLIONAIRES

M. S. PARKER

BELMONTE PUBLISHING, LLC

CHAPTER

One

XANDER

THE CHAMPAGNE BUBBLES TICKLED my nose, tiny explosions of overpriced bubbles that did absolutely nothing to dull the edge. Three glasses in and still painfully sober. Still painfully me.

"Christ, you're not going to believe this shite." Leo's face was pressed against the Gulfstream's window, his breath fogging the glass like an excited kid on Christmas morning. "Look at those beaches. Look at the water. Miami's going to be bloody brilliant."

I lowered my drink. "You said the same thing about London."

"London was cold and full of stuck-up models." He turned to me, blue eyes bright. "Miami is different. It's paradise."

Paradise. Right.

Leo's phone buzzed. "Mystery billionaire buys expansion team, immediately drops twenty million on Scottish bad boy..." he read, scrolling through what looked like ESPN. "They're really leaning into that angle."

Bad boy. The label clung to me like tar. Maybe not without reason: Five months ago, some dickhead with a press badge ambushed me outside the bar in Chelsea, jammed his phone in my face and talked shit about my family. A scandal about my twin brother, Sean McCrae, getting mixed up with a Scottish socialite. I told him to fuck off with his lies—Sean would've called me if he was even in the country. But this press asshole just wouldn't quit. He kept pushing and pushing until—bam —I decked him. What else was I supposed to do?

Unfortunately, a photographer documented the entire showdown.

The pictures made me look like a complete jackass, plastered all over the news and gossip sites, and just like that, my Chelsea career went straight into the gutter. Banished to the reserves like some rookie fuck-up, I needed an escape hatch. Then thirty days ago, this absurdly fat offer from Miami appeared out of nowhere. Too perfect, too convenient, but hey —new continent, clean slate, and all that bullshit.

"They still won't say who's financing the team," Leo said. "Some oil tycoon probably. Somebody who thinks football is played with their hands."

"As long as the checks clear and they keep me away from California," I said, my tone deliberately casual despite the sudden tightness in my chest.

Leo didn't notice the change. He never did. That was why I kept him around as my assistant—that and the fact that he was the only person who'd stuck by me demanding nothing but proximity to the mess that was my life.

"Another?" He gestured to my empty glass.

"Why not?" It wasn't like I had anywhere important to be.

Just a new team. A new city. A new place to disappoint people who expected the eighteen-year-old wonder kid I once was instead of the burnout adult I'd become.

The flight attendant—Melanie, probably—swooped in with another champagne, flashing a smile that could outshine the Miami sun. Unlike most airplane staff who blend into the cabin walls, this one wanted to be noticed.

"Fresh drink for Mr. McCrae," she announced, leaning close enough that her citrus-flower perfume hit my nostrils. "Getting the Miami party started early?"

My autopilot charm kicked in without permission. "You could say that," I replied, my face arranging itself into a practiced half-grin. "Or just making this flight more bearable."

Her blue eyes locked onto mine for one Mississippi too many. "If you need any other... comforts during your journey, just flag me down." Her fingers grazed my arm while setting down the glass—a move straight out of the "I'm interested" playbook.

"Noted," I said between sips, throwing her a wink. Just my default setting with hot women who showed interest. No effort required. No thought needed. Just what I do.

She turned with a promising look, hips doing that calculated rhythm down the aisle. I tracked her exit, my brain already running its tired program: grab number, hotel bar meetup, lose myself for a night between expensive sheets and unfamiliar perfume.

I cut my stare short, pivoting from the aisle to face the window. Miami's coastline approached—a dazzling ribbon of white and turquoise that supposedly represented my do-over. The whole point of this transfer, the one vow I'd made to myself after I'd torched my Chelsea career, was to knock off the bullshit. To pump the brakes. No more 3 AM "Leo, I'm in trouble" phone calls, no more mornings where my skull felt like someone took a hammer to it while shame crashed over me in waves. This was my shot to dominate on the field.

Beyond the glass, Miami stretched out like a billboard for second chances. White buildings, turquoise water, palm trees dancing in what had to be a breeze warm enough to make you forget your mistakes.

I remembered my last Florida trip. A high school tournament when I was sixteen. Jimmy stood right beside me. We'd crushed it. Just a year before everything exploded in our faces.

That memory stuck. Jimmy's victory-red face. His arm draped across my shoulders. That trophy weighing down our hands. The moment he locked eyes with me: "We're unstoppable, man. Fucking unstoppable."

But reality check—we weren't. Just dumb teenagers who thought death and consequences were for other people.

I finished half of the champagne in one gulp.

"...and there's this club on South Beach that has underwater speakers, so you can feel the bass while you're in the pool," Leo was saying, still scrolling through his phone. "And during Art Basel, they have these parties where everyone's basically naked but covered in body paint. And the Brazilian models, bro. They do yoga on the beach at sunrise."

"Sounds great," I said, with little interest. "We should check it out."

Leo beamed, satisfied with my response. "Hell yeah, we should. Miami's going to be epic."

The captain's voice crackled over the intercom, announcing our descent into Miami International. Leo buckled his seatbelt without pausing his monologue about South Beach nightlife. I finished my drink and handed the empty glass to Melanie, who took it with another seductive smile.

Miami, forty-five hundred miles from Palo Alto—from the ghost of Jimmy. A different coast. A different climate. A different life.

It should have felt like enough distance.

For some strange reason, it didn't.

———

The penthouse the team had provided us was obscene. Floor-to-ceiling windows offered a view of water so blue it looked artificial. The furniture was all cream leather and glass, the stuff that showed every fingerprint, every stain. Not exactly practical for someone who spends half his time covered in grass and mud, but I supposed that was what cleaning services were for.

Leo whistled as he wandered through the open-concept living area. "They're not fuckin' around, are they?"

"Guess not."

The Miami heat nearly knocked me over as I walked onto the balcony.

Below me, thirty floors down, cars crawled along the streets like brightly colored insects. People moved in and out of shops, restaurants, and office buildings. Normal people with normal lives, untouched by the guilt that had shaped mine.

"Mate, come and look at all this booze!"

I followed Leo's voice to one of the giant bedrooms. King-sized bed, more windows, another balcony. A bathroom bigger than my first apartment in Glasgow.

"Check out the welcome basket." Leo gestured to a ridiculous arrangement on the dresser—a giant wicker basket wrapped in cellophane and tied with a navy blue ribbon in the team's colors.

I approached it warily, half-fearing to find a severed horse's head. But it was just expensive booze—Dom Perignon, Macallan 18, Grey Goose—along with some fancy snacks and...

"Is that Throat Coat tea?" I grabbed the distinctive yellow box, turning it over in my hands.

"What's Throat Coat tea?" Leo asked, already opening the Macallan.

"It's this herbal tea I started drinking after my voice cracked during that post-game interview in Glasgow seven years ago. The one where I sounded like I was going through puberty again."

"Aye, I remember that. That was fuckin' brilliant."

I wasn't laughing. That specific brand—not something you'd guess at. It wasn't something you'd include in a standard welcome basket, unless you were welcoming a singer, or motivational speaker like Sean.

Someone knew me. Someone had been studying me.

"Weird coincidence," Leo said, pouring himself a generous measure of scotch.

But I didn't believe in coincidences. Not anymore.

My phone buzzed in my pocket. Unknown Miami number. A text: *Welcome home, Xander.*

My eyes were fixed on the screen, and goose bumps prickled my skin.

Miami wasn't home. Palo Alto had been home. Glasgow and then Chelsea were my exiles. Miami was just a big paycheck.

"You look like someone just pissed in your cornflakes," Leo said, scotch sloshing in his glass. "What is it? A ghost pop out of your phone or something?"

Maybe it fucking did. But I just mumbled, "Just the jet lag making me tired."

"It's only a five-hour time difference, you daft git."

"I'm old. My body's betraying me at every turn."

Leo snorted. "You're twenty-nine, not collecting Social Security. Have a drink, mate. We've got that team thing tonight."

Right. The team event. Some fancy party at the owner's mansion, where I'd meet my new teammates, coaching staff, and the rich clown who'd decided I was worth twenty million despite my game going to shit lately.

"What time is that again?"

"Eight. The car is picking us up at seven-thirty." Leo sipped his scotch. "You've got an hour. Plenty of time to settle in."

I nodded, still reading the text message.

Welcome home, Xander.

Who the fuck would send that? Who even had my number?

The team, obviously. Management. PR. But something about the wording—*home*—turned my blood cold.

I didn't delete the message.

"I'm going to shower," I said, heading for the bathroom.

I closed the door before he answered, slumped against it, and let out a breath. This bathroom was ridiculous—marble and chrome everywhere, a rainfall shower big enough for the entire starting lineup, and a tub that could host a water polo match.

Just another luxury space wasted on my undeserving ass.

The mirror didn't lie. I looked like complete garbage—a human dumpster fire running on empty, held together with duct tape and bullshit.

I cranked the shower until it was practically boiling,

turning my skin lobster-red and making my muscles throb in that weird, not-quite-pain way.

I stood there cooking myself until I felt somewhat like a person again. When I stepped out into the fog, I found the suit Leo had picked out. Tom Ford. Black on black. Not an outfit—a goddamn shield. By the time I buttoned up, my "couldn't-give-less-of-a-fuck" face was locked and loaded.

Leo was waiting by the door. "Car's downstairs," he said, giving my suit an approving nod.

I straightened my cuffs, the motion feeling strangely final. "Good. Let's go meet the rich motherfucker who bought me for twenty million."

————

The house—mansion, really—was precisely the over-the-top display of wealth I'd expected. Mediterranean-inspired architecture, a circular driveway lined with palm trees, valets in crisp uniforms taking keys from guests who arrived in luxurious cars.

Our driver pulled up to the entrance, and Leo bounced out of the car. "Are ye ready to meet the man who built a whole team just tae sign ye?"

"Can't wait," I said, my tone flat.

The foyer was marble and gold, a chandelier the size of my first car hanging from a ceiling at least twenty feet high. Staff in black and white circulated with trays of champagne and canapés. A string quartet played something classical in one corner. The whole thing screamed new money trying very hard to look like old money.

I grabbed champagne from a server and checked out the

crowd. A parade of power players—MLS bigwigs, politicians, C-list celebrities, and every soccer VIP with a pulse, all crammed in to witness this franchise's big, expensive birth.

"That's Diego Mano," Leo pointed to a tall guy wearing what looked like a designer suit that fit him like a trash bag. "Columbian striker. They brought him over a few months ago. Word from trainin' is he's a right hothead with a massive ego, but the lad can play. He's been outperforming everyone."

I knew the type. Talented but a total ball hog, the type of player who'd rather blast it into row Z than pass to an open teammate. Mano caught me staring and lifted his glass, a smug smirk on his face. I did the same, mentally preparing for the dick-measuring contest that was definitely on the horizon.

"And there's Ben Carter," Leo pointed to some baby-faced kid chatting up a reporter. "Last year's number one draft pick."

"Anyone else I need to fake interest in?" I asked, gulping my champagne.

"The entire roster, and—"

The screech of microphone feedback shut him up. Everyone went quiet as the MLS commissioner waddled up to a podium.

"Ladies and gentlemen, welcome!" the Commissioner said. "For years, one man has pursued a singular vision: to bring another world-class soccer team to the heart of Miami. Tonight, that dream becomes a reality. It is my distinct honor to celebrate the official launch of Miami's new MLS franchise, the Miami Pirates FC!"

The room exploded with applause. Miami's mayor stood up front, pumping the senator's hand, both grinning like they'd won the lottery. This wasn't a party—it was a goddamn coronation built on cash mountains and ego. And I was the priciest bauble in their collection. I focused on my champagne bubbles, the only thing not screaming for attention.

"And now, the man who bankrolled it all," the Commissioner bellowed. "Please welcome your team owner, Hank Swanson, and the team's new head of sports medicine, Dr. Tara Swanson!"

My glass didn't drop—it fucking detonated with glass chunks stabbing into my palm, blood and champagne creating a modern art piece on the marble.

"Shite, Xander, you alright?" Leo jumped in, snatching napkins, jamming them against my bleeding hand.

But I couldn't hear him over the roaring in my ears. Couldn't feel the pain in my hand. Couldn't focus on anything but the two figures now standing at the podium.

Hank Swanson. Older, grayer, but those eyes—those cold, accusing eyes—were exactly the same as they'd been twelve years ago at his son's funeral.

And beside him...

Fuck.

Tara.

Not sixteen-year-old Tara with braces and tears at a funeral.

Twenty-eight-year-old Tara in a dress that was professional but also absolutely not, with Jimmy's eyes and Jimmy's stubborn jaw but also curves that made my mouth go dry and my cock shamefully hard.

She was looking right at me; her expression perfectly composed despite the scene I was making. And her eyes. Her eyes said: *Gotcha.*

The room came back into focus slowly, sound filtering in past the rushing in my ears. Leo was still fussing over my hand. A server had appeared with a dustpan and brush for the broken glass. People were staring, whispering.

And then Hank was walking toward me, his steps deliberate, as if he were an executioner approaching the block.

"Xander McCrae," he said, loud enough for everyone nearby to hear. "Welcome to Miami."

He glanced down at my bleeding hand, his expression unreadable. "Someone get a first aid kit," he called over his shoulder. "Dr. Swanson, perhaps you could assist?"

Tara grabbed my bloody hand.

"We need to wash this out," she said, her voice deeper than memory served. "Could have glass bits stuck in there."

I gaped at her, brain short-circuiting as I tried to connect this grown woman to the teenager from twelve years back. The teenager I'd nearly...

The cemetery was quiet except for the soft sound of sobbing. Tara in the black dress that was too big for her stood across from me, Jimmy's coffin between us like a barrier.

I found her alone behind the church afterward, her face streaked with tears, her thin shoulders shaking. I didn't know what to say, what to do. I just knew I couldn't leave her alone.

"Tara," I said, and she looked up at me. And for one insane second, one grief-drunk, pain-filled second, I almost kissed her...

"Mr. McCrae?" Tara's voice cut through my thoughts, all business and ice-cold distance. "If you'll follow me, we can get this taken care of."

I nodded, my mouth suddenly useless. Leo moved to tag along, but Hank blocked him.

"I'm sure your friend is in good hands with Dr. Swanson," he said. "Why don't you tell me about your first impressions of Miami?"

Leo froze, his eyes finding mine for direction. I gave him the tiniest nod. *I'm fine. Go.*

He surrendered to Hank's guidance, throwing worried

looks over his shoulder as he went. I trailed behind Tara through the crowd, feeling every damn eyeball in the room drilling into my back.

She brought me to a small study off the main foyer, shutting the door with a click that might as well have been a prison cell locking. The whole place reeked of dusty books and unspoken accusations.

"Sit," she said, gesturing to a leather armchair.

I obeyed, dropping into the chair while she dug through a desk drawer and pulled out a first aid kit. She snapped on latex gloves, then kneeled in front of me and took my bleeding hand.

"This might hurt," she said, finally looking me in the eye.

"I've had worse," I said, my voice coming out like I'd gargled gravel.

Her mouth twitched with what might've been a smile—gone so fast I questioned if I'd seen it at all. "I'm sure you have."

She started cleaning the cut with antiseptic wipes. Her touch was gentle, but as the alcohol bit into my open wound, I flinched.

"Sorry," she said, not sounding remotely apologetic.

I couldn't help staring at her while she worked. Everything about her had blossomed with age—no more braces, just perfect teeth. Her hair stopped at her shoulders now instead of flowing down her back. But those eyes hadn't changed a bit. Same shade as Jimmy's.

"There's a piece of glass," she announced, picking up tweezers. "This is gonna sting."

I nodded and braced myself. She leaned over my hand, focused entirely on her task. The scent of vanilla drifted from her skin—subtle but unmistakable.

The tweezers dug into my cut, and I sucked air through my teeth.

"Almost got it," she said, her voice unexpectedly soft. "There."

She held up a bloody glass shard like a trophy before dropping it into a dish and returning to clean my wound.

"So," I said. "Sports medicine."

"Yes." She kept her eyes on my hand. "I've been on staff for three months, getting everything ready for the launch."

"And your father bought the team."

That got me a quick look, amusement flashing in her eyes. "He didn't buy it, Mr. McCrae. He created it."

The correction dangled between us, and my jaw clenched. "Quite a coincidence," I said. "Me being hunted for this team. Not to mention becoming available at the exact moment your father was completing his roster."

She dabbed antiseptic cream on the cut, her touch businesslike, completely unbothered by my accusation. "I don't believe in coincidences, Mr. McCrae."

Neither did I.

She wrapped gauze around my hand, taping it with mechanical efficiency. Her fingers burned hot against my skin.

"So," I said. "How long have you known?" I blurted out the question that'd been stuck in my throat since I spotted her at that podium.

"Known what?" Her voice played innocent, but when her eyes locked on mine, they told a completely different story.

"That I was coming to Miami."

She finished my bandage and rocked back, stripping off her gloves. "About as long as you have, I imagine."

"Bullshit."

A tiny smile crept across her face. "Keep this clean and dry. New bandage every day."

She stood, collecting the first aid supplies while turning her back on me. I pushed myself up from the chair.

"Why?" I demanded. I wasn't letting her off the hook that easily.

She spun around, face blank. But her eyes held something I couldn't decode.

"Why what, Mr. McCrae?"

"Why am I here? Why are *you* here? Why did your father create this team?"

She dropped the first-aid kit on the desk. "Why am *I* here? This is my home, Mr. McCrae. My dad moved us from California right after the funeral. I finished high school here, got my doctorate at U-Miami."

She took a breath, letting that bomb detonate before switching back to Dr. Professional. "So, I'm here because I'm the best at my job, and my father created the team because he loves football. And you're here because you've got talent. That's all."

Total bullshit answer. Maybe she spent half her life in this humidity hell, but that changed exactly dick.

"Twelve years," I growled. "Twelve years, and now we're all magically on the same team. That's not random, and it's not about scoring goals."

She moved closer, near enough that I spotted tiny freckles scattered across her nose.

"What do you think it's about, then?" She whispered so quietly I had to lean in.

Before I could answer, the door opened, and Hank Swanson stepped into the room. He glanced between us, his eyes narrowing, sizing up the situation.

"Everything alright in here?" he asked, his tone pleasant but his eyes cold.

Tara stepped back. "Just finishing up, Dad. Mr. McCrae should be fine, but he'll need to keep the wound clean and change the bandage daily."

Hank nodded, his gaze shifting to me. "Ugly gash," he said. "Accidents happen though, right, Xander? Especially when booze enters the picture."

The words were innocent enough, but the implied meaning was clear. A reference to that night and Jimmy.

I met his gaze steadily. "I'd better get back to the party."

He stepped aside, gesturing for me to precede him out of the study. As I passed him, he added, "I hope your hand heals quickly. We have a lot of work to do, you and I."

I didn't respond, didn't trust myself to. Instead, I walked back into the crowd, searching for Leo, for a drink, for anything that might anchor me in this surreal reality I'd stepped into.

CHAPTER

Two

TARA

MUCH EARLIER THE SAME DAY...

The steady rhythm of my feet against the pavement at 5:03 AM was a kind of peace to my soul. One-two, one-two, each impact sending a satisfying jolt up my calves. Miami Beach was still sleeping, just the occasional early-morning jogger and the homeless guys who recognized me now with sleepy nods.

I'd been running this exact route every morning for the past month. Not because I was a creature of habit, though I was. Not because the sunrise over the Atlantic was spectacular, though it was. I'd been running it because the route passed the row of luxury penthouses where the team housed some of its VIP players.

My earbuds were not playing music. Instead, a British sports commentator's voice filled my head: "McCrae was never a fit for Chelsea. He's always been Miami's type of player—flash, style, a bit of danger."

Danger. If they only knew.

"—and as I expected, sources at Chelsea say the management isn't heartbroken to see him go. Too many late nights, too many missed practices. Talent can only take you so far when your lifestyle's working against you—"

I rounded the corner, slowing as I approached the glass-fronted building where the team had three penthouse suites reserved. One of them would be his later today.

My eyes darted to the top floors. Empty for now. But soon… tonight.

I kicked it up a notch, focusing on not dying. In through the nose, out through the mouth. Steady. Controlled. The exact opposite of how I'd been since the day Xander left Palo Alto.

The rest of my five-mile run went by in a haze. I knew Leo Martin would be glued to his side—his babysitter for the past decade, the only person who hadn't jumped ship from the shit-show of Xander McCrae.

I knew every detail about him that Google and gossip could provide without actually breathing the same air. And tonight, finally, that would change.

Back in my apartment, I stuck to my morning ritual of showering with my stupidly expensive Chloé vanilla and jasmine shampoo. Why that specific one? Because twelve years ago, a seventeen-year-old soccer prodigy casually mentioned he dug some random girl's vanilla scent. Pathetic? Absolutely. I remembered everything he'd ever said to me. Every. Single. Word.

I wrapped myself in a plush towel and padded to my bedroom, where three dresses lay arranged on my king-sized bed. The black one: sophisticated, serious, a statement that I was a professional to be reckoned with. The navy blue: team colors, showing my allegiance, my father's daughter through and through. And then the deep emerald one: the exact shade of Xander's eyes.

My phone buzzed on the nightstand.

Dad: *"Car will pick you up at 6 PM. Remember, you're representing the organization tonight."*

I stared at the message, my wet hair dripping onto the screen. Was it a warning or just logistics? With my father, you never knew.

I typed back: *"I'll be ready."* Simple. Noncommittal. The perfect daughter response.

I opened the charter flight app. It confirmed Xander's plane had touched down right on schedule. The team's car service had probably collected him already. Xander was now breathing the same Miami air as I was. I hammered out a quick "welcome home" text and fired it off to his number. Because of course I had his number. What kind of obsessed stalker would I be if I didn't?

I set my phone down and looked again at the three dresses. I'd decide later. Right now, I had to get to work.

———

For the past three months, I'd basically lived in the sports medicine wing at the training facility. Top-shelf equipment, twelve staff members I'd handpicked myself, and the unspoken power that comes with being brilliant at my job— oh, and Daddy owning the team.

I flipped through injury reports at my desk, making notes on treatment plans for two midfielders with minor hamstring strains and a goalkeeper recovering from wrist surgery. This wasn't pretense; I genuinely cared about these athletes and their recovery. My obsession with Xander had never been at the expense of my professional integrity. It had simply been the engine driving it.

There was a knock at my door.

"Dr. Swanson?" My assistant, Lauren, stood there with a stack of manila folders. Forty-ish, divorced, with the efficient manner of someone who'd spent decades making other people look good. I'd hired her precisely because she wasn't young or pretty or interested in football players. She was interested in organization and discretion.

"The new player files arrived," she said. "Should I distribute them to the team, or—"

"I'll handle them myself." I kept my voice neutral, even as my heart rate ticked up.

She set the stack on my desk without comment. Lauren never asked questions, which was another reason she was perfect.

When the door closed behind her, I waited thirty seconds— counting them in my head—before reaching for the files. These were the final player acquisitions for this transfer window. I flipped through them until I found the one with Chelsea's seal.

Xander McCrae. DOB: 29/05/1994. Height: 6'3". Weight: 84 kg.

I opened it with steady hands, the steadiness that comes from actively telling your muscles not to shake. The medical history was extensive. Football at that level took its toll. Old ankle sprain from his Glasgow days. Hyper extended knee three years ago. Broken finger from what was listed as "training incident" but what I knew from news reports was actually a bar fight in London.

And then, in the more recent notes: "Patient reports stress-related insomnia following a personal matter. Sleep aid prescribed: Ambien, 10mg PRN."

Personal matter? What are you hiding, Xander?

I chose the emerald dress.

Not because it matched his eyes—though it did, perfectly—but because it was a weapon. The cut was standard, but the fabric stuck to my curves like it had something to prove—a dress that makes a man forget his own name.

My father's car arrived promptly at 6 PM. The driver—Lenny, who'd worked for my father since before I was born—gave me an approving nod as I slid into the back seat.

"You look lovely, Miss Tara."

"Thank you, Lenny." I smoothed the dress over my thighs, my hands betraying none of my anxiety. "Is my father already at the house?"

"Yes, miss. He's been there since four overseeing the preparations."

Of course, he had. Hank Swanson left nothing to chance, especially not tonight. This was the culmination of... what? That was the question that had been gnawing at me for over two years, since he'd first mentioned his interest in creating the team. What exactly was my father's endgame here?

The car pulled up to Dad's waterfront mansion, where valets in team colors were already parking guests' cars. I froze with my finger on the doorknob.

"Lenny," I said, "has my father been acting... weird lately?"

Lenny's eyes caught mine in the rearview. "Weird how, miss?"

"I don't know. All detached and intense."

Lenny was silent for a moment. "Your father has always been a man who plays the long game, Miss Tara. Perhaps he's simply seeing a plan come to fruition."

Perhaps. I nodded, gathered my clutch, and stepped out of the car.

The house was already filling with guests—team executives, coaching staff, local celebrities, and players. I didn't immediately scan the place for Xander. That would be too obvious, too eager. Instead, I worked the room, shaking hands, making small talk, being the poised, professional daughter Hank Swanson expected.

But I was hyperaware, every nerve ending attuned to the entrance. Every tall, dark-haired figure in my peripheral vision made my pulse spike. I'd been waiting twelve years, but I could hardly wait another twenty minutes.

As I was discussing rehabilitation protocols with the assistant coach, I felt a shift in the air, a prickle at the back of my neck. I didn't turn around. I didn't need to. I knew he was here.

"Excuse me," I said to the coach. "I need to check in with my father before the announcements."

I made my way toward the back of the room.

My father stood near the small podium that had been set up, talking with the team's PR director. He looked up as I approached, his eyes taking in the emerald dress with a flicker of concern.

"Tara." He kissed my cheek, the gesture perfunctory. "Right on time."

"Always." I smiled. "Is everything ready?"

"Just about." He dismissed the PR director with a nod and turned to me fully. "You remember what we discussed?"

"Of course." Though we hadn't discussed much, really. Just that I was to be polished and represent the organization well.

"Good." He squeezed my arm, a rare physical gesture. "This is an important night for both of us."

The PR director was back, signaling that it was time for the announcements.

My father moved to the podium, and I took my place slightly behind him, my eyes searching the room as he welcomed the guests. And then—there. By the bar. Dark hair, green eyes, wide shoulders in a black suit. Xander, with a man I assumed was Leo next to him, whispering something in his ear.

My breath caught. All the photographs and video clips hadn't prepared me for the reality of him. He was broader than he'd been at seventeen, his jawline sharper, his eyes—even from across the room—harder. But it was him. The boy who'd haunted me for over a decade, now a man standing twenty feet away.

He hadn't seen me yet. He was looking down at his champagne glass, nodding absently at whatever Leo was saying.

"And now," the Club President's voice cut through my fixation, "the moment you've all been waiting for. Please welcome your new team owner, Hank Swanson, and our new head of sports medicine, Dr. Tara Swanson!"

I stepped forward, my smile firmly in place. And that's when Xander looked up.

Our eyes locked across the room, and the champagne glass shattered.

Leo was immediately at his side with napkins, tending to his hand. But Xander wasn't looking at Leo. He was looking at me, his face a study in shock.

My father was already moving toward Xander. He glanced down at Xander's hand and called for me to assist.

I took Xander to my father's study, and as I began cleaning the wound, my mind flashed back to that day at the cemetery.

The world felt like it was stuffed with cotton, all sound muffled except for my own hiccupping sobs. He found me later, hiding behind the church. His strong shoulders were shaking; I'd never seen him cry before. My arms moved around his neck, a desperate attempt to hold together the pieces of my shattered world. I whispered his name, and he looked down at me, his eyes so green, like moss after it rains. He leaned in, and I felt his breath on my cheek. He was going to kiss me, and for one impossible second, I thought maybe the world wouldn't feel so broken for us anymore. But then he flinched back as if I'd burned him. "I'm sorry, I can't—you're Jimmy's sister."

A month later, he was gone, but that almost-kiss remained, seared into my brain.

"There's a piece of glass," I said, snapping back to reality. I grabbed the tweezers. Leaning over his hand, I tried to ignore the scent of his cologne as I extracted the shard.

I wrapped up my first-aid treatment quickly before the door swung open. Dad. He surveyed us—the closeness, the electric current between us—his eyes missing nothing.

"Everything alright in here?" he asked.

"All done, Dad," I said, my tone all business. "Mr. McCrae's good to go, just needs to keep that cut clean".

My father's gaze shifted to Xander. "Ugly gash," he said, the words dripping with unspoken meaning. "Accidents happen though, right, Xander? Especially when booze enters the picture."

I watched Xander's face tighten, a flicker of pain crossing his features before being replaced by a mask of indifference. My father clapped him on the shoulder with forced camaraderie and ushered him out, leaving me alone in the quiet study.

Daddy was up to something, no doubt. I couldn't pinpoint his exact game plan, but my gut screamed that we'd barely scratched the surface of whatever twisted plot was unfolding.

CHAPTER
Three

XANDER

I HADN'T SLEPT. Not even close.

I'd spent the entire night on the penthouse balcony, watching the city's lights flicker and fade as dawn crept over the Atlantic. My hand throbbed under the bandage—a tiny, persistent drumbeat. *She's here. She's here. She's here.*

I knocked back another gulp of whisky. The bottle was nearly empty now. I should've felt something—drunk, numb, anything—but my body had long ago built up a tolerance that would impress medical students. The alcohol just sat there, burning my throat, doing jack shit for the chaos in my head.

Last night played on an endless loop: Hank's smug welcome, the champagne glass shattering in my grip, the crowd's murmurs. But mostly Tara's eyes. Those weren't the eyes of a girl anymore. They were assured. Determined. Hungry.

I flexed my bandaged hand, feeling the cut beneath the gauze stretch and burn. Her fingers had been so careful wrapping it. But I'd felt it—the tiny hesitations, the barely notice-able pressure changes. She'd enjoyed it. Enjoyed touching me.

"Jesus fucking Christ," I muttered, tipping my head back against the lounge chair. The sky turned that peculiar pre-dawn gray, the color of indecision.

Jimmy was six months older than me and would have been thirty by now. Would have had a career, maybe a family. Instead, he was dust and memory, and his sister—his baby sister—was all grown up and armed with medical credentials.

The sliding door behind me whispered open. Leo. Always Leo.

"You look like absolute shite," he said, settling into the chair beside me. He was already dressed in pressed chinos and a polo, looking every inch the professional assistant, despite the early hour. "Didn't sleep?"

I raised the nearly empty whisky bottle in silent answer.

Leo sighed. "Give me that." He plucked it from my hand and set it on the small table between us. "We've got the facility tour in an hour. You need to shower and look less like you're auditioning for 'Intervention.'"

"Cancel the tour."

"Can't. Owner's orders." Leo's voice was casual, but I caught the slight edge. He'd been watching me like a hawk since the party, his usual easygoing front slipping to reveal something more urgent. "Apparently, Hank Swanson is very excited to show off his new toy."

"Me or the facility?" My laugh was brittle.

"Both, probably." Leo stood, stretching his arms above his head. "Come on. Shower. Coffee. Advil. In that order."

I didn't move. "She's his daughter."

Leo paused mid-stretch. "Aye, I gathered that from the

matching surnames and the whole 'let me introduce my daughter' carry on."

"Not just his daughter. She's Jimmy's sister."

Leo's arms lowered slowly. In the years we'd been friends, I'd mentioned Jimmy's name exactly twice. Once, blackout drunk in Glasgow, sobbing on a bathroom floor. The second time, in London, after I'd gotten the tattoo: his initials and the date.

"Jimmy," Leo repeated carefully. "Your friend from California. The one who died."

I nodded, eyes fixed on the horizon where the first golden rays of sun were spilling over the ocean. "Car accident."

Leo was quiet for a long moment as he connected the dots. "And the lass—Dr. Swanson—she was his sister."

"Yeah, Tara." Her name felt strange in my mouth after so long. "She was sixteen when it happened."

Leo's expression shifted. "When what happened, exactly?"

I stood abruptly, the chair scraping against the balcony floor. "I need that shower."

I brushed past him, ignoring the question. Leo knew the broad strokes of my past—driving accident, best friend dead, guilt and exile—but not the details.

Some shame cuts too deep to share, even with the person who's seen you at your worst.

The hot water hammered my shoulders without mercy, but my brain kept right on playing the greatest hits of my fucked-up past. I slapped my palms against the fancy slate tile, dropping my head under the spray like I might drown the thoughts if I tried hard enough. My bandaged hand was turning into soggy gauze origami—perfect ammunition for Dr. Tara's next round of "how to take care of yourself, dumbass."

What the fuck was wrong with me?

I turned the water to cold, gasping as it hit my skin. Better. Pain was clarifying. It reminded me I was still alive, still paying for what had happened that night.

By the time I emerged from the bathroom, a towel wrapped around my waist, Leo had coffee and Advil waiting. He handed me both without comment. We'd perfected this dance over the years—his quiet efficiency managing my self-destruction, neither of us acknowledging the codependency of it all.

"Car's downstairs in fifteen," he said, scrolling through his phone. "The team facility is about twenty minutes away, traffic permitting."

I swallowed the pills dry, chasing them with scalding coffee. "What's the dress code for these things?"

"Athletic casual. I laid something out." He nodded toward the bed, where a pair of designer joggers and a fitted team polo waited. Of course, he had. Leo always thought of everything.

I yanked on the clothes like a zombie, my brain stuck in rewind mode. The polo squeezed my shoulders too damn tight, with that team logo sitting over my heart like I'd been cattle-branded.

Congratulations! You now belong to Hank Swanson.

Leo hovered by the door, jingling keys and thumbing through emails. He looked up as I shuffled over, his face giving away exactly nothing.

"Ready?"

"Not even close," I admitted. "But since when has that stopped the world from kicking my ass, anyway?"

The Miami training facility was a glass-and-steel middle finger to fiscal responsibility. The team's logo dominated the façade in letters big enough to be seen from space, practically screaming, "We have more money than we know what to do with."

"Fuckin' hell," Leo whispered as we pulled into VIP parking. "They're no' messin' aboot. Chelsea's digs look like a wee YMCA compared to this."

Our coach named Wilkes waited for us in the lobby. His expression said, plain as day, "I'd rather be getting a root canal."

"McCrae," he greeted, extending his hand. "Welcome to the facility."

His grip was firm, yet his eyes betrayed a different truth—the judgment of a man who'd already decided who I was based on tabloid headlines and social media threads.

"This is Leo Martin, my assistant," I said. Leo, ever the charmer, quickly engaged Wilkes, offering me a much-needed reprieve.

The tour was exactly what I expected: a blur of state-of-the-art bullshit designed to impress players and justify exorbitant contracts. Hydrotherapy pools with underwater treadmills. Anti-gravity training machines that looked like something out of a sci-fi film. A nutrition bar that served protein shakes with ingredients I couldn't pronounce.

I nodded with the right intervals, made vague sounds of appreciation, and tried to ignore the pounding in my temples. The Advil was barely touching the hangover, and every bright light and nerve-grating sound in the cavernous facility felt like a personal attack.

"The locker room's through here," Wilkes was saying,

leading us down yet another pristine corridor. "You've got a permanent spot with your name already on it. Owner's orders."

Of course.

We rounded a corner, and my eyes caught on a sign: SPORTS MEDICINE WING. My steps faltered.

"Medical facilities are top of the line," Wilkes continued, not noticing my hesitation. "MRI, X-ray, the works. Dr. Swanson built quite the department."

We passed an open door, and I glimpsed a series of examination rooms. At the end of the hallway was a larger office, a plaque beside the door: *DR. TARA SWANSON, HEAD OF SPORTS MEDICINE.* The letters seemed to burn into my vision, each one pulsing in time with the throbbing in my head.

"Speaking of Dr. Swanson," Wilkes said, checking his watch, "you're scheduled for your physical assessment at noon. Standard procedure for all new players."

My stomach twisted. "Today?"

"Owner's orders," Wilkes repeated, the phrase becoming an ominous mantra. "He wants you cleared ASAP so you can start training with the team tomorrow."

Well, shit.

The waiting room of the medical wing was quiet. I'd been sitting here for twenty-three minutes. I knew because I'd been counting the seconds, watching the digital clock on the wall tick forward like a sadistic tortoise on Xanax.

Leo had abandoned me after the tour, claiming he needed to "sort out some contract rider details" with management.

The betrayal pissed me off more than it should have. I was a grown man, for fuck's sake. I didn't need a babysitter for a routine physical.

Except this wasn't routine. Nothing about this situation was routine.

I could hear her voice through the closed door of an examination room, calmly discussing another player's recovery protocol. It was the voice of a stranger, not the girl I remembered. That girl had been all raw emotion and wide eyes. This woman sounded controlled.

Dangerous.

The door to the examination room opened, and a young midfielder limped out. Sánchez, if I remembered correctly from the roster Leo had shown me. He looked dazed but relieved, like he'd just escaped an IRS audit with both kidneys intact.

He spotted me, a flicker of recognition in his eyes. He gave a weird, sympathetic half-smile. "Good luck in there, mate."

What the hell does that mean?

Before I could ask, Tara appeared in the doorway. She wore fitted navy scrubs that somehow looked tailored, her dark hair pulled back in a neat ponytail.

"Mr. McCrae," she said, her voice crisp. "Come in."

I stood, my legs feeling strangely unsteady.

The door clicked shut behind me. The examination room smelled of antiseptic and... vanilla. The combination was dizzying, triggering a sensory memory I'd spent years trying to bury.

Her hair smelled of vanilla when I leaned in. Her face tilted up to mine, eyes wet with tears but so trusting, so open...

"McCrae," Tara said, interrupting my thoughts. "Let's start with that hand."

There was no preamble, no small talk. She gestured for me to sit on the edge of the table. I obeyed, my muscles tight, feeling like I was walking into a trap I couldn't see.

She didn't ask for permission, just took my injured hand in hers. Her touch was firm, but the heat of her skin radiated through mine. I noticed her nails—short, no polish.

Her fingers stilled for a second. She finally looked up, and our eyes locked. The air crackled with a volatile combination of anger and desire.

"You got this wet," she observed, her tone mildly accusatory.

"Shower."

"You need to keep it dry for at least twenty-four hours." She removed the bandages and reached for a fresh packet of antiseptic wipes. "This might sting."

It did, but I didn't flinch. Pain was an old friend at this point.

Tara's fingers, steady and sure, pressed the antiseptic-soaked gauze against the gash on my hand, each swipe sharp with something more than medicine, as if she were pouring all the years I'd left her behind into that sting.

She finished wrapping my hand, her touch lingering a beat too long, then stepped back, her hazel eyes unreadable. "Alright, McCrae. Full physical now. Standard for all new players. Shirt and shorts off."

I stared, my pulse hammering. "You're kidding."

Her lips twitched, a ghost of a smirk. "You can have Dr. Mitchell do it instead. Sixty-three, hands like a freezer, and he's got zero patience for cocky forwards."

I stood, tugging my shirt over my head in one fluid motion, my eyes locked on hers. Her gaze stayed professional, but I caught the slight flare of her nostrils as it swept over my chest, the lean muscle honed from years in the gym. When my fingers paused at the waistband of my training shorts, her brow arched, daring me to hesitate.

"I've seen plenty of athletes in various states of undress, McCrae," she said, her voice cool but edged with something softer, something that remembered us. "You're not my first."

But the faint catch in her breath told me I wasn't just another player. Not to her.

I dropped the shorts, standing there in black briefs that left little to the imagination. My body was a machine, built for speed and power, but under her scrutiny, I felt like that 17-year-old kid again, half-hard, and fighting to keep my head straight. I tried to focus on anything else—corner kicks, ice baths, the smell of wet grass—anything but Tara, with her steady hands and eyes that saw too much.

She circled me, her sneakers soft on the tiled floor, like she was sizing me up for more than just a physical. "Any injuries I should know about?"

"Besides the ones from crashing into defenders?"

She stopped behind me, close enough that I felt the warmth of her breath on my shoulder. "Specifics, McCrae." Her fingers brushed the tattoo on my ribs—Jimmy's initials, the date of his accident etched into my skin. Her touch was light, but it burned, dragging me back to the summer we lost him, the summer I lost everything.

"My brother," she said, her voice quieter now, heavy with memory. "When did you get this?"

"Years after it happened."

"The accident." Her fingers pressed harder, tracing the ink as if she could feel the shared grief beneath it. "And then you left without a word."

The accusation knocked me on my ass worse than any

cheap shot on the field. After Jimmy died, I bolted—grabbed the first contract waved in my face just to get as far away as possible from everyone's sideways looks and hushed gossip, from that goddamn guilt that gnawed through my insides. I never considered what my vanishing act did to her.

"I got signed to Glasgow, Tara. Besides, your father—"

"Stop." Her hand pressed flat against my ribs, her palm hot against my hammering heartbeat. "Not here."

She stepped around to face me, her composure a thin veil over the flush creeping up her neck. "Lie on the table. Range of motion."

I glanced at the narrow exam table, cold and clinical. "Is this really necessary?"

"It's protocol," she said, her tone sharp but her gaze soft, conflicted. "Unless you want to explain to my dad why you bailed on your physical."

I flopped onto the table, flat on my back, eyes locked on the ceiling. Forty-two fucking tiles. I counted every single one as if it might save me from the fact that Tara was standing close enough for me to smell her shampoo.

"Arms up," she ordered from behind me.

I lifted them, feeling weirdly naked in a way that had nothing to do with being in my underwear. Her hands wrapped around my wrists. Each time her fingers moved, my body felt things it had no business feeling during a medical exam.

"Range looks good," she said, her voice dropping to a tone that made my brain short-circuit. "Let's check those rotator cuffs."

Her thumbs bulldozed into my shoulders, hunting down knots. I let out a grunt when she found a tender spot.

"Jesus, you're tight here," she said. "Better start stretching, or you'll be useless on the pitch."

"I'll make it a priority, Doc," I said through clenched teeth.

"You better." Her fingers dug deeper—not a suggestion but a command. "Roll over. Gotta check your spine."

I rolled onto my stomach, grateful for the brief shield from her gaze. The table was hard and unyielding, and I shifted, trying to ease the pressure of my growing erection. I cursed my cock for its betrayal, but in Tara's presence it seemed to have a mind of its own.

Tara's hands moved down my back, her thumbs tracing my spine, pressing at intervals. When she reached the small of my back, just above my briefs, her touch slowed, her fingers brushing the sensitive skin there.

"Slight curvature," she said, her voice closer, her breath warm against my ear. "Postural, probably. Core strength?"

"Strong enough," I managed, my voice rough.

"We'll test that." Her hands slid to my hips, fingers digging into the muscle where my lower back met my glutes. "Pain?"

"None." Not the kind she meant, anyway.

"Good." She stepped back. "Turn over."

I froze, because turning over meant one thing—Tara getting an unobstructed view of the hard-on I'd been praying would go away. "Give me a minute."

"Problem?" Her voice carried a teasing lilt.

"You know what the problem is," I muttered, low and raw.

"I'm a professional, Xander. The body's just biology." But the flush on her neck, spreading to her collarbone, said she wasn't as detached as she claimed.

I rolled onto my back, jaw clenched, refusing to acknowledge the obvious strain in my briefs. Her eyes flicked down, then back to my face, a spark of heat breaking through her cool facade, causing her to falter for the briefest second.

Then she continued, "Hamstring flexibility." But when she spoke, her voice was huskier now. She lifted my right leg, pressing it toward my chest, standing between my spread thighs. The position was intimate, vulnerable, her hands steady but her proximity undoing me.

"Decent flexibility," she murmured, her hand on my thigh firm, almost possessive. "But you're tight. Feel any pulling?"

"Only where it's obvious," I said, my voice a low growl.

A smile flickered across her lips, gone as fast as it came. "Pain, Xander. I'm talking about pain."

"None."

She lowered my leg but didn't step back. Instead, she lifted my left leg, positioning it over her shoulder, bringing her face inches from mine. Her ponytail brushed my chest, and I fought the urge to tangle my fingers in it, to pull her closer.

"Discomfort?" she asked, her breath warm against my jaw, her eyes locked on mine.

"Define discomfort," I shot back, my control fraying like a worn-out cleat.

Her smile was slow, dangerous. "Push against my shoulder."

I did, feeling the stretch in my hamstring and the maddening heat of her body so close. When she shifted, her hip grazed my erection, deliberate and unapologetic. I sucked in a sharp breath, my hands twitching toward her.

"Sorry," she said, her voice low, not sorry at all.

She switched to my right leg, repeating the motion, but this time her fingers brushed the front of my briefs, slow and intentional. My control snapped like a taut string.

"Tara," I warned, my voice rough with need.

"Yes, Xander?" Her eyes were dark, her mask slipping.

Before I could answer, the door swung open, no knock, no warning. Diego, the team's cocky striker, leaned against the frame, grinning like he'd caught us in the act. "Well, damn, Doc. This the new warm-up routine? Count me in."

Tara spun toward the door, her professional mask slamming back into place. The transformation was instant—eyes hardening, spine straightening.

"Diego, what have I told you about knocking?" Her tone was sharp and scolding. "This is a medical examination."

Diego's smirk didn't falter as his eyes traveled from my position on the table to Tara's flushed face. "Seems like a very thorough examination."

I sat up, swinging my legs off the table, every muscle in my body tight with frustration. Diego's eyes flicked to my briefs, his smirk widening into something that made me want to rearrange his perfect teeth.

"I have the test results from the practice field," he said, waving a manila envelope. "Hank asked me to bring them directly to you. Said it was urgent."

Bullshit. What a liar. And a bad one at that. This was a power move—marking territory, letting me know where I stood in the locker room pecking order.

Tara snatched the envelope from his hand. "You could have left these with my assistant."

"And miss this?" Diego's eyes lingered on me. "Welcome to Miami, superstar. Better get used to the heat."

"That's enough," Tara snapped. "Out. Now."

Diego raised his hands in mock surrender, backing toward the door. "Whatever you say, Doc." He threw me one last look before disappearing, his message delivered: *she's off-limits.*

Tara tossed the envelope onto her desk without opening it.

"We're done here." Her voice was clipped, all business. "You can get dressed. Your test results will be filed with the coaching staff by the end of the day."

I reached for my shorts, yanking them on with more force than necessary. "That guy's a piece of work."

"He's the team's top scorer." Her tone gave nothing away. "And you're the new star player threatening his position."

I pulled my shirt over my head, feeling the heat of her gaze even as she pretended to write notes on her clipboard. Part of me wanted to grab her, finish what we'd started. The smarter part knew that was suicide.

"Same time tomorrow for the cardio assessment," she said, not looking up.

I nodded, wariness battling in my gut. If Diego hadn't interrupted... Christ, I don't know what would've happened. Something stupid. Something we couldn't take back.

"Tomorrow," I mumbled, and left without another word, the door clicking shut behind me, separating us once again.

CHAPTER

Four

TARA

WHEN THE DOOR shut on Xander's retreating figure, my knees buckled beneath me. I slid down against the cool surface and hit the floor. My hands trembled as I raised them to my face, staring at my fingers—the same fingers that had just traced the outline of my brother's initials tattooed on Xander's skin.

"Breathe," I whispered to myself. "Just breathe."

But my lungs refused to cooperate. Every inhalation caught halfway, trapped by the thundering of my heart. My skin still buzzed where it had touched his—alive in a way I'd never experienced before. Nothing had prepared me for the reality of him.

The heat of his skin.

The flex of muscle beneath my hands.

The scent of him—expensive soap layered over something raw and masculine.

The insistent bulge of his cock that rubbed against his

briefs was impossible to ignore when I hooked his leg over my shoulder.

A laugh bubbled up from my chest—half triumph, half disbelief. I'd done it. After years of planning, of maneuvering myself into the perfect position, I'd finally gotten my hands on Xander McCrae.

And he had responded exactly as I'd hoped.

I pushed myself up from the floor, smoothing my navy scrubs as I took a deep breath, centering myself. Control was everything. I'd spent twelve years building this version of myself—competent and untouchable. I wouldn't let one encounter, no matter how charged, unravel me.

I glanced at the clock. Five hours until dinner with my father. Five hours to prepare for the subtle interrogation that would inevitably come. Because tonight wouldn't be a simple family meal. It would be a debriefing.

I needed to be ready.

———

The restaurant my father had chosen was exactly his style—expensive, and impersonal. The kind of place where the menu had no prices, and the waitstaff moved like ghosts, appearing only when needed.

My father stood as I approached the table, his tall frame impeccable in a tailored suit. At sixty, Hank Swanson still cut an imposing figure with silver hair precisely styled, his posture military-straight. The physical resemblance between us was minimal. I had my mother's coloring, her delicate features. But the set of my jaw, the stubborn line of my mouth —those were pure Swanson. Jimmy had inherited more from him.

"Tara," my father said, leaning in to brush a perfunctory kiss against my cheek. "You look lovely."

I'd chosen my outfit carefully—a navy sheath dress, professional but feminine. Armor for the battle ahead.

"Thank you for making time," I said, settling into the chair a waiter had pulled out for me. "I know how busy you are with the team launch."

My father waved a dismissive hand. "Family comes first. Always has."

The words should have been comforting. Instead, they raised the fine hairs on my arms. In my father's world, "family" wasn't about love or connection—it was about loyalty, about falling in line.

"Speaking of the team," he continued, "the launch party was a resounding success. Commissioner Wilson called me personally to say how impressed he was with our setup."

"That's wonderful," I said, accepting the glass of wine a server poured for me. "The facility is certainly state-of-the-art."

"It should be, for what it cost." My father's eyes crinkled with pride. "But worth every penny. We've assembled quite a roster. Mano, Banda, Carter... and of course, McCrae."

And there it was, the name landing between us with the weight of a challenge. I took a careful sip of wine, using the moment to compose my features.

"How did you find him today?" My father's tone was casual. "Physically, I mean."

I met his gaze, keeping my expression neutral. "His overall condition is excellent. Exceptional cardiovascular fitness, no major injury concerns. Some muscular imbalances that need addressing—primarily in the shoulders and lower back. Nothing unexpected for a player at his level."

"And mentally?"

I tilted my head, feigning confusion. "I'm not a psychologist, Dad. My assessment was purely physical."

"Come now, Tara. You're more observant than that." He leaned forward slightly. "Did he seem... stable to you?"

I couldn't quite decipher the question. Was he concerned about his investment?

"He seemed focused," I said carefully. "Professional. Cooperative with the examination."

"Hmm." My father took a sip of his whisky, studying me over the rim of his glass.

The server arrived with our appetizers, momentarily breaking the tension. I used the interruption to steer the conversation to safer ground—the team's upcoming schedule, the marketing campaign, the charity events planned for the season. My father played along, but I felt his focus wavering.

As I finished a point about community events, he reached across the small table and his index finger brushed away a tiny, nonexistent crumb from the tablecloth next to my bread plate. The gesture was slight, proprietary, and utterly dismissive of what I'd just said. It was a silent correction, a reminder that he controlled the space, the conversation, and everything in it. He leaned back, his point made without a single word.

"You've prescribed physical therapy for McCrae, I understand?" he asked, his voice casual again now that he had reestablished command.

I nodded. "Bi-weekly sessions to start, then we'll reassess. His muscular tension needs aggressive treatment if he's going to perform at his best."

"Bi-weekly?" My father raised an eyebrow. "Is that standard protocol?"

"For elite athletes? Absolutely." The lie came easily. "The

sooner we address these imbalances, the better he'll integrate with the team."

My father studied me for a long moment, his expression unreadable. Then he nodded, satisfied with my explanation. I took a deep breath, sensing an opening. Time to test the waters.

"It was incredibly fortunate for us," I said, keeping my tone neutral, "that a player of his caliber became available at the exact moment you were completing the roster." I paused, observing him. "The incident in Chelsea that got him transfer-listed was perfect timing for us."

My father gave a dismissive, paternalistic laugh. "Tara, men like McCrae are walking liabilities. Trouble doesn't find them; they invite it in for a drink." He signaled to the server for another whisky. "Besides, his marketability alone justified the expense. Miami loves a bad boy, and McCrae sells tickets. His jersey sold out the first day."

He swirled the amber liquid in his glass. "Frankly, Chelsea was looking for an excuse to get rid of him. A hot-headed player picking a fight with some loudmouth blogger isn't exactly a mastermind plot."

I froze, my wine glass halfway to my lips. *Blogger.*

The word lodged in my brain like a splinter. Every article I'd read, every report I'd combed through had described the man as a "paparazzo" or "member of the press." But my father had called him a "blogger"—a more specific, more dismissive term.

I set my glass down carefully, concealing the tremor in my hand. "I wasn't suggesting a conspiracy, Dad. Just commenting on the timing."

"Timing is everything in business," he said, his eyes crinkling with a smile. "And in life."

The rest of dinner passed in a blur. We spoke of inconsequential things—the Miami weather and the upcoming hurricane season. But beneath the surface pleasantries, my mind raced.

That one word—*blogger*—had cracked the smooth narrative my father had presented. It was a tiny inconsistency, insignificant on its own. But combined with everything, it raised questions I wasn't sure I wanted answered.

Had my father manipulated events to bring Xander to Miami? And if so, why?

By the time the check arrived (which my father paid without glancing at the total), a cold certainty had settled in my stomach. This wasn't just about me or Xander. My father was playing a longer game, one with rules I didn't fully understand.

"I'll take you home," he said as we stood to leave.

"That's unnecessary. I have my car."

"Nonsense. You've had two glasses of wine. The valet can take your car home." His tone brooked no argument. "Besides, I'd like a few more minutes with my daughter."

Outside, a sleek black Bentley waited at the curb with Lenny at the wheel. My father's hand at my elbow guided me inside, his grip firm. The interior was cool and dark, smelling of leather.

As the car pulled away from the restaurant, my father turned to me. "I'm proud of you, Tara. The way you've established yourself with the team, the respect you've earned. Your brother would be proud too."

The mention of Jimmy made my throat tighten. "Thank you."

"I just want what's best for you. You know that, don't you?"

I simply nodded, not trusting my voice.

"Good." He patted my hand. "Because sometimes what's best for us isn't what we think we want."

The warning was clear, if oblique. I forced a smile. "I'm a big girl, Dad. I can take care of myself."

"Of course you can." His answering smile was indulgent. "But even big girls need their fathers sometimes."

The car glided to a stop in front of my building. My father leaned over to kiss my cheek.

"Get some rest," he said. "You have a busy day tomorrow. McCrae again, yes?"

"Yes," I confirmed.

"Good luck with that." Something in his tone made me glance sharply at him, but his expression revealed nothing. "Goodnight, Tara."

"Goodnight, Dad."

I stepped out of the car, watching as the Bentley pulled away from the curb.

Inside my apartment, I kicked off my heels and headed straight for the shower, as if I could wash away the unsettling dinner conversation along with the day's sweat. The hot water did nothing to ease the tension that had settled there.

My father's words repeated in my head: *A hotheaded player picking a fight with some loudmouth blogger isn't exactly a mastermind plot.*

Blogger was a clue. What if my father, with his connections and his millions, had orchestrated the entire thing? Created the perfect scandal to force Chelsea's hand, to make Xander available when my father was building his team?

I dressed in my sleeping shorts and tank top, then padded to my home office. The space was organized with medical journals lined up on shelves, physical therapy equipment neatly stored, and a large desk facing the window with a beautiful view.

I sank into my desk chair, opening my laptop. The screen illuminated, displaying the photos I'd taken of Xander's medical file from Chelsea. I zoomed in on the note about his insomnia:

The patient reports difficulty falling asleep and staying asleep. Attributes to stress. Prescribed Ambien 10mg PRN. The patient advised limiting alcohol consumption while using medication.

Insomnia. A common symptom of PTSD; of unresolved trauma.

I stared at the warning listed in Xander's file. Ambien and alcohol—a potentially lethal combination. The recommended limit was one drink, maybe two at most. But I'd seen the tabloid photos. Xander wasn't having "a drink." He was drowning himself night after night.

Was he trying to self-destruct? Or just desperate for dreamless sleep?

I made a note on my phone to address it during tomorrow's session. It would be tricky—confronting him about his drinking would likely trigger defensiveness. But I couldn't ignore a genuine medical concern, especially not when it affected a player under my care.

I closed my laptop and stood, stretching tired muscles. Tomorrow would be another predawn run past his building, another day of calculated interactions. Another step in my plan.

Back in my bedroom, I set my alarm for 4:45 AM and crawled into bed, wondering which of us was more damaged.

CHAPTER

Five

XANDER

THE WHISKY WASN'T WORKING ANYMORE.

I stood on the penthouse balcony, gripping the glass railing with white knuckles, watching dawn break over Miami Beach. The city was already stirring—early joggers dotting the shoreline, delivery trucks rumbling along Ocean Drive, fishing boats heading out for the morning catch. Normal people doing normal things while I stood above it all, trapped in a gilded cage of my own making.

The bottle of Macallan beside me was nearly empty. I'd started drinking around midnight, hoping to find that familiar numbness, the blessed quiet that usually came after the fourth or fifth glass. But it hadn't come. Now, the alcohol had only sharpened every jagged thought.

Sleep had been impossible. Every time I closed my eyes, I saw Tara—not as she was now, composed and clinical, but as she'd been twelve years ago. Sixteen years old, dark hair falling around her tear-stained face as she'd looked up at me behind the church after Jimmy's funeral. The moment I'd almost ruined everything by nearly kissing her.

I drained the last of my whisky, the burn in my throat barely registering anymore. Below, a lone female figure caught my eye—a runner moving along the beach with purpose. Dark hair pulled back in a ponytail, athletic build.

It couldn't be.

I leaned forward, straining to see better. The distance made it impossible to be sure, but something about the way she moved... I swore it was Tara.

Christ, you're losing it, McCrae.

I rubbed a hand on the back of my neck, disgusted by the paranoid turn of my thoughts. This was Miami, for fuck's sake. Half the women here had dark hair and athletic builds. It wasn't Tara. It couldn't be.

But the seed of doubt had been planted, and in my exhausted, alcohol-soaked brain, it took root. I made a note to buy a pair of high-powered binoculars.

"Morning, sunshine."

Leo appeared beside me, two steaming mugs of coffee in hand. He was wearing crisp linen shorts and a button-down shirt, looking infuriatingly put-together. He handed me a mug, his nose wrinkling at the empty whisky bottle.

"Did ye sleep at all?"

I grunted, accepting the coffee. "What do you think?"

"I think you're going to regret this when you have to perform for your new team in—" he checked his watch, "—about two hours."

I took a sip of the coffee. Black, scalding hot, and strong enough to strip paint. Just how I needed it.

"Don't forget," Leo continued, scrolling through his phone, "you've got your first PT session with Dr. Swanson at eight."

Something inside me snapped. The mention of her name—so casual, so normal—as if she were just another team doctor and not the architect of my current nightmare.

"How did you not know?" The words came out low and dangerous.

Leo glanced up from his phone, brow furrowed. "Know what?"

"Your one job—your *only* job—was to do the research before I sign my life away." I set the coffee mug down with enough force to slosh liquid over the rim. "You let me walk into a trap because you didn't do your homework."

Comprehension dawned on Leo's face, followed quickly by hurt. "Xander—"

"Hold on," I said, my voice rising with each accusation. "You didn't know the owner was Hank Swanson? Or that his daughter was head of sports medicine? What am I paying you for, Leo? To organize my social calendar? To make sure I have enough whisky?"

Leo's expression hardened. "That's no' fair, and you know it."

"Fair? You want to talk about *fair*?" I laughed, the sound harsh. "Fair would have been knowing what I was walking into. Fair would have been having a fucking choice."

"The team's ownership was hidden behind a series of LLCs," Leo shot back, his temper rising. "The high-level staff weren't publicly listed until the launch. I'm your assistant, Xander, not a corporate spy! They obviously wanted it kept quiet and disguised their tracks!"

"Bullshit. You could have found out. You *should* have found out." I jabbed a finger at him. "But you were too busy planning parties and chasing tail to do your actual job."

Leo recoiled as if I'd slapped him. "That's what you think I do? After twelve years? After everything we've been through?"

"I think you dropped the ball on the most important transfer of my career, and now I'm fucking trapped by a CEO billionaire who hates my guts." I turned away from him, staring back at the beach where the dark-haired runner had disappeared from view. "I think you let me walk into an ambush."

"An ambush?" Leo's voice was incredulous. "You're acting like this is some kind of conspiracy. It's a football team, not the fucking CIA."

"You don't know what you're talking about." The words came out tired, defeated. "You don't know what they're capable of."

"Then enlighten me! Because from where I'm standing, you're having a meltdown over seeing your old friend's family again." Leo stepped closer, lowering his voice. "I get that Jimmy's death was traumatic, but this? This isn't normal, Xander."

I whirled on him, fury coursing through me, anew. "Normal? You want to know what's normal? Normal is not having the father of the kid you basically killed manipulate your entire fucking career. Normal is not having the sister you almost—" I cut myself off, the words too dangerous to say aloud.

Leo's face softened with concern. "The sister you almost what?"

"Nothing." I ran a hand over my face. "Forget it."

"Xander, whatever happened—"

"I need to get ready for practice." I pushed past him, heading for the door. "I'll get a car service. Don't wait up."

"Xander, wait—"

But I was already inside, the sliding glass door shutting behind me with a final-sounding click. I leaned against it for a moment, hating myself for the hurt I'd seen in Leo's eyes. He didn't deserve my rage. None of this was his fault. But I needed someone to blame, someone to absorb the toxic cocktail of guilt and fear churning inside me.

Because the alternative was admitting the truth: that I'd brought this all on myself, and I was still paying the price.

———

I showed up early at the Pirates' training facility for two reasons: to dodge Leo at the penthouse and to get my showdown with Tara out of the way. My skull felt like it was hosting a rave, thanks to last night's booze festival, zero sleep, and emotional baggage playing on loop.

But whatever game Tara had planned, I was ready to play.

At 8 AM sharp, the sports medicine wing was dead quiet. I passed through the glass doors, looking for Tara. Instead, I got a tiny blonde in scrubs behind the reception desk.

"Mr. Xander McCrae," she announced without bothering to look up from her screen. "Dr. Swanson asked me to inform you that your physical therapy session is canceled because of a scheduling conflict."

I stood there like an idiot. "Canceled?"

"Yes." She finally granted me eye contact, her face revealing her boredom. "You're free to join team practice at nine. Coach Wilkes expects you."

"When is it rescheduled for?"

"Dr. Swanson will be in touch." Back to her screen, conversation over.

I lingered, knocked off my game and pissed. This was textbook power-play bullshit—Tara establishing dominance, making it clear she controlled when and where we'd interact. Part of me felt relieved for the delay, but mostly I was fuming at being so easily jerked around.

"Fine," I said, turning to leave. "Tell Dr. Swanson I said thanks for the consideration."

The assistant didn't give enough of a shit to respond.

The locker room was half-full when I entered, with players in various states of dress preparing for the morning session. The conversation died as I walked in, replaced by a heavy silence that followed me to my assigned locker. I recognized a few faces from the welcome party—Diego Mano, the team's star striker; Banda, a veteran defender; and a handful of younger players whose names I couldn't recall.

I nodded at everyone, expecting the same enthusiasm you'd get from a DMV employee on a Friday afternoon. Being the new guy always sucked balls, especially when you're the fancy import with a "problem child" reputation. Throw in being Hank Swanson's pet project, and I basically had "SOCIAL LEPER" branded on my ass.

I changed into my training gear, moving like someone who wasn't nursing a hangover. Over a decade in pro soccer taught me locker room politics—the pecking order, the silent judgment, the "prove yourself, asshole" gauntlet everyone runs. My strategy remained simple: shut up and show my domination on the field.

"So, McCrae." Diego Mano's voice sliced through the quiet. "Settling in okay?"

I glanced up to find the Columbian striker posted up against the neighboring locker, arms folded like he was posing for his next underwear ad. At thirty-two, Mano was soccer's equivalent of a classic car—not as fast as he once was, but still dangerous and overpriced.

"Getting there," I said, yanking my shirt over my head.

"Good, good." Mano faked a smile. "Miami's a great city. Lots to enjoy. Beaches, clubs, beautiful women..." He paused like he was about to drop wisdom. "Though some women around here are off-limits, you understand?"

I met his stare, having already read his territorial pissing contest invitation. "I'm just here to play football, Mano."

"Of course." He smacked my shoulder with enough force to qualify as low-key assault. "But since we're teammates now, let me give you some friendly advice. The doctor? Dr. Swanson?" His voice dropped to a rough hush. "I saw your little performance on her table yesterday. I don't give a fuck what you've got planned, but she's team property. Hands off!"

The way he talked about Tara—like she was the community coffee machine—made my blood boil, but I kept my poker face. "Noted."

"Good." Mano straightened up, mission accomplished. "See you on the pitch, superstar."

He sauntered away. I'd just been marked as competition—not just for playing time, but for Tara's attention. The irony would have been laughable if it weren't so fucking depressing. Here I was, trying to avoid Tara at all costs, while Mano had me tagged as a threat to whatever he had going on with her.

I finished changing and was lacing up my boots when a shadow fell across me. A younger player, maybe twenty-one or twenty-two, was hovering awkwardly. I think Leo called him Bill something.

"Mr. McCrae? I'm Ben Carter." The kid extended his hand, his expression a mix of nervousness and barely contained excitement. "Welcome to the team, sir. It's an honor to play with you."

I shook his hand, surprised by the genuine warmth in his greeting. "Thanks, Ben. And it's just Xander. 'Sir' makes me feel ancient."

Ben grinned, his nervousness falling away. "Right, sorry. Xander." He hesitated, then added in a rush, "I grew up watching you at Rangers. That free kick goal against Celtic in the 2016 derby? Changed my life. Made me want to be a forward."

Despite my foul mood, I smiled. There was something refreshing about the kid's unabashed admiration. "That was a lucky shot."

"Bullshit," Ben said, then looked mortified at his outburst. "I mean—it was perfect. Textbook. Thirty yards out, top corner."

I laughed, the sound rusty but genuine. "Well, when you put it that way."

A whistle blew from the corridor outside, signaling it was time to head to the pitch. Ben bounced on his toes, still grinning.

"Anyway, I just wanted to welcome you. I've only been here a month, but if you need anything, or have questions about the city or whatever..." He trailed off, suddenly self-conscious.

"Thanks, Ben. I appreciate it." And I did, more than the kid could know. In a locker room full of cold shoulders and thinly veiled hostility, his friendly overture felt like finding water in a desert.

We headed out together, joining the stream of players moving toward the indoor pitch. Ben kept up a steady stream of chatter about the team, the coaches, the tactical system they'd been working on. I let his words wash over me, grateful for the distraction from my darker thoughts.

The practice facility had a full-sized pitch under a soaring dome, the artificial turf a perfect replica of the stadium playing surface. Coach Wilkes, a grizzled veteran of the MLS, stood at the center circle with his assistants, clipboard in hand.

"Gentlemen," he called as we gathered around him. "As you know, we're just two weeks away from our season opener. Today we focus on integrating our new players into the system." His gaze found me in the crowd. "McCrae, you'll start with the first team. Let's see what you've got."

I nodded as dozens of eyeballs bored into me. Nothing new here—the classic "show us you're worth the money" moment. Football made sense to me. I could handle this shit.

We kicked off with basic warm-ups, then passing drills and mini-games. My body went through the motions automatically while my brain took a vacation. My hangover still knocked around in my skull, but it backed off once I got into the flow.

During a water break, I spotted a group watching from the edge—coaches, medical team, and slightly removed from the pack, Hank Swanson in the flesh. Our eyes connected for a hot second before he turned to chat with some lackey. Message received, boss: I'm under the microscope.

Practice wrapped with a full-team scrimmage, starters versus backups. They stuck me in attacking midfield, just behind Mano and another forward. As we lined up, Mano bumped past me.

"Don't count on getting the ball," he hissed. "New hotshots don't get the VIP treatment here."

I ignored him. Fuck it. My game would do the talking.

When the whistle shrieked, everything played out exactly how Mano promised—my so-called teammates deliberately froze me out, testing how long before I'd crack. Amateur hour bullshit I'd seen before. I stayed patient, kept finding open space, making myself an option, waiting for their competitive nature to overpower their petty crap.

It came as a loose ball in midfield. I jumped on it before the other guy could get there, spinning away from pressure like I was dodging an ex at the grocery store. The field in front of me? Wide open. Mano sprinted right, his face screaming, "PASS ME THE BALL, ASSHOLE." Instead, I gunned it forward, the ball stuck to my feet while I danced between two defenders.

The keeper charged out straight at me. Out of the corner of my eye, Mano stood there waving his arms, completely unmarked. The old Xander would've blasted it himself, because of ego, and to make a point. But that wasn't me anymore.

I slipped Mano a perfect pass. All he had to do was tap it in. When the ball hit the net, everyone shut up for a beat. Then Ben Carter broke the silence with a "HELL YEAH!" and a few others clapped.

Mano looked like he'd swallowed something sour but tasty —happy about the goal, pissed the opportunity came from me. He gave me the world's most reluctant nod as he jogged past me.

"Nice vision," he mumbled.

"Nice finish," I shot back.

For the rest of the scrimmage, guys actually passed to me. I kept it simple, showing I could control the game's heartbeat rather than just showing off tricks. When Coach Wilkes blew his whistle, I'd dished three assists and created enough scoring chances to fill a highlight reel.

"Good work today, gentlemen," Wilkes announced to our

circle. "Especially you, McCrae. That's the kind of unselfish play we need."

I nodded at the compliment, feeling the vibe around me change just a little. I hadn't won these fuckers over—not even close—but I'd earned a sliver of professional respect. Baby steps.

As the team dispersed toward the locker rooms, Wilkes approached me. "Hank needs you in his office," he said, his expression giving nothing away. "And don't forget the team dinner tonight. Seven sharp at La Mar."

"Yes, Coach."

Getting called to Hank's office? About as promising as a prostate exam from Edward Scissorhands. And tonight's team dinner meant another round of psychological warfare with the Swansons.

Fucking perfect.

One battle at a time, I told myself. Handle Hank first. Dinner drama later.

I found my way through the building to the executive section, where Hank's corner office commanded a view of the training grounds. His secretary—a woman who reminded me of my old tax audit—flicked her hand toward the door without speaking.

Hank stood at the window, back turned like the rich snob he'd always been. He didn't bother turning around when I walked in.

"Close the door, Xander."

I shut it and stood like an idiot, not daring to sit uninvited.

"Impressive session out there," he said to the window. "You haven't lost your touch."

"Thank you, sir." The word "sir" came out of my mouth before I could stop *it*.

He finally turned, fixing me with those X-ray eyes. Time had worked him over—silver hair replaced the brown, his face more creased and worn. But those eyes? Still cut right through you.

"I wanted to see how you're settling in." He pointed to a chair. "Please, sit."

I perched on the edge. "I'm settling in fine."

"Good, good." Hank lowered himself into his throne behind an enormous desk. "And the accommodations? The penthouse is to your liking?"

"It's very nice."

"I'm glad." He examined briefly. "You know, when I brought you to Miami, there were those who questioned my judgment. Your reputation precedes you, after all."

I kept my mouth shut, waiting for whatever trap he'd laid.

"But I told them, 'I know Xander McCrae. I know what he's capable of, both the good and the bad'." He leaned forward, eyes on mine. "I believe in second chances, Xander. Even for those who may not deserve them."

"I appreciate the opportunity," I said carefully.

"I'm sure you do." His smile remained cold. "One thing I've always admired about you, Xander, is your resilience. Most people wouldn't have recovered from the trauma that night. The guilt alone would have destroyed them."

My fingernails dug into my palms. "Is there something specific you wanted to discuss, Mr. Swanson?"

"Just making conversation." He reclined in his chair. "And call me Hank. We're practically family, after all."

The jab cut deep. I fought to keep my face blank while my insides twisted.

"Now, about tonight's dinner," Hank continued. "It's a

tradition with new signings—a chance for the team to bond off the pitch. I expect you to be on your best behavior."

"Of course."

"Good." He checked his watch. "That's all for now. I've kept you long enough. I'm sure you want to rest before tonight."

I stood up, taking the hint. "I appreciate your time."

At the door, Hank called out: "Oh, and Xander? I've asked Tara to keep a close eye on your physical condition. Your medical history shows some concerning patterns with alcohol. We wouldn't want any... accidents."

I stopped dead, hand on the doorknob.

"No," I said without looking back. "We wouldn't."

———

La Mar was "pretentious as fuck" just as I expected—all modern edges, giant windows flaunting magnificent sweeping views, and a private room where the Pirates could pretend to like each other over fancy cutlery.

I showed up at seven on the dot. No way I'd give Hank ammunition by being late. Most of the team was already there, playing nice with drinks. I grabbed a soda water with lime at the bar. After last night's binge and today's hangover, alcohol was the last thing I craved.

"Xander McCrae, choosing sobriety?" The gossip rags would be stunned.

Tara materialized beside me, wine in hand, rocking a black dress that walked the tightrope between "respectable" and "holy shit." Her dark hair tumbled loose, red lips turned in a half-smile.

"Dr. Swanson," I said, voice tight. "You bailed on me this morning."

"Emergency with a defender." She took a sip of her wine, her eyes staying on mine. "We'll fix your shoulder soon. That knot isn't going anywhere."

The server interrupted before I could respond. "Mr. McCrae? Your seat awaits."

Of course, they'd put me next to Tara. But at least Ben Carter sat on my other side—one friendly face in this shark tank.

"Lucky me," Tara whispered as she sat. "The golden boy all to myself."

Pure torture followed. Every move she made brushed against me. Her perfume hijacked my brain. I tried to bury my attention in the menu, in Ben's football talk—anything but the woman whose elbow kept bumping mine.

Dinner dragged on with fake laughs and team-bonding bullshit. I fielded questions about Europe, keeping everything light. Across the table, Mano glared daggers at every interaction between me and Tara.

As the plates disappeared, Hank rose with champagne in hand. The room went quiet.

"A toast," he announced, commanding attention without effort. "To new beginnings, new challenges, and new family."

Agreement rippled around us.

"When I brought a team to Miami, I wanted something special. Not just winners, but family. Legacy." His eyes found me like heat-seeking missiles. "Some of you just joined us. Others have been here from day one. But you're all part of something bigger now."

He raised his glass higher. "It's been twelve years since we lost my son, Jimmy, in a tragic accident."

Holy shit, is he really going there?

The name dropped like a bomb. Tara froze beside me.

"But I built a new legacy in his memory, a new family." Hank's eyes burned into mine. "Welcome to it, Xander."

Silence crushed the room. Players squirmed, sensing the weird vibe but clueless about why. Twenty-something curious stares weighed on me.

Tara shoved back her chair. "Excuse me," she muttered, barely audible. She bolted toward the exit, cracking at the seams.

I sat paralyzed between rage at Hank's calculated bullshit and worry for Tara. Bringing up Jimmy—so deliberate, so public—was a strike meant to wound us both.

"You okay, man?" Ben whispered. "You look like death warmed over."

In a way, yeah. Jimmy Swanson's ghost now haunted this fancy dinner, courtesy of my new boss.

"I'm fine," I lied. "Need air."

I followed Tara's escape route and found her tucked in an alcove by the bathrooms, back against the wall, eyes closed, fighting for breath.

"Tara."

Her eyes popped open, wet with unshed tears. "Go away, Xander."

"Are you alright?"

She barked a harsh laugh. "Can you believe it? My father wants a new family. He already has a family he ignores. Me. And then he dares to bring Jimmy into this, although he knows it hurts me."

I moved closer, pulled by something primal—guilt, shared pain, or some toxic cocktail of both.

"He's trying to break us both," I hissed.

"It's working." Tara looked up, facade crumbling. "You left," she said, voice cracking. "You just left me. I've been frozen at sixteen, waiting—"

Her raw pain gutted me. Without thinking, I stepped closer, cupped her cheek. Her skin felt soft, her breath warm.

"I'm sorry," I whispered, though for what exactly—leaving, returning, or this whole fucking mess—I couldn't say.

She leaned into my touch, eyes closing briefly. When they opened, they burned with a need matching mine. I leaned in, pulled by forces I couldn't fight, didn't want to fight.

Our lips hovered inches apart when a kitchen crash yanked us back to reality. We jumped apart like guilty teenagers.

Tara recovered first, smoothing her dress with shaky hands. "This never happened," she declared with surprising steadiness. "None of it."

She brushed past me, heading back with her chin up, leaving me to wonder how the fuck I screwed up so badly to end here.

CHAPTER
Six

TARA

MY HANDS WERE STILL SHAKING as I fumbled with my keys at the apartment door. The metal jangled cheerfully, like tiny church bells, when all I wanted was silence. Blessed, empty silence to drown out my father's voice saying Jimmy's name.

I closed the door hard enough to rattle the abstract paintings on the hallway wall. The sound satisfied something primal in me, something that wanted to break things, to make the external world match the chaos inside my chest.

You left. You just left me.

God, had I actually said that? Out loud? To Xander?

I loosened my heels, sending them skittering across the hardwood floor, and went straight for the kitchen. The wine bottle had already been open since the day before. I poured a generous glass, then thought better of it and took the entire bottle with me to the living room.

The apartment was dark except for the streetlights filtering through the windows. But all I saw was Xander's face, the way his green eyes had gone soft when I'd started crying like some pathetic teenager.

I've been frozen since sixteen, waiting—

"Fuck." The word came out as a groan. I collapsed onto the couch, pressing the cold wine bottle against my forehead. All this careful planning, building myself into someone untouchable, and I'd crumbled at the first mention of my brother's name.

No, that wasn't fair. It wasn't just Jimmy's name. It was how my father had wielded my dead brother like a scalpel, cutting precisely where he knew it would hurt most. And Xander—Xander had been right there to witness my unraveling.

I took a long pull from the bottle, not bothering with the glass anymore. The wine was crisp and cold, burning slightly as it went down. I replayed the hallway scene over and over.

The way Xander had found me. The concern in his voice as he'd called out my name. The tentative step forward, like he was approaching a wounded animal. And then—

His hand on my cheek. Warm and gentle.

I'd leaned into that touch like a drowning woman reaching for shore. And when he'd leaned in, when his mouth had been inches from mine, I'd wanted it with a desperation that terrified me. Not as part of my plan, not as Dr. Swanson manipulating her patient, but as Tara. Just Tara, who'd been fascinated by this man since she was a teenager.

The almost-kiss burned on my lips like a brand. I could still smell him—something uniquely Xander that hadn't changed.

If that dish hadn't clattered—

I stood abruptly, the wine sloshing dangerously in the bottle. No, I couldn't think about what might have happened.

It was a repeat of what had happened twelve years ago at Jimmy's funeral. But back then I was only sixteen, hopelessly in love with Xander. Not anymore. I was an adult with a plan. Take control. Make Xander depend on me, and then I would reject him the way he abandoned me. Make him pay for what he did.

I needed to regain that control. To remember who I was and what I was doing here.

The wine bottle found its home on the table as I padded barefoot to my home office. I hesitated at the door. This room was my command center. It was where I plotted and planned.

I opened the door and flicked on the lights.

The wall was covered with close to a hundred photos, articles, and screenshots of Xander McCrae's life. Here was Xander scoring the winning goal for Rangers. There was Xander stumbling out of a London nightclub, clearly intoxicated. A paparazzo shot of him with a blonde model in Ibiza. His transfer announcement to Chelsea. The fight that had gotten him suspended.

In the center, barely visible beneath layers of more recent additions, was an original photo. The one on Jimmy's Instagram, taken just a week before the crash. Xander and Jimmy at the beach, arms slung around each other's shoulders, grinning at the camera like they had all the time in the world.

I stood before my wall of obsession, forcing myself to really look at it. This was who I was. This was what I'd chosen. Every decision in my adult life had led to this moment, to having Xander McCrae finally within reach.

He followed you.

The thought came unbidden, shifting something fundamental in my chest. He'd followed me when I'd fled the dinner. He'd sought me out, touched me, almost kissed me. Not because I'd manipulated him into it, but because...

Because he'd wanted to.

His guilt made him vulnerable. His attraction made him weak. And that almost-kiss? That proved he was just as fucked up about this as I was.

I could work with that.

I moved to my desk, my mind already plotting, strategizing. Tomorrow, I'd reassert control. I would remind him exactly who was in charge.

My hand was on my laptop, ready to pull up my email, when my phone buzzed on the desk beside it. A text from an unsaved number, but I knew who it was from the arrogant tone.

Diego Mano: *Still thinking about that dance you owe me, Doc. Let me know when you're ready to pay up.* 😏

I rolled my eyes, a wave of annoyance washing over me. The team's pre-launch party, a few weeks before Xander had even arrived. I'd had two glasses of champagne on an empty stomach and had been circulating to build rapport with the key players. Diego had cornered me by the bar. I'd engaged in some harmless, professional flirting—the kind of ego-stroking necessary to keep a high-maintenance star striker happy. I vaguely remembered him asking me to dance, and me demurring with a laugh. "You'll have to catch me later."

Apparently, in his mind, "later" had arrived.

I tossed the phone onto the desk without responding. It was a minor annoyance, a gnat to be swatted away later. My focus was singular. My focus was on Xander.

———

The next morning, the physical therapy room was my stage, and I was the director. I'd deliberately chosen the private room at the end of the medical wing—the one without windows. I'd dressed strategically—black athletic leggings that hugged every curve, a fitted Miami Pirates polo that was technically professional but left little to the imagination.

Dr. Swanson was in residence.

When Xander arrived, I put him through his paces. Every command, every touch was designed to re-establish the boundary between doctor and patient, to remind him of my authority. I made him take off his shirt and lie face down on the table, a position that left him vulnerable. Perfect.

I started with a general assessment, my hands moving across his back, cataloguing areas of tension. "Tell me when you feel pain."

"I always feel pain," he muttered into the headrest.

I ignored the comment, though something in my chest twisted at the honesty. My fingers found the knots along his spine, the places where he held his stress, his guilt, his twelve years of self-punishment.

"Breathe," I commanded when I felt him tense. "This won't work if you're fighting me."

"Story of our lives," he said so quietly I almost missed it.

I pressed harder in response, finding a tight spot between his shoulder blades. He hissed in pain.

"That's your rhomboid major," I explained, my voice staying steady even as my hands softened slightly. "You've been compensating for that old shoulder injury for years. Your entire posterior chain is a mess."

I worked the muscle, feeling it slowly release under my fingers. My hands moved lower, to the small of his back where the muscles were practically frozen with tension. Each touch was firm enough to be therapeutic, yet gentle enough to be something else entirely.

"Turn over," I said after twenty minutes of working on his back.

He shifted, and I caught the briefest glimpse of his face before he settled on his back.

I moved onto his shoulders, standing at the head of the table. This position required me to lean over him, my chest inches from his face as I worked the front of his shoulders. I felt more than heard his sharp intake of breath.

"Relax," I said, my voice dropping lower despite myself.

"Trying," he ground out.

My hands moved to his left shoulder, the one with the old injury. I felt the scar tissue beneath my fingers and began working the area.

Then my thumb found it—a deep knot, probably adhesions from the original trauma. I pressed into it, working to break it up.

Xander's breath caught, his whole body going rigid. It wasn't just pain—it was memory. His eyes flew open, finding mine, and for a moment he looked exactly like the seventeen-year-old boy who'd been pulled from that wreckage.

My mask slipped. I saw him—really saw him—not as my obsession but as someone who'd been destroyed by the same night that had destroyed me.

"Does that hurt?" My voice came out soft.

He stared up at me, those green eyes wide and vulnerable. "It's an old injury."

We both knew we weren't talking about the muscle anymore.

"I know," I whispered, my thumb still on that damaged spot, feeling his pulse race beneath the skin. "I know it is."

The moment stretched between us. My hands had gone still on his shoulder. His hand came up, fingers wrapping around my wrist. Not to stop me, just to touch.

"Tara—"

The sound of my name, not "Dr. Swanson" but "Tara," broke whatever spell had fallen over us. I jerked back, my mask slamming back into place so hard it felt like whiplash.

"We're done for today," I said, my voice sharp.

He sat up slowly, confusion flashing across his face. "But it's only been—"

"I said we're done." I turned away, busying myself with meaningless paperwork. "You can schedule your next session with my assistant."

I heard him pull his shirt back on, his soft footfalls as he moved to the door. He paused there, and I could feel him looking at me, wanting to say something. But I kept my back turned, my spine rigid.

The door opened, then closed. His footsteps faded down the hallway.

Only then did I allow myself to breathe, my hands braced on the counter as my legs threatened to give out. For one moment, we'd just been two damaged people recognizing each other's pain.

I was still trying to process the intense emotional whiplash of the session when I left the private room and walked back toward my office.

"Doc! There you are."

I turned to find Diego Mano leaning against the wall in the corridor, blocking my path. He was still in his practice gear, a towel slung around his neck, a predatory smile on his face.

"I was just coming to see you," he said, pushing off the

wall to stand directly in front of me. "You didn't answer my text."

"I've been with a patient, Mr. Mano," I said, my tone crisp and professional.

"Diego," he corrected smoothly. "And I think you owe me that dance. Or maybe a drink, to start." He was standing too close, invading my personal space in a way that was clearly intentional.

"I don't recall owing you anything," I said, trying to step around him. He shifted his body subtly, blocking me again.

"Come on, Tara," he purred, his eyes raking over me. "That night at the party... you wanted to. Don't play shy now. How about tonight? That new place on Collins."

He was backing me into a corner, and I could feel my annoyance curdling into genuine anger. I was about to agree to a "one-drink date" I had no intention of keeping, just to create an exit, when a new voice cut in.

"Dr. Swanson? Sorry to interrupt."

I looked past Diego's shoulder to see Ben Carter standing there, a water bottle in his hand. His expression was open and friendly, but his eyes, when they flicked to Diego, were hard.

"Ben," I said, a wave of relief washing over me. "What can I do for you?"

"I just had a quick question about the new hamstring exercises," he said, stepping forward and positioning himself neatly between me and Diego, creating a welcome buffer. "Am I supposed to be feeling the stretch more in the belly of the muscle or near the insertion point?"

Diego's jaw tightened, his frustration at being interrupted by a rookie palpable. He shot Ben a look of pure venom before turning his charming smile back on me.

"We'll talk later, Doc," he said, his voice a low promise. He brushed past Ben, deliberately bumping his shoulder as he went.

Ben didn't flinch. He waited until Diego was out of earshot before turning to me, his "question" about his hamstring forgotten. "You okay?" he asked, his voice quiet.

"I'm fine," I said, though I was more shaken than I wanted to admit. "Thank you, Ben."

He just nodded, a silent understanding passing between us. "Anytime, Doc."

He gave me a small, respectful smile and walked away.

I watched Ben until he disappeared around the corner.

This morning I'd been so certain, so smug in my belief that I was in control of this game. I'd manipulated Xander's body on my table. I'd orchestrated every touch. I'd convinced myself I was the puppet master.

What a joke.

CHAPTER
Seven

XANDER

I COULDN'T FEEL my legs.

My back pressed against the frigid metal of my locker, shirt still bunched in my fist. Everyone else had hustled out to the practice field, but I remained frozen. Brain offline.

Her touch lingered on my skin—methodical one second, weirdly intimate the next. How her fingers found that exact spot on my shoulder where old injuries had healed over deeper wounds. The shift in her eyes when she pressed into it, like she was x-raying straight through to my fucked-up soul.

I yanked my shirt over my head, flinching as my newly prodded muscles complained. Before common sense kicked in, I grabbed my phone and fired off a reply to the "Welcome home" message I was sure had been from Tara.

You felt it too.

The message zoomed away. Three dots popped up almost instantly, vanished, then reappeared. My heart knocked against my ribs while I waited.

Felt what?

Classic deflection. Pure Dr. Swanson mode. But I'd finished with the bullshit games. Done running from old ghosts. I was exhausted. So fucking exhausted.

That we're both broken in exactly the same places.

I stared at the screen, waiting for the three dots to return. Nothing. Just dead air stretching forever.

Whatever. If she wanted to play pretend, I could join in. Nothing left to lose anyway. I typed: *Tomorrow night. Team party at The Basement. I know you'll be there.*

I paused, then added:

Wear the green dress.

A direct challenge. A poke in the ribs. I knew she'd never do it, but I wanted her to know I remembered the dress that matched my eyes. Did she really give that much attention to detail that she dressed to match my eye color? Hmm. Maybe. If so, what did that say about her motives?

Her reply arrived faster this time.

I'll wear whatever I want.

A smile crept onto my face despite everything. There she was—the fighter, the woman who refused to be pushed around.

Good. Surprise me.

I set the phone down, a weird rush replacing the empty ache in my chest. I'd thrown down the challenge. Her move now.

"McCrae! You planning on joining us this century?"

Coach Wilkes blocked the doorway, arms crossed. Behind him, the Florida sunshine blazed, and I heard the shouts and whistles from practice already underway.

"Sorry, Coach. Physical therapy ran long."

He checked his watch. "Five minutes to get your ass on that field. Owner's watching again today."

Perfect. Just what I needed. Hank Swanson's icy stare tracking my every move, hunting for weakness, for evidence that he'd been right about me being a drunken fuck-up.

"I'll be right there."

———

The practice field sparkled like a golf course on steroids, sunshine pouring over the grass while I hauled ass to join warm-ups. Same as yesterday, everyone watched me like I was the new zoo exhibit.

Ben Carter gave me a bro-nod as I lined up next to him.

"You okay?" he muttered.

"Yeah. Whatever."

"Dr. Swanson seemed a little upset this morning."

I shot him a look. "Yeah?"

He paused. "I've seen how you react with her. Just saying, if you needed to talk—"

"How about we don't?" I snapped.

Ben winced. "Got it."

Fuck. The kid was just being nice. Before I could fix it, the coach's whistle sounded across the field.

"Move your asses! First team west, second team in pinnies east. Scrimmage in fifteen!"

I jogged to first-team territory where Diego Mano stood waiting, eyeballing me like I'd keyed his car.

"McCrae," he called. "You're with me."

The drill was simple—one player would send a ball in, and the other would control it, then lay it off to a third player making a run. Basic stuff we'd done a thousand times before.

But as Diego sent the ball toward me, it came in hard and high, nowhere near my feet.

I brought it down with my chest, but before I could settle it, Diego was there, coming in with a tackle that was late and deliberate. His cleats raked down my shin as I tried to jump away, sending a shot of pain up my leg.

"Fuck!" I stumbled but stayed upright, blood already seeping through my sock where his studs had caught me.

"Oops," Diego said with all the sincerity of a politician. He leaned in close. "I thought I told you to stay away from the doctor's office? You're not the only one getting 'special treatment'."

Bingo. There it was again. This wasn't about soccer. This was about Tara.

"Everything cool over there?" Coach yelled.

"All good, Coach," Diego chirped, suddenly Mr. Innocent. "Just miscommunication."

Coach turned away, and Diego shot me one final death-glare before trotting off.

"You good?" Ben appeared beside me, eyeing my bloody sock.

"Peachy," I tested my weight. Hurt like hell, but nothing busted. "Just a scratch."

"He's a total asshole," Ben said. "Thinks he owns the place —and everyone in it."

I raised an eyebrow. "Not a fan, huh?"

Ben shrugged. "I hate bullies. Plus, I've seen how he looks at Dr. Swanson. Like she's his property."

Something ugly twisted in my gut. I squashed it. Tara wasn't mine to get territorial over, no matter what weird energy buzzed between us in that PT room. She was still part of her father's scheme to bring me to Miami.

"Thanks," I nodded toward Diego. "For the warning."

"No problem." Ben hesitated. "Some of us are actually glad you're here. Not everyone buys the 'washed-up party boy' bullshit."

Coach's whistle cut him off. "Enough gossip! Full-field scrimmage!"

I limped into position, shin throbbing.

Practice finished without more drama. By the end, my legs felt like concrete, and my shin pulsed with every heartbeat.

As we left, Coach grabbed my arm. "McCrae. Hold up."

I braced for a lecture, but he surprised me. "Good work today."

"Thanks, Coach."

"Don't get excited yet." He nodded toward Hank, who was talking with Tara. "The boss wants to see you after your shower."

My stomach dropped. "Again. Why?"

"No idea, didn't ask." Coach's face softened. "Look, I don't know what's happening between you and the Swansons, and I don't care. But after thirty years in MLS, I know talent, and you've got it in spades. Don't let this bullshit derail that."

I nodded, speechless, watching Hank and Tara walk away, wondering what fresh hell awaited in the owner's office.

————

The shower did little to ease the tension knotting my shoulders. I stood under the spray longer than necessary, letting the hot water pound against my skin, trying to wash away the memory of Tara's hands, of Diego's threat, of Hank's icy stare.

By the time I emerged, the locker room was mostly empty.

A few stragglers were still getting dressed, including Ben, who gave me a small wave as he headed out.

"The party tonight at Basement," he called over his shoulder. "You coming?"

I forced a smile. "Wouldn't miss it."

Once I was alone, I checked my phone. No new messages from Tara. I wasn't sure what I'd been expecting—an apology? A continuation of our tense exchange? Some acknowledgment of what had passed between us in that PT room?

Instead, there was nothing. Just the hollow silence of a conversation cut short.

I dressed quickly in jeans and a simple black t-shirt, still damp from the shower. I took the elevator to Hank's office on the top floor.

His assistant gave me a tight smile as I approached. "Mr. McCrae, Mr. Swanson is expecting you."

She buzzed me in without another word.

Hank was standing at the window, his back to the door, hands clasped behind him as he gazed out at the Miami skyline. He didn't turn when I entered.

"Xander," he said, my name sounding like an afterthought. "Have a seat."

I remained standing. "I'll stand, thanks."

Now he turned, a small smile playing at the corners of his mouth. "Still defiant, I see. Some things never change."

"What do you want, Hank?"

He moved to his desk, sitting down in a leather chair. "Direct, as always. I've always appreciated that about you."

I said nothing, waiting him out.

"I wanted to discuss your... progress," he said finally. "Dr. Swanson tells me your shoulder is still giving you trouble."

The casual mention of Tara sent a spike of anger through me. "My shoulder is fine."

"That's not what her assessment says." He tapped a folder on his desk. "She's recommending continued physical therapy, now three times a week."

Of course, she was. More opportunities to get me alone, vulnerable, under her hands. More chances to play whatever game we'd started.

"Is that all?" I asked, already turning to leave.

"Not quite." Hank's voice hardened. "I also wanted to remind you of the morality clause in your contract."

I froze. "Excuse me?"

"Section 12, paragraph 3. Players are expected to maintain professional relationships with all team staff. Any violation of this clause is grounds for immediate termination."

The implication was clear. Whatever Tara and I were doing, whatever we might do, Hank knew about it. And he was warning me off.

"I'm well aware of my contract," I said, my voice tight. "Is there anything else?"

Hank studied me for a long moment. "Just one thing. The party tonight at Basement. I expect all my players to represent the organization with dignity and restraint."

"I'll be on my best behavior," I said, the words tasting like ash in my mouth.

"See that you are." He turned back to his window, a clear dismissal. "That will be all, Xander."

I left without another word, the door swinging shut behind me with a soft click.

The chains were tightening.

The penthouse was quiet when I returned. Late afternoon sunlight streamed through the windows, casting long shadows across the minimalist furniture. I moved to the bar, poured myself two fingers of whisky before collapsing onto the couch.

The day's events played on a loop in my head. That moment of electric connection with Tara, followed by her cold dismissal. Diego's threat on the field. Hank's thinly veiled warning in his office.

I was being played from all sides, caught in a web of manipulation and secrets that stretched back to a night I'd spent the better part of my adult life trying to forget.

The sound of the front door opening pulled me from my thoughts. Leo walked in, his arms full of shopping bags, his face neutral.

"There you are," he said, setting the bags down on the kitchen counter. "I was beginning to think you'd moved out."

The tension between us from our earlier fight hadn't eased. I took another sip of whisky, letting the burn coat my throat.

"I'm sorry," I said finally.

Leo's eyebrows shot up. "For what?"

"For blaming you. For the contract, for not knowing about the Swansons. None of that was your fault." I set my glass down, meeting his eyes. "This whole thing is a setup, and I took it out on you. I'm sorry."

For a moment, Leo just stared at me. Then his shoulders slumped, the mask of indifference falling away.

"I should have done more digging," he said, moving to sit across from me. "The ownership structure was deliberately hidden behind a bunch of shell companies and investment groups. I should have been more thorough."

"It wouldn't have mattered," I said. "Hank wanted me here. He would have found a way."

"So what now?" Leo asked, eyeing my whisky. "You planning on drinking yourself into oblivion before the party tonight?"

I snorted. "Tempting, but no. I need to be clear-headed for this one."

"Because...?"

I hesitated, then decided Leo deserved the truth. "Because Tara's going to be there. And things between us are... complicated."

Leo's expression shifted, concern replacing relief. "Xander, you need to be careful. If Hank finds out—"

"He already knows," I cut in. "He called me into his office today to remind me of the morality clause in my contract. Fraternizing with team staff is grounds for termination."

"Jesus," Leo muttered. "So that's his game? Bring you here just to fire you if you get too close to his daughter?"

I shook my head. "I don't think so. It's not that simple." I thought of the way Hank had looked at me in his office. All calculating. "He wants something from me, but I don't think it's my career. Not yet, anyway."

"What then?"

"I don't know," I admitted. "But I'm going to find out."

Leo studied me for a long moment. "Just... be careful, aye? Whatever history you have with the Swansons, it's clearly not over. And I don't want to see you get hurt."

The sincerity in his voice caught me off guard. In all the years we'd known each other, through all the clubs and parties and scandals, Leo had been the one constant in my life. My friend, my protector, the one person who'd stuck by me even when I was at my worst.

"I'll be careful," I promised, though we both knew it was a lie.

Leo seemed to sense this. "What time should we head to the club?"

"We?" I raised an eyebrow.

"You think I'm letting you walk into that lion's den alone?" Leo grinned, some of his usual spark returning. "Besides, someone's got to be sober enough to get your drunk ass home when this all goes sideways."

How about that? I wasn't entirely alone in this mess.

"Ten," I said. "We'll head over around ten."

———

The Basement was exactly what its name suggested, an underground club nestled beneath one of South Beach's most exclusive hotels. The line to get in stretched around the block, but Leo led me past it to a side entrance where a massive bouncer nodded in recognition.

"McCrae," he said, unclipping the velvet rope. "The team is in the VIP section."

The club was a sensory assault—bass pounding in my chest, strobe lights turning the dance floor into a blur of moving bodies, the sharp-sweet scent of perfume mixed with sweat and booze. I followed Leo through the crowd, nodding at the occasional fan who recognized me despite the dim lighting.

The VIP section was elevated above the main floor, offering a perfect view of the chaos below while remaining somewhat insulated from it. Most of the team was already there, spread across a collection of low couches and hightables. Diego held court at the largest table, surrounded by a group of women who laughed too loudly at whatever he was saying.

Ben Carter caught my eye from a quieter corner and raised

his drink in greeting. I nodded back, scanning the room for the one face I really wanted to see.

And then I saw her.

She wasn't wearing the green dress. She was in red, a deep blood-red dress that clung to every curve before ending mid-thigh. Her hair was down, falling in loose waves around her shoulders. She looked nothing like the severe Dr. Swanson who'd tortured me in that PT room. This was Tara—fierce, beautiful, and utterly untouchable.

She was standing at the bar, her head tossed back in laughter. Diego's eyes kept darting to her, possessive and hungry. As I watched, he excused himself from his table and moved toward her, placing a proprietary hand on the small of her back as he leaned in to say something in her ear.

An ugly twist knotted in my gut at the sight of his hand on her. The memory of what he said on the practice field echoed in my head: *"You're not the only one getting 'special treatment'."*

"Down, boy," Leo murmured beside me, noticing the direction of my gaze. "You've got that 'punch first, think later' look again."

I forced myself to look away, accepting a drink from a passing waitress without checking what it was. The liquor burned going down, and I welcomed the heat, the momentary distraction from the sight of Diego's hand on Tara's back.

The night stretched on, a blur of music and drinks and meaningless conversation. I made the rounds, playing the part of the team's new star, shaking hands and making small talk with sponsors and club officials. But my eyes kept finding her across the room, and more often than not, I found her watching me too.

It was torture, this silent communication across a crowded

club. Each glance felt like a continuation of our text exchange, a challenge thrown and accepted.

I dare you. I double-dare you.

Diego hovered around her like he owned the place—and her. The longer the night went on, the harder it was to miss the way he kept trying to stake his claim. At one point, he tried to drag her onto the dance floor, but she shook her head, extracting herself from his grip with a smile.

I lost sight of her for a while after that, caught in a conversation with the nightclub's owner, who was a big soccer fan and wanted to discuss European tactics. By the time I extricated myself, Tara was nowhere to be seen.

"Looking for someone?"

Ben appeared at my elbow with a knowing smile on his face.

"Just getting some air," I lied.

Ben's smile widened. "She's at the bar. Alone for once. Diego got called away to deal with an issue at the door. One of his buddies couldn't get in."

I glanced toward the bar, and sure enough, there she was. Standing alone, her red dress a beacon in the dim light, her fingers wrapped around a glass of something clear.

"Thanks," I said to Ben, already moving.

"Watch yourself," he called after me. "Diego's got a temper."

I weaved through the crowd, my heart pounding in my ears louder than the bass that shook the floor. She saw me coming, her eyes tracking my approach in the mirror behind the bar. She didn't turn, didn't acknowledge me, but I felt her awareness like a physical touch.

I took the empty spot beside her, not looking at her directly, just watching her reflection as she watched mine.

"You didn't wear the green dress," I said, my voice low but clear over the music.

Her lips curved into a small smile. "I told you I'd wear whatever I wanted."

"The red suits you."

"I didn't ask for your approval."

The bartender approached, and I ordered a whisky neat. In the mirror, I could see Diego re-entering the club, his eyes scanning the crowd. It wouldn't be long before he spotted us.

"Your boyfriend's back," I said, nodding toward the entrance.

Tara's smile tightened. "Diego is not my boyfriend."

"Does he know that?"

"What I do or don't do with Diego Mano is none of your business." She turned to face me fully now, her eyes challenging. "Just like what I do or don't do with you is none of his."

The bartender set my whisky in front of me. I took a sip, letting the liquor coat my tongue before I spoke again.

"So, what exactly are we doing, Tara?"

"I don't know what you mean."

"I think you do." I set my glass down, turning to face her. "The PT session. The texts. Whatever happened in that room... that wasn't just doctor and patient."

Her eyes flashed with something that might have been anger, or desire, or both. "You're delusional."

"Am I?" I stepped closer, close enough to smell her perfume, and the light floral scent made my head spin. "Tell me you didn't feel it. Tell me you haven't been thinking about it all day, just like I have."

She opened her mouth to respond, but her eyes suddenly widened, looking past me. I turned to see Diego approaching, his face dark with fury.

"Game over, McCrae," he barked. "She doesn't want your bullshit."

I glanced at Tara, watching emotions battle across her face. Want versus fear. Risk versus reason. We stood on the edge of something dangerous. One more move and we'd both crash with no safety nets.

But I'd had enough of caution. Enough of the hints, the unsaid things, the near misses.

"Fuck it," I muttered, loud enough to cut through the bass.

No dark corners. No private moment. Right there, with Diego and half the team gawking, I took her face in my hands and kissed her.

For one terrifying second, she didn't move. Then, with a noise that sounded like victory and defeat combined, she kissed me back. Her mouth opened against mine, her fists grabbing my shirt, yanking me closer. The kiss burned hot and hungry, bottled words and denied wants compressed into one fucking reckless moment.

It wasn't pretty. It wasn't gentle. It was a middle finger to the past, to her father, to all the secrets keeping us apart. We were mutually assured destruction, fire meeting gasoline, and God help anyone caught in the blast radius.

Somewhere beyond us, Diego sucked in a breath, the crowd buzzed with shock. But who cared? Nothing existed except Tara in my arms, her taste, my heart hammering like it might crack my ribs.

In this stolen moment, we were just Xander and Tara. Not doctor and patient. Not the owner's daughter and a fallen star. Just two people broken by the same shit, finally connecting in the middle of chaos.

And if Hank Swanson wanted to can me for it, let him. Some things were worth burning for.

CHAPTER
Eight

TARA

HIS LIPS WERE STILL on mine. My hands still clutched his shirt. The world had narrowed to this; his taste, his scent, the slight stubble against my skin, the heat of his body against mine. The bass vibrated loudly through the club, but all I could hear was the rush of blood in my ears and the soft sound he made when I parted my lips against his.

Twelve years of waiting.

Twelve years of planning.

Twelve years of obsession.

And in one reckless moment, Xander had just taken all the power I'd so carefully cultivated and thrown it right out the window.

Reality crashed back in. I realized every eye was on us—the shocked faces of my medical staff, the slack-jawed expressions of the players, the gleeful looks of those already pulling out phones to document the moment.

And there was Diego on the sideline, his face twisted into an ugly smirk.

My survival instinct kicked in with brutal clarity. This wasn't just about regaining control of our twisted game. This was about my career. My life.

I shoved Xander back hard enough that he stumbled. Oxygen rushed back into my lungs.

And then, without thinking, I raised my hand and let it fly —flat-palmed, sharp, catching him square across that perfectly chiseled jaw.

The sound cracked through the club's momentary lull in music. My hand burned from the impact. His head snapped to the side, a red mark already blooming on his cheek.

"Who do you think you are?" I snarled, my voice dripping with ice. "You are a player. I am your doctor. Don't you *ever* forget that again."

The shock on his face was so raw, so genuine, that for a heartbeat I almost broke character. Almost reached for him. Almost told him I was sorry, that I didn't mean it, that the kiss had been everything I'd dreamed of.

But Diego's satisfied laugh cut through the tension, and Xander's expression hardened into something cold. Without a word, he turned away and walked out of the club.

I'd won. So why did victory taste like ash in my mouth?

"Guess he can't handle rejection," Diego said, sidling up beside me, voice thick with false sympathy. "Some guys just don't know how to take no for an answer."

I rounded on him, channeling all my conflicted emotions into a glare so cold it made him take a step back.

"I handled it, Diego. Stay out of it."

"I was just—"

"I don't need your protection. I don't need anyone's protection." I smoothed down my dress, hyper-aware of every eye still on me. "What I need is for everyone to remember that I am a medical professional, and this kind of behavior will not be tolerated."

I could feel the narrative solidifying around me. Poor Dr. Swanson, accosted by the team's newest troublemaker. The talented but unstable Xander McCrae, living up to his party-boy reputation. Just another incident in a long history of bad behavior.

I spotted Coach Wilkes across the room, his expression grim. Time for damage control.

I made my way over to him, my chin held high. The crowd parted before me, whispers following in my wake. This was a performance, and I needed to nail every beat.

"Coach," I said, my voice steady. "I want to apologize for that unfortunate spectacle."

Wilkes studied me, his weathered face unreadable. "You have nothing to apologize for, Doc. McCrae was out of line."

"It wasn't entirely his fault." I kept my voice low and steady.

Wilkes nodded, but there was something in his eyes. "You two have a history?"

"A long time ago. Nothing relevant to the present situation."

"If you say so." He didn't look convinced. "You heading out?"

"Yes. I think I've had enough excitement for one night." I managed a tight smile. "I'll see you tomorrow."

I turned to leave, feeling the weight of his gaze on my back. The whispers followed me through the club, but I kept my head high, my pace measured. I was Dr. Swanson, completely in control of the situation.

It wasn't until I was alone in the elevator, the doors sliding shut on the chaos behind me, that the first crack appeared in my facade. My hand—the one that had struck Xander's face—trembled as I pressed the button for the lobby.

I stared at my palm, still faintly pink from the impact. I could still feel the heat of his skin, the slight roughness of his stubble. I could still taste him on my lips.

The slap had been a lie.

The kiss had been the truth.

By the time I reached the lobby, I had composed myself once more. I nodded to the doorman, walked calmly to the valet, and gave a generous tip as my car was brought around. I drove home on autopilot, the Miami night a blur of neon and palm trees beyond my windshield.

My apartment building was quiet at this hour. The doorman nodded as I entered, and I forced a smile in return. The elevator ride was mercifully empty, giving me the privacy to close my eyes and lean against the wall, trying to gather the strength for the last steps of this charade.

The moment my apartment door closed behind me, the adrenaline that had carried me through the night vanished, leaving me shaking. I kicked off my heels, letting them lie where they fell, and made my way to the bathroom, shedding clothes as I went.

The bathroom was my sanctuary—all white marble and chrome, with a deep Jacuzzi tub big enough to stretch out in. I turned the taps on full, watching as steam rose from the water. I added a generous pour of bath oil, something lavender and supposedly calming, though I doubted anything could calm the storm raging inside me now.

I caught sight of myself in the mirror as I waited for the tub to fill. My lips were slightly swollen, my pupils dilated, a flush still visible on my chest and neck. I looked... *wrecked*. Like someone who had been thoroughly kissed and then left wanting.

Which, of course, was exactly what had happened.

I stepped into the bath, hissing as the hot water enveloped me. I sank down until only my head remained above the surface, letting the heat and the scented steam work their way into my tense muscles.

It didn't help. If anything, the sensual warmth of the water only heightened my awareness of my body—of the way my skin still tingled where he'd touched me, of the heavy ache between my thighs, of the hollow emptiness in the pit of my stomach.

I closed my eyes, trying to focus on my breathing, to center myself the way I'd learned in med school to handle stress. In for four, hold for seven, out for eight. A simple technique to calm the sympathetic nervous system.

But with my eyes closed, all I could see was Xander's face as I slapped him. The shock, the hurt, the way his eyes had gone from burning with desire to cold in the space of a heartbeat.

I'd hurt him. I'd meant to, of course—that was the point. To reassert control. To reestablish boundaries. To remind him and everyone watching that I was Dr. Swanson, not some conquest to be had against a bar.

But I hadn't expected it to hurt me too.

I traced my fingers over my lips, remembering. He'd tasted like whisky. His hands had been gentle on my face, despite the urgency of the kiss. And for that brief, perfect moment before reality crashed in, I'd felt something I hadn't felt in my entire adult life: whole.

My hand drifted down, skimming over my collarbone,

between my breasts, across my stomach. I imagined it was his hand, his touch. What would have happened if we hadn't been in that club? If Diego hadn't been watching? If I hadn't been so caught up in my need to maintain control?

Would we have ended up here, in my bathroom? Would he be in this tub with me, his body pressing mine against the smooth marble, his hands exploring every inch of me?

I let my hand drift lower, under the water, between my thighs. I was already swollen, aching with need. I bit my lip to stifle a moan as I touched myself, imagining it was him.

In my fantasy, he wasn't gentle. He was demanding, almost angry—as angry as I'd pretended to be in the club—we'd be in the shower and he would push me against the wall, his body hard and unyielding against mine. His hands would pin my wrists above my head as he kissed me, deep and possessive.

"Is this what you want?" he'd growl. "To be fucked by a player? By someone beneath the great Dr. Swanson?"

"Yes," I gasped, both in my fantasy and in the reality of my bath. "God, yes."

In my mind, he spun me around, pressing me face-first against the cool tile. One hand kept my wrists pinned, the other snaked around to find me wet and ready. He teased me, his fingers circling but never quite giving me what I needed.

"All those years," he said, his voice rough with desire. "Just thinking about you. Dreaming about you. And now you're going to come for me, Tara. You're going to come around my fingers, and then you're going to come around my cock, and you're going to remember who you belong to."

"Please," I begged, my hips moving against my hand, chasing the pleasure that built with each stroke. "Please, Xander."

In my fantasy, he finally relented, pushing two fingers deep inside me as his thumb circled my clit. In reality, I did the same, matching the rhythm I imagined he would set—hard and fast and merciless, exactly what I needed.

The orgasm hit me like a wave, sudden and overwhelming. I cried out, my back arching, water sloshing over the edge of the tub as my body convulsed with pleasure. I rode it out, gasping his name into the empty bathroom, until the after-shocks subsided and I was left floating in the cooling water, breathless and spent.

As the haze of pleasure faded, reality crept back in. I was alone in my bathtub, having just gotten myself off to a fantasy of the man I'd publicly humiliated hours before. The man whose career I could destroy with a word to my father. The man I'd spent twelve years obsessing over, planning to seduce and then discard.

But that wasn't the plan anymore, was it? The "hunt" I'd so carefully orchestrated wasn't a game I controlled. It was a need that had consumed me, body and soul. A need that might just destroy everything I'd worked for.

I climbed out of the tub, water dripping onto the marble floor as I reached for a towel.

I wrapped it around myself and padded into my bedroom, the plush carpet soft beneath my bare feet. My phone sat on the nightstand, screen dark. I picked it up, my thumb hovering over his name in my messages.

I could text him. Apologize for the slap. Explain that I'd panicked, that I'd been afraid of what people would think, of losing my job, my reputation. Tell him that the kiss had been everything I'd dreamed of for twelve years.

Or I could double down. Be Dr. Swanson. Send a cold message reminding him of the boundaries and warning him of the consequences if he ever tried something like that again.

I set the phone down without doing either. There was no middle ground here, no safe path forward. Either I surrendered to this need and accepted the consequences, or I buried it deep and pretended it had never existed.

I crawled into bed, not bothering with pajamas, the towel falling away as I slipped between the cool sheets. Sleep wouldn't come easily, if at all. Not with my mind racing and my body still humming with residual pleasure and unfulfilled need.

CHAPTER
Nine

XANDER

THE STING of her slap burned on my cheek as I pushed through the crowd. Bodies parted before me like water, their whispers trailing in my wake. I kept my head down, jaw clenched so tight my teeth ached, my only focus on getting the fuck out of this club before I did something even more stupid than kissing Dr. Tara Swanson in front of half the Miami Pirates organization.

I shouldered past the bouncer and burst into the humid Miami night. I gulped down air that tasted of ocean salt, trying to steady myself.

What the fuck was I thinking?

I wasn't. That was the problem. One moment I'd been watching her across the bar, all cool confidence in that dress red as sin that wiped every warning from my head.

Next, I was pulling her against me, claiming her mouth with mine, consequences be damned.

And for that one perfect moment, she'd kissed me back.

Her lips had parted, her body had melted into mine, her hands had clutched at my shirt like she was drowning and I was air.

Then she shoved me off her and slapped me. Hell of a hit—she didn't hold back.

"You are a player. I am your doctor. Don't you *ever* forget that again."

Her words echoed in my head, each syllable another twist of the knife. I'd misread everything. The tension between us, the loaded glances, the almost-kiss at dinner—all of it meaningless.

I paced in front of the club entrance. My car was with the valet, but I couldn't face dealing with that right now. I needed to walk, to move, to do something with this restless energy coursing through my veins.

Idiot. Fucking idiot. You've just torched your career. Again.

I'd violated every professional boundary. Forced myself on the team doctor. In public. With witnesses. With fucking *camera phones*.

By morning, the video would be all over social media. By afternoon, Hank would have me in his office. By evening, I'd be back on the transfer list, my reputation somehow even more tarnished than before.

Chelsea would laugh their asses off. *Told you so. Once a liability, always a liability.*

"Xander!"

I turned to see Leo pushing through the crowd leaving the club, his face a mask of concern.

"If you're here to say 'I told you so,' save it," I snapped.

Leo ignored me, grabbing the valet ticket from my numb fingers. "I'm driving," he said. He handed the ticket to the valet and stood beside me, the silence between us heavy.

When the Audi was brought around, Leo opened the passenger door for me. "Get in."

I hesitated, then slumped into the seat, the familiar scent of the leather doing nothing to soothe me. Leo got behind the wheel, the engine purring to life as he pulled away from the curb and merged into the steady flow of Miami nightlife traffic.

We drove in silence for several blocks. I stared out the window, watching the blur of South Beach slide past. I expected a lecture. A reminder of all the ways I'd fucked up. A rundown of the damage control we'd need to do. The contracts we'd need to review. The lawyers we'd need to call.

Instead, Leo reached over and turned up the radio. A pop song I didn't recognize filled the car.

"Well," he finally said, glancing at me with a hint of his usual sardonic humor, "that's one way to make an impression on your new teammates."

I let out a surprised bark of laughter. "Yeah. Not exactly the first impression I was going for."

"I don't know. That kid Ben looked pretty impressed. I think you just became his hero."

I snorted. "Great. The only person in my corner is the one guy on the team who's too young to know better."

Leo navigated through a yellow light, his profile illuminated briefly by the passing streetlamps. "Not the only one."

The simple statement lingered. I glanced at him, but his eyes were fixed on the road ahead, his expression unreadable.

We drove the rest of the way to the penthouse in companionable silence. Leo handed the keys to the valet and followed me into the lobby, his presence steady and grounding at my side. In the elevator, he leaned against the wall, arms crossed over his chest.

"You want to talk about it?" he asked as we ascended.

I stared at my reflection in the polished doors. The red mark on my cheek had faded, but I could still feel the ghost of her touch. "Not really."

"Fair enough."

The elevator dinged, and we stepped out into the private foyer of the penthouse. I fumbled with the keys, suddenly exhausted, the adrenaline crash hitting me all at once. Leo took them from my hand without comment and unlocked the door, pushing it open. Slinging an arm around my shoulders, he steered me inside like he'd done a hundred times before.

I headed straight for the bar, but Leo intercepted me, steering me toward the kitchen instead.

"Water first," he said. "You can drink yourself stupid after you're hydrated."

I slumped onto a barstool at the kitchen island, watching as Leo filled a glass from the filtered tap and set it in front of me. I drained it in one long swallow, not realizing until that moment how thirsty I was.

Leo refilled it without being asked, then leaned against the counter, studying me. "For what it's worth, I don't think you're going to get fired."

I raised an eyebrow. "No? You got a direct line to Hank Swanson I don't know about?"

"No, but I've got eyes. And a brain." Leo crossed his arms. "If he wanted you gone, he wouldn't have brought you here in the first place. Whatever game he's playing, it's not over yet."

"Maybe not," I conceded. "But he warned me off Tara specifically. Said there was a morality clause in my contract that could get me sacked if I crossed any lines with any of the staff." I laughed bitterly. "Pretty sure making out with her in a club counts as crossing a line."

"She kissed you back," Leo pointed out. "Before the slap, I mean. I saw it. Half the fuckin' club saw it."

I rubbed a hand over my face, remembering the feel of her lips, soft and yielding, before they turned hard and unyielding. "Doesn't matter. She made her position pretty clear afterward."

Leo was quiet for a moment, his expression thoughtful before he pushed away from the counter. "You should get some sleep. Tomorrow's going to be a long day."

I nodded, suddenly too tired to argue. Leo was right. Whatever fallout was coming, I'd face it better with a clear head.

He walked me to my bedroom door, pausing with his hand on the knob. "For what it's worth..." he said, his voice unusually serious, "I've got your back. Always."

"I know," I said, the words inadequate but sincere. "Thanks."

He nodded once, then turned and headed down the hall to his own room, leaving me alone with my thoughts.

I stripped off my clothes and fell into bed, every muscle aching with tension. The ceiling fan whirred softly overhead, stirring the cool air-conditioned breeze across my bare chest. I closed my eyes, but all I could see was Tara's face—first soft with desire, then hard with rejection.

I'd been so sure I wasn't imagining the connection between us. The electricity that crackled whenever we were in the same room. The way her breath caught when I said her name. The heat in her eyes when she'd worked on my shoulder in the therapy room.

Had I manufactured all of it? Projected my own twisted obsession onto her professional detachment?

No. She'd kissed me back. For that one perfect moment, she'd wanted me as much as I wanted her.

Fuck it. Whatever happens tomorrow, the kiss was worth it.

———

A knock on my bedroom door jolted me awake. I blinked in the darkness, disoriented. The digital clock on the nightstand read 2:37 AM. I'd been asleep for less than an hour.

The knock came again, more insistent this time. I switched on the bedside lamp and swung my legs over the side of the bed, pulling on a pair of sweatpants before crossing to the door.

Leo stood in the hallway, looking uncomfortable. His hair was mussed, like he'd been sleeping too. "You, uh... you have a visitor."

I frowned, still foggy with sleep. "What? Who?"

Leo stepped aside, gesturing toward the living room. "See for yourself."

I pushed past him, confused and wary. The penthouse was dark except for a single lamp in the living room, casting long shadows across the polished floor. And there, silhouetted against the Miami skyline, stood Tara.

She was still wearing the red dress from the club, though her hair was looser now, falling in soft waves around her shoulders. She turned as I entered the room, and the breath caught in my throat. Her eyes were wild, her expression a storm of emotions I couldn't decipher.

"What are you doing here?" I asked, my voice rough with sleep and surprise.

She didn't answer immediately, her gaze traveling slowly down my bare chest before returning to my face. The intensity in those dark eyes made my skin prickle with awareness.

"I'll, uh... I'll give you two some privacy," Leo muttered,

retreating down the hallway. I heard his bedroom door close with a soft click.

Tara took a step forward, then another, closing the distance between us with deliberate grace. "I shouldn't be here."

"No," I agreed, not moving. "You shouldn't."

"This is a mistake."

"Probably."

We stared at each other, the air between us charged with the same electricity I'd felt at the club, and in every moment we'd been alone together since I'd arrived in Miami.

"How did you know where I was staying?" I asked, breaking the tense silence.

She laughed, a soft, breathless sound that sent a shiver down my spine. "I've been running past this building every morning."

"I knew it was you," I said, the pieces clicking into place. The figure on the beach that morning, the one I'd dismissed as paranoia. "I saw you. I thought I was losing my mind."

"You're not," she said, taking another step closer. We were almost touching now, close enough that I could smell her perfume. "Not about that, anyway."

I reached for her, unable to resist any longer. My hand cupped her cheek, thumb brushing across her lower lip. She inhaled sharply but didn't pull away.

"What about the slap?" I asked, my voice low. "What about 'you're a player, I'm your doctor'?"

"I panicked," she admitted, leaning slightly into my touch. "Everyone was watching. My staff, the team... I have a reputation to maintain. A position to protect."

"And now?"

Her eyes met mine, dark and fathomless. "Now I'm here."

I closed the remaining distance between us, capturing her

mouth with mine. This kiss differed from the one at the club—
slower, deeper, more deliberate. Her lips parted beneath mine,
her tongue sliding against my own in a dance that made my
blood sing.

Her hands were everywhere—in my hair, on my chest,
trailing fire down my back. I pressed her against me, feeling
the heat of her body through the thin fabric of her dress. She
made a soft, needy sound in the back of her throat that nearly
undid me.

I backed her toward the wall, pinning her there with my
body. Her head fell back as I trailed kisses down her neck,
tasting the salt of her skin, feeling her pulse race beneath my
lips.

"Enough kissing," she gasped, her voice rough with desire.
Her hands moved to my waistband, tugging at the drawstring
of my sweatpants. "Let's fuck."

Her words sent a jolt of heat straight to my groin. I pulled
back slightly, searching her face. Her eyes were dark with
need, her lips swollen from my kisses. But there was something else there too—a desperation, an urgency that went
beyond mere physical desire.

"Tara—"

"Don't," she cut me off, her fingers digging into my
shoulders. "Don't overthink this. Don't make it more than
it is."

Her hands were sliding down my chest, dipping below my
waistband, wrapping around me with confident precision.
And suddenly, thinking was the last thing on my mind.

I hoisted her up, her legs wrapping around my waist, and
carried her to my bedroom. We fell onto the bed in a tangle of
limbs, my hands already working the zipper of her dress. She
arched her back, helping me slide the fabric down her body,

revealing inches of smooth skin that I immediately covered with my mouth.

Her underwear was black lace, a stark contrast against her pale skin. I hooked my fingers into the waistband, looking up at her for permission. She nodded, lifting her hips to help me remove them.

And then she was naked beneath me, all soft curves and sharp angles, more beautiful than anything I'd ever seen. I took a moment just to look at her, to commit this image to memory—Tara Swanson, splayed across my sheets, her hair a dark halo around her face, her eyes heavy with desire.

"Stop staring," she said, a hint of vulnerability creeping into her voice.

I shook my head, lowering myself to kiss her again. "Not a chance. You're fucking gorgeous."

A flush spread across her chest and up her neck, but she didn't look away. Instead, she reached for me, pulling me down on top of her, her body arching to meet mine. I slid a hand between her thighs, finding her wet and ready. She gasped as I stroked her, her nails digging into my back.

"Now," she demanded, her voice a ragged whisper. "I need you now."

I reached for the nightstand drawer, fumbling for a condom. She watched through hooded eyes as I rolled it on, her tongue darting out to wet her lips in a gesture so unconsciously sensual it damn near knocked me to my knees.

I lined myself up and pushed into her, slowly at first, the heat of her so tight and perfect it took my breath away. I had to stop, just for a second, braced above her, fighting for control. She was real. This was real. And, fuck, if it didn't feel better than anything I'd ever imagined.

Her legs wrapped tight around my waist, demanding

more, and I gave her everything she was asking for, driving into her harder, faster, until the only sound in the room was her gasping my name, her head thrown back against the pillows like she was offering herself up to me.

We crashed together hard in a raw frenzy, like neither of us could get close enough, fast enough, every thrust sharp, punishing, desperate. We weren't careful, weren't gentle. Her nails scored my back, my grip on her hips turned punishing, neither of us letting go as we chased the only healing we knew.

She came with a cry that she muffled against my shoulder, her body tightening around mine in waves that pulled me over the edge with her. For a moment, we were suspended together in that perfect, mindless bliss—no past, no future, just the present and the exquisite sensation of being completely, utterly connected.

Reality crept back in slowly. The sound of our breathing, harsh in the quiet room. The feel of her skin, slick with sweat beneath my palms. The weight of what we'd just done, settling over us.

I rolled to the side, not wanting to crush her with my weight, but kept an arm around her waist, unwilling to break contact completely. She didn't resist, but she didn't curl into me either. We lay side by side, staring at the ceiling, neither of us quite ready to face what came next.

"Well," I finally said, when the silence had stretched too thin, "that was unexpected."

She laughed, the sound startled and genuine. "That's one word for it."

I turned my head to look at her, drinking in the sight of her profile in the dim light. Her hair was a mess, her makeup slightly smudged, her lips still swollen from my kisses. She'd never looked more beautiful.

"Do you regret it?" I asked, the question slipping out before I could stop it.

She went quiet, staring at the ceiling. "I don't know," she whispered. "Ask me tomorrow." A beat passed, then she glanced at me, her expression unreadable. "Funny thing is, I was already in bed, ready to sleep when..." She left it hanging, unfinished, like even she wasn't sure how to explain it.

I nodded, accepting that it was the most honest answer she could give. Whatever this was between us—obsession, attraction, the ghost of something that had started twelve years ago —it wasn't simple. It would not be resolved with one night of mind-blowing sex, no matter how much we might have hoped it would be.

She shifted, turning onto her side to face me. Her hand reached out, fingers tracing the network of scars on my shoulder—the same ones she'd touched in the therapy room, but this time, there was no power play in the gesture. Just curiosity, and something softer I couldn't name.

"How did you get these?" she asked.

I closed my eyes, the memory washing over me. "You know. Glass from the windshield," I said, the words sticking in my throat.

Her fingers stilled for a moment, then resumed their gentle exploration. "Jimmy's crash."

I nodded, not trusting myself to speak.

She was quiet for a long time, her touch a balm against the old wound. "I never stopped thinking about you," she finally said, her voice so low I almost didn't hear it. "All these years. Even when I hated you for leaving, I couldn't stop."

The admission cracked something open inside me, something I'd kept carefully sealed. "I never stopped thinking about you either," I confessed, the words raw and honest in the darkness. "Not for a single day."

She looked up at me, her eyes wide and vulnerable in a way I'd never seen before. For a moment, I caught a glimpse of the sixteen-year-old girl who'd looked at me across her brother's casket, her heart in her eyes. The one I'd almost kissed behind the church, in a moment of shared grief and connection that had haunted me ever since.

But then the moment passed. She sat up, the sheet falling away. "I should go."

I didn't stop her. We both knew this couldn't last, couldn't continue. Not with who we were, not with our history, not with Hank Swanson standing between us like a specter.

I watched as she gathered her clothes, slipping back into the red dress. She didn't look at me as she zipped it up, as she ran her fingers through her tangled hair, as she checked her reflection in the mirror above my dresser.

Only when she was fully dressed, standing at the foot of my bed like a stranger, did she meet my eyes again. "This can't happen again," she said, but there was a question in her voice, a hesitation that belied her words.

I sat up. "Can't it?"

She shook her head, but it seemed more like she was arguing with herself than with me. "It's too complicated. Too dangerous. For both of us."

"I'm not afraid of dangerous," I said, holding her gaze. "I'm not afraid of complicated."

"I have to go," she repeated, more firmly this time. "It's almost dawn."

I nodded, accepting the inevitable. But as she turned to leave, I called after her. "So what happens now, Dr. Swanson?"

She paused in the doorway and looked back at me with an

expression that mirrored all the confusion and longing I felt. "I have no idea," she admitted, and then she was gone.

I fell back against the pillows, my body satisfied but my mind racing. The sheets still smelled like her—her perfume, her sweat and sex. I closed my eyes, trying to hold on to the memory of her touch, her taste, the sound of her voice when she'd said my name.

Whatever came next, whether punishment from Hank, awkwardness at the facility, or the inevitable fallout from crossing this line, I'd face it. For the first time in a very long time, I felt something other than guilt and self-loathing.

I felt alive.

CHAPTER

Ten

TARA

I WOKE WITH A JOLT, my body tensing before I even opened my eyes.

I'd slipped out of Xander McCrae's penthouse just before dawn, my body still humming with the aftershocks.

"Fuck," I whispered, pressing the heels of my hands against my eyes until stars burst behind my eyelids.

Sunlight streamed through the gaps in my blinds, painting bright stripes across my pristine white duvet. My bedroom looked exactly as it always did—minimalist, organized, controlled. Everything in its place. Nothing to betray the fact that less than eight hours ago, I had stood outside Xander's door, heart hammering in my chest, and told him—

"*Let's fuck.*"

Oh god.

I cringed so hard my entire body curled in on itself. Had those words actually come out of my mouth? Had I really

shown up at his door in the middle of the night and proposi-
tioned him like some desperate groupie?

Yes. Yes, I had.

And then I'd let him carry me to his bedroom. Let him
undress me, touch me, taste me. Let him see me fall apart
beneath him, my careful control shattered by his hands, his
mouth, his hard cock.

I flung back the covers and headed for the shower. Under
the hot spray, I took inventory of the evidence. The slight soreness between my thighs. The shadow of a bruise forming on
my hip where his fingers had dug in. The faint sting of his
stubble burned on my neck and chest.

Physical proof it hadn't been a dream. That Dr. Tara Swanson, head of sports medicine for the Miami Pirates, respected
professional and consummate control freak, had come
completely undone in Xander McCrae's bed.

What was I thinking?

That was the problem. I hadn't been thinking at all. I'd
been feeling—raw, desperate, and out of control.

Pathetic.

I shut off the water and wrapped myself in a towel. As I
wiped the steam from the mirror, I stared at myself. "This
stops now," I told my reflection firmly. "You are not some
lovesick teenager. You have a reputation to maintain and a
career to protect."

My reflection stared back at me, unconvinced.

As I dried my hair, a new perspective took shape in my
mind. Maybe last night hadn't been a mistake after all. Maybe
it had been exactly what I needed—what we both needed.
Years of tension, of wondering, of what-ifs... all of it released in
one night of mindless, physical pleasure.

I'd gotten him out of my system. That was all. I'd satisfied my curiosity, scratched the itch that had been plaguing me since I was sixteen.

And I'd done it on my terms. I'd gone to him. I'd dictated what would happen between us. I'd left before dawn, before things could get messy or complicated.

I hadn't lost control at all. I'd exercised the ultimate control. I hadn't fallen victim to any uncontrollable desires. I'd made a strategic decision to neutralize the distraction he represented. And now that it was done, I could move forward. Focus on my job. On my future.

I dressed with renewed confidence, choosing a casual sundress for my Saturday brunch plans. As I applied a light touch of makeup, I avoided thinking about how Xander's eyes had tracked my every movement as I'd dressed in his room. How he'd watched me from his bed, the sheets pooled around his waist, his expression unreadable in the pre-dawn light.

"So what happens now, Dr. Swanson?"

I pushed the memory away. Nothing would happen now. We'd had our moment, and now it was over. Back to reality. Back to our respective roles—player and team doctor. Nothing more.

———

"You fucked him."

I nearly choked on my mimosa. "Jesus, Chloe. Keep your voice down."

Chloe Durand, my best friend since undergrad and the most unapologetically blunt person I'd ever met, leaned across our table at Havana Café, her eyes gleaming with mischief. Her wild curls were dyed a vibrant turquoise this month, a vivid contrast to the bohemian white sundress that made her look like some kind of ocean goddess.

"Well, did you?" She pressed on, undeterred by my glare.

The trendy brunch spot was packed with beautiful people in designer sunglasses, sipping overpriced drinks and pretending not to eavesdrop on each other's conversations. I glanced around, paranoid that someone from the team might be nearby.

"Can we not do this here?" I hissed.

Chloe rolled her eyes but settled back in her chair. "Fine. But you're not getting out of this conversation, T. I've waited for God knows how long to hear how the ghost boy measures up to your fantasies."

I winced at the nickname. Ghost boy. That's what Chloe called Xander. The one who haunted my dreams, my relationships, my entire adult life.

"It's not what you think," I said, picking at my avocado toast.

"So you didn't sleep with him?" Her arched eyebrow called bullshit on my evasion.

I sighed, resigned to her persistence. "Okay, yes. I did. But it's not a big deal."

"Not a big deal?" Chloe let out a burst of laughter that turned heads at nearby tables. "Honey, you've been obsessed with this man since you were in braces. You've stalked his social media, dated guys who looked like him, and literally chosen your entire career path just to get close to him again. And now you've slept with him. That's the *fucking* definition of a big deal."

Put that way, it did sound slightly unhinged. But Chloe didn't understand. She lived her life like one of her art installations—chaotic, vibrant, open to interpretation. She'd never understood my need for structure, control, and carefully laid plans.

"It was just sex," I insisted, lowering my voice. "I needed to get him out of my system. And now I have."

Chloe studied me over the rim of her glass, her artist's eye missing nothing. "Is that what you're telling yourself?"

"It's the truth."

"Mmm-hmm." Her skepticism was palpable. "And that's why you're positively glowing this morning? Because you got him 'out of your system'?"

I felt heat rise to my cheeks. "I am not glowing."

"Oh, sweetie." She reached across the table to pat my hand condescendingly. "You're practically radioactive. I've known you for eight years, and I've never seen you look like this after sex. Not even with what's-his-name, the CrossFit instructor with the eight-pack."

"Connor," I supplied automatically. "And that was different."

"Yeah, because you weren't in love with Connor."

"I'm not in love with Xander either," I snapped, more sharply than I intended. "I was... fixated. Obsessed, maybe. But that's over now."

Chloe's expression softened. "Tara. Come on. You can't close a book by skipping the middle and reading the last page. You just made yourself want to read it all over again."

I hated how right she was, and I busied myself with my food, avoiding her too-perceptive gaze.

"Look," she continued, "I'm not judging. God knows I've made some questionable choices in the name of great sex. Remember the fire dancers from Art Basel?"

I couldn't help but smile at the memory. "The ones who almost burned down your apartment?"

"Worth it," she said with a wink. "My point is, if this was just a one-night stand to scratch an itch, great. But be honest with yourself about what it meant."

"It didn't mean anything," I insisted. "It was... closure."

Chloe snorted. "Closure rarely involves orgasms, honey."

"Can we please change the subject?" I begged, glancing around the café again. "How's the installation coming for your opening tomorrow?"

She allowed the deflection, launching into an animated description of her latest mixed-media project—something involving reclaimed driftwood, copper wire, and projections of ocean waves. I nodded in all the right places, but my mind kept drifting back to Xander's hands on my skin. His mouth on mine. The way he'd looked at me in the darkness, like I was something precious.

"I never stopped thinking about you either. Not for a single day."

I shook the memory away, forcing myself to focus on Chloe's words.

"—and the lighting is still giving me fits, but I think it's going to be amazing," she was saying. "You're coming, right? I reserved a special space for your brother's piece."

The mention of Jimmy brought me back to the present. "Of course I'm coming. I wouldn't miss it."

Jimmy had been an artist too, though his medium had been photography rather than Chloe's eclectic installations. After his death, I'd kept several of his pieces in storage—moody black and white landscapes that captured something essential about his soul. I haven't looked at them for years, but when Chloe asked about using one in her show, I gave her the key to the storage unit.

"You should bring him," Chloe said suddenly, her eyes lighting up with inspiration.

"Bring who?"

"Ghost boy. Xander. Your one-night stand that definitely meant nothing at all." Her voice dripped with sarcasm.

I stared at her, aghast. "Are you insane? I can't bring him to your opening."

"Why not? If you're really over him, it won't be a big deal." She leaned forward, her expression turning sly. "Prove it. To me. And to yourself."

She was daring me to put my money where my mouth was —to prove that last night really had been nothing more than physical release.

"It would be inappropriate," I argued. "He's a player. I'm his doctor."

"Didn't seem to bother you last night," she countered.

I glared at her. "That was different. That was private."

"And this would be public. Neutral ground. Just two colleagues attending a cultural event in the name of charity." She spread her hands, the picture of innocence. "What could be more appropriate?"

I knew what she was doing. She was poking at my defenses, testing the story I'd constructed to protect myself from the truth that last night hadn't resolved a single thing. If anything, it had only deepened the connection between Xander and me, made it more immediate, more dangerous.

But I couldn't admit that. Not to her, and certainly not to myself.

"Fine," I said. "I'll invite him. But only because I know you won't let this go if I don't."

Chloe's triumphant smile was insufferable. "Perfect! And wear that backless black dress...the one that makes your ass look spectacular."

"I hate you," I muttered.

She blew me a kiss. "Love you too, T. Now, about the fire dancers..."

———

Back at my apartment, I paced the living room, phone in hand, trying to compose a text to Xander that sounded casual, yet professional.

Me: *McCrae, I'm attending an art opening tomorrow evening at Galleria Durand in Wynwood. The artist is a friend of mine. Some of the team sponsors will be there. Your presence would be appreciated by the board. 7 PM.*

I read it over three times, making sure it struck the right tone—cool, detached, focused on the work-related connection rather than the personal one. Satisfied, I hit send before I could overthink it.

His response came almost immediately.

Xander: *Sounds lovely, Dr. Swanson. Should I bring a plus one?*

The question made my stomach clench with an emotion I refused to name. The thought of Xander bringing someone else —standing beside some beautiful woman, his hand on her lower back, whispering in her ear the way he'd whispered in mine—made me want to throw my phone across the room.

Me: *Not necessary.*

Xander: *Then it's a date. See you at 7.*

I stared at the word "date," my heart racing. This wasn't a date. It was a professional obligation. A test of my composure. Nothing more.

I was typing a reply back—using several curse words— when my phone rang with an unknown number. Frowning, I answered.

"Dr. Swanson speaking."

"Dr. Swanson." The voice was male, vaguely familiar. "This is Leo Martin."

I froze. Xander's loyal assistant.

Shit.

"Mr. Martin," I said, my voice impressively steady. "What can I do for you?"

There was a pause, as if he was choosing his words carefully. "I was hoping we could meet. To discuss... a matter of mutual concern."

The vague phrasing set alarm bells ringing in my head. Was this about last night? Had Xander sent his assistant to warn me off? To threaten me with consequences if I didn't keep my distance?

"I'm not sure what we would have to discuss," I said coolly.

"It's about Xander," Leo said, his voice dropping. "I need to talk to you. About him. And about what happened twelve years ago."

The reference sent ice through my veins. What did Leo know? How much had Xander told him?

"I'm quite busy today, Mr. Martin—"

"Please," he interrupted, with a note of genuine urgency in his voice. "It's important. I wouldn't ask if it wasn't."

Something in his tone made me hesitate. This wasn't just about last night. This was something more serious.

"Fine," I conceded. "There's a coffee shop called Cafecito on 8th Street. I can meet you there in an hour."

"Thank you," Leo said, relieved. "I appreciate it, Dr. Swanson."

Cafecito wasn't too busy. The Saturday afternoon lull was perfect for a conversation that required privacy. I spotted Leo at a corner table, hunched over a mug, his expression pensive.

He looked up as I approached, rising slightly in his seat. "Dr. Swanson. Thank you for coming."

I slid into the chair across from him, setting my purse on the table like a barrier between us. "Mr. Martin."

"Please call me Leo."

I nodded but didn't reciprocate the invitation to use my first name. Whatever this was about, I wanted to maintain as much professional distance as possible.

A barista appeared at my elbow, and I ordered a cortadito, needing the jolt of Cuban coffee to steady my nerves. Leo waited until the server had departed before speaking again.

"I'm not here to interfere," he began, his voice low. "What happens between you and Xander is... well, it's not my business."

I raised an eyebrow, skeptical. "Then why are we here?"

Leo sighed. Up close, I could see the strain around his eyes. He looked like a man carrying a heavy burden.

"I've been with Xander for a long time," he said. "Since he came to Glasgow. I've seen him at his worst—drunk, self-destructive, drowning in guilt. I've picked up the pieces more times than I can count."

I remained silent, unsure where this was going but unwilling to give anything away.

"He's not who you think he is," Leo continued. "He's not the callous playboy the tabloids make him out to be. He's... he's haunted. By what happened to your brother. And what happened between the two of you."

The mention of Jimmy sent a rush through my chest. "Mr.

Martin...Leo...I appreciate your concern for Xander, but I don't see how this—"

"I don't know what game you and your father are playing," he interrupted, leaning forward so his forearms rested on his knees. "Revenge, closure, whatever it is. But I can't let you hurt him. Not when he's already spent twelve years punishing himself."

A flare of pure fury went through me. "Punishing himself? For getting drunk and killing my brother? Or for disappearing without a word afterward?"

Leo's expression hardened. "Is that what you really think happened? That he *killed* Jimmy?"

"It's exactly what happened," I snapped, my voice rising. "He was driving drunk, he crashed the car, and my brother died. The end."

"He was drunk, yes," Leo acknowledged, his voice low and serious. "But I've held his hair while he puked his guts out from guilt. I've heard the nightmares. I've seen a man torture himself for more than a decade." He leaned even closer, his eyes boring into mine. "I don't know everything that happened in that car, but I would bet my life on one thing... Xander wasn't driving."

The words slammed into me, knocking the air from my lungs. The entire foundation of my life—the grief, the rage, the vengeance—cracked beneath me.

"That's not possible," I whispered. "Jimmy didn't have a license. And Xander confessed. He *said* it was his fault."

"He blamed himself," Leo corrected, his gaze unwavering. "That's not the same thing. And just because Jimmy didn't have a license doesn't mean he couldn't drive."

The coffee cup trembled in my hand, hot liquid sloshing

dangerously close to the rim. I set it down before I could spill it, my fingers suddenly numb.

"You're lying," I said, but there was no conviction in my voice. "Why would you...why would he—"

Leo's expression softened. "Trust me. I've known him for almost half my life. Whatever happened in that car, whatever role Xander played in your brother's death, he wasn't behind the wheel."

My mind raced, trying to reconcile this new information with everything I'd believed. With the narrative that had shaped my life.

Xander and Jimmy were at the party. Xander had been drinking. He'd gotten into the car with Jimmy, and they crashed into a tree.

Those were the facts. The immutable truths around which I'd constructed my understanding of that night.

"Why are you telling me this?" I asked, my voice barely steady.

Leo met my gaze. "Because whatever is happening between you two, it needs to be based on truth. Not from an old misunderstanding that's destroyed both your lives."

I stared at him, momentarily speechless.

"You expect me to believe that Xander let everyone think he killed my brother when he didn't?" I shook my head. "Why would he do that?"

"I don't know," Leo admitted. "He doesn't talk about it. But I think... I think he believes he deserved the blame. That even if he wasn't driving, he feels he was still responsible."

"I need to go," I said abruptly, gathering my purse. The coffee sat untouched, cooling in its cup.

Leo didn't stop me. "Just think about what I've said," he

urged. "And maybe... maybe ask him yourself. About what really happened that night."

I nodded stiffly, unable to form words around the lump in my throat. As I stood to leave, Leo's voice stopped me one last time.

"He cares about you, you know. More than he should. More than is safe for him."

I didn't turn around, couldn't bear to see the sincerity in his eyes. "Goodbye, Leo."

My mind reeled as I exited the coffee shop, every moment replaying through a new, warped filter. If Xander hadn't been driving... if Jimmy had... No. It couldn't be possible, could it?

CHAPTER
Eleven

XANDER

I GRABBED THE MEDICINE BALL, dropped it, caught it in a fluid motion, and slammed it against the floor with all my might. The heavy thud reverberated through the empty gym, a brief and unsatisfying release for the tension that had been building inside me since Tara had left my bed before dawn.

"I have no idea."

Her last words to me. I'd asked her what happened next, and she'd given me the most honest answer possible. Neither of us knew what the hell we were doing. What we were to each other now or what any of this meant.

I picked up the ball again, twisted my torso, and slammed it down with even more force. Sweat dripped into my eyes, my breath coming in hard gasps. I'd been at this for over an hour, pushing my body to exhaustion, hoping it might quiet my mind.

It wasn't working.

The memory of her kept intruding. The softness of her skin

under my hands. The way she'd looked at me in the darkness, her eyes reflecting the faint glow from the city lights outside my window. The taste of her. The sound of her breath catching when I—

I hurled the ball against the wall this time, the impact jarring enough to snap me back to the present. This was pathetic. I was Xander McCrae, for fuck's sake. I'd had more women than I could count. Beautiful women. Famous women. Women whose names and faces blurred together in a meaningless parade of temporary distraction.

So why couldn't I stop thinking about this one?

I knew why. Because she wasn't just any woman. She was Tara. Jimmy's little sister. The girl who'd haunted me since I left Palo Alto. The woman who'd shown up at my door in the middle of the night, looked me dead in the eye, and said, *"Let's fuck."*

God.

I grabbed a towel and wiped the sweat from my face, taking deep breaths to slow my racing heart. This was supposed to be my day off. A chance to recover, to process everything that had happened since I arrived in Miami. Instead, I was here, in the team's training facility on a Saturday afternoon, trying to outrun thoughts of Tara Swanson.

When Leo had left earlier, saying he had errands to run, I'd nearly crawled out of my skin with restlessness. The penthouse felt too empty, too quiet. Every room reminded me of her—of leading her through the living room to my bedroom, of waking up beside her, of watching her slip out before dawn.

So I'd come here, hoping a rigorous workout would center me. Hoping, if I was being honest with myself, that she might be here too. That I might run into her in the hallway, or glimpse her through the glass walls of her office, and get some sign of what last night had meant to her.

But the medical wing was dark and empty when I passed it, and the rest of the facility was nearly deserted on a Saturday afternoon. Just a skeleton security crew and the occasional staff member going about their business.

And me, all alone with my thoughts and a medicine ball. Pathetic.

The sound of the door opening made me turn. Ben Carter, with a gym bag slung over his shoulder, walked in, then stopped short when he saw me.

"Oh, sorry," he said, already backing toward the door. "I didn't realize anyone was in here."

"It's fine," I said, gesturing for him to stay. "I was just finishing up."

He hesitated, then came further into the room. "You sure? I don't want to interrupt your workout."

"You're not," I assured him, grabbing my water bottle. "Besides, there's plenty of equipment for both of us."

Ben nodded, setting his bag down and pulling out a pair of training shoes. "I didn't expect to see anyone here today," he said, lacing up his shoes. "Most guys take Saturdays off."

"I needed to clear my head," I admitted, not sure why I was telling this to a kid I barely knew.

"Yeah, I get that." He stood and started a series of stretches. "Sometimes the apartment gets too quiet, you know? Especially when you're new to a city."

I nodded, surprised by his perceptiveness.

"You played well yesterday," I told him, meaning it. "The cross you sent in during the third drill was perfect."

Ben's face lit up at the compliment. "Thanks, man. That means a lot, coming from you."

"What are you working on today?" I asked, changing the subject. I'd never been comfortable with praise, even when it was genuine.

"Just some conditioning," Ben said. "I want to improve my stamina for the full ninety."

"Mind if I join you? I could use a workout partner."

He looked surprised, then pleased. "Yeah, sure. That would be great."

For the next hour, we moved through a series of exercises together. Sprints on the treadmill. Box jumps. Core work. Throughout it all, our conversation flowed naturally from football to music to favorite places in our respective hometowns.

It was... nice. Uncomplicated. Ben didn't seem to care about my reputation or my past. He was just a new player who loved the game and was eager to learn. His enthusiasm was infectious, reminding me of how I'd felt at his age, before the weight of expectation and notoriety had settled on my shoulders.

"So what's the deal with Mano?" I asked as we took a water break. "He seems to have it out for me."

Ben's expression darkened slightly. "Diego's... territorial. About the team, about his position." He hesitated. "About Dr. Swanson."

The mention of Tara sent a jolt through me. "What do you mean?"

Ben looked uncomfortable, clearly regretting bringing it up. "It's nothing, really. He just... he flirts with her a lot. Gets possessive when other guys talk to her."

"Are they together?" The question came out sharper than I had intended.

"No," Ben blurted. "I mean, not that I know of. She always shuts him down. But he doesn't seem to take the hint."

I nodded, trying to appear casually interested rather than intensely relieved. "He seems like the type who doesn't hear 'no' very often."

"He's got a lot of pride," Ben agreed. "And a lot of problems."

Something in his tone caught my attention. "What problems?"

Ben glanced around the empty gym, then lowered his voice. "You didn't hear this from me, but... he's got a gambling issue. Serious one. Word is he owes money to some people you don't want to owe money to."

That was interesting. Potentially useful information if Diego's aggression toward me continued to escalate.

"Thanks for the heads up," I said. "I appreciate it."

Ben looked nervous. "Just... don't mention it to anyone, okay? If it got back to management..."

"It won't," I assured him. "The secret's safe with me."

We finished our workout with a series of cool-down stretches. Then as we were gathering our things to leave, Ben turned to me with an earnest expression.

"Hey, I just wanted to say... I'm glad you're here. On the team, I mean. I know some of the guys have been giving you a hard time, but they'll come around. You're exactly what we need to make a real run at the championship."

"Thanks, Ben," I said. "That means a lot."

He nodded suddenly embarrassed and headed for the door. "See you at practice on Monday!"

I watched him go, feeling a strange mix of emotions. It was nice to know I had at least one ally on the team. But his words also reminded me of the pressure I was under. The expectations. The scrutiny. All of which would only intensify once the season started.

And then there was Tara. My doctor. My one-night stand. My... what? What were we to each other now?

I have no fucking idea.

I grabbed my gym bag and headed for the showers, no closer to an answer than I had been when I arrived.

———

"This place is incredible," I said, eyeballing the vibrant chaos of Versailles, Miami's Cuban food mecca. "How'd you score a table on a Saturday night?"

Leo flashed a grin, looking less twitchy than he had all week. "I have my ways. Plus, the hostess is a fan. I promised her an introduction."

I glanced over to where the hostess stood, arranging menus at her station. She caught me looking and smiled, giving a little wave.

I immediately looked away.

Fuck.

It wasn't the first time Leo had hooked me up with a beautiful woman. His talent for social engineering had led to countless hookups over our years together. At any other time, I'd have been grateful for the setup with the gorgeous hostess.

But tonight? I couldn't summon even a flicker of interest.

"You're welcome," Leo said, misreading my silence as appreciation.

"Not tonight, man."

Leo raised an eyebrow. "She's exactly your type. Tall, blonde, legs for days..."

I took a long swig of water, wishing it was something stronger. Only one woman occupied my thoughts, her dark eyes and stubborn jaw haunting me. The one woman I absolutely couldn't have. The one who'd left my bed with a whispered goodbye.

"I'm just not in the mood," I muttered.

Leo studied my face, his expression shifting from confusion to realization. "Oh shit. It's the doctor, isn't it? Tara's got you all twisted up."

Before I could think of a decent response, our appetizers landed—croquetas and fried plantains. Happy for the save, I attacked the food like I hadn't eaten in days.

"This is amazing," I mumbled through a mouthful. "We should eat here every damn night."

Leo nodded, but his smile looked fake. He just pushed food around his plate.

"What?" I asked.

Leo put down his fork and took a deep breath. "I met with her today."

"Who?" I halted my next bite of food mid-air.

"I met with Tara," he said, keeping his voice steady while my face turned hot. "This afternoon. For coffee."

I stared at him, trying to compute. Leo had gone behind my back to meet Tara. After everything.

"What the fuck, Leo?" I kept my voice down despite wanting to flip the table. "Why would you do that?"

"Because I was worried about you," he said simply. "Because I needed to understand what was happening between you two."

"That's not your call to make," I snapped. "My relationship with Tara is none of your fucking business."

"It is when it's hurting you," Leo fired back. "When it's part of this self-destructive bullshit you've been pulling for years."

I wanted to argue but couldn't. His words hit too close to

home. I just glared, waiting.

"I didn't go there to interfere," Leo softened his tone. "I went because I couldn't watch her hurt you over a misunderstanding."

"What misunderstanding?"

Leo leaned in, dead serious. "She thinks you were driving the car that night, Xander. She thinks you killed her brother driving totally shit-faced."

The words knocked the air out of me. I couldn't breathe for a second.

"That's... that's not what happened," I finally croaked, slumping back. If Tara believed I'd killed her brother...

"Oh God," I whispered, my stomach turning. "All this time, she thought..."

Leo nodded grimly. "That's why I had to talk to her. To tell her the truth. She'd spent years thinking you were directly responsible for Jimmy's death."

My brain scrambled to process this bombshell. Every interaction with Tara since I'd hit Miami took on a new, fucked-up meaning. Her coldness. Her anger. Her control issues.

"Did she believe you?" I asked, dreading the answer.

Leo paused. "I don't know. She was... rocked. But it's a lot to take in. To have your understanding of such a monumental event challenged after so many years."

I nodded, food totally forgotten.

Tara believed I'd been drunk driving, crashed the car, and walked away while Jimmy died. No wonder she hated me. No wonder she'd tracked me, planning her revenge.

And last night... was that part of her plan too? To seduce me, make me vulnerable, all as some twisted payback?

The thought made me want to puke.

"I'm sorry," Leo said, watching me. "I know this is heavy. But you needed to know."

I nodded, speechless. My phone buzzed—a momentary escape from my mental shitstorm. I pulled it out.

A text from Tara.

Just a reminder about the art opening tomorrow evening. Here's the address...

I stared at the message. Hours ago, this would've felt promising, her making sure I'd show up. A sign that last night meant something. Now it felt like a bad omen.

The art opening. A public event where I'd have to face her, knowing what I now knew. Knowing all this time she'd been viewing me as her brother's killer.

"Xander?" Leo broke through my thoughts. "What is it?"

I handed him my phone without a word. He read it, his face grim.

"You don't have to go," he said, passing it back. "I can make an excuse. Say you're sick."

I shook my head. "No. I have to go." I needed to talk to her and find out if what Leo told her had changed anything.

"Are you sure that's smart?" Leo asked, concerned.

"Probably not," I admitted. "But I ran from her once. I can't leave things like this."

Leo nodded. "Want me to come with you?"

I considered it. Having Leo there would be a safety net. But this was my mess to clean up.

"No," I decided. "This is between Tara and me."

I texted back a simple reply: *I'll be there.*

CHAPTER

Twelve

TARA

I'D ALWAYS BELIEVED in the power of organization. Control the information, control the narrative. Control the narrative, control the outcome. My office was a testament to this. Twelve years of Xander McCrae's life, captured and contained on my walls.

But tonight, my carefully curated shrine to obsession might as well have been abstract art. Meaningless. A collection of pixels and paper that suddenly told me nothing at all.

"Xander wasn't driving."

Leo's words from our coffee meeting yesterday were still in my head as I sat cross-legged on the floor, surrounded by printouts of old newspaper articles. My laptop balanced precariously on my knees as I scrolled through digitized archives of the Palo Alto Weekly, searching for something— anything—that might confirm or refute his claim.

I'd been at this for hours, combing through every report of the accident, every interview, every public statement. My eyes burned from staring at the screen, but I couldn't stop. The truth had to be here somewhere, buried in all these words.

The earliest reports were frustratingly vague: *Local Teen Killed in Late-Night Crash. Alcohol Found at the Scene. Survivor in Stable Condition.*

Later articles hinted at Xander's "involvement" in the crash, noting his blood test showed he was twice over the limit, yet he was never arrested. Instead, the story took shape in the unsaid, through careful hints and things left out.

I glanced at the police report summary, the public version, scrubbed clean of anything too sensitive, just enough to keep people satisfied. Detective Richard Morrison was the name attached. I burned it into my mind. Rick Morrison. The guy who wrote the official story of my brother's death. The source of that vague report that let the whole twisted tale take hold.

What if Leo was right? What if Xander hadn't been driving? What if...

I closed my eyes, forcing myself to confront a possibility I'd never allowed myself to consider: What if Jimmy had been behind the wheel?

Jimmy didn't have a license—my father wouldn't let him get one until he turned eighteen—but I remembered catching him sneaking out with Dad's car keys late at night, his finger pressed to his lips as he winked at me. "Our secret, Tara-bean," he'd whispered, using the nickname that only he was allowed to call me.

The memory made my stomach lurch. I rushed to the bathroom, barely making it before emptying the contents of my stomach into the toilet. I retched until there was nothing left, then sank to the cold tile floor, pressing my forehead against the porcelain.

"Fuck," I whispered to the empty bathroom. "Fuck."

If Jimmy had been driving... if Xander had been the passenger... then my entire understanding of that night—of Jimmy's death, of Xander's guilt, of my father's grief—would have been built on a lie.

A lie that had shaped... everything.

I dragged myself up from the floor, rinsed my mouth, and splashed cold water on my face. I thought of the wall in my office, covered with images of Xander. The Instagram accounts I'd created to follow him. The Google alerts set to notify me of every mention of his name. The career path I'd chosen specifically to position myself in his world.

And now... what if it had all been for nothing?

I walked back to my office on unsteady legs, looking at the collage of Xander's life with fresh eyes. The teenage boy with the haunted expression at press conferences. The young man who escaped to Scotland. The professional athlete whose smile never reached his eyes. The reputation for reckless behavior, for self-destruction.

Had I been tracking the evolution of a killer? Or witnessing the slow implosion of a man crushed by misplaced guilt?

I sank back down to the floor, pulling my laptop closer. This wasn't enough. News reports and sanitized police summaries couldn't give me the truth. I needed to hear it from him. From Xander.

My phone buzzed with a text from Chloe: *You still coming tonight? The main sponsor (aka your dad) is asking if his star player will be there.*

The art opening.

Yes, I'll be there. And so will he. I texted back, my fingers steady despite the turmoil in my mind.

———

The gallery was packed, a sea of Miami's art elite mingling with the nouveau riche and the genuinely curious. Galleria Durand was Chloe's latest venture, a converted warehouse in Wynwood with exposed brick walls, polished concrete floors, and strategic lighting that made even the most mundane objects appear profound.

I stood just inside the entrance, surveying the crowd. My black dress was backless, with a neckline that dipped just low enough to be interesting without crossing into inappropriate.

"Tara! You made it!"

Chloe materialized beside me, resplendent in a flowing kimono-style dress with her signature chunky jewelry and purple-streaked hair piled high on her head. She pulled me into a tight hug, smelling of the faint, herbal scent that always clung to her.

"Wouldn't miss it," I said, returning the embrace. "The place looks amazing, Chloe. You've outdone yourself."

She beamed, gesturing to the packed gallery. "It's going well, right? The new collection is already half sold." She leaned in closer, her voice dropping to a conspiratorial whisper. "It's good you're wearing the dress I suggested. He's by the bar. You weren't kidding about the eyes. He's hot as fuck."

My heart rate kicked up a notch. I followed the direction of Chloe's subtle nod. And there he was.

Xander stood with his back against the bar, a glass of what looked like sparkling water in his hand. He was dressed in dark jeans and a charcoal gray button-down, the sleeves rolled up to expose his forearms. He looked uncomfortable, out of place among the art world denizens with their affected poses and exaggerated gestures.

Chloe was right. He was beautiful. The harsh gallery lighting cast shadows across the planes of his face, highlighting the firm jaw, the full lips, the eyes that were indeed the exact shade of the dress I'd worn to the team launch.

As if sensing my gaze, he looked up. Our eyes met, and for a moment, everything else—the noise, the people, the art— faded away, leaving just the two of us, locked in a silent, charged exchange.

Then someone jostled me, breaking the connection. When I looked back, Xander had turned away, saying something to a gallery assistant who had approached him.

"Well?" Chloe nudged me. "Aren't you going to go talk to him? That's why you brought him here, right?"

"Not yet," I said, accepting a glass of champagne from a passing server. "Let him stew longer."

Chloe rolled her eyes. "You and your games. Fine, but don't wait too long. I need to do the sponsor announcement in about twenty minutes, and then I'm taking a select group up to the rooftop for the private viewing."

"The rooftop?" This was news to me. "What's up there?"

A secretive smile played across Chloe's lips. "Something special. A surprise. Trust me, you'll want to be part of that group." She squeezed my arm. "I've got to circulate. The woman in the red dress is a potential major donor. Go get your man."

Before I could correct her—Xander wasn't "my man" in any sense of the word—she was gone, floating through the crowd.

I took a sip of champagne, using the moment to gather my thoughts. I needed to approach this carefully. The gallery was too public, too crowded for the conversation I needed to have with Xander. I'd have to wait for an opportunity to get him alone.

With a deep breath, I made my way through the crowd

toward the bar. Several people stopped me to chat—friends from college, acquaintances from my father's social circle, a few of the team's administrative staff. I made polite conversation all the while aware of Xander's presence, like a magnetic pull I couldn't ignore.

When I finally reached him, he was alone again, staring into his glass.

"McCrae," I said, slipping into my professional persona as a shield. "Glad you could make it. The sponsors appreciate your support of the community."

He looked up, his expression guarded. "Dr. Swanson. Wouldn't miss it." His voice was neutral, giving nothing away. "Your friend has quite an eye. The gallery is impressive."

"Chloe's one of the best curators in Miami," I agreed, leaning against the bar beside him. "She has a talent for finding beauty in unexpected places."

A muscle ticked in his jaw. "Is that why you invited me? As an unexpected ornament for your friend's gallery opening?"

The bitterness in his tone caught me off guard. "No, I—"

"Ladies and gentlemen!" Chloe's amplified voice cut through the noise of the crowd. She stood on a small platform near the center of the gallery, microphone in hand. "First, thank you all for coming to the inaugural exhibition at Galleria Durand. Your support means the world to me and to the artists we're showcasing tonight."

A round of applause rippled through the crowd. Chloe waited for it to die down before continuing.

"I'd especially like to thank our major sponsors, without whom this space would not exist. Hank Swanson of Swanson Enterprises." She gestured to my father, who stood near the front of the crowd, raising his glass in acknowledgment. "And the Miami Pirates FC, represented tonight by their star acquisition, Xander McCrae, and their physical therapist, Dr. Tara Swanson."

All eyes turned to us. I managed a smile, raising my glass slightly. Beside me, Xander did the same.

"In a few minutes," Chloe continued, "I'll be taking a few of our key sponsors up to the rooftop terrace for a private viewing of a special acquisition."

She stepped down from the platform, handing the microphone back to an assistant. As the crowd dispersed, returning to their conversations and contemplation of the art, Chloe made her way toward us.

"Tara!" she called. "Why don't you bring Mr. McCrae up? I'm sure our principal benefactor would love a word with the team's new star."

I glanced at Xander, who looked as puzzled as I felt. "Of course," I said, matching Chloe's volume. "We'd be honored."

Chloe led us through the crowd to a private elevator. My father was already inside, along with two board members from the team and their wives.

"Dr. Swanson, McCrae." My father nodded to us as we entered, his expression unreadable. "Quite the event your friend has put together."

"Yes, Chloe has outdone herself," I agreed, positioning myself as far from him as the small elevator would allow. Xander stood beside me, his presence solid and warm against my side.

The elevator ride was mercifully short. When the doors opened, we stepped out onto a beautifully lit rooftop terrace. String lights were draped overhead, creating a warm, intimate atmosphere. Miami's skyline spread out before us, a glittering backdrop to the scene.

But it was the centerpiece that made my breath catch.

A single spotlighted photograph hung on a freestanding wall. Black and white, moody and evocative, a landscape I recognized instantly. A lone tree on a windswept hillside, the sky above it heavy with storm clouds. The composition was perfect, the balance of light and shadow masterful.

It was Jimmy's photograph.

"She hung his best work," I whispered, my voice barely audible.

Beside me, Xander had gone rigid. "Jimmy's," he said, the word sounding as if it had been torn from him.

Chloe approached us, her expression soft. "I found it in the storage. His last photograph."

I couldn't speak. My throat had closed up, emotion threatening to overwhelm me. Jimmy had loved photography, had dreamed of becoming a professional. This image—this piece of him—preserved and displayed with such care, felt like a gift I wasn't worthy of.

My father and the other guests had moved to the far side of the terrace, where servers were pouring champagne. Chloe squeezed my hand once, then left us alone with the photograph.

For an eternity, neither of us spoke. We were side by side, looking at this tangible reminder of the person we'd both loved and lost. The ghost that had always been between us.

"What really happened that night, Xander?" The question came out of me unbidden, quiet but intense. "I need you to tell me the truth."

He turned to me, confused. "What?"

"That night. The crash." I met his gaze. "I've always been made to believe you were the one driving. Drunk. But Leo told me you weren't driving. I need you to tell me exactly what happened."

Understanding dawned in his eyes. "Leo shouldn't have told—"

"Please." I interrupted him, my voice breaking slightly. "Just tell me what you remember."

Xander looked back at the photograph, as if seeking permission from Jimmy's ghost. When he spoke at last, his voice was low, and raw with emotion.

"You're right. I was drunk. First time ever. We were at a party, and I... I wanted to forget something." His eyes flicked to me briefly, then away. "Jimmy was sober. Insisted on taking me home."

I nodded, eager for him to continue.

"I remember getting in the car. Jimmy helped me with the seatbelt. I was pretty far gone." He paused, inhaling deeply. "The next thing I remember is the crash. The sound of it. Metal crunching. Glass breaking. I woke up. Jimmy was..." His voice faltered. "He was hurt badly. There was so much glass and blood. I tried to help him, tried to stop the bleeding, but..."

He trailed off, lost in the memory. I waited, heart pounding, for him to continue.

"The paramedics arrived. Then the police. They kept asking me questions. Who was driving? How much had I had to drink? I couldn't... I couldn't focus. The only thing on my mind was Jimmy."

"But everyone said you were driving?" I pressed. "And Jimmy didn't even know how to drive."

Xander shook his head. "I don't know for sure. I don't remember starting the car, much less driving it. But..." He looked at me, his eyes haunted. "...know this: if I hadn't gotten drunk, *I* would have been the one driving, and the accident would never have happened. So it doesn't matter who drove... I was to blame."

The raw self-hatred in his voice was unmistakable. This wasn't the confession of a man who had walked away from a crime. This was the broken testimony of someone who was punishing himself for a tragedy he couldn't fully remember.

I couldn't stop staring at him, this man I had trained myself to hate, now realizing he was just as much a victim as I was, if not more.

"Tara?" Xander's voice invaded my thoughts. "Say something."

"I don't—" I began, but was interrupted by Chloe approaching us again.

"Sorry to break this up," she said, glancing between us with curiosity, "but your father is asking for you, Tara. Something about an early morning meeting tomorrow."

I nodded, grateful for the interruption. "Tell him I'll be there in a second."

Chloe hesitated, then retreated, leaving us alone again.

Xander's eyes were still on me, waiting. Demanding a response I wasn't ready to give.

"We can't talk here," I said finally. "Not with all these people."

"Then where? When?" The intensity in his voice matched the urgency I felt.

I thought of my apartment, with its wall of evidence. Not something I'd like to show Xander. Of the training facility, where we were constantly under my father's surveillance. Of Xander's penthouse, where we had already crossed one line we couldn't uncross. None of those places felt right. I needed space. Air.

"I run the beach path every morning. South Pointe Pier. I'm there at 6 AM." I met his gaze. "If you want to talk, you'll have to keep up."

Surprise crossed his face, followed by a slow nod. "I'll be there."

"I have to go," I said, gesturing toward where my father stood watching us with narrowed eyes. "Before he comes over."

As I walked away from Xander, my father's gaze tracked my movement. He intercepted me near the elevator.

"Enjoying the art?" His voice carried a deceptively casual tone I'd learned to fear.

"It's beautiful. Chloe's a master at curating this stuff."

"Yes, she is." He glanced back toward where Xander still stood beneath Jimmy's photograph. "That piece is particularly moving. Your brother had such talent."

The way he said it made my chest tighten. "He did."

"It's fitting that McCrae is here to see it. Full circle, wouldn't you say?"

There was a satisfaction that made my skin crawl. As if this entire evening had been orchestrated for that purpose.

"I suppose."

CHAPTER
Thirteen

XANDER

SLEEP WAS A JOKE. For the second night—or third, who was counting—I was back on the penthouse balcony, watching the city breathe below. The lights weren't a fuzzy blob anymore. They were sharp, distinct. Too clear.

For twelve years, I'd worn the guilt. Played the part of the drunken fuck-up because it was the only role I had left. It's a hard habit to break.

The sliding door whispered open behind me. Leo.

He didn't ask if I couldn't sleep. He knew better. He just joined me at the railing, two glasses in his hand. He passed one to me. Whiskey.

We stood there for a minute, the silence easy.

"She thought I was driving," I said, not to him, but to the skyline.

Leo took a slow sip from his glass, his gaze fixed forward. "Yeah," he said, his voice low. "She did."

"What is it?" The question had been bugging me for hours. "What makes you so sure I wasn't?"

He leaned against the railing. "It was the little things over the years when you were wasted or half asleep. The way you'd talk about Jimmy—not with guilt, but confusion. Like you couldn't put the pieces together." He paused, looking straight at me. "And honestly? It never made sense that you'd drive drunk. Not you. The guy I know fucks himself up, sure. But you don't gamble with other people's lives."

He was right. I wouldn't have put Jimmy at risk. Never.

"But what I could never figure out," Leo continued, his voice dropping, "is why the cops never made it clear-cut. They're experts at crash reconstruction. They should've known who was driving from the evidence. It's almost like they didn't want to."

He was *right*. At seventeen, I'd been so scared and so damn grateful not to face vehicular manslaughter charges that I never questioned the vague official report. I just accepted my banishment. But that missing official conclusion—that's where the rumors started. The space where gossip grew, and why my guilt festered.

"I can't recall what happened that night," I admitted, my voice raw. "Not really. And I think that's been the whole fucking problem all along."

"So what's the plan? How do we fix it?" Leo asked quietly.

I thought of Tara's challenge, her invitation to meet at sunrise. Not a showdown anymore. A goddamn rescue rope.

"I'm going to solve the mystery," I said, a new determination hardening my voice. "Not just for me and Tara, but for Jimmy."

Leo studied me, then nodded. "Good. It's about damn time."

I arrived at South Pointe Park at exactly six o'clock, the sky barely brightening with dawn's first hint. The air tasted like salt; the beach was empty except for a few crazy-early joggers and their dogs.

Tara was impossible to miss, standing at the jetty entrance, hair in a ponytail, wearing expensive running clothes that showed off every athletic curve. She was mid-stretch, one leg kicked behind her, arms up, her body a perfect cutout against the pale sky.

I just stared for a second. This woman who'd been my personal ghost for twelve years. Who'd slapped me in public, then showed up in the middle of the night. Who'd believed I killed her brother, but was now meeting me at dawn to better understand what actually had happened.

She clocked me approaching, her face neutral but not pissed off anymore. Something had changed between us on that rooftop.

"You showed," she said, dropping her stretch.

"Thought I'd bail?"

She gave a tiny shrug. "Wasn't convinced either way."

I pointed to the shoreline path. "So we're... running?"

"I run every morning," she stated it as if the fact was obvious. "Five miles minimum. Can you handle it?"

The question came with a dare, and, fuck it, I smiled. "I'm a seasoned athlete, Dr. Swanson. I think I'll survive."

Her mouth twitched—almost a smile. "We'll find out."

Then she bolted down the path, setting a pace just shy of brutal. I followed, matching her stride. The first mile passed without words, just our breathing and feet hitting packed sand.

I'd expected a casual jog while we talked. But Tara ran like she had demons on her heels, form perfect, focus total. By mile two, I was genuinely working to keep up, seriously impressed by her speed and stamina.

She didn't just jog to stay fit. She ran like a pro, like someone with years of training. It hit me. I knew jack shit about her beyond our trauma connection and her job as team doctor. What else had I missed about Tara Swanson?

We rounded a curve, and Miami's skyline appeared—a wall of luxury buildings catching the first sunlight. My penthouse stood among them, a shiny cage I'd walked into without seeing the trap.

At mile three, Tara veered off the main path, leading me up a narrow trail toward the jetty. We slowed on the rough ground until she stopped at a lookout with a killer view of the ocean and city.

We stood there breathing hard, sweat everywhere, the run having burned away some of our awkwardness. Right then, we weren't victim and perpetrator. We were just two people, hearts hammering, lungs burning, fucking alive.

"You can run," I said, breaking the quiet. I watched her, trying to connect this disciplined athlete with the vengeful doctor who'd tormented me in the exam room. "There's a lot I don't know about you."

"There's a lot you don't know, period," she shot back. She turned fully toward me, intense as hell. "I've been digging. Looking at old news about the crash."

I braced myself. "And?"

"They're vague. Very vague. Alcohol was 'believed to be a factor.' You were 'involved' in the crash. Nothing actually says who was driving." She crossed her arms. "The public police report summary is just as unclear."

I nodded, goosebumps rising despite the heat. "Leo said the same thing last night. He always thought it was weird they never made a solid conclusion."

Tara's eyes widened slightly, as if surprised I was backing her research instead of fighting it. "The whole town believed what they were made to believe," she said, voice stronger. "What *we* were all made to believe."

"Right."

"The investigating officer," she continued, voice tight, "was Detective Rick Morrison. His name's all over the reports, but the conclusions... they're missing. Or someone deliberately left them out."

"Morrison," I repeated, noting the name. First real clue I'd ever had. "He wrote the report?"

"He's the one who didn't write the entire conclusion," she corrected, eyes sharp. "I'm sure he'll remember you. And he knows what really happened that night."

The gray water smashed itself against the jetty rocks, a pointless, repetitive violence I understood. For twelve years, I'd done the same thing to myself. I'd swallowed the story whole, never once asking if it was poison.

Now I had a name. Morrison. A target. It wasn't hope, but it was a direction to point the anger.

I turned to her. The look in her eyes wasn't soft. It was the sharp, jagged edge of a world that had just been shattered. Good. We were on the same page.

"He fed us a lie," I said. It was all that needed saying.

"And we both got fat on it," she shot back, her voice tight. "So we find him. We find Morrison."

There was no question in her tone. It was a damn order. An order I was ready to follow.

"A cop who cashes out on a kid's death doesn't just vanish," I said. "He buys a quiet life."

"Then we make his life loud," she said, already turning from the water. "He has to be in the system somewhere. Pension, property records... something."

"And Hank?" I asked.

Her jaw tightened. "He can't know. He finds out we're digging, he'll bury Morrison for good."

I nodded. "Just us, then."

She started walking back toward the path, her pace quick, deliberate. "There's a coffee shop down the road. They'll have Wi-Fi."

The coffee shop screamed hipster heaven—outdoor tables, chairs that didn't match, and enough plant life to qualify as a mini-jungle. We snagged a corner spot away from the morning zombies still waiting for caffeine to kick in. Tara ordered two black coffees and whipped out her laptop from the backpack she'd lugged during our run.

"Let's start with the basics," she said, fingers flying across the keyboard. "Richard Morrison, a former detective with the Palo Alto Police Department."

Her fingers flew across the laptop keys, fast and certain. She attacked a keyboard the same way she did everything else —like she was trying to solve a problem that pissed her off. Her hair was still damp from our run, pulled back tight, but a few strands had escaped, clinging to the flushed skin of her neck.

And just like that, my head was somewhere else entirely. A few nights ago. Her skin, salty under my tongue. The taste of her. My name, a ragged sound torn from her throat in the dark. A low heat coiled in my gut, and I had to shift in the shitty cafe chair, adjusting my legs. Pathetic.

"He retired about five years ago," she said, clicking through search results like I wasn't having a full meltdown across the table. "Thirty years on the force. Decorated officer who specialized in traffic incidents and vehicular homicides."

"So he'd know his shit," I said, fighting for a normal voice. "The kind of guy who could look at a crash and tell exactly what went down."

She nodded, eyes glued to the screen. "Exactly. Which makes the vagueness of that public report even more suspicious."

I leaned closer. "Does it say where he located to after retirement?"

She clicked another link and let out a surprised "Huh."

"Naples, Florida."

"Florida?" I repeated, shock temporarily cooling my hormones. "He's in the same fucking state as us?"

"Looks that way." She spun the laptop toward me. The screen showed a local news piece with a photo of an older dude sporting gray hair and a face that had seen some shit. Caption read: "Retired Detective Richard Morrison, now serving as a volunteer with the Naples Marine Conservation Society."

"Naples is what… three hours from here?" I asked suddenly buzzing with possibility.

"About that," she confirmed, excitement coloring her cheeks. "We could drive there. Talk to him face-to-face."

This wasn't just talk anymore. We could actually do this— find Morrison, grill him about that night, finally get the truth.

"When?" I asked, mentally canceling whatever bullshit I had scheduled.

Tara frowned. "We both have tight schedules. The team, practice, my patients." Her fingers drummed on the table. "This weekend? Saturday? We could drive down early, be back the same day."

"Saturday," I nodded. "I'll make Leo clear my schedule."

She hesitated. "Xander... we need to be careful. If my father finds out what we're doing..."

She didn't finish. We both knew what that prick was capable of.

"We'll be sneaky as fuck," I promised. "Nobody needs to know our business."

She closed her laptop with a snap. "Saturday, then. I'll pick you up at six. We should get an early start."

I couldn't help grinning. "Another six AM meetup? You really get off on torturing people with early mornings, don't you?"

Her mouth twitched. "It's the best time to get stuff done without people bothering you."

"I can think of other activities that are better without interruption," I said, voice dropping as I eyed her lips.

Her cheeks went pink, and she looked away. Then she stood up fast, gathering her stuff, the softness gone from her face as quickly as it had come.

"I'll see you at the facility tomorrow, McCrae," she said, all business. "Don't be late for your session."

As she turned, I nodded toward the cups. "What about your coffee? You didn't even take a sip."

She hesitated, a ghost of a smile tugging at her mouth. "Guess I was already wired enough." Her eyes flicked to mine,

softer for a heartbeat, before it was gone. "You can have it."
Then she was gone, walking out without looking back.

I watched her go, grinning like an idiot. Too fucking late for
walls now. We both knew it. This truth-hunting mission was
already tangled up in something way more complicated.

CHAPTER
Fourteen

TARA

I TAPPED my pen against Xander's medical file, the rhythmic sound matching my pulse. Inhale. Exhale. The clock on my office wall showed 1:53 p.m. Seven more minutes until his appointment. Time to get myself together.

But focusing on paperwork wasn't doing it today. Not when my mind kept replaying our weekend run along the shore, the way his eyes had locked with mine when we'd agreed to find Morrison, the heat in his voice when he'd leaned close at that coffee shop.

"I can think of a few other things that are better without interruption."

I slammed the folder shut and pressed my palms against my eyes. This was madness.

My phone buzzed with a text, jolting me from my thoughts.

Chloe: *Thanks again for coming to the opening! So... how's Ghost Boy this morning? Still broken in all the right places?* 😏

Of course. Leave it to Chloe to cut straight through my pretense. I hesitated for just a moment before responding.

Me: *I have a session with him in 5 minutes, and I'm freaking out. I don't think I can do this.*

Her response was immediate.

Chloe: *Of course you can. You've got a wall full of diplomas and probably the most expensive pair of yoga pants in Miami right now.*

Me: *That's not helping.*

Chloe: *Honey, just picture him as a sentient anatomical chart with really great abs. All business, no pleasure. You've got this.*

I smiled despite myself. She wasn't entirely wrong. I could handle one soccer player with haunting green eyes and a talent for dismantling my defenses.

Me: *Sentient anatomical chart. Got it.*

Chloe: *And if that doesn't work, remember you've already seen him naked, so the mystery's gone* 😏

I ignored her when the knock came at my door. Three sharp raps. I knew without checking it was him.

I straightened, smoothed my navy scrubs, and took a deep breath.

"Come in," I called, pleased at how steady my voice sounded.

The door opened, and there was Xander, wearing the team's standard training gear—a fitted blue shirt and black shorts—his dark hair still damp from a shower, those moss-green eyes burning into me like he could strip me bare with a look. My grip on composure faltered for a dangerous second.

"Dr. Swanson," he said, his voice wrapping around my name in a way that made my pulse trip.

It took me a heartbeat too long to find my voice. "McCrae," I replied, gesturing to the chair across from my desk. "Have a seat. How's the shoulder feeling after Saturday's practice?"

He sat down, his tall frame making my office chair look almost comically small. "Better. The exercises you recommended helped."

I nodded, forcing myself to look at the file rather than at the way his shirt stretched so magnificently across his shoulders. "Good. Today, I'd like to try something different. I've scheduled us for the hydrotherapy room."

His eyebrows rose slightly. "Hydrotherapy?"

"The buoyancy of the water will take pressure off your joints while still allowing for a full range of motion," I explained, falling back on the comfortable rhythm of medical jargon. "It's effective for someone with your combination of old injuries."

What I didn't say was that I'd chosen hydrotherapy specifically because it would put a literal barrier between us. Water. It was safe. Impersonal.

"If you say so, Doc," he replied, a hint of amusement in his voice.

I stood, gathering my tablet and a towel. "Follow me."

The hydrotherapy room was at the end of the medical wing, a large space dominated by a pool roughly the size of a small hotel's. Unlike a standard swimming pool, this one featured adjustable water jets, underwater treadmills, and a variable depth floor that could be raised or lowered depending on the therapy needs. The water was kept at a therapeutic 94 degrees, warm enough to relax muscles without overheating during exercise.

"I've booked the room for the next hour," I said, setting my tablet on a small table near the edge of the pool. "There's a changing area through that door. You'll find shorts in your size."

He nodded and disappeared into the changing room. The

moment he was gone, I exhaled shakily. No worries. Piece of cake. Just another routine hydrotherapy session, that's all.

I quickly changed into the athletic swimwear I kept at the facility—a modest but fitted black one-piece with short sleeves, designed for therapeutic work rather than sunbathing. Over it, I wore black athletic shorts, creating a look that was functional and professional. I pulled my hair into a tight bun and was reviewing the session plan on my tablet when I heard the changing room door open.

I looked up, and my jaw nearly dropped. Xander stood there in nothing but navy swim shorts, his torso bare and magnificent, and my body reacted before my brain could catch up.

I'd seen him shirtless before, of course, but something about the context—the steamy room, the blue water reflecting ripples of light across his skin—made it different. His body was a masterpiece of muscle, honed by years of elite sports rather than vanity workouts. And there was that sexy tattoo sprawled across his left shoulder and chest, the intricate Celtic design only making it harder not to stare at the sculpted planes of his pectorals.

I swallowed hard and forced my gaze back to my tablet. "Let's get started. Use the steps. I'll be right behind you."

He followed my instructions, descending into the water. I set my tablet aside and joined him.

"We'll begin with some basic mobility work," I said, my voice remarkably steady considering the riot of my pulse. "Stand with your feet shoulder-width apart."

For the next fifteen minutes, I guided him through a series of stretches and controlled movements, focusing on his problem areas—the shoulder, the knee, the chronically tight hip flexors common in soccer players. I maintained a running commentary of instructions, using the language of my profession like a shield.

But the water, which I'd thought would be a barrier, was proving to be the opposite. Each time I needed to adjust his form or stabilize a movement, my hands made contact with his wet skin. Water wasn't a barrier at all—it was a conductor, amplifying every touch, making each point of contact feel electric.

Shit.

"Now we'll work on core rotation," I said, moving to stand behind him. My teeth caught my bottom lip before I could stop myself—God, from this angle it would be so easy to slide my arms around his shoulders. But I chastised myself and continued, "This will engage your obliques. Now twist from the waist while keeping your hips stable."

I placed my hands on his hips to show the position, and I could feel the subtle shift of muscle beneath my palms. Ugh, he was making this impossible, and he didn't even know it.

"Like this?" he asked, executing a perfect rotation.

"Good," I said, my voice betraying nothing of the desire building low in my belly. "Now, in the other direction. Keep your hips facing forward."

He twisted again, and I felt the powerful engagement of his core muscles. Things were going along well. Just a doctor working with a patient. That I could smell his soap, could remember exactly how those muscles had felt under my fingertips in a very different context, was irrelevant.

"We'll do ten more repetitions," I instructed. "I'll count them out." I moved around to face him, positioning myself in front so I could monitor his form more closely.

We were on number seven when it happened. The pool was equipped with therapeutic jets that could be programmed to activate at specific intervals. I'd forgotten to disable this feature before our session, and suddenly, a powerful jet near where we were standing switched on with a mechanical hum.

The forceful stream of water hit the back of Xander's legs, pushing him off balance. The pool floor was slick, offering little traction. He stumbled forward, his feet sliding. Instinctively, he reached out to catch himself, his hands finding my waist just as I stepped forward to stabilize him.

The momentum carried us both backward until my back hit the pool wall. His body followed, pressing against mine, his hands still gripping my waist, my palms flat against his chest in a failed attempt to maintain distance.

The heat of him, the slick strength of muscle under my hands, the thud of his heartbeat against my palm—it was all too much. The warm water swirled around us, but it might as well have been fire licking at my skin.

We froze there, breaths mingling, his face inches from mine, droplets clinging to his lashes. His pupils were blown wide, green swallowed in black, and every ounce of restraint I'd been clinging to threatened to shatter.

"Sorry," he murmured, but he didn't move away. "Lost my footing."

I should have stepped aside. I should have made a comment about the importance of proper footing in aquatic therapy. I should have done anything except stand there, my hands still pressed against the wet, warm skin of his chest, feeling his heart hammer beneath my palm.

"It's okay," I said, my voice barely audible over the hum of the water jets. "The pool floor can be slippery."

His eyes dropped to my mouth, and I felt something inside me unravel. The walls I'd constructed, they all dissolved in the steam-filled air between us.

"Tara," he said, my name a question on his lips.

I knew what he was asking. Acknowledgment that whatever was happening between us was real and mutual and inevitable.

I gave a small, almost imperceptible nod.

His mouth was on mine before I could draw another breath, hot and insistent. This kiss was different—not desperate or angry or tinged with revenge. It was slow, deep, exploratory. He tasted of mint, and I answered with a desperate heat, my lips parting, my tongue tangling with his as if I'd forgotten the meaning of restraint.

My hands slid up his chest to his shoulders, then into his wet hair, pulling him closer. His hands moved from my waist to my back, pressing me against him until there was no space between us, just the warm water and the heat of our bodies.

The rational part of my brain—the part that had graduated top of my class, that knew exactly how many ethical boundaries we were obliterating—was screaming at me to stop. We were at the facility. During working hours. Anyone could walk in.

But the part of me that had obsessed over this man, the part that had finally tasted what it was like to be with him, was louder.

His hands slid lower, cupping my ass through my shorts, lifting me slightly so that I was pinned between his body and the pool wall. I wrapped my legs around his waist, a small sound of need escaping me as the new position brought him flush against my center.

"God, I've thought about this every minute since the other night," he murmured against my neck, his accent thicker with desire. "Can't focus on anything else."

"Me too," I admitted, the confession torn from me as his teeth grazed my collarbone. "It's driving me crazy."

He captured my mouth again, the kiss deepening as his hips pressed against mine in a rhythm that made my breath catch. The water lapped around us, creating small waves that seemed to echo the building tension in my body.

Even though we were in a therapy pool, in our swimsuits, in the middle of the day, it still felt more intimate than when we hooked up at his penthouse. That wasn't all about years of anger and obsession finally letting loose. This was totally different—a conscious decision, made with clear heads and open eyes.

His hand slid between us, fingers dipping beneath the edge of my shorts, seeking. I gasped against his mouth as he found his target, my hips bucking involuntarily against his touch.

"Xander," I breathed, both a warning and a plea. "We can't... not here."

He withdrew his hand immediately, pressing his forehead against mine, both of us breathing hard. "You're right," he said, his voice rough.

The acknowledgment should have been a relief, but instead, I felt a crushing disappointment. I wanted him—now, consequences be damned. The realization was terrifying in its intensity.

I disentangled myself from him reluctantly, putting a few inches of water between us. His eyes were dark, his breathing uneven, his desire clear even through the distortion of the water.

In that moment, I made a reckless, potentially career-ending decision that flew in the face of all my careful planning. But I was tired of planning. Tired of calculating every move, of keeping my wants and needs buried beneath layers of career ambition and old grudges. And for once, I was going to take what I wanted without overthinking it.

"My place," I said, my voice low and steady despite the rapid pounding of my heart. "Tonight."

His eyes widened slightly, surprise giving way to heat. "Your place?" he repeated, as if making sure he'd heard correctly.

I nodded, a strange, exhilarating sense of freedom washing over me. "Use the back entrance. The one by the recycling bins. There's a smaller chance of being seen."

A slow smile spread across his face, transforming his features from merely handsome to devastating. "What time?"

"Nine," I said, already calculating how long it would take me to get home, to prepare, to make sure there was no evidence of my research wall or the years I'd spent stalking him. "And Xander..." I leaned closer, my lips brushing his ear, "don't be late."

I pulled away before he could respond, before I could change my mind. With a composure I didn't feel, I waded to the steps and climbed out of the pool.

"That's enough for today, McCrae," I said, my voice impressively steady as I grabbed a towel. "We'll continue this on Wednesday."

I didn't look back as I headed to the changing room, but I felt his eyes on me the entire way. As the door closed behind me, my heart was still racing, my body humming with unfulfilled desire.

What had I just done? Invited a player—a patient—to my home for what would undoubtedly be a night of breaking every ethical code I was bound by. Risked my career and my reputation.

And I didn't regret it for a second.

CHAPTER

Fifteen

XANDER

THE MEMORY of Tara's whispered invitation played on a loop in my head as I tossed a soccer ball from hand to hand, my fidgety ass unable to sit still.

"My place. Tonight."

Her voice had been low, dripping with want, the words tickling my ear as water trickled down our bodies in the hydrotherapy pool. Hours later, I could still feel her body pressed against mine, wet fabric stuck to curves my hands knew by heart. Shit, I'd turned into a horny sixteen-year-old, watching the clock like it might speed up if I stared hard enough.

I squeezed the ball with both hands, trying to compact my wild thoughts into something less stupid. Nine o'clock felt like a damn eternity away, but I could see myself walking up those back stairs.

Then I had a realization so obvious I almost laughed at myself.

I had no clue where Tara lived.

"Fuck," I muttered, collapsing onto the sofa. "Fuck, fuck, fuck."

She'd been clear about the time. About using the back entrance. But in that steamy moment with water swishing around us and horniness fogging my brain, we'd both forgotten the most basic detail—her fucking address.

I pulled out my phone, thumb hovering over her contact. The fix was easy: text her and ask. Done. But something stopped me.

This wasn't Tara forgetting. This was Tara being Tara.

Everything between us had been a calculated power game. Even our first hookup happened on her terms, in my space, when she decided it was time.

And now this—an invitation with a critical piece missing. Not a mistake. A goddamn test.

I hurled the ball at the wall, snatching it on the bounce.

Asking for her address felt like surrendering before our new game even started. If I wanted to be her equal—her partner in this dangerous fling—I needed to prove I could keep up, predict her moves, and beat her at her own game.

"Easy there, tiger. What's up?"

I looked up to see Leo in the living room doorway, eyebrows raised. His hair was perfect, wearing his crisp button-down and slim chinos—his standard "babysitting Xander" uniform.

"Nothing," I said automatically, then changed my mind. Leo was my friend, and I needed advice. "Actually, something. Tara invited me over to her place tonight."

Leo's face switched from curious to horrified faster than a ref pulling a red card. "Tell me you're not actually considering this."

I threw the ball again, harder. "Already decided. I'm going."

"Xander," Leo used the tone reserved for when he thinks I'm about to fuck up spectacularly, "did you forget who she is? That her dad owns the team? We're talking about the woman who's been quietly obsessed with you for over a decade?"

"I remember all that," I said, putting the ball down. "But things are different now. We both know there's more to Jimmy's death. And there's something between us, Leo. Something real."

Leo dropped into the armchair, messing up his hair in frustration. "There's something alright. Mutual destruction, maybe. Career suicide, definitely."

He wasn't wrong. I understood exactly how many boundaries we were smashing. But logic took a backseat when Tara Swanson walked back into my life.

"Look," I said, leaning forward, "I know the risks. But I'm going. That's not the problem."

"What's the problem, then?"

I paused, knowing how stupid this would sound. "She didn't give me her address."

Leo stared blankly before erupting with laughter. "That's your issue? Just text her and ask, dumbass."

"I can't."

"Why the fuck not?"

I stood, too jittery to stay seated. How could I explain the unwritten rules between Tara and me and the precise balance we'd built through every interaction?

"Because she left it out on purpose," I said finally. "It's a test."

Leo's face was pure skepticism. "A test. Sure. Or maybe—

crazy thought here—she just forgot to mention it while you two were getting handsy."

I shook my head. "You don't know her like I do. This is classic Tara. She wants to see if I can figure it out myself."

"And if you can't?" Leo asked, his voice softening. "If this is some weird test and you fail by simply asking for directions like a normal person, then what? She cancels? Is that really the kind of fucked-up relationship you want?"

Fair question, one that made me stop. What kind of relationship did I want with Tara? Whatever we had was messy, intense, and potentially catastrophic. But it also made me feel more alive than ever.

"I need to do this," I said firmly. "I need to show her I understand the game."

Leo sighed, recognizing my stubborn expression. "Fine. How do you plan to find her address without asking?"

I checked my watch. Almost four. "I'll start at the training facility. There must be staff records or emergency contacts somewhere."

"And if there isn't?"

I grabbed my car keys from the coffee table. "Then I'll wing it."

———

The training facility was quieter than usual when I arrived, most of the players and staff having gone home for the day. Perfect. The fewer people around to question my presence, the better.

I made my way past the empty practice fields and through the main building, nodding casually to a few maintenance workers. The facility was designed like a small campus, with different wings for various departments—medical, coaching, administration, and player development.

As I rounded the corner toward the administrative wing, I spotted Ben Carter coming out of the weight room, gym bag slung over his shoulder. His face lit up when he saw me.

"Xander! Didn't expect to see you here this late."

I smiled, slowing my pace. "Just wanted to get some extra work in. You know how it is."

Ben nodded enthusiastically. "For sure. It never hurts to push harder, right?"

"Exactly." I hesitated, trying to frame my next question carefully. "Hey, quick thing—is there some kind of team directory anywhere? I need to check something with Dr. Swanson about my therapy schedule, but I don't have her contact details."

Ben's expression was open, without a hint of suspicion. "Oh, all the high-level staff information is kept in the admin office for emergencies. Phone numbers, addresses, everything. They should still be open if you want to head over there now."

Bingo. I kept my expression neutral, even as satisfaction coursed through me. "Thanks, mate. I appreciate it."

"No problem," Ben replied. "Hey, a bunch of us are grabbing dinner at that Cuban place near the beach tomorrow. You should come. The team's still getting to know you, and it'd be cool to hang out off the pitch."

The invitation threw me. At Chelsea, especially after the rumors started, teammates avoided me like the plague. "I'll check my schedule," I said, genuinely touched. "Thanks for the invite."

Ben grinned. "Cool. See you at practice tomorrow, then?"

"Definitely."

Ben was a good kid, straight-up honest. He'd given me

exactly what I needed without question, trusting me completely.

The administration wing sat at the far end of the building—corporate central where the suits handled the business side. Most doors were closed, but light leaked from a few. I approached the main office, where a middle-aged woman with short hair hammered away at her keyboard.

I knocked on the open door, flashing my million-dollar smile. "Excuse me. Sorry to bother you so late."

She looked up, her smile dropping when she recognized me. "Mr. McCrae. How can I help you?"

"Please, call me Xander," I said, stepping in. "I need to update my emergency contact info. My agent reminded me I never filled out that part."

Believable enough. In the chaos of transferring to Miami, shit definitely fell through the cracks.

"Of course," she said, turning to her computer. "I can pull up your file right now."

"That would be great, thank you..." I checked her name-plate, "...Ms. Connor."

She lit up at the personal touch, fingers dancing over keys. "It'll just take a moment. We've had network issues today."

Right on cue, her phone rang. She frowned at the caller ID. "Sorry, I need to take this. It's about next week's away game."

"No problem," I said, leaning against the doorframe. "Take your time."

She answered and jumped straight into hotel and bus talk. I waited until she was deep in conversation, half-turned away from me.

I slid over to the file cabinets along the wall. Standard office shit with neat labels. Top drawer: "Player Personnel." Second: "Coaching Staff." Third: "Medical and Support Staff." *Jackpot.*

I eased the third drawer open, quiet as a cat burglar, hyper-aware of Ms. Connor yakking away feet from me. Files organized alphabetically. I flipped through: Peterson... Richards... Santos... Swanson.

I pulled Tara's file just enough to see her info sheet. Boom —her address right there: 1800 Meridian Avenue, Apartment 1102. I burned it into my brain and carefully put everything back exactly as I found it.

I was closing the drawer when a man's voice boomed down the hall, getting louder with each word.

"—just wanted to check if she's still around. Had a question about my knee."

Fuck. Diego Mano. His cocky voice was unmistakable, and he was heading straight here.

I looked around frantically. Ms. Connor was still on the phone, her back to me. No escape route. Then I spotted a door —a supply closet with a keypad lock.

Without thinking, I slipped across and tried the handle. It opened, and I ducked inside, leaving just a crack to peek through. Cramped as hell, stuffed with office crap. I flattened against the wall, barely breathing.

Diego appeared in the doorway, oozing with that dickhead confidence that made me want to punch him.

"Excuse me," he interrupted Ms. Connor. "I'm looking for Dr. Swanson. Seen her?"

Ms. Connor covered the phone, her face cooling like a freezer door. "Dr. Swanson left over an hour ago, Mr. Mano. If you have a medical concern, schedule a proper appointment."

Diego leaned against the doorframe, exactly where I'd stood. "It's not urgent. Just wanted to ask her something... personal."

The way he said "personal" made my teeth grind. His obsession with Tara was getting creepier by the day.

"I'm afraid I can't help you," Ms. Connor replied, ice-cold. "Dr. Swanson's schedule and whereabouts aren't something I discuss with players."

Diego stiffened like he'd been slapped. "Fine. If you see her, tell her I was looking for her."

"I will pass that along," she said, in a tone that screamed "fuck off," if such a sweet lady were to use the f-word. You go, Ms. Connor.

Diego hung around like a bad smell, then stormed off, stomping down the hall. I exhaled. Too fucking close. And his possessive tone about Tara just confirmed what a threat this asshole was.

I waited until Ms. Connor resumed her call, then snuck back to my spot by the door. When she hung up, I flashed an apologetic smile.

"Sounds like you've got your hands full with those travel plans."

She sighed, returning to her computer. "It's always something. Now, let's update your emergency contact."

I spent the next few minutes giving Leo's details, playing along to sell my story. When we finished, I thanked her and walked out, strutting through the facility like I hadn't just pulled off a heist.

Mission accomplished—I had Tara's address. I passed the test. And that close call with Diego only cranked up my excitement for tonight.

———

1800 Meridian Avenue turned out to be a sleek, modern apartment building in South Beach. I circled the block once, familiarizing myself with the layout before parking my car a street over—less chance of being recognized that way.

Following Tara's instructions, I approached from the rear of the building. Sure enough, there was a service entrance near a neatly organized recycling station. The door required a key fob for entry, but as I approached, a maintenance worker exited, holding the door open with unconscious courtesy. I nodded my thanks and slipped inside.

The service corridor led to a utility elevator, which I took to the eleventh floor. The hallway was quiet, lit by recessed lighting. 1102 was at the end of the hall, a corner unit.

I stood outside her door for a moment, gathering myself. This wasn't just about sex. It wasn't even just about our complicated shared history. By seeking out her address, by accepting her unspoken challenge, I was agreeing to something deeper in whatever dangerous game we were creating together.

I raised my hand and gave three sharp raps against the polished wood.

Seconds ticked by, and then the door swung open. Tara stood there, dressed in a simple black tank top and yoga pants, her dark hair loose around her shoulders. The initial shock on her face was worth every moment of the day's elaborate quest —pure, unguarded surprise that quickly morphed into something more complex: respect, desire, and a slow, impressed smile.

"You're here," she said, her voice betraying a hint of wonder. "How did you...?"

I grinned, leaning against the doorframe. "You said not to be late."

She stepped back, gesturing for me to enter. "I did say that."

I stepped into her apartment, taking in the sleek, minimalist design—clean lines, neutral colors, expensive furniture that looked barely used. It was exactly what I would have expected from Tara, yet there was something almost impersonal about it, as if it were a showroom rather than a home.

The door closed behind me, and suddenly the air between us was electric. We stood facing each other in her entryway.

"You didn't ask me for my address," she said, but there was no reproach in her tone, only a hint of admiration.

"I didn't," I agreed, taking a step toward her. "That wouldn't have been nearly as interesting, would it?"

She matched my movements, closing the distance between us until we were inches apart. "How did you find me?"

"Let's just say I have resources."

"Team directory?"

I raised an eyebrow. "Maybe I followed you home."

A smile played at the corners of her mouth. "Now that would be interesting. Stalking the stalker."

There was something liberating about acknowledging the twisted nature of our connection so openly.

"I passed your test," I said, my voice low. "What's my reward?"

Her answer was to close the final distance between us, her mouth finding mine. This kiss was slower, like two people who knew they had all night to explore each other.

I backed her against the wall, my hands finding her waist, fingers slipping beneath the hem of her tank top to touch warm skin. She arched into me, her hands threading through my hair.

"Bedroom," she murmured against my lips. "Down the hall."

I lifted her, her legs wrapping around my waist as I carried her through the apartment. The bedroom was as minimalist as the rest of the place—a queen-sized bed with crisp white linens, a sleek dresser, and little else. I set her down gently on the edge of the bed, taking a moment to look at her—flushed cheeks, dark eyes wide with desire, lips slightly swollen from our kisses.

"What?" she asked, suddenly self-conscious under my gaze.

"Just making sure this is real," I said honestly. "That we're really here."

Her expression softened. "It's real, Xander."

I kneeled before her, pushing her tank top up slowly, revealing inch by inch of smooth, golden skin that glowed under the soft bedroom light. She raised her arms without a word, letting me peel the fabric over her head and toss it aside like it was nothing. No bra—just her, bare and perfect, her breasts rising and falling with each quickened breath. Full and firm, nipples already pebbled from the cool air or anticipation, I couldn't tell which. My cock twitched in my jeans, straining against the denim, but I forced myself to take it slow. This wasn't a race; this was a conquest, a mapping of every curve and secret.

"You're beautiful," I murmured, my voice rough with need. The words felt too simple, too tame for the storm raging inside me, but they were true. Tara, offering herself up like a gift I didn't deserve.

She reached for the hem of my shirt, her fingers brushing my abs in a way that sent electricity shooting through me. "Your turn," she said, her voice husky, commanding in that quiet way of hers. I let her pull it off, then stood to shuck my jeans and boxers in one fluid motion, my erection springing free, hard and aching for her. Her eyes darkened as she took me in, her tongue darting out to wet her lips. Fuck, that look alone could undo me.

We came together on the bed, skin to skin, her body soft and yielding against my harder frame. I captured her mouth in a deep, devouring kiss, my hands roaming—tracing the dip of her waist, the swell of her hips, the firm globes of her ass. She moaned into my mouth, her nails scraping lightly down my back, leaving trails of fire that made me growl. Our first time had been raw, furious, a clash of bodies fueled by hate and history. This? This was deliberate, a slow burn that promised to consume us both.

I broke the kiss, trailing my lips down her neck, nipping at her collarbone before moving lower. My mouth closed over one nipple, sucking hard, teasing with my tongue until she arched off the bed, her fingers tangling in my hair. "Xander," she gasped, and hearing my name like that—breathless, needy —stoked the fire in my veins. I switched to the other breast, my hand sliding between her thighs, finding her yoga pants damp with arousal. I hooked my fingers into the waistband and tugged them down, along with her panties, exposing her completely.

She was glistening, ready for me, and the sight made my mouth water. I spread her legs wider, settling between them on my knees. "I've wanted to taste you since that night," I confessed, my breath hot against her inner thigh. She shivered as I kissed my way up, teasing, nipping, until my tongue flicked over her clit. Her hips bucked, a sharp cry escaping her lips. I held her down with one hand on her hip, the other parting her folds as I licked and sucked, savored her sweetness, the way she trembled under my assault.

"God, yes," she panted, her hands fisting the sheets. I slipped a finger inside her, then two, curling them to hit that spot that made her tighten around me. She was so wet, so responsive, her body clenching as I worked her higher. But I wanted more—I wanted to push her, to see how far this twisted connection could go.

I pulled back just as she was on the edge, her frustrated whine music to my ears. "Not yet," I said, my voice low and commanding. I grabbed her wrists, pinning them above her head with one hand, using my free one to trace down her body. "You like control, don't you, Tara? But tonight, I'm taking it."

Her eyes flashed with challenge, but there was heat there too, desire mingling with defiance. "Is that so?" she breathed, testing my grip. I tightened it just enough to make her gasp, then reached for the drawer of her nightstand—hoping, praying she'd have something I could use. Luck was on my side: a silk scarf, probably for her hair, but perfect for what I had in mind.

I wrapped it around her wrists, tying them loosely to the headboard—not tight enough to hurt, but enough to restrain her. "Tell me to stop if it's too much," I whispered, searching her face. She nodded, her pupils blown wide with lust. "Don't stop."

Kinky little minx.

I grinned, dark and predatory, as I kissed my way back down her body. With her hands bound, she was at my mercy, writhing as I teased her breasts again, pinching her nipples until they were red and sensitive. Then lower, my mouth on her core once more, but this time I added a twist—lightly spanking her thigh, the sharp slap echoing in the room. She jolted, moaning louder. "Again," she demanded, and fuck if that didn't make me harder.

I obliged, alternating slaps with soothing licks, building her up until she was begging, her body slick with sweat. When she shattered, coming hard against my tongue, her cries filled the room, her bound hands straining against the scarf.

I untied her quickly, rubbing her wrists as she came down, but we weren't done. Not by a long shot. She pushed me onto my back, straddling me with a fierce grace that took my breath away. "My turn," she said, her voice a sultry purr. She grabbed the scarf from where I'd tossed it, tying my wrists now—loose, but symbolic. The role reversal sent a thrill through me; this woman, so composed in her daily job, was unleashing something wild.

She kissed down my chest, her teeth grazing my nipples, making me hiss. Her hand wrapped around my cock, stroking firmly as she licked the tip, tasting the pre-cum beading there. "You taste like sin," she murmured, before taking me deep into her mouth. I groaned, hips thrusting involuntarily, but she held me down, controlling the pace. Slow, torturous suction, her tongue swirling, until I was throbbing, on the brink.

"Enough," I growled, tugging at the scarf.

She released me with a wicked smile, and in one fluid motion, I flipped us, pinning her beneath me. My hand found my jeans, and I dove into the back pocket, pulling out the condom I'd had the foresight to bring. My fingers were surprisingly steady as I ripped the packet open with my teeth and sheathed myself.

Then I entered her in one swift, certain thrust, burying myself to the hilt. She was tight, hot, perfect, her walls clenching around me like a vice. We moved together in that classic rhythm, missionary but so damn intense—her legs wrapped around my waist, pulling me deeper, our eyes locked as I drove into her.

But I wanted to claim her in every way. I pulled out, ignoring her protest, and turned her onto her stomach. "On your knees," I commanded, my hand landing a light smack on her ass. She complied, arching her back, presenting herself to me. I gripped her hips, entering her from behind, the angle hitting deeper, harder. She pushed back against me, meeting every thrust, her moans muffled by the pillow. I reached around, fingering her clit, spanking her lightly again— reddening that perfect skin just enough to sting sweetly.

"Fuck, Tara," I grunted, the slap of our bodies filling the room. She came again, her pussy fluttering around me, pulling me closer to the edge. But I held back, flipping her onto her side next, lifting one leg over my shoulder for a new angle. This position let me go slow, deep, grinding against her as I kissed her ankle, nipping at her calf. Her hands roamed my chest, nails digging in, marking me as hers.

Finally, I rolled us so she was on top, riding me like the goddess she was. Her breasts bounced with each movement, her hands braced on my chest as she ground down, circling her hips in a way that made stars explode behind my eyes. I sat up, wrapping my arms around her, our bodies slick and fused. "Come with me," I whispered, thrusting up into her.

She did, her head thrown back in ecstasy, and I followed, spilling into the condom with a roar, waves of pleasure crashing over me until we were both spent.

Afterward, we lay tangled in the sheets, her head on my chest, my fingers tracing lazy patterns across the smooth skin of her back. The sweat cooled on our skin, and the silence in the room was heavy with the truth of what we'd just done. This wasn't just sex. It was a treaty signed in the dark.

"This changes things," she whispered, her breath a warm puff against my skin.

"It changed the second I saw you the first day at the launch party," I said, my voice rough. "This just made it real."

She propped herself up on an elbow, her expression serious in the dim light filtering through the blinds. "We have to be careful, Xander. My father... and Diego. He was asking about me at the facility today, making comments."

A cold knot formed in my stomach. So she knew. Of course she did. "I know. I was there. I heard him."

Her eyebrows shot up. "You were *there*? In the admin offices?"

I couldn't help but grin, a real one for a change. "I was conducting my little research."

Understanding dawned on her face. "The file cabinet. That's how you got my address."

"It was a multi-pronged intelligence operation," I said, enjoying the spark of reluctant admiration in her eyes. "Very professional."

She shook her head, a slow smile finally breaking through. "You are going to be so much trouble, aren't you?"

"Sweetheart," I said, my voice dropping as I pulled her down for another slow, deliberate kiss. "I've been trouble since the day I was born."

I woke up slowly, dragged from a deep, dreamless sleep I hadn't had in years. The first thing I registered was the scent.

Not the stale smell of my penthouse, but something else. Something clean, with a hint of vanilla. Tara.

My eyes cracked open. She was gone, but the indentation of her head was still on the pillow next to mine. The events of the night before came rushing back—the raw desperation, the way she'd come apart under me. A slow heat spread through my chest.

I found her in the kitchen, wearing a t-shirts that hung down to her mid-thigh. Her back was to me as she stood at the counter, her hair a messy knot on top of her head. For a second, I just watched her, this woman who had consumed my thoughts for twelve years, first as a ghost of the past and now as a wildfire in my present.

"Morning," I said, my voice a gravelly mess.

She jumped, spinning around. A faint blush crept up her neck. "Morning. Coffee's on."

"I'm starving," I said, leaning against the doorframe. "Got any food in this place that doesn't require a medical degree to pronounce?"

A small smile touched her lips. "I think I can handle some eggs."

As she turned to the fridge, I felt the need to move, to walk off some of the nervous energy buzzing under my skin. The apartment was neat, impersonal. Muted colors, modern furniture. It felt more like a hotel suite than a home.

"Hey, where's the bathroom?" I asked, heading down the short hallway.

"First door on your right," she called from the kitchen.

My hand was on the knob of the first door when I saw another one, slightly ajar at the end of the hall. Curiosity, or maybe just a subconscious need to know more about the woman I'd just spent the night with, pulled me toward it. I pushed the door open, expecting a spare bedroom or a closet.

It wasn't a bedroom. It was a goddamn command center.

One entire wall was an organized collage of my life. Press clippings, paparazzi shots, game stats going back to my rookie year. Red string connected dates and locations, a spiderweb of my personal history. A grainy photo of me from the night of the accident was tacked right in the center, my face a mask of youthful arrogance and stupidity. It was a shrine to my downfall.

The air left my lungs in a single, silent punch. This wasn't research. This was obsession. Every move I'd made, every mistake, every public triumph and private failure, all cataloged and displayed like a serial killer's trophy room.

My blood ran cold. The heat from a moment ago turned to ice.

"Tara," I said, my voice flat, dead. "Get in here."

I heard a pan clatter in the kitchen. A second later, she appeared in the doorway, a questioning look on her face. "What's wrong?" Then her eyes followed my gaze to the wall.

The color drained from her face so fast I thought she might faint. The carton of eggs she was holding slipped from her numb fingers and crashed to the floor, splattering yellow yolk across the hardwood. She didn't even flinch. She just stared at the wall, then at me, her expression one of pure, unadulterated horror. She hadn't just been caught; she'd been exposed.

"What the fuck," I whispered, turning to face her fully, "is this?"

"Xander, I... I was going to take it down."

"Take it down?" I let out a harsh, barking laugh that had no humor in it. "You've been tracking me. For years. Every part of this was a plan, wasn't it? Getting me to Miami, becoming my doctor... getting me into your bed last night?" The last question came out like a snarl, the taste of betrayal bitter in my mouth.

"No!" she said, taking a step forward. "Last night wasn't part of the plan. It was the moment the plan fell apart." Her eyes were pleading. "This," she gestured wildly at the wall, "this was about revenge. It was built on the lie that you killed my brother. It was how I kept the anger burning."

She walked past me, right up to the wall. With a sharp, sudden movement, she ripped the photo of me from the accident off the corkboard. The paper tore. Then she tore down another clipping, and another, her movements becoming frantic. The red string snapped, falling limp to the floor.

I just watched, silent, as she dismantled twelve years of her own rage, piece by piece. She didn't stop until the wall was bare, leaving only the ghost impressions of where the photos had been. She stood in the middle of the paper debris, her chest rising and falling rapidly, her eyes blazing.

"I'm done chasing ghosts, Xander," she said, her voice shaking but firm. "This was for a man I thought you were. A monster. It had nothing to do with the man who was in my bed last night."

I looked from the wreckage on the floor to her defiant, vulnerable face. The ice in my gut began to thaw. She hadn't just built this wall; she had lived in the prison it created. And she had just torn it down for me.

Slowly, I closed the distance between us, stepping over a picture of myself celebrating a championship win. I reached out and brushed a tear from her cheek with my thumb.

"Okay," I said, my voice quiet but steady. "No more ghosts."

CHAPTER
Sixteen

TARA

I'D BEEN WATCHING the clock on my office wall for the past twenty minutes, trying not to seem obvious about it. The cleaning staff had already come and gone, leaving behind the antiseptic smell that permeated the medical wing after hours. Most of the other office lights were off—just a few security lamps casting long shadows down the corridor.

Seven-fifty-eight on a Friday night, and I was pretending to catch up on paperwork.

I shifted in my chair, uncrossing and recrossing my legs. The motion sent a delicious reminder of last night's activities shooting through my body—little aches in places that made me bite my lip to suppress a smile. Professional decorum be damned, I couldn't wait to see him again.

Seven-fifty-nine.

The past week had been the most exhilarating of my life. After years of watching Xander McCrae from a distance, I was finally getting to know the real Xander. The one who laughed with his whole body. The one with a scar on his hip from falling off a bicycle when he was nine. The one who kissed like he was drowning and I was air.

I traced my collarbone, remembering the feel of his lips there. We'd found a moment between his training and my patient rounds, ducking into a supply closet like teenagers. His hands had been everywhere at once, and I'd had to bite down on his shoulder to keep from crying out when he slid his fingers inside me.

Eight o'clock.

A soft knock at my door sent my heart rate skyrocketing. I took a deep breath before calling out, "Come in."

The door opened, and there he was—all six feet three inches of him, freshly showered, his dark hair still damp at the temples. He wore jeans and a simple gray t-shirt that clung to his shoulders in a way that made my mouth go dry. The door shut behind him, and his face broke into that devastating smile I was still getting used to seeing directed at me.

"Dr. Swanson," he said, his voice a low rumble. "Working late again? You know what they say about all work and no play."

I leaned back in my chair, allowing myself to drink him in. "I thought that's why you were here, Mr. McCrae. To help me with the 'play' part of that equation."

His eyes darkened as he moved toward my desk, his gait unhurried but purposeful. "Happy to be of service."

He rounded the desk, and I swiveled my chair to face him. He was intoxicating.

"You're staring," he said, the corner of his mouth quirking up.

"I am," I admitted. "Is that a problem?"

"Not at all." He braced his hands on the arms of my chair,

effectively caging me in. "I like it when you stare. Reminds me of how you looked at me last week during my physical. Like you were cataloging every inch."

I tilted my head back to maintain eye contact. "I was. Professional interest, of course."

"Of course." His face was inches from mine now. "And is your interest still... professional?"

I reached up, running my finger along his jawline, feeling the slight stubble there. "Not even remotely."

His laugh was warm against my lips as he closed the distance between us. The kiss started slow, almost chaste, but quickly deepened as I parted my lips for him. His tongue slid against mine, and I couldn't help the small sound that escaped me. He groaned in response, his hands leaving the chair to tangle in my hair.

When we finally broke apart, we were both breathing hard.

"I've been thinking about doing that all afternoon," he confessed, his forehead resting against mine.

"Just that?" I teased, my hands sliding under his shirt to feel the warm skin beneath.

His eyes, mossy green and alive with desire, held mine. "No. Not just that."

He straightened, pulling me up with him. I let him guide me backward until I felt the edge of the examination table against the backs of my thighs. The same table where I'd first asserted my dominance over him during his physical. The irony wasn't lost on me.

"Turnabout is fair play, Doctor," he murmured, as if reading my thoughts. He lifted me easily, setting me on the edge of the table, my skirt riding up as he stepped between my legs.

"Is that what this is? A game?" I asked, even as my body

betrayed my desire, my legs wrapping around his waist to pull him closer.

He paused, his hands stilling on my thighs. "No. This is not a game to me, Tara."

The sincerity in his voice made my chest tighten. I reached up, tracing the outline of his lips with my finger. "Good. Because it's not a game to me either. Not anymore."

The admission was full of implications neither of us was ready to voice aloud. Instead, we let our bodies speak for us. His hands resumed their exploration, pushing my skirt higher, his fingers tracing patterns on my inner thighs that made me shiver. I pulled his shirt over his head, revealing the taut muscles of his chest and abdomen, marked here and there with the scars of his profession.

"You know, I was thinking. Taking down that obsession wall of me," he said. "That couldn't have been easy."

"It wasn't," I admitted. "It felt like erasing a part of myself. But I don't need it anymore. I have you now. The real you."

His smile was soft, almost vulnerable. "You do have me. All of me."

The moment stretched between us, something profound and fragile taking shape. Then he kissed me again, and thought became impossible. My hands fumbled with his belt as his lips traced a path down my neck, making me gasp when he found the sensitive spot just below my ear.

"You're wearing too many clothes," he murmured against my skin.

I couldn't agree more. We undressed with urgent movements, afraid the spell might break if we took too long. When we were both naked, he stood back for a moment, his eyes roaming over me with a hunger that made me feel powerful and vulnerable all at once.

"God, you're gorgeous," he said, his voice rough with desire.

I reached for him, pulling him back to me. "Show me how gorgeous you think I am."

He did. Right there on the examination table, he worshipped every inch of me. His hands and mouth were everywhere, drawing sounds from me I didn't know I could make. When he finally slid inside me, the sense of completion was overwhelming. We moved together with a synchronicity that felt both new and familiar, as if our bodies had always known how to dance together.

"Look at me," he commanded softly as I felt myself nearing the edge. I opened my eyes to find his gaze intense on mine. "I want to see you come undone."

It was his eyes that did it—the raw vulnerability and desire I saw there. I came with his name on my lips, my body clenching around him. He followed moments later, his face buried in my neck, his breath hot against my skin as he pulsed inside me.

We stayed like that for a long moment, our breathing gradually slowing, his weight a comforting pressure on top of me. I ran my fingers through his hair, marveling at how right this felt—how right he felt.

"We should probably get dressed," I said eventually, though I made no move to do so. "Security does rounds every hour."

He groaned but pulled away, reaching for his discarded clothes. "Always the voice of reason, Dr. Swanson."

I sat up, watching as he pulled on his jeans. "One of us has to be. And since you're the one who suggested sex in my office..."

He grinned, unrepentant. "I didn't hear any complaints. In fact, I'm pretty sure I heard the opposite of complaints."

I felt my cheeks heat as I slid off the table, grabbing my blouse from where it had landed on my desk chair. "I'm not complaining. Just pointing out the facts."

He stepped behind me as I buttoned my blouse, his arms wrapping around my waist, his chin resting on my shoulder. "Fact 1… that was amazing. Fact 2… you're amazing. Fact 3… I can't wait for tomorrow."

Tomorrow. Our Naples trip to confront Rick Morrison. The real reason we'd met tonight—to finalize our plans before setting out early in the morning. The reminder sobered me.

"About tomorrow," I said, turning in his arms to face him. "Are you sure you're ready for this? Whatever Morrison tells us… it could change everything."

Xander's expression grew serious. "I'm ready. I've lived with half-truths and guilt for too long. I need to know what really happened that night. Even if I was the one driving."

I nodded, understanding completely. "I'll pick you up at seven, then. We should get there by early afternoon."

"Actually," he said, a hint of his earlier smile returning, "I thought I could drive."

"Fine," I conceded. "But I'm bringing the coffee and snacks."

"Deal." He sealed it with a quick kiss before releasing me to finish dressing.

———

The highway unfurled in front of us like an endless black belt through Florida's scenery. Palm trees disappeared, replaced by scruffy pines as we drove north, the morning sunlight splashing across the road.

I checked out Xander from my seat, taking in his profile while he handled the wheel. That strong jaw, the little crease between his eyebrows when he focused, those hands gripping the steering wheel like he owned it.

"You're doing it again," he said without taking his eyes off the road.

"Doing what?"

"Staring. Analyzing."

I smiled, not bothering to deny it. "Force of habit, I guess. A life of observation is hard to break."

He glanced at me, his expression softening. "I'm not complaining. I enjoy being the focus of your attention. Always have."

The admission caught me off guard. "Always?"

He returned his gaze to the road, a slight flush coloring his cheeks. "Even back then. When you were sixteen, I noticed you watching me when you thought I wasn't looking."

"You knew?" I felt heat rise to my face. "And you never said anything?"

"What was I supposed to say? 'Hey, Jimmy, I think your little sister has a crush on me, and the really messed up part is I kind of like it'?" He shook his head. "I was horrified by my own feelings. You were my best friend's sister. It was... complicated."

I gave a humorless laugh. "Forget complicated... this is a full-blown train wreck with no brakes."

Xander snorted. "Yeah, look at us... sneaking around behind your father's back, risking both our careers, trying to uncover the truth about your brother's death. I'd say complicated doesn't even begin to cover it."

I turned to look out the window, watching the landscape blur past. He was right, of course. What we were doing was reckless at best, potentially catastrophic at worst. And yet...

"I wouldn't change it," I said, surprising myself with the truth of it. "Any of it."

His hand found mine across the console as we drove on, the miles disappearing beneath us. The conversation flowed more easily now, veering away from the heavy topics of the past and the uncertain future. I learned about his childhood. He told me about his first soccer ball, a gift from his father on his fifth birthday.

In return, I shared stories of growing up as the youngest Swanson, always in Jimmy's shadow but never resenting it. I told him about my mother's death when I was ten, how Jimmy, only two years older, had stepped up to fill the void she left.

"He would have been happy about this, you know," Xander said after a poignant story about Jimmy teaching me to ride a bike. "About us working together to uncover the truth."

The thought had never occurred to me. "You think so?"

Xander nodded, a sad smile playing on his lips. "I'm sure of it. We were his two favorite people."

We were silent, lost in thought. As we neared the coast, the scenery shifted—more buildings, lusher plants. We stopped for gas and a quick bathroom break.

Back on the road, the mood lightened. Xander found a radio station playing 90s hits, and we sang along to songs that had been popular when we were kids. I discovered he knew all the words to "Wannabe" by the Spice Girls, a fact I promised to use against him at the earliest opportunity.

I was feeling great by the time we pulled over for a late lunch at this classic Florida diner. Think turquoise booths, shiny chrome, and all the comfort food you could want. We snagged a booth in the back, away from the few other people, and ordered burgers and milkshakes.

"So," Xander said after the waitress left with our order, "what's the plan when we get to Morrison's place? Do we just knock on his door and say, 'Hey, remember that fatal car crash twelve years ago? We have some questions about your investigation.'"

I grimaced. "I was thinking we'd be a bit more subtle than that. Maybe introduce ourselves as researchers working on a book about unsolved or controversial cases in Palo Alto."

He raised an eyebrow. "And you think a retired detective won't see through that in about two seconds?"

"You have a better idea?"

He leaned forward, his voice dropping. "I think honesty might be our best approach. Tell him who we are, why we're there. Appeal to his conscience."

I considered this. "And if he refuses to talk to us?"

"Then we know he has something to hide." Xander's expression was determined. "But I don't think he will. If he took a bribe to alter his report, it's been eating at him ever since. People like that, they're often looking for a chance to unburden themselves."

Our food arrived, halting the conversation. I took a bite of my burger, surprised by how hungry I was. Across the table, Xander was equally focused on his meal, though his eyes kept finding mine over the top of his milkshake glass.

"What?" I asked after the third meaningful glance.

He set down his glass, a slow smile spreading across his face. "Nothing. Just thinking about how surreal this is. You and me, on a road trip, eating burgers like a normal couple."

A normal couple. The phrase sent a flutter through my stomach. "Is that what we are? A couple?"

His smile faltered slightly. "I don't know what we are, Tara. I just know that right now, sitting across from you, I'm happier than I've been in a long time. And I don't want it to end."

The honesty in his voice made my chest ache. I reached across the table, taking his hand in mine. "I don't want it to end either."

Something shifted in his gaze, a heat replacing the vulnerability. His thumb traced circles on my palm, sending shivers up my arm. "Good to know we're on the same page."

The air between us practically crackled. Suddenly, the burger in front of me was replaced by a different hunger. I glanced around the diner—two other tables were occupied, both by elderly couples engrossed in their own meals. The server was nowhere to be seen.

"Let's get out of here," I said, my voice lower than I intended. "We still have an hour's drive ahead of us."

Xander's eyes darkened, and he nodded. He threw down money to cover the tab, and led me out to the parking lot with a hand at the small of my back. The touch was innocent enough, but the promise it held made my skin tingle.

The Audi was parked at the far end of the lot, partially obscured by a large delivery truck. As soon as we were around the side of the vehicle, out of sight from the diner windows, Xander pressed me against the passenger door, his body flush against mine.

"Tell me if you want me to stop," he murmured, his lips hovering just above mine.

"Don't you dare," I breathed, pulling him down to me.

The kiss was hungry, desperate, fueled by the freedom of being away from Miami and the watchful eyes that constantly surrounded us. His hands were everywhere—in my hair, at my waist, sliding under my shirt to cup my breast through my bra. I arched into his touch, my own hands equally busy, tracing the hard planes of his chest beneath his t-shirt.

"Car," I gasped as his lips found my neck. "Inside."

He fumbled with the key fob, unlocking the doors without breaking contact. The back door opened, and he lifted me inside, climbing in after me and pulling the door shut. The tinted windows provided a shield from any potential onlookers, though the isolated location of the car already offered significant privacy.

"I've wanted to do this since we left Miami this morning," he confessed, his voice rough as he pulled me onto his lap, my knees straddling his thighs.

"Then what are you waiting for?" I challenged, my fingers already working at his belt.

There was no slow buildup this time, no gentle exploration. This was pure need, the culmination of a morning spent in close proximity, sharing painful truths and building a new understanding between us. We undressed each other with clumsy movements, hampered by the confined space but driven by a desire that wouldn't be denied. My elbow knocked against the window as I yanked his shirt over his head, and he let out a muffled curse when his knee banged the center console while shucking off his jeans. "Bloody hell, this car's not built for tall guys," he grumbled, but his grin was wicked, eyes blazing with heat as he finally freed himself, his cock springing up hard and thick, already glistening at the tip.

I laughed breathlessly, the sound turning into a moan as his hands shoved my shorts and panties down in one rough tug, my ass bumping the ceiling in the process. "Ouch—watch it, soccer star. You're supposed to be agile." But the teasing died on my lips when he opened a condom wrapper, equipped himself before gripping my hips, and positioning me over him. God, the way he looked at me—like I was the only thing in his world—made my core clench with anticipation.

"Agile enough for you?" he growled, thrusting up just as I sank down, sheathing him inside me in one slick, mind-blowing slide. We both groaned, the fit so tight, so perfect, but the angle in this damn backseat had me half-twisted, my head grazing the roof every time I tried to move. I bit my lip to stifle a giggle as I adjusted, rocking experimentally—only to have my foot slip off the seat and kick the door handle. The car let out a beep, the hazards flashing once before he slapped the button to kill them. "Shit, Tara, you're going to get us arrested before we even finish."

"Shut up and fuck me," I demanded, but I was laughing too, the absurdity of it all mixing with the raw heat building between us. His hands dug into my thighs, guiding me as I rode him harder, the leather seats creaking under our weight like a bad soundtrack. Sweat slicked our skin, the windows fogging up faster than a teenage make-out session, and every thrust sent jolts of pleasure spiking through me. He leaned forward, capturing a nipple in his mouth through my bra— wait, no, he'd shoved that up too, exposing me to his hungry gaze. His tongue swirled, teeth grazing just enough to make me arch, which only drove him deeper, hitting that spot that made stars burst behind my eyes.

"Fuck, you're so wet, so tight," he rasped, his accent thick-ening with lust, one hand sliding between us to circle my clit with rough, precise strokes. I ground down, chasing the fric-tion, but the limited space turned every movement into a comedy of errors—his elbow hit the seatback release, nearly flattening us both, and I had to brace one hand on the foggy window to steady myself, leaving a perfect handprint like some erotic crime scene. We burst out laughing mid-thrust, the sound vibrating through our joined bodies, but it only fueled the fire, making everything hotter, more urgent.

"Look at me," he commanded, his voice strained with the effort of control, cupping my face to lock our gazes.

I met his eyes, drowning in the intensity I found there—the raw need, the vulnerability, the way he saw straight through to my soul. In that moment, with his body buried deep inside mine, the car rocking subtly with our rhythm, a terrifying clarity washed over me: I was completely, irrevocably in love with him. Not the obsession I'd nursed all those years, not the revenge fantasy I'd constructed, but real love—messy and frightening and exhilarating.

The realization pushed me over the edge, my release crashing through me with unexpected force, my walls pulsing around him in waves that had me crying out, muffled against his shoulder. He followed moments later, thrusting up hard one last time, spilling into the condom with a guttural groan, his face buried in my neck, my name a prayer on his lips.

We stayed like that for several minutes, our breathing gradually slowing, my forehead resting against his. The reality of what we'd done—having sex in a public parking lot in broad daylight, complete with accidental hazard lights and foggy windows—should have horrified me. Instead, I felt a giddy rush of liberation. I'd acted purely on impulse, driven by desire, and it had been hotter than hell.

"We should probably get back on the road," Xander murmured eventually, though he made no move to release me.

I nodded reluctantly, and we dressed in silence—though not without a few more mishaps, like me nearly putting my shirt on backward, and him struggling to zip his jeans in the confined space. Once presentable, we moved to the front seats, and Xander started the engine.

As we pulled back onto the highway, his hand found mine across the console again. "No regrets?" he asked, a hint of vulnerability in his voice.

I squeezed his hand, offering a smile. "Not a single one."

The rest of the drive passed in a comfortable haze. We talked about our favorite movies and dream vacations. It felt like the most natural thing in the world, being with him like this.

As we approached Naples, however, the mood in the car shifted. The reality of our mission reasserted itself, the weight of the past settling over us once more. Xander's grip on the steering wheel tightened, and I checked the address on my phone with increasing frequency.

"Turn right at the next light," I instructed, my voice more clinical than it had been all day. "Then it should be the third street on the left."

Xander nodded, following my directions without comment. We turned onto a quiet, suburban street lined with modest single-story homes. Palm trees and well-tended gardens spoke of a peaceful, middle-class neighborhood—the kind where people knew their neighbors and kept their lawns neatly trimmed.

"Number 1542," I said, scanning the houses. "There. On the right."

The house was unremarkable—pale yellow stucco with white trim, a small front porch with a pair of rocking chairs, a neatly kept lawn with a few decorative shrubs. A mailbox at the end of the driveway confirmed it: "R. Morrison" in simple black letters.

Xander pulled the car to a stop at the curb in front of the

house. We sat in silence for a long moment, staring at the inno-
cent-looking dwelling. It seemed impossible that the man
inside held the key to the truth that had defined both our lives
for twelve years.

"What if he's not home?" I asked, suddenly anxious.

"Then we wait," Xander replied, his voice steady despite
the tension showing in his posture. "Or we get a hotel room
and come back tomorrow. We've come too far to turn back
now."

I nodded, drawing a deep breath to steady myself. "What if
he doesn't want to talk to us?"

Xander turned to face me, his expression serious. "Then we
make him listen. This isn't just about clearing my name
anymore, Tara. It's about finally learning the truth... for both
of us."

The conviction in his voice steadied me. He was right.
Morrison's words could change everything, but the prison of
not knowing was worse.

"Ready?" Xander asked, his hand finding mine.

I met his gaze, drawing strength from the determination I
saw there. "Ready."

We got out of the car and walked up the driveway side by
side. The concrete path to the front door seemed much longer
than it actually was, each step bringing us closer to answers
we'd sought for over a decade.

At the door, we paused, exchanging one last look. "We're in
this together," he hissed.

I nodded, squeezing his hand before releasing it. Then,
before I could lose my nerve, I raised my fist and knocked on
Rick Morrison's door.

CHAPTER
Seventeen

XANDER

I DIDN'T KNOW what I expected when the door swung open, but it wasn't this—a man who looked like he'd been carved from weathered stone, his silver hair neatly combed, wearing pressed khakis and a polo shirt like he was heading to a retiree golf tournament.

Rick Morrison had the eyes of a man who'd spent decades watching people lie to him. Those eyes swept over us now, narrowing slightly as he assessed the threat level of the young couple on his doorstep.

"Can I help you?" His voice had the neutrality of someone who'd conducted thousands of interviews, revealing nothing while taking in everything.

Tara stepped forward. "Detective Morrison? My name is Dr. Tara Swanson, and this is Alexander McCrae. We'd like to speak with you about a case you worked on twelve years ago in Palo Alto."

The transformation was instant. At our names, Morrison's

entire demeanor shifted. His spine straightened, his jaw tightened, and those assessing eyes turned cold and distant. I'd seen that look before—on opponents across the pitch right before they committed a brutal foul. The look of someone about to do something they knew was wrong.

"Not interested," he said flatly, already moving to close the door. "Good day."

I reacted on instinct, my hand shooting out to block the door. "Please," I said, keeping my voice calm despite the adrenaline surging through me. "Five minutes. That's all we're asking."

Morrison's eyes flicked to my hand on his door, then back to my face. For a second, I thought he might try to force it closed anyway. Instead, he let out a sharp exhale through his nostrils.

"Five minutes," he conceded with visible reluctance. "Then you fucking leave, and you don't come back."

He stepped back, allowing us entry into a living room that looked like it had been assembled from a catalog labeled "Retired Bachelor." Beige walls, beige furniture, a few generic landscapes on the walls. No personal photos, no mementos. The room of a man who either had no past or was deliberately trying to forget it.

"Sit," he instructed, gesturing to a sofa that looked barely used.

Tara and I sat side by side, close enough that I could feel the tension radiating from her body. Morrison remained standing, arms crossed over his chest, making it clear this was not a social call.

"You're here about the Swanson boy," he said, not bothering to frame it as a question. "James. The crash."

"Yes," Tara confirmed, her voice steady despite the slight tremor I could see in her hands. "My brother."

Morrison's expression didn't change. "It was more than a decade ago. Tragic accident. The report is public record. I have nothing more to say."

"With all due respect, Detective," I said, leaning forward, "the public report is why we're here. It's... incomplete."

Morrison's jaw ticked.

"The report never explicitly states who was driving the car," Tara pressed. "Don't you find that odd for an official accident report?"

A muscle worked in Morrison's cheek. "As I said, the report contains all relevant information."

"All relevant information?" I couldn't keep the edge from my voice. "I was seventeen years old. I was told I killed my best friend. I've carried that guilt ever since, Detective. Don't you think whether I was *actually* driving the car is relevant?"

For half a second, something darted behind Morrison's eyes—a flicker of shame, maybe—before his face locked back into place.

"What happened that night was a tragedy," he said, his voice flat. "But the case is closed. The report stands."

Tara's voice had taken on a dangerous edge. "Was your job to write a deliberately vague report that allowed my father to use that ambiguity to destroy Alexander's life?"

"I don't know what you're implying, Dr. Swanson," Morrison's expression hardened, "but I suggest you be very careful."

Something snapped in his carefully maintained facade. His face flushed, and he jabbed a finger toward Tara.

"I filed the report based on the evidence available!" he barked, defensive heat replacing his cold detachment. "The official report was the final conclusion. It's not my fault if my original notes suggested something different!"

The room went still. Morrison froze, his face draining of color as he realized what he'd just admitted. Tara and I locked eyes, the same realization hitting us both.

Original notes. A second, unredacted version of the truth existed.

"What did your original notes say, Detective?" I asked, my voice quiet but intense.

Morrison's expression shuttered. "I misspoke," he said, his voice an icy rasp. "I think your five minutes are up. Get the hell off my property before I call the cops."

I placed a gentle hand on Tara's arm. We'd gotten what we came for. A lead. We walked out into the oppressive Florida heat, the door slamming shut behind us.

"Original notes," she whispered as we reached the car, her eyes bright with a mix of anger and triumph.

"Original notes," I confirmed, gripping the steering wheel. I yanked the car away from Morrison's neighborhood, desperate to get some space before I completely lost my shit. We drove without talking for a good five minutes, both of us crushed by the bomb that asshole had just dropped on us.

Just as I was merging onto the highway, my phone buzzed, the screen flashing a picture of a familiar, grinning face.

Sean.

I almost ignored it. The last thing I wanted was to drag him into this.

"Who is it?" Tara asked quietly.

"My brother."

"You should answer it," she said. "Maybe you need to talk to him."

I took a breath and hit the speakerphone button. "Hey. Fair warning, you're on speaker, and I've got company."

"There he is!" Sean's voice was disgustingly cheerful, the charismatic energy he used on stage bleeding through the phone. "I heard you were transferred to Miami. Figured I'd check in, see if you've been behaving yourself."

"Something like that," I mumbled, my eyes fixed on the road.

Sean's tone shifted instantly, the public persona dropping away. "Cut the bullshit, Zan. I know that tone. That's the 'world's ending but it's my own damn fault' voice. What's really going on?"

"It's nothing, Sean. Just… stuff."

"Stuff," he repeated flatly. "Listen to yourself. You sound like you're carrying a mountain. You carry every problem like you're the only one strong enough, and you refuse to let anyone help you hold the damn thing up."

I flinched. His words, a perfect blend of his professional motivational speaking and brotherly love, hit their mark.

"I don't want to bother you with my shit," I said, my voice low.

"You're my twin, you idiot. Your shit is my shit," Sean said, his voice softening. "Listen to me. It's time to let us in. Let the family help. It's not a burden. It's what we do. Stop trying to be the hero in your own tragedy and let someone else share the load for once."

The dam cracked. I looked over at Tara, at her determined, beautiful face, and knew he was right. I couldn't do this alone anymore.

"It's about the accident," I said, the words feeling heavy in my mouth. "Jimmy's death, remember? I just spoke with the lead detective. He accidentally let it slip that he had 'original notes' that *could* prove I wasn't driving."

Sean was silent for a beat, processing. When he spoke again, his voice was calm and strategic, the "Commander" personality taking over. "Okay. And these notes are where?"

"Hi Sean. This is Tara, Jimmy's sister. The notes must be in the police archive in Palo Alto," Tara answered for me. "We can't get to them without tipping off my father."

"You can't," Sean corrected. "But Cory can."

The suggestion was so simple, so obvious, I felt like an idiot for not thinking of it myself. Cory. Our older half-brother. The quiet, workaholic investor who lived right there in Stanford.

"He's a research machine. He can dig into anything without leaving a trace. He's local. Call him. Tell him everything. He'll help. You know he will."

Sean was right. I'd just been isolating myself.

"Alright. Thank you, Sean," I said, my voice thick.

"Trust me," he said, his voice quiet but certain. "Now go make the call. It's about damn time you let your brothers have your back."

He hung up, leaving a profound silence in the car.

Tara turned to me, hope flickering in her eyes. "That's good news. It sounds like Cory's in your corner."

Of course. It wasn't a question of if he'd help, but whether I should finally let him. For all these years, I'd deliberately kept my family out of this.

"I'm from a big, blended family," I said, no hesitation in my voice. "Half, step, cousin—it doesn't matter. We always have each other's backs. Cory will help. The real question is whether he'll forgive me for not asking sooner.

"Then call him," Tara said, her decision made. "We need those notes. They could be the key to everything."

I eased onto the shoulder, hazard lights flashing, and pulled up Cory's name. My chest felt tight as I hit call. Two rings, and then his voice came through

"Xander. Is everything alright?" No surprise, no preamble. Just immediate concern. That was Cory.

"Not really," I said, my voice rough with emotion. "I'm in some trouble, Cory. I need a favor. A big one."

"Whatever it is, you've got it," he replied instantly. "Where are you? What do you need?"

The immediate, unquestioning support almost broke me. I explained everything—Morrison, his slip about "original notes," our belief that they contained the truth.

"So you need someone to access police records in Palo Alto without alerting Hank Swanson," Cory summarized when I finished.

"Yes," I confirmed. "I know it's a lot to ask—"

"It's done," Cory said, cutting me off. "You're my brother, Xander. I've been waiting for you to finally let us in on this."

The simple statement crushed me. All this time...

"Thank you, Cory. This means... everything."

"You got it," his voice was quiet but certain. "I'll start looking into it right away. And Xander? Be careful. I remember Hank Swanson. He won't go down easy."

My gaze flicked to Tara. She didn't know the details of the call, but she caught enough of Cory's warning in my expression to tense, her knuckles whitening against her knees.

"We'll watch our backs."

"Good. I'll call soon." And with that, he hung up.

I lowered the phone, relief and a renewed sense of hope.

Tara angled toward me. "So? How did it go?"

"He's in," I said, sliding the phone back into the console. "Cory's got us covered."

I merged back onto the highway, and just as a fragile calm began to settle in the car, Tara's phone buzzed. She glanced at the screen, and her entire body went rigid.

"What is it?" I asked, catching the color drain from her face.

Her jaw tightened. "It's from my father." Her voice was clipped as she read aloud: "Family dinner at the house tomorrow night. Seven o'clock. Don't be late."

It wasn't a request; it was a summons. A clear power play.

"I can go with you," I offered, keeping my eyes on the road.

Tara swiped the screen, closing the text messages, her expression hardening with a new, steely resolve. She shook her head. "No," she said, her voice firm. "That's what he'd expect. He's testing me." She met my gaze, a strategist already planning her next move. "We can't show our hand yet. I'll handle him."

She was right. This was a game of chess, and we couldn't afford a single misstep.

CHAPTER
Eighteen

TARA

THE EMERALD green dress tempted me from its hanger. That dress was reserved for Xander. I shoved it deeper into my closet, my fingers lingering on the silky fabric. I wished I could wear it but this wasn't a night for Xander's favorite color.

Tonight was about armor, not seduction.

I pulled out a sleek navy shift dress instead. The kind of outfit that says, "I'm here because obligation demands it, not because I want to be." Perfect for a dinner with my father that we both knew was really an interrogation.

My phone buzzed on the dresser. A text from Xander.

Good luck tonight. I'll be thinking of you the whole time.

A second message followed almost immediately.

And no, before you ask, I'm not going to tell you to "be careful." You know your father better than anyone.

I smiled despite myself. In just two texts, he'd managed to both support me and acknowledge my autonomy.

I'll call you after, I texted back. *Don't wait up though. These dinners have a way of stretching into endless psychological warfare.*

I set the phone down and returned to my preparation. I applied makeup and put my hair up in a sleek chignon, not a strand out of place. I slipped on the navy dress, a pair of modest heels, and a simple necklace of pearls that were my mother's.

As I hooked the clasp at the back of my neck, the thought came unbidden: Who was that woman in the back seat of the Audi, legs wrapped around Xander, reckless and alive? And who was this one now, zipped into a stark navy dress, the dutiful daughter of Hank Swanson?

Which one was real? I wondered, not for the first time. Or had I learned to perform so well that I no longer knew where the act ended and I began?

Before leaving, I went to my home office. The wall that had once displayed Xander's life was now bare, the materials carefully packed away in storage boxes—not destroyed, but hidden. I couldn't bring myself to get rid of them completely.

Instead of the obsession wall, I now had a new focus: a small corkboard with the few facts we knew about the night Jimmy died. Detective Morrison's name. The mention of "original notes." The deliberately vague official report. It wasn't much, but it was a start.

"I'm coming, Jimmy," I whispered. "I'm going to find out what really happened."

I grabbed my purse and keys, running through my mental checklist one last time. It wasn't just about deflecting my father's questions about Xander. It was about finding evidence. I knew my father too well to believe he didn't keep records of everything. The trick would be finding a way to access his office during dinner.

The drive to my father's Miami mansion took twenty minutes, each one stretching my nerves a little tighter. Before I pulled up to the gates, I'd rehearsed a dozen different responses to the questions I knew would come. The security guard recognized my car and waved me through without stopping.

I parked in the circular drive and took a deep breath, shifting into character: Dr. Tara Swanson, devoted daughter and perfect team physician who's definitely not sleeping with the team's star forward.

Before I could ring the bell, the massive front door swung open. My father stood there, a tumbler of scotch in his hand, his expression arranged in what passed for warmth on his features.

"Tara." He leaned in to kiss my cheek. I forced myself not to flinch at the contact. "Right on time, as always."

"Hello, Father." I returned the kiss, the gesture as empty as the crystal vase on the entry table. "I hope I haven't kept you waiting."

"Not at all." He gestured me inside, his hand hovering just above the small of my back without actually touching me—a pattern established years ago. My father rarely touched anyone unless he was making a point. "Can I get you a drink? Wine? Something stronger?"

"Just water for now, thank you." I needed to keep my wits about me.

He nodded approvingly and led me through the soaring foyer toward the formal living room.

"How's the team shaping up?" he asked, his tone casual as he poured me a glass of sparkling water from the bar cart. "I've been watching practice. Some of the new acquisitions seem promising."

And there it was—the first probe. Not directly about Xander, but close enough. A fishing expedition disguised as small talk.

"The roster has potential," I replied, matching his casual tone. "Coach Wilkes has been integrating the new players well. A few minor injuries to manage, but nothing serious."

"And McCrae?" The question landed with deceptive lightness. "I've noticed he's been performing exceptionally well in practice. Your sessions must be having quite an effect on him."

I took a careful sip of water, using the moment to compose my face into a facade of indifference.

"He's responding well to treatment," I said, keeping my voice detached. "His shoulder issues require regular maintenance, but he's compliant with the protocols I've established."

My father studied me over the rim of his glass. "Compliant? Why wouldn't he be?"

I shrugged, the gesture deliberately dismissive. "He's a talented athlete, but he requires a lot of maintenance. He's still a liability... the drinking, the partying. You knew what you were getting when you signed him."

The words felt like acid on my tongue, but I forced them out anyway. This was the game. This was how I survived.

My father's expression shifted subtly, the tightness around his eyes easing just a fraction. I'd passed the first test.

"Well, as long as he performs on the field, the rest is manageable," he said, setting his glass down. "Shall we move to the dining room? Dinner should be ready."

I followed him through the house, past walls adorned with expensive art chosen for investment value rather than aesthetic appeal. The dining room was a study in tasteful opulence, a long mahogany table that could seat sixteen set for an intimate dinner for two. Or so I thought.

Just as we entered, the doorbell chimed. My father checked his watch and smiled—a small, satisfied expression that set off alarm bells in my head.

"Oh, I forgot to mention," he said, though the calculated gleam in his eyes made it clear this was no oversight. "I invited Diego Mano. I know you two have been exchanging glances."

My stomach dropped.

I stood frozen as my father went to greet him. The trap was so obvious it was almost insulting. After the scene at the night-club—Diego's possessiveness, Xander's kiss, my slap—my father was making his move. He knew damn well Diego had been hitting on me since day one, his flirtations as relentless as they were unwelcome. And now, Father was shoving him in my face, not because he truly cared about matchmaking, but to rattle me, to remind me who pulled the strings in my life. To mess with my head and keep me off-balance, especially now that Xander was in the picture.

I heard them before I saw them—Diego's too-loud laugh, my father's measured response. Then they rounded the corner into the dining room. Diego Mano was dressed in an expensive suit that looked like it had been selected to impress rather than for style, his dark hair slicked back, his smile wide and predatory as his eyes landed on me.

"Dr. Swanson," he said, moving forward to take my hand before I could avoid the contact. "You look beautiful tonight."

He lifted my hand to his lips, and it took every ounce of self-control not to pull away. I forced a polite smile instead.

"Mr. Mano. This is a surprise."

"A pleasant one, I hope," he replied, his thumb brushing across my knuckles before finally releasing my hand. "Your father has been telling me about how you skipped two grades in high school. Fascinating."

"How thoughtful of you, Father," I said, the words coated in enough sugar to cause diabetes. "Though I'm sure Mr. Mano has better things to do on a Friday night than discuss my high school days."

"Not at all," Diego replied, his eyes never leaving my face. "And please, call me Diego. I think we've moved beyond formalities, don't you? Especially after our... moment at the club."

I felt my face heat at the reference. Of course he would bring that up—the night I'd slapped Xander after our kiss. In Diego's mind, that action had been a rejection of Xander, not a desperate attempt to salvage my professional reputation.

"Well," my father interjected smoothly, "shall we sit? Carmen has prepared her famous paella."

The next hour and a half was an exercise in controlled torture. Diego sat to my right, my father at the head of the table. Throughout the meal, Diego found every excuse to touch me—his hand brushing mine as he passed the bread, his knee pressing against my thigh under the table, his fingers grazing my arm as he emphasized a point in conversation. Each touch made my skin crawl, but I endured it with a fixed smile, knowing my father was watching every reaction, gauging how far he could push me before I cracked.

The conversation drifted from team dynamics to Diego's career aspirations to Miami's social scene. Diego made pointed references to clubs and restaurants he thought I might enjoy, clearly angling for a date. My father encouraged him at every turn, praising Diego's judgment and taste with nauseating enthusiasm, all while shooting me subtle, knowing glances that said, See? This is what I choose for you.

"You know, Tara rarely takes time to enjoy the city," my father said, signaling Carmen to clear the dinner plates. "She's always been so focused on her work. Perhaps you could show her what she's missing, Diego."

Diego's smile widened. "It would be my pleasure, sir. In fact, there's a charity gala at the Vizcaya Museum next weekend. Very exclusive. I happen to have an extra ticket."

The trap was closing. I could feel it tightening around me with every passing minute. If I refused outright, my father would question why. If I accepted, I'd be encouraging Diego's pursuit. I needed a third option—one that wouldn't raise suspicions.

"That's very kind," I said carefully, "but I'm not sure my schedule will permit it. We have away games coming up, and I need to make sure the medical team is prepared."

"Surely you can spare one evening," my father pressed, his eyes gleaming with that manipulative spark. "The team will survive without you for a few hours."

I was saved from having to respond by Carmen's return with dessert—a delicate flan that I had no appetite for but pretended to enjoy anyway. As Diego launched into a story about his last charity event (which seemed to involve more celebrities and alcohol than actual charitable work), I noticed my father checking his watch.

"I just remembered," he said, interrupting Diego mid-anecdote, "I need to take a call from our Tokyo investors. They're considering a significant stake in the team, and with the time difference..." He stood, smoothing his trousers. "Please, continue with dessert. This shouldn't take long."

He left the dining room, his footsteps echoing down the hallway toward his office. I could practically feel the smugness radiating off him—he thought he was so clever, leaving me alone with Diego to foster this unwanted connection, to throw me off my game and remind me of his control.

Little did he know, he'd just handed me exactly what I needed: access to the house while he was occupied.

"Finally," Diego said as soon as my father was out of earshot. He shifted his chair closer to mine. "I've been wanting to get you alone all night."

I forced a tight smile. "Mr. Mano—"

"Diego," he corrected, his hand coming to rest on my knee under the table.

I removed his hand firmly. "Mr. Mano, I think there's been a misunderstanding. My father may have given you the impression that I'm interested in pursuing something personal with you. I'm not."

His expression hardened briefly before smoothing into a confident smile. "You're playing hard to get. I respect that. But we both know what happened at the club. You rejected McCrae publicly. That sent a message."

"The only message I intended to send was professional," I replied, my voice cooling several degrees. "I don't mix my personal and professional lives."

He laughed, the sound grating on my already frayed nerves. "Come on, Tara. Your father approves. We'd be good together. What's holding you back?"

The fact that I'm in love with Xander McCrae, I thought. The fact that even if I weren't, you'd be the last man on earth I'd consider.

But I couldn't say either of those things. Not when I needed to maintain the facade long enough to search my father's office.

"I have a headache," I said abruptly, pressing my fingers to my temple for emphasis. "I'm sorry, but I need to find some aspirin. If you'll excuse me?"

I stood before he could protest, leaving my barely touched flan on the table. Diego rose as well, but I waved him back down.

"Finish your dessert. I know where my father's medicine cabinet is. I'll be back shortly."

I didn't wait for his response, already moving toward the doorway with measured steps—not too fast to suggest urgency, but quick enough to discourage him from following. Once in the hallway, I paused, listening. I could hear my father's voice from behind his closed office door, the low murmur of business being conducted.

I moved swiftly toward the grand staircase, my heels silent on the plush carpet. The main bathroom was on the second floor, providing perfect cover for my absence. But instead of turning right at the top of the stairs, I turned left, toward my father's private study.

Unlike his formal office downstairs where he conducted team business, the study was where he kept his personal files —the ones that didn't need to withstand scrutiny from part-ners or investors. If there was evidence of his deal with Detec-tive Morrison, it would be here.

The door was unlocked, as I'd expected. My father's arro-gance extended to his security practices; he never imagined anyone would dare invade his private spaces. I slipped inside, closing the door silently behind me.

The room was exactly as I remembered it—wood-paneled walls lined with leather-bound books he'd never read, a massive oak desk positioned to command the space, and filing cabinets on the side. Everything in its place, every item a reflection of the control he valued above all else.

I hurried to the cabinets, scanning the labels. "Legal Documents." "Financial Records." "Team Acquisitions." My eyes landed on a cabinet in the far corner, labeled simply: "Archived - Palo Alto."

My heart rate kicked up. There it was—the physical repository of our past life in California. I crossed to it, my hands already reaching for the drawer labeled "S-Z."

It was locked.

Dammit.

I glanced at the desk, remembering a habit from my childhood. My father had always kept spare keys hidden under the blotter—not out of forgetfulness, but because he couldn't bear the thought of being locked out of his own records, even temporarily. I lifted the corner of the leather desk pad, and there it was—a small brass key.

My hands trembled slightly as I returned to the cabinet and fitted the key into the lock. It turned, and the drawer slid open smoothly, revealing neatly labeled hanging files. I rifled through them quickly: "Stanford Medical Center," "Swanson Investments - West Coast," "Swanson Residence - Palo Alto."

A receipt of a recent money transfer was mixed up with all the folders. Could be important, so I snapped a picture with my phone.

And then I saw it. A thick file labeled simply: "J.S. - ACCIDENT."

I grabbed the folder just as I heard footsteps in the hallway approaching the study. My father.

Shit.

The steps stopped outside the door. I heard my father's voice, still on his call: "Yes, I understand the concerns about the expansion timeline. Let me pull up those projections for you."

The door opened, and my father stepped into the study, phone pressed to his ear. He froze when he saw me, his expression shifting from surprise to cold fury in the space of a heartbeat.

"I'll need to call you back," he said into the phone, his eyes never leaving my face. He ended the call without waiting for a response, slipping the phone into his pocket with deliberate calm.

"Tara," he said, his voice dangerously soft as he took in the open file cabinet, the folder in my hands. "What exactly do you think you're doing in my private study?"

I didn't flinch. I didn't stammer excuses or pretend I'd gotten lost looking for aspirin. The time for pretense was over. My fingers tightened around the manila folder, burning into my palm like a brand.

"Looking for the truth," I said. "The truth about what happened to Jimmy."

My father's expression hardened, his features arranging themselves into the disapproval I'd known my entire life. He closed the door behind him with a soft click that somehow felt more threatening than if he'd slammed it.

"Put that back," he said, each word precise and clipped. "Now."

"No." The refusal was simple, but it felt monumental—perhaps the first time I'd directly defied him since I was a child. "I want to know why the police report about Jimmy's accident is so vague about who was driving. I want to know why there's no conclusive finding in the official record."

He moved further into the room. He was a predator assessing his prey, determining the most efficient way to neutralize the threat. I'd seen him use this tactic in countless business negotiations—the slow advance, the calculated silence designed to make the other party nervous, to prompt them into filling the void with ill-considered words.

I held my ground.

"This is grief talking," he finally said, his tone shifting to something resembling concern—a perfect imitation of paternal worry that might have fooled anyone who didn't know him as well as I did. "You're becoming emotional. Irrational. This obsession with reopening old wounds... it's not healthy, Tara."

"Grief?" I repeated, unable to keep the edge from my voice. "It's been twelve years, Dad. This isn't grief. This is about uncovering the truth."

"The truth?" His eyebrows rose slightly. "The truth is what it's always been. Your brother died in that car accident. Xander McCrae was drunk. He admitted it himself. Or have you forgotten?"

How could I? Many times I heard the story of seventeen-year-old Xander, pale and broken at Jimmy's funeral, saying those words—"I was drunk, this is all my fault." But now I understood those words had been twisted, manipulated, their meaning changed.

"He said he was drunk. He said it was his fault. He never said he was driving," I pointed out. "And the police report never officially concluded who was behind the wheel. Why is that?"

My father sighed heavily, as if I were a child refusing to accept an obvious reality. "You're overthinking this. The report is clear enough for anyone with common sense to understand what happened."

"Clear enough?" I opened the file in my hands, quickly scanning the pages. "Then why doesn't it state explicitly that Xander was driving? Why are there no witness statements? No toxicology reports included? This is a police report that goes out of its way to avoid making definitive statements."

"You don't know what you're talking about," he snapped, his patience visibly fraying. "You're not a lawyer or a police officer. You're a doctor who should focus on her patients instead of playing detective."

I slammed the file shut. "I know enough to recognize when key information is missing. I know enough to see a cover-up when it's staring me in the face."

His eyes narrowed. "A cover-up? That's absurd. You've been spending too much time with McCrae. He's poisoning your mind with his version of events, trying to absolve himself of guilt after all these years."

"Xander's not trying to absolve himself," I shot back. "If anything, he blames himself more than anyone. But that doesn't mean he was driving."

I watched my father closely, cataloging every micro-expression, every tell. The slight tightening around his eyes. The almost imperceptible clench of his jaw. He's getting uncomfortable, and open for making mistakes. *Good.*

"Detective Morrison," I said suddenly, dropping the name like a bomb.

There it was—the reaction I was looking for. A flicker of something in his eyes. A momentary lapse in control. It lasted less than a second, but it was enough. Confirmation.

"The police investigator on Jimmy's case," I continued, pressing my advantage. "You know him, don't you? You spoke to him after the accident."

"I spoke to many people after your brother died," he replied, his voice too even. "I don't remember every name."

"That's a lie."

My father's expression hardened further. "Tara, you're

being disrespectful. And ungrateful. All I've ever done is protect you, and look after you, like any father would. This conversation is over." His voice was cold, final. "Put that file back where you found it."

"You paid him off, didn't you?" I said, my voice dangerously steady. "Detective Morrison. Paid him to bury his conclusion, to leave the report just ambiguous enough for you to write your own story."

His face was a mask of stone. "Get out of my house." Each word was a shard of ice. "Now."

I didn't flinch. For the first time, I wasn't looking at my father, the grieving parent I'd spent a lifetime trying to please. I was looking at a stranger. A puppeteer who'd just had a string cut. The grief I'd always seen in his eyes wasn't for his lost son; it was for the flaw in his perfect narrative.

"That's not a denial," I whispered, the realization hitting me hard. "You still owe me an explanation."

He took a step closer, his voice dropping to a low, patronizing calm. "An explanation for what, Tara? For protecting this family? For shielding your brother's memory from a fantasy you've concocted?" He gestured vaguely at my head. "You've been under a great deal of stress."

My hand was steady as I placed the file back in the drawer. The slide of the wood was the only sound in the room. I pushed it shut with a soft, final click, my eyes locked on his the entire time. The sound was a period on a sentence I didn't know I was writing.

"This isn't over," I said, the words quiet but absolute.

A flicker of annoyance crossed his face before it vanished. "Oh yes, it is." He stepped aside, gesturing toward the door as if dismissing a servant. "Go home, Tara. When you've had time to think rationally, we can discuss your future with the team."

The threat was thinly veiled. My position, my career, my life's work—all of it hung in the balance. He was reminding me of his power, of how much I stood to lose if I pushed this further.

I walked past him without another word, my head held high. I didn't run. I wouldn't give him the satisfaction of seeing me flee.

The door of the study clicked shut behind me, the sound unnervingly final.

The second I was out of his sight, the strength drained from my legs. I leaned against the cool wood, the polished surface doing little to calm the tremor in my hands. The air I sucked into my lungs felt thin, useless. It was over. Not the search for the truth, but the lifelong, fruitless campaign for his approval. The man I had worshipped was a fabrication. A ghost. A single, hot tear escaped, and I swiped it away with a vicious-ness that surprised me. No more.

I took one more deep, shuddering breath, straightened my shoulders, and turned toward the dining room, my face a care-fully constructed mask of indifference.

Diego was still there, nursing a glass of wine. He rose when he saw me, a smile spreading across his face.

"Feeling better?" he asked, moving to intercept me.

"No," I replied, not breaking stride. "I'm leaving."

His smile faltered. "What? But we haven't even had coffee yet. Your father said—"

"My father doesn't speak for me," I cut him off, already reaching for my purse on the side table. "Goodnight, Mr. Mano."

I was out the front door before he could respond, the cool night air hitting my face like a blessing after the suffocating atmosphere inside. I slid behind the wheel of my car, and pulled away from the house before my father could emerge to try to stop me.

Only when I turned the corner, when the house was no longer visible, did the first crack appear in my composure. A tremor in my hands. A tightness in my chest that made it hard to breathe, as I pulled over to the side of the road.

The tears came suddenly, violently, wracking sobs that bent me double over the steering wheel. I cried for the brother I'd lost. For the years wasted on a misplaced vendetta. For the father I'd thought I had—strict but loving, controlling but protective—who had never really existed at all.

———

I'd promised to meet Xander at his penthouse after dinner, and I parked in the visitor's section of his building's garage and took the private elevator directly to his floor, grateful that I didn't have to pass through the lobby in my current state.

I knew the code to his door, of course, and I stepped inside to find Xander standing on the balcony, his back to me, a drink in his hand. Leo was nowhere in sight.

I closed the door behind me, and he turned, his eyes finding mine across the room. He didn't speak, just watched as I crossed the space between us and stepped out onto the balcony.

He took in my tear-stained face, my disheveled appearance, and without a word, set his glass down and opened his arms. I stepped into them, burying my face against his chest, breathing in his scent—something uniquely him that I'd come to associate with safety.

"Hey," he murmured against my hair, his arms tightening around me. "I've got you."

Those simple words broke something loose inside me. I clung to him, allowing myself this moment of vulnerability.

"What happened?" he asked, his voice low and steady.

I took a deep breath. "I found the file on Jimmy's accident in my father's study. He caught me looking at it."

Xander's body tensed, but he didn't interrupt, giving me space to continue at my own pace.

"When I mentioned Detective Morrison, there was a reaction. Just for a second, but it was there. He knows him. He did something… bribed him, threatened him, I don't know… but I'm sure he tampered with the official record so it would be ambiguous. And then he could spin the narrative any way he wanted."

Xander's jaw tightened, a muscle jumping in his cheek. "Did he admit it outright?"

"No," I shook my head. "He stonewalled me. Ordered me out of the house. Threatened my position with the team, indirectly."

"Bastard," Xander muttered, his hands gentle on my arms despite the anger in his voice. "Are you okay?"

The question was simple, but was I okay? How could I possibly answer that?

"No," I said honestly. "I'm not okay. But I will be." I met his gaze directly. "We're going to uncover the truth, Xander. All of it. No matter what it takes."

He studied my face for a long moment, as if searching for something. Whatever he saw there must have reassured him, because he nodded once, decisively.

"We will," he promised.

He led me back inside, guiding me to the plush sectional

sofa that dominated the living area. I sank into it gratefully, suddenly aware of how exhausted I was. Xander disappeared briefly into the kitchen, returning with a glass of water and a damp cloth.

"For your face," he explained, handing me the cloth. "Unless you want to keep the raccoon eyes. They're actually kind of badass."

A surprised laugh escaped me. "Very funny," I said, accepting the cloth and gently wiping away the remnants of my mascara. "I must look a mess."

"You look beautiful," he said simply, sitting beside me. "You always do."

The sincerity in his voice made my heart twist. This man who had carried the weight of my brother's death, who had been vilified and exiled because of my father's lies, was looking at me like I was something precious despite it all.

"I'm sorry," I said suddenly, the words tumbling out before I could stop them. "For believing the worst of you for so long. For not questioning the story. For—"

"Stop," he interrupted gently. "You were sixteen, Tara. A teenager who'd just lost her brother. You believed what the adults around you told you to believe. That's not your fault."

I shook my head, not ready to absolve myself so easily. "I wasn't that young. I should have known better. I should have questioned it."

"Why would you?" he asked. "Everyone believed the same thing. It was the accepted truth. And I never denied it, did I? I said it was my fault. I believed it was."

"But it wasn't," I insisted. "At least, not the way everyone thought."

He was quiet for a moment, his gaze drifting to the city lights beyond the windows. "We still don't know exactly what happened that night," he said finally. "Not for certain. But we're getting closer."

I thought about the file I'd found, the reaction I'd seen in my father's eyes. And then, my mind flashed to Diego—his unwanted touches, his persistent advances, the way my father had shoved him at me like a weapon. But I pushed the thought away. No need to mention that to Xander. No need to stir up unnecessary drama when we had enough real battles to fight. "Yes," I agreed. "We are."

CHAPTER
Nineteen

XANDER

THE AIR WAS FILLED with the smell of garlic and cumin as we chilled at an outdoor table in Little Havana. Miami's perfect twilight blue hung above us, with strings of lights zigzagging between buildings. A three-piece band cranked out tunes in the patio corner—guitar strums and bongo beats backing our dinner conversation.

"So this loaded collector… who just dropped twenty grand on Chloe's installation… asks her if the piece is 'supposed to be ironic,'" Tara said, leaning in with her elbows on the table, wineglass in hand.

Chloe rolled her eyes hard. "I told him art isn't a fucking riddle. It either speaks to you or it doesn't."

"What did he say to that?" Leo asked, eyes twinkling with mischief.

"He bought another piece," Chloe replied with a grin. "For thirty thousand."

Leo howled with laughter, raising his mojito. "To bullshitting the wealthy!"

"I'll drink to that," I said, clinking my glass against his.

This night felt almost normal. Just four friends out eating, drinking, and laughing. It was hard to imagine such en evening after the recent shit-storm of Tara confronting her father, and the growing certainty we'd been played. But we'd promised to forget all that for one evening. To breathe. To remember what it felt like to just be people, not chess pieces in Hank Swanson's game.

Watching Leo and Chloe across the table, I noticed their easy vibe. At first, Leo questioned inviting Tara's bestie to dinner, but I thought they connected instantly. Same smart ass humor, same talent for spotting life's absurdities.

"You know," I whispered to Tara as Leo and Chloe launched into a heated debate about whether a banana ducttaped to a wall counted as art, "I think they're hitting it off quite well."

Tara turned to me, eyebrows shooting up. "Leo and Chloe?"

"Yeah," I nodded, glancing their way. "They've been flirting all night."

She stared at me, then erupted into laughter so explosive that Leo and Chloe paused mid-argument to look over.

"What's so funny?" Leo asked.

"Nothing," Tara managed, wiping tears. "Inside joke."

They shrugged and resumed their debate. Tara leaned close, voice hushed.

"Leo is gay," she said, eyes sparkling with humor. "You've known him since Glasgow and you didn't know he was gay?"

I blinked, brain buffering. Leo? Gay? I looked at my best friend—his perfect hair, his spotless designer clothes, his smooth charm. I'd always thought his fashion knowledge came from being European, but suddenly, other things clicked. How he set me up with women but dodged when I suggested girls for him.

"Huh," I said brilliantly. "I guess it never came up."

Tara shot me a droll look. "Never came up? Xander, he's wearing a pink shirt with flamingos on it."

"I thought that was just... you know, Miami fashion."

She shook her head, dark hair bouncing around her shoulders. "You are hopelessly oblivious sometimes."

"In my defense, I've been a little busy for the last decade," I said, half-joking. "Trying to outrun my demons and shit."

Her smile softened, and she reached for my hand. "Well, you don't have to run anymore."

Her words hit home and I squeezed her hand, my throat tightening as I tried to swallow it down.

"Anyway," she continued, mercifully changing topics, "Leo and Chloe aren't flirting. They're bonding over a mutual love of judging people."

I looked back at them. Now that she mentioned it, they did have more of a "partners in crime" energy than a romantic one. Leo showed Chloe something on his phone, both hunched over it, cackling like evil masterminds.

"They're probably rating men on Tinder," Tara said.

"How did you know? About Leo, I mean."

"Gaydar," she said with a shrug. "Also, he checked out the server's ass when he walked away earlier."

I laughed, shaking my head. "I can't believe I never noticed."

"To be fair, I don't think he was trying to hide it. It just wasn't relevant to your friendship." She sipped her wine, watching me. "Does it change anything for you?"

"No," I said instantly, surprised she'd even ask. "Of course not. He's still Leo. Still my best friend."

She smiled, genuinely this time. "Good answer."

The conversation shifted as our food arrived—a feast of ropa vieja, lechon asado, tostones, and black beans and rice. Miami's Cuban food scene was one of the few bright spots in my unexpected relocation, and this restaurant, tucked on a side street, was quickly becoming my go-to spot.

"So, McCrae," Chloe said after a while, pointing her fork at me, "Tara tells me you're quite the soccer superstar."

I glanced at Tara, who looked slightly embarrassed. "I wouldn't say superstar," I replied.

"Don't be humble," Leo jumped in. "Three-time top scorer in the Premier League, two Champions League titles, Sports Illustrated cover..."

"Alright, alright," I laughed, hands up in surrender. "I did okay."

"More than okay," Tara murmured, and something about her proud tone made my chest tighten again.

"What about you, Chloe?" I asked, desperate to shift focus. "Tara mentioned you're an artist?"

"Mixed media, mostly," she nodded, eyes lighting up. "I create immersive installations that challenge perceptions of space and identity. Or at least that's what my gallery bio says." She grinned. "Really, I just like making weird shit that makes people uncomfortable."

"She's being modest," Tara said. "Her last exhibition was written up in Artforum. She's kind of a big deal in the Miami art scene."

"Stop it," Chloe waved her off, but looked pleased. "Anyway, it pays the bills and lets me spend my days covered in paint and resin instead of stuck in an office. Can't complain."

"I've always envied that creative freedom," I admitted. "Soccer's been my whole life since I was a kid. Never really had the chance to explore other interests."

"It's never too late," Chloe said. "What are you into besides kicking balls around?"

I laughed at her bluntness. "I don't know, actually. Never really thought about it."

"You like photography," Leo offered. "Remember that vintage Leica you bought in Prague?"

"Yeah, I still have it," I said, surprised he remembered. I'd bought it on a whim during a post-season trip years ago. "Haven't used it much, though."

"Jimmy was into photography too," Tara said softly. Then, with a glance toward Chloe, she added, "And Chloe knows all the best spots around Miami if you ever want to try it."

Chloe lit up. "Oh, definitely. The light here is incredible. The Wynwood Walls, the Art Deco district at sunrise, the mangroves at Oleta River State Park... I could show you sometime."

"I'd like that," I said, meaning it. The idea of having a hobby, something separate from soccer and its constant pressure, sounded damn good. And in memory of Jimmy. "Thanks."

The conversation flowed after that, bouncing from art to travel to embarrassing stories about Tara and me. By the time we finished dinner and lingered over coffee and flan, I was stuffed.

"We should do this again," Leo said as we waited for the check. "Next time at that new fusion place in Brickell? I know the chef."

"Of course you do," I teased, elbowing him.

"What can I say? I'm connected," he grinned.

"I'm in," Chloe agreed.

After settling the bill (I insisted on paying, over everyone's protests), we stepped into the warm Miami night. The street buzzed with life—music pouring from open doors, people laughing and dancing on sidewalks. It felt like a party without a reason.

"Night's still young," Chloe observed. "There's a great little jazz club around the corner. Anyone interested?"

Leo checked his watch. "I'm game if everyone else is."

I looked at Tara, trying to read her face. She met my gaze, a silent question in her eyes. I raised an eyebrow slightly, and the barest tilt of her head was all the confirmation I needed.

"Actually," I said, turning back to Leo and Chloe, "I think we're going to call it a night. Rain check on the jazz club?"

Leo's eyes darted between Tara and me, a knowing smile spreading. "Sure thing, boss. Rain check it is."

"You kids have fun," Chloe added with a wink that made Tara blush.

We said goodbye, promising another dinner soon. As Leo and Chloe headed toward the jazz club, I turned to Tara.

"Your place?" I asked softly.

She nodded, her eyes dark and inviting under the street lights. "My place."

We'd barely made it through the door when Tara kicked off her heels and turned to me with that sly smile that always made my pulse kick up a notch. "Nightcap?" she offered, heading toward the kitchen like she hadn't just spent the whole dinner driving me crazy under the table.

"Just water," I replied, following her, my eyes glued to the sway of her hips in that little black dress. "I'm trying to cut back on the drinking."

She turned to look at me, one eyebrow arched in surprise, and yeah, maybe a little pride gleaming in those dark eyes. "Really? The infamous Xander McCrae, turning down a scotch? Who are you and what have you done with my bad boy?"

I shrugged, suddenly feeling a bit exposed under her gaze, but in a good way—like she was seeing the real me, not the tabloid version. "Yeah, well... it's time. Been using it as a crutch for too long. Plus, I figure if I'm gonna keep up with you, I need to be at my best. You're exhausting, woman."

She laughed, and filled two glasses with water from the fridge. When she handed me one, her fingers brushed mine, lingering just long enough to send a spark up my arm. "I'm proud of you," she said simply, her voice soft but sincere.

Four words. Just four ordinary words, but from her, they hit like a winning goal in stoppage time. I'd spent my life letting people down—coaches, teammates, fans, myself. The idea that I could make someone proud, especially her, felt better than any high I'd chased. I set my glass on the counter and took hers, placing it beside mine. Then I pulled her close, one hand at the small of her back, pressing her against me, the other cupping her face like she was the most precious thing I'd ever held.

"Tara," I murmured, my thumb tracing her bottom lip, not sure what to say next, only knowing I needed to express the fucking hurricane of feelings she stirred in me. Love, lust, gratitude—all tangled up in a mess I wasn't great at articulating.

She saved me from fumbling through it by rising on her toes and pressing her lips to mine. The kiss started soft, a question, an invitation—her tongue teasing the seam of my mouth like she was testing if I'd bite. Spoiler: I did. I answered by deepening it, my hand sliding from her face to her neck, fingers tangling in her hair as I tilted her head back for better access. She tasted like the mojito she'd sipped at dinner, minty and sweet, with a kick that made me groan.

We stumbled toward her bedroom, a trail of chaos in our wake—my jacket tossed over the couch, her purse dumped on the floor, my shirt buttons popping open as her fingers worked them. "You're terrible at multitasking," she teased between kisses, her breath hot against my ear as I nearly tripped over her discarded heels.

"Says the woman who's about to walk into a wall," I shot back, spinning her just in time to avoid the hallway corner, my hands already unzipping her dress. The fabric slid down her shoulders, revealing smooth skin and a lacy black bra that made my mouth go dry. "Fuck, Tara, did you wear this for me?"

"Maybe," she purred, shoving my shirt off and raking her nails down my chest, light enough to tease but hard enough to leave faint red lines. "Or maybe I just like feeling sexy. Problem?"

"No problem at all," I growled, backing her into the bedroom door with a thud that made us both laugh. "Except now I have to decide where to start." I hoisted her up and carried her the last few steps to the bed, our mouths never breaking contact. We hit the mattress in a tangle, me on top, but she flipped us with surprising strength—years of sports paying off—and straddled me, her hair falling like a curtain around us.

"Impatient much?" I grinned up at her, my hands gripping her thighs as she ground against me, the friction through our remaining clothes driving me insane.

"Says the guy who's already rock hard," she countered, her hand slipping down to palm me through my pants, squeezing just right. I bucked into her touch, a curse slipping out, and she laughed again—that wicked, triumphant sound. "See? Told you."

"Keep that up, and this'll be over before it starts," I warned, but I was already undoing her bra, tossing it aside to reveal her perfect breasts. I sat up, capturing one nipple in my mouth, sucking hard while my thumb teased the other. She arched, her fingers digging into my shoulders, a moan escaping that was half gasp, half my name.

"Not if I have anything to say about it," she breathed, pushing me back down and shimmying out of her panties. She made quick work of my belt and zipper, freeing me with a stroke that had me seeing stars. "Hold on…"

I watched as she leaned over to the nightstand, giving me a glorious view of her ass, and I couldn't resist—I gave it a light smack, just enough to sting playfully.

She yelped, spinning back with mock outrage, a condom packet in hand. "Oh, it's like that, huh?"

"Absolutely," I said, grinning as she tore it open with her teeth—hot as hell—and rolled it on me with torturously slow strokes. "Payback for that foot thing under the table at dinner."

"Fair enough." She positioned herself over me, sinking down, her tightness enveloping me until we both groaned. She started slowly, rolling her hips in that hypnotic rhythm, her hands braced on my chest. But I wasn't content to just lie there—I thrust up to meet her, flipping the script, and soon we were moving together, sweat-slicked and breathless.

"God, Xander," she panted, her nails scraping my abs. "Harder."

I obliged, sitting up to wrap my arms around her, changing the angle so I could go deeper. We were face-to-face now, her breasts pressed against my chest, our breaths mingling as we kissed through the building heat. But I wanted more—I flipped us again, to her back, and hooked one of her legs over my shoulder for that perfect, mind-blowing depth. She cried out, her hands fisting the sheets, and I reached between us, circling her clit with my thumb until she was trembling.

"Close," she whispered, her eyes locking on mine, dark and wild.

I grunted, picking up the pace, the bed creaking like it might give out. "Come for me, Tara."

She did, shattering around me with a cry that echoed off the walls, her body clenching in waves that pulled me right over the edge. I followed with a roar, burying my face in her neck as pleasure crashed through me.

Afterward, we lay twisted in her sheets, her head on my chest. The city lights twinkled beyond her bedroom window like distant stars, but I couldn't look away from her.

"I could get used to this," she murmured, voice thick with satisfaction, her hand idly drawing circles on my pec.

"Me too," I replied, pressing a kiss to the top of her head. "But next time, let's see if we can break the bed for real."

She lifted her head, smirking. "Challenge accepted." And just like that, we were laughing again, tangled up in each other, the night stretching out with endless possibilities.

———

Sunday unfolded with the languid pace of a dream, the kind where time stretches like taffy and every moment feels indulgent. I woke to the soft warmth of Tara's body curled against mine, her dark hair fanned across my chest like a silk blanket, her leg thrown over my thigh in that possessive way that made my morning wood twitch with interest. Golden light filtered through her curtains, casting a hazy glow over the rumpled sheets, and I couldn't help but trace my fingers along the curve of her spine, down to the dip of her waist, savoring the feel of her skin—smooth, warm, and all mine.

She stirred, letting out a contented hum that vibrated against my skin, her eyes fluttering open to meet mine. "Morning, soccer star," she murmured, her voice husky from sleep and last night's exertions. A slow, wicked smile spread across her face as she felt my arousal pressing against her hip. "Already? You're insatiable."

I grinned, rolling her onto her back in one fluid motion, pinning her gently beneath me. "Blame yourself, Doc. Waking up to you like this? It's a miracle I lasted this long." I dipped my head to kiss her neck, nipping at the sensitive spot just below her ear that always made her gasp. She did, arching into me, her hands sliding up my back to tangle in my hair.

"Flattery will get you everywhere," she teased, but her breath hitched as I trailed kisses lower, across her collarbone, down to the swell of her breasts. "But if you think you're getting round two without earning it—"

"Oh, I'll earn it," I growled, capturing a nipple in my mouth and swirling my tongue around it until she moaned, her hips bucking up to meet mine. We moved together in that lazy, unhurried rhythm of morning sex—slow builds, teasing touches, her nails scraping my shoulders as I slid into her, filling her completely. "Fuck, Tara, you feel like heaven."

"And you feel like trouble," she shot back, wrapping her legs around my waist to pull me deeper, her eyes locked on mine with that intense, challenging gaze that drove me wild.

We laughed through the gasps, the bed creaking under us as we chased release, her coming first with a cry that echoed in the quiet room, pulling me over the edge right after.

Eventually, hunger—the real kind—drove us to the kitchen. I rummaged through her fridge while she perched on the counter beside me, wearing nothing but my discarded shirt from last night, the hem riding up her thighs in a way that was distracting as hell. "French toast it is," I declared, cracking eggs into a bowl. "But if you keep swinging your legs like that, breakfast is gonna burn."

She stole a slice of bread from the loaf, nibbling on it with mock innocence. "Me? Distracting? Never." Then she leaned in, pressing a sticky, maple-syrup-flavored kiss to my cheek. "Though if it burns, we could always order in... or skip to dessert."

I turned, caging her against the counter with my arms, my lips brushing hers. "Woman, you're gonna be the death of me. But what a way to go." I kissed her properly then, deep and hungry, until the sizzle of butter in the pan reminded me of the food. "Alright, back off, temptress. Let the master work."

"Master, huh?" She hopped down, swatting my ass with a dish towel. "We'll see about that. If this French toast isn't Michelin-star worthy, you're doing the dishes naked."

"Deal," I said, flipping the bread with a flourish. "But if it is, you're joining me in that shower after."

Spoiler: It was damn good—crispy edges, custard center, topped with fresh berries she'd had stashed away. We ate at the counter, her feeding me bites between laughs, the domesticity of it all hitting me like a warm wave. Who knew playing house could feel this sexy?

After breakfast, we showered together, which—predictably —led to another delay. The steam-filled bathroom turned into our playground, her soapy hands gliding over my chest, down my abs, lower until I had her pressed against the tiled wall, water cascading over us as I thrust into her from behind. "God, Xander," she panted, her palms flat against the wall for leverage. "We were supposed to be quick."

"Quick is overrated," I rasped in her ear, one hand between her legs, circling her clit until she shattered again, her cries muffled by the spray. I followed suit, groaning her name like a prayer.

By the time we finally made it out of her apartment, it was past noon, both of us flushed and grinning like idiots. We spent the afternoon wandering through a local farmer's market, her arm linked through mine as we sampled artisanal cheeses and fresh mangoes. "Try this," she said, holding a slice to my lips, her eyes sparkling with mischief. "It's almost as sweet as you."

I nipped her fingers playfully. "Careful, or I'll drag you behind that stall and show you sweet." She laughed, pulling me along to the next booth, where we haggled over handmade candles that smelled like ocean breeze.

From there, a long walk along the beach, our fingers intertwined, toes sinking into the warm sand. We talked about everything and nothing—her favorite books (medical thrillers, go figure), my disastrous first pro game (tripped over the ball, face-planted in front of 50,000 fans), and more talk about dream vacations (hers: secluded Greek islands; mine: anywhere with her and a bed). The sun beat down, waves lapping at our feet, and for a few hours, we pushed aside the shadows of the past and the uncertainty of the future. We were just a man and a woman enjoying a beautiful day together, stealing kisses when no one was looking.

As the sun set, we returned to her apartment with

takeout from a Thai place near her building—spicy pad see ew for me, green curry for her. We ate on her balcony, cross-legged on the cushioned loungers, watching the sky turn from blue to orange to deep purple, the first stars appearing overhead.

"I wish every day could be like this," Tara said softly, leaning back in her chair, a glass of sparkling water in her hand, her bare feet propped in my lap.

I massaged her instep absently, my thumb circling the arch. "It could be," I replied, the words out before I'd fully thought them through. "Maybe not exactly like this—practice and all—but... good. Together. No more sneaking around, no more bullshit."

She looked at me, her expression unreadable in the fading light, a mix of hope and hesitation flickering in her eyes. "Xander..."

Whatever she was about to say was interrupted by my phone ringing. I pulled it from my pocket, ready to silence it, but paused when I saw the caller ID.

"It's Cory," I said, my pulse suddenly spiking. I hadn't expected him to get back to me this quickly.

I answered, putting the phone on speaker out of habit. "Hey Cory."

"Xander," my brother's voice came through, crisp and busi-nesslike as always. "I've got updates on your situation. Is now a good time?"

I glanced at Tara, who nodded encouragingly. "Yeah, now's fine. You're on speaker, by the way. Tara's here with me."

There was a brief pause. "Dr. Swanson," Cory acknowl-edged. "Good evening."

"Good evening, Mr. McCrae," she replied formally. "Thank you for your help with this."

"Cory, please," he said, his tone warming. "And you're welcome. Though I'm afraid I have mixed news."

I sat up straighter, my relaxed mood evaporating. "What did you find?"

"Good news/bad news situation," Cory said, getting straight to the point as he always did. "The bad news first: there are no 'original notes' in the police archives. The file has been scrubbed clean."

My heart sank. "Completely?"

"From what my contact could tell, yes. Either the notes were never filed officially, or they were removed at some point. Possibly when Morrison retired."

Tara's face fell, and I reached across the table to take her hand. "And the good news?" I asked, not sure there could be any.

"The good news," Cory continued, "is that I tracked down Morrison's former partner, a Detective Miller. He's retired now too, but he was willing to talk off the record."

Hope flickered back to life. "What did he say?"

"He confirmed what you suspected. Morrison was dirty. Apparently, he was forced into early retirement to avoid an internal affairs investigation. Miller wouldn't go into details, and he made it very clear he won't testify or go on record."

"So we're back to square one," I said, frustration creeping into my voice.

"Not exactly," Cory replied, and I could hear the slight smile in his voice—the one he got when he'd found a clever solution to a problem. "Miller gave me what he called 'the key to unlocking Morrison.' Something that might persuade him to talk to you."

Tara leaned forward eagerly. "What is it?"

"Two words: Valdez case."

I frowned, looking at Tara, who appeared equally confused. "What's the Valdez case?"

"According to Miller, it was a major drug trafficking case that Morrison tanked," Cory explained. "He wouldn't elaborate, but he seemed confident that mentioning it would get Morrison's attention."

"Thank you, Cory," I said, my mind racing with the implications. "This could be exactly what we need to make him talk."

"Don't thank me yet," he cautioned. "This is still a long shot. And if what Miller implied is true, you could be stepping into something dangerous."

"We're already in something dangerous," I replied grimly. "Might as well see it through."

"Your call," Cory said. "Just be careful, little brother. And keep me updated."

"I will," I promised. "And Cory? I owe you one."

He chuckled. "Add it to your tab. Goodnight, Xander, Dr. Swanson."

"Goodnight," we replied in unison as the call ended.

For a moment, we sat in silence, processing what we'd learned. Then Tara squeezed my hand, drawing my attention back to her.

"The Valdez Case," she mused, her brow furrowed in concentration. "I've never heard of it."

"Me neither," I admitted. "But if it gives us leverage over Morrison..."

"We need to use it," she finished my thought. "When can we go back to Naples?"

I considered our schedules. "Next Saturday? We both have the morning off."

She nodded decisively. "Saturday it is. We'll confront him

again, this time armed with a key to open him up."

———

Monday morning arrived with the harsh buzz of my phone alarm at 5:30 AM. I groaned, reaching out blindly to silence it on the nightstand, my body still heavy with the lingering haze of sleep and the sweet ache from the weekend's indulgences.

Tara shifted beside me, her warm, naked form pressed against my side like she'd been molded there overnight. I froze for a second, not wanting to disturb her, but damn if the sight of her didn't make it hard to move.

She was on her back, one arm draped lazily over her head, the sheet tangled low around her hips, exposing the perfect curve of her breast—the soft swell rising and falling with each slow breath, her nipple pebbled from the cool morning air sneaking through the curtains.

Her runner's body was a masterpiece in the dim light: lean, toned legs stretched out, the subtle definition of her abs from all those dawn jogs, the gentle flare of her hips that I'd gripped so tightly just hours ago. She looked like sin wrapped in silk sheets, peaceful and vulnerable in sleep, her dark lashes fanned against her cheeks, lips slightly parted as if whispering secrets to her dreams.

God, I was tempted—tempted to roll over, wake her with my mouth on that breast, tease her awake until she was arching and begging for another round, her nails digging into my back as I slid into her heat.

My cock stirred at the thought, hardening against her thigh, but I held back. She needed the rest; we'd pushed each other to the brink all weekend, and with the week ahead—practice, the looming trip to Naples, the shadows of her father's bullshit hanging over us—I couldn't be the selfish prick who stole her sleep. Not today.

I pressed a soft kiss to her shoulder instead, inhaling her scent—vanilla and sex—before forcing myself to slip out of bed.

She stirred anyway, her eyes fluttering open, hazy and unfocused. "Time to go already?" she murmured sleepily, her voice a husky rasp that went straight to my groin.

"Yeah," I said, leaning down to press a lingering kiss to her forehead, my hand brushing a strand of hair from her face. "Early practice. Go back to sleep, beautiful."

She nodded, a small smile curving her lips as her eyes drifted shut again, already surrendering to the pull of slumber. I watched her for another moment, struck by how peaceful she looked—how right it felt to wake up next to her, like this was the start of something real, something worth fighting for. It was hard to leave the warmth of her bed for the long day ahead, but I forced myself to get up, pulling on my clothes quietly before slipping out.

I was one of the first to arrive at the practice facility, which wasn't unusual. Despite my party-boy reputation, I'd always been serious about training. I changed quickly in the empty locker room and was heading toward the gym for some pre-practice stretching when my phone buzzed with a text.

It was from Reyes, the team manager: *Mr. Swanson wants to see you in his office immediately.*

I frowned at the screen. It was barely 7 AM. Hank must have seen me arrive.

On my way, I texted back, changing direction toward the administrative wing of the facility.

As I walked, I mentally prepared myself for a confrontation. This had to be about Tara, about what she'd found in his study. He must know we were getting closer to the truth. Would he threaten me? Try to buy me off? Or would he go straight to ruining my career, as he'd done before?

I knocked on the door to his office, squaring my shoulders, ready for battle.

"Come in," Hank's voice called from inside.

I pushed open the door, stepping into the spacious office with its view of the practice fields. Hank was seated behind his massive desk, immaculately dressed as always in a tailored suit despite the early hour. But it wasn't the sight of him that made me freeze in my tracks.

It was the woman seated in one of the chairs facing his desk, who turned to look at me with a predatory smile I remembered all too well.

Brittany Ashworth. Instagram model. Professional groupie. A woman I'd banged a few times when I was wasted and spiraling in London. A woman who hadn't crossed my mind for months.

"Xander, thank you for joining us," Hank said, his tone pleasant but his eyes cold. "I believe you know Ms. Ashworth?"

"Brittany," I acknowledged stiffly, not moving from the doorway. "What are you doing here?"

She popped up, tugging at her skintight dress, her cosmetically enhanced lips forming a fake-ass smile. "Xander, honey," she cooed, dramatically placing her hand on her noticeably swollen belly—a sight that made my blood run cold. "We need to talk... about the baby."

CHAPTER

Twenty

TARA

I STARED at the rows of PT schedules on my laptop screen, the cursor blinking mockingly at me like it knew my mind was a million miles away. The gentle soreness between my thighs— a delicious, lingering ache—served as a constant reminder of the weekend with Xander. His rough hands gripping my hips as he thrust deep, his mouth hot and demanding on my neck, the way he'd pinned me against the shower wall yesterday morning, water cascading over our slick bodies while he growled my name like a curse and a prayer. And later, across the breakfast table, those moss-green eyes locking on mine with an intensity that made my core clench, like I was something he couldn't get enough of. God, the man knew how to unravel me.

But now? The Valdez Case.

The phrase kept circling in my thoughts like a shark in chummed waters, pulling me under. Whatever this mysterious case was, it might be the key to unlocking the truth about

Jimmy's death—about the accident that had shattered us all. I shook my head, forcing myself to focus on the rehabilitation plan for Ben Carter's hamstring injury. With proper care, he'd be good to go for Saturday's kickoff, his explosive speed back on the field.

I actually managed to get some work done for about fifteen minutes, typing notes, before someone banged on my office door like they were serving a warrant.

"Come in," I called, not looking up from my laptop, my fingers hovering over the keys.

The door swung open with a whoosh, and Jess, one of the junior physical therapists, burst in. Her eyes were wide as saucers, her phone clutched in her hand like a lifeline. "Dr. Swanson, have you seen this?" she asked breathlessly, thrusting her phone toward me.

I frowned, taking the device from her, my thumb brushing the screen. "Seen what?"

The display lit up with a celebrity gossip site, the kind that thrived on scandal and half-truths. My stomach dropped as I registered the headline screaming in bold, lurid font: SOCCER BAD BOY XANDER MCCRAE EXPECTING FIRST CHILD WITH MODEL GIRLFRIEND. Below it was a photo of a stunningly beautiful blonde woman—flawless skin, lips curved in a coy smile, perfect makeup that screamed "camera-ready." Her hand rested protectively on a visibly pregnant belly, the swell unmistakable under her form-fitting dress. She stood outside our training facility, looking both vulnerable and victorious, like she'd just won some twisted game.

"They're saying she flew in from London yesterday," Jess was babbling, her voice distant as blood rushed in my ears, drowning out everything but the pounding of my heart.

"Apparently, they've been together for a while. Like, on-and-off secret romance or something."

I couldn't tear my eyes from the image. The woman—Brittany Ashworth, according to the caption—was exactly the type I'd seen Xander with in countless paparazzi shots over the years, the ones I'd obsessively collected in my digital dossier of his downfall. Tall, blonde, model-thin except for that undeniable baby bump, her curves engineered for maximum allure. My throat tightened, a cold sweat prickling my skin as I scrolled down, skimming the article's salacious details.

"Dr. Swanson? Are you okay?" Jess's voice cut through the fog, concern etching her young features.

I blinked, realizing I'd been staring silently at the phone for too long, my grip white-knuckled. I handed it back to her, hiding behind the same cool front I used with my father. "I'm fine," I said, my voice steady, even as my insides twisted like a wet rag. "But we shouldn't be gossiping about team members, Jess. It's unprofessional."

Her face fell slightly, cheeks flushing. "Oh, right. Sorry. I just thought... with you working so closely with him..."

"Thank you for your concern," I cut her off, turning back to my laptop. "Could you close the door on your way out? I need to finish these schedules."

She nodded, mumbling another apology before slipping out. Once alone, I sat perfectly still, yet the room seemed to tilt around me, the air thickening like humidity before a storm. With trembling fingers, I picked up my phone and opened my browser, typing "Xander McCrae Brittany Ashworth pregnant" into the search bar, my heart hammering against my ribs.

The results flooded in like a tidal wave. Every major sports and entertainment site had the story, splashed across their homepages with gleeful abandon. Some included quotes from "sources close to the couple" claiming they were "overjoyed" and "working through some issues but committed to co-parenting." Others had paparazzi shots of them together in London clubs months ago—his arm slung possessively around her waist, her face turned up to his, both laughing in that hazy, alcohol-fueled glow. Five months ago, according to one article's meticulous timeline.

Five months ago, when I was still secretly following his every move online, cataloging his exploits like a deranged archivist in my hidden wall of obsession. Five months ago, when I was plotting my revenge against the man I believed had killed my brother, running past his penthouse at dawn to unsettle him. Five months ago, when he had no idea I even existed anymore, lost in his spiral of self-destruction.

A cold, sickening feeling spread through my chest, coiling like nausea. I'd known about his reputation, of course—the drinking, the partying, the endless parade of beautiful women who'd grace his arm for a night or two before being discarded. I'd seen the photos, analyzed them like evidence in a trial. There was nothing wrong with that; we weren't together then. Hell, I was the one who'd hated him. But somehow, in the whirlwind of our reconnection—the stolen kisses, the heated nights where he'd worshipped my body like I was his salvation—I'd convinced myself that was all in the past. That he'd changed. That we were different.

Yet here was living, breathing proof—curved and swollen—that his old life was about to collide spectacularly with whatever fragile thing we'd been building these past weeks.

My fingers itched to text him, to demand answers, but then doubt crept in like fog. The timing was a little too perfect, a voice in my head whispered. This has my father's fingerprints all over it—another calculated strike to shatter us.

The thought should've given me some peace, a lifeline to cling to. If Daddy Dearest was pulling strings again, maybe there was an explanation for all this, a way to unravel the lie. But damn if those photos from five months ago weren't burned into my brain—Xander standing next to Miss Perfect, the timeline matching up with every tabloid snapshot of their "dates." God, what a mess. My chest tightened, breaths coming shallow as I forced myself to close the browser, shoving the phone away like it burned.

My phone buzzed again, this time with a text from my father's assistant: Mr. Swanson requests your presence in his office immediately regarding an urgent team matter.

I closed my eyes, drawing a deep, steadying breath. Of course he wanted to see me. This was probably exactly what he'd been waiting for—the perfect opportunity to drive a wedge between Xander and me, to prove he'd been right all along about the "toxic" man who'd "destroyed" our family. Part of me wanted to ignore the summons, to march straight to Xander's locker and demand the truth from his lips, watch those green eyes as he explained. But that wasn't an option. Whatever my personal feelings, I was still the head of Sports Medicine for this team, and my father was still my boss.

I stood, smoothed the wrinkles from my top, and headed for my father's office, each step feeling like I was walking through quicksand, the weight of betrayal and suspicion dragging me down.

He was on the phone when I entered, but he gestured for me to take a seat. I perched on one of the sleek leather chairs, back ramrod straight, face neutral—the same posture I'd adopted in this office countless times, a shield against his probing gaze.

"Yes, I understand the PR implications," he was saying, his voice calm and authoritative. "We'll issue a statement by end of day... No, I don't want him doing interviews yet... Yes, that's exactly right. Thank you, Davis."

He hung up with a decisive click and turned his attention to me, his expression a false picture of perfect paternal concern —eyes softening at the edges, mouth curving in what passed for sympathy. "Tara," he said softly, leaning forward slightly. "I'm so sorry you've been caught up in this mess."

The genuine-sounding sympathy in his voice almost fooled me. He was good—had always been good—at modulating his tone to get exactly the response he wanted, like a conductor leading an orchestra of emotions.

"I'm not 'caught up' in anything," I replied, my voice cool and clipped, refusing to give him an inch. "I'm here because you summoned me."

He sighed, leaning back in his chair with exaggerated weariness, steepling his fingers. "I know things have been... strained between us lately. But I'm still your father, and I still care about you. When Ms. Ashworth told me the news this morning, my first thought was of you."

"How thoughtful," I said, not bothering to hide the sarcasm in my words. "And did you invite Ms. Ashworth to Miami, or did she come on her own initiative?"

A flicker of annoyance crossed his face—there and gone in a blink—before his expression smoothed again. "I didn't invite her, no. She contacted our PR department yesterday, after having just arrived from London, saying she needed to speak with Xander as soon as possible about their child. She was waiting for me when I arrived at the office this morning. As you can imagine, I was caught completely off guard."

"I'm sure you were," I murmured, my tone laced with doubt, watching him closely for any tell.

He studied me for a moment, his gaze sharp as a scalpel. "You don't believe me."

"Let's just say the timing seems convenient."

"For whom?" he asked, spreading his hands in a gesture of innocence. "Certainly not for the team. Not for our image. And certainly not for you."

I said nothing, unwilling to give him the satisfaction of seeing how deeply this had affected me—the way it clawed at my insides, stirring up insecurities I'd thought buried.

"I had truly hoped he had changed, Tara," he continued, his voice soft with feigned regret, like a disappointed parent. "For your sake."

The words hit their target, a precise strike. Had I been a fool to believe Xander could change? To think that the damaged, self-destructive man I'd stalked for years—the one who'd drowned his guilt in booze and bodies—could suddenly transform into someone stable and trustworthy?

"My sake has nothing to do with this," I said, hating how defensive I sounded. "Why am I here?"

My father leaned forward, resting his elbows on his desk, his eyes locking onto mine with that unyielding intensity. "You're here because, as head of Sports Medicine, you need to be aware of any situation that might impact team dynamics. And because, as your father, I'm concerned about how closely you've been working with McCrae."

"My work with Xander has been completely professional," I said, the lie tasting bitter.

He gave me a look that said he knew better. "Regardless, I think it's best if you maintain a strict distance from him going forward. For your own sake, and most certainly for the team's image."

There it was—the real purpose of this meeting, slithering out like a snake. Using the scandal he may have orchestrated to enforce the separation he'd wanted all along, to clip my wings and keep me under his thumb.

"Are you ordering me to avoid a player under my medical care?" I asked, refusing to rise to the bait.

"Of course not," he replied smoothly. "I'm suggesting you delegate his sessions to other therapists on your staff. You would still oversee his treatment plan, of course, but the day-to-day interactions could be handled by others."

"That's not how I run my department," I said flatly, meeting his gaze without flinching.

"Tara," he sighed, his patience visibly thinning, a muscle ticking in his jaw. "This isn't just about protocols. This is about protecting you. McCrae is toxic. He destroys everything he touches."

"Including Jimmy?" The words slipped out before I could stop them, sharp and accusatory.

My father's face hardened, the mask cracking for a split second to reveal the steel beneath. "We're not discussing that again. I thought I made myself clear the other night."

"Crystal," I said, rising from my chair, my legs steady despite the storm inside. "If that's all, I have patients waiting."

"One more thing," he said as I reached the door, his voice stopping me cold. "The press will be all over this. If anyone approaches you for comment, direct them to the PR department. No exceptions."

I nodded curtly and left without another word, my mind racing like a fever dream. As I walked back to the medical wing, I felt like I was moving through a fog, my thoughts a jumbled mess of hurt, confusion, and suspicion—Xander's touch still ghosting my skin, warring with the image of that swollen belly.

———

By late afternoon, I was exhausted. I decided to leave early, something I rarely did. As I gathered my things—laptop in bag, keys in hand—I instructed my assistant to reschedule my last two appointments.

"Even McCrae?" she asked, glancing at the schedule on her screen. "He's due in fifteen minutes."

My heart stuttered, a sharp pang in my chest. I had forgotten he was on today's schedule. For a moment, I considered staying—facing him, demanding answers, watching those lips that had kissed every inch of me form the truth. But the thought of confronting him now already, with the wound still so fresh and raw, was unbearable, like salt on exposed nerves.

"Especially McCrae," I said. "Tell him... tell him I had an emergency."

It wasn't entirely a lie. This felt like an emergency—the kind that left you gasping for air, unsure which way was up, your world tilting on its axis.

I took the back exit, hoping to avoid running into anyone who might want to discuss the day's gossip, their pitying eyes or whispered speculations. I was almost to my car, the humid Miami air clinging to my skin, when I heard his voice, rough and urgent.

"Tara! Wait!"

I froze, keys in hand, my pulse spiking like I'd been caught mid-sprint. Then slowly, I turned to face him. Xander was jogging toward me across the parking lot, his practice clothes still damp with sweat, clinging to the hard lines of his chest and thighs in a way that made my traitorous body respond despite everything. His face was etched with desperation, hair tousled, eyes wild.

"Please," he said as he reached me, slightly out of breath, his scent washing over me like a memory. "Can we talk?"

Up close, he looked terrible—eyes bloodshot and shadowed, hair disheveled as if he'd raked his hands through it a hundred times. Part of me ached to reach out, to smooth the worry lines from his forehead, trace the stubble on his jaw like I had yesterday morning. I kept my arms firmly crossed like armor.

"I don't think that's a good idea right now," I said, my voice steadier than I felt, even as my knees threatened to buckle.

"Tara, it's not what you think," he said urgently, stepping closer. "It's a setup. You have to believe me."

I laughed, a short, humorless sound that echoed bitterly. "Do I? Why is that, exactly?"

He ran a hand through his hair, his frustration evident, muscles flexing under his shirt. "Because we're in this together. Because after everything we've shared—the way you moaned my name last night, the way you looked at me like I was your everything—you know me."

"Do I?" I repeated, softer this time, the words laced with pain. "Because from where I'm standing, it seems like there's a lot I don't know about you."

He flinched as if I'd slapped him, his broad shoulders

slumping slightly. "What you saw—what everyone's seeing—it's not the truth. Brittany and I were never a couple."

"What was she, then?" I asked, needing to hear him say it. He hesitated, and in that moment of silence, I saw the truth written across his face—guilt, regret, the shadows of his past.

"She was... we hooked up a few times," he admitted finally, his eyes never leaving mine, pleading. "In London. It was nothing serious—just drunk nights, empty mornings."

"So you did sleep with her," I said, each word like glass in my throat, slicing deep.

"Yes," he said, his voice raw, stepping closer until I could feel the heat radiating from his body. "But it was months ago, Tara. Before I came to Miami. Before us—before you walked back into my life and turned everything upside down in the best way."

My stomach clenched, a mix of jealousy and hurt twisting like a knife. "Many months?" I asked, my voice trembling now. "Like, five-months-pregnant amount of months?"

The color drained from his face, leaving him ashen. "I... I don't know exactly when... but yes, the timing could fit. But Tara, she also slept with half of my old team. I'll demand a paternity test. This whole thing reeks of a setup—"

"Including you," I cut him off, the words falling between us like stones, heavy and final. "She slept with half your team, including you."

He didn't deny it, just looked at me with those moss-green eyes full of anguish and desperation, the same eyes that had darkened with lust as he'd buried himself inside me. "Tara, please. You know what your father is capable of. This is exactly the kind of manipulation he excels at—twisting the knife to keep us apart."

"Maybe," I conceded, wrapping my arms around myself

tighter, the breeze chilling my skin. "Maybe this is all some elaborate scheme. But the fact remains that you slept with this woman, and now she's pregnant, and the timing fits. Those are facts, Xander, not manipulations."

"I can explain—"

"Can you?" I interrupted, suddenly exhausted, the fight draining from me like blood from a wound. "Can you explain why I had to find out about this from a junior therapist showing me a gossip site? Why you didn't call me the moment she showed up? Why, after everything we've shared—your body on mine—your first instinct wasn't to come to me?"

He looked stricken, his hands clenching at his sides as if fighting the urge to touch me. "I was ambushed this morning. Your father called me into his office, and she was just... there, with that smug smile and her hand on her belly. I've been trying to get to you all day, but you weren't answering my texts, and then your assistant said you had an emergency..."

I checked my phone, the screen lighting up with several missed texts from him, all variations of *"We need to talk* and *It's not what you think."* I'd been so caught up in my own spiral that I hadn't noticed them, the notifications buried under the avalanche of news alerts.

"I don't know what to believe right now, Xander," I said, my voice breaking slightly, tears pricking my eyes. "I want to trust you. I want to believe this is just another of my father's schemes. But..."

"But what?" he pressed when I trailed off, his voice a rough whisper, stepping so close I could see the flecks of gold in his eyes.

I looked at him—really looked at him. The man whose every move I'd tracked across continents, whose body I now knew as intimately as my own. The man who, just yesterday, had made me breakfast, kissing me like I was the only woman in the world.

"But I also know how you've been acting these many years," I said quietly, the words heavy. "The drinking. The partying. The women. I've followed it all, Xander—every self-destructive choice, every meaningless hookup splashed across the headlines. I wanted to believe you'd changed, that what we have is different. But maybe I've just been fooling myself."

He reached for me, his hand stopping just short of touching my arm, hovering like a promise unfulfilled. "What we have *is* different," he insisted, his voice pitching higher with emotion. "Tara, you're the only one who's ever seen me—the real me. You're the one who makes me want to be better."

"Don't," I cut him off, taking a step back, the space between us feeling like a chasm. "Not now. I need... I need time to process this."

The look of devastation on his face nearly broke my resolve —his strong jaw clenched, eyes glistening with unshed tears. For a moment, we stood there in painful silence.

"What about Morrison?" he asked finally, his voice cracking. "What about finding out the truth about Jimmy? We were going to do this together."

I closed my eyes briefly, the reminder hitting like a fresh wave. In the shock of the day's revelations, I'd almost forgotten our plan to confront the detective again, armed with the Valdez leverage.

"I don't know," I admitted, opening my eyes to meet his gaze one last time. "I need to think."

"Tara—"

"I have to go," I said, turning away before I could change my mind, before the pull of him dragged me back. "I can't do this right now."

I got into my car without looking back, my hands shaking so badly I could barely insert the key into the ignition. As I pulled out of the parking lot, I caught him in my rearview mirror—standing exactly where I'd left him, shoulders slumped, looking utterly lost, like a man watching his world drive away.

CHAPTER
Twenty-One

XANDER

THE SOUND of Brittany's fake sobbing filled the penthouse like a bad porno soundtrack—overacted and making me want to hurl. I stood in the middle of my living room, a tumbler of scotch dangling from my fingers, watching her face on the enormous TV screen. God, she was good at this shit, I'll give her that. Those big blue eyes welling up just right, not a single tear daring to streak her war paint.

"It's been so difficult," she sniffled. "For months, I've wanted Xander to take responsibility. Our baby deserves a father."

The interviewer—some blonde vulture from a gossip sports channel faking sympathy—nodded like she was auditioning for an Emmy. "And how has Xander responded to the news?"

Brittany's lower lip trembled on cue. "He... he said he needed time. That he wasn't ready." Her hand moved protectively to her rounded belly, stroking it like it was a goddamn prop. "But this little one isn't going to wait."

I hurled my glass at the wall with a snarl. It shattered spectacularly, scotch splashing across the pristine white surface. "That's a fucking lie!" I roared at the TV, my voice bouncing off the high ceilings. "You ambushed me in that bastard's office, you scheming bitch! That was the first I'd heard of your little 'miracle'—and we both know it ain't mine!"

Leo appeared from the kitchen, taking in the broken glass and the scotch dripping down the wall without so much as a flinch. The man's seen worse from me over the years. Without a word, he grabbed the remote and muted the TV, cutting off Brittany's crocodile tears mid-sniffle.

"That's enough of that bollocks," he said firmly, though his eyes were gentle with that annoying concern he always showed. "You're just torturing yourself, mate. And the wall didn't deserve it."

I ran a hand through my hair, my fingers shaking like I'd just come off a bender—which, let's be honest, I was itching for. "Did you hear the crap that woman's spewing? That I abandoned her? That I've known for months?" I paced the length of the room, unable to stand still, my blood boiling. "She waltzes into Hank's office like it's a bloody stage, drops this bomb, and now she's playing the victim card on every channel? Fuck me, Leo, it's a masterclass in bullshit."

Leo sighed, moving to clean up the broken glass. "I know, Xander. But shouting at the telly won't change the narrative she's spinning. It'll just give you a headache."

My phone buzzed for the hundredth time that day, vibrating angrily on the coffee table. Leo plucked it up before I could snatch it and smash that too.

"ESPN," he reported after checking the screen, his tone flat. "Third time they've called in the last hour. Persistent wankers."

"Tell them to fuck off," I muttered, stalking to the bar to pour another drink. My hands were still trembling, making the bottle clink against the glass like a drunk's Morse code. "Or better yet, tell 'em I've got a paternity test lined up that'll blow this fairy tale to hell."

"Already did," Leo replied, declining the call with a swipe. "Along with TMZ, Sports Illustrated, and that slimy bloke from the Daily Mail who keeps texting like we're old pals. 'Exclusive interview, Xander? Spill the tea on your baby mama drama?' Cheeky bastard."

I knocked back half the fresh drink in one swallow, the burn sliding down my throat. The last twenty-four hours had been a nightmare straight out of Dante's Inferno, Miami edition. After Tara had driven away from me in the parking lot, leaving me standing there like a gutted fish, I'd tried calling her repeatedly, each unanswered ring twisting the knife deeper. I'd even gone to her apartment, pounding on the door like a desperate fool, but she wouldn't open up—though I could hear her moving around inside.

Meanwhile, Brittany had launched a full-scale media assault, her sob story spreading. Somehow, she'd booked interviews with every major gossip outlet, each one featuring her tearful account of our "relationship" and my supposed abandonment of her and our unborn child. That we'd never actually been in a relationship, and that I'd only slept with her a handful of times—always drunk off my ass, always meaningless, regrettable romps in some hazy club bathroom or hotel suite—was conveniently omitted. She was a pro at this game and probably had a publicist on speed dial.

"I need to make a statement," I said, more to myself than to Leo. "Set the record straight. 'Ladies and gents, the kid ain't mine—it's probably half of Chelsea's backline's love child.'"

Leo shook his head, dumping the glass shards into the bin with a clink. "Not without a lawyer present, you daft Yank. She's making serious allegations, Xander. One wrong word from you, and she could sue for defamation. You'd be handing her the rope to hang you with."

"But she's the one lying!" I protested, my voice rising as I resumed pacing, the room feeling smaller by the second. "She's dragging my name through the mud, and I'm just supposed to sit here and take it up the ass?"

"For now, yes," Leo said firmly, straightening up to meet my glare. "The lawyer's coming tomorrow. Until then, radio silence. No tweets, no rants, no more glasses meeting their maker."

I leaned against the bar, suddenly exhausted, the scotch settling. "This is Hank's doing," I said quietly. "All of it. He's orchestrated this whole circus—the blonde bombshell, the baby bump, the media frenzy. Bastard's probably popping champagne right now."

Leo didn't disagree, just crossed his arms and nodded. "It does seem too convenient. The timing, especially. And just when you and Tara were getting close? Smells like Hank Swanson's cologne: expensive and rotten."

I took another swig. It had been a week since I'd had more than a beer or two—trying to clean up my act, be the man Tara deserved, the one who didn't drown his demons in a bottle. But what was the point now? She wouldn't even look at me.

"He's winning, Leo," I said, hearing the defeat in my voice. "He's always been ten steps ahead of me, the wily old prick. Even when I think I'm making progress—sobering up, scoring on the pitch, winning her over—he finds a way to rip it all away. I'm just a pawn in his twisted game."

Leo watched me pour a third drink, concern in his eyes, but

he knew better than to lecture. "Maybe you should slow down on the sauce," he suggested gently anyway, because that's Leo —ever the optimist.

I laughed bitterly. "Why? This is who I am, isn't it? The drunk, the screw-up, the man who destroys everything he touches... and apparently knocks up gold-diggers in his spare time. Isn't that what everyone's saying? Might as well live up to the hype."

"That's not who you are," Leo said firmly, stepping closer. "That's who you let people think you are... big difference, mate. The real Xander? He's the one who dragged his arse out of bed at dawn for practice, the one who's been fighting tooth and nail for the truth about Jimmy. Don't let this bollocks define you."

I didn't answer, just stared at the scotch in my glass, swirling it like it held answers at the bottom. It was easier this way—to let the alcohol blur the edges of my thoughts until Tara's devastated face, Jimmy's ghost, Brittany's lies all faded into a manageable haze. But even through the buzz, I knew Leo was right. Drowning myself wouldn't fix this; it'd just prove Hank's point.

On the muted TV, Brittany was now showing the interviewer a sonogram, waving it like a trophy. I couldn't bear to watch anymore, the sight twisting my gut.

"Turn it off," I said hoarsely, setting the glass down untouched—for now.

Leo complied with a nod, the screen going black, reflecting my haggard face back at me. "You should try to get some sleep. You've got practice tomorrow... can't show up looking like you lost a fight with a bottle."

The thought of facing the team, of enduring their judgment, the whispers in the locker room, Diego's smug face grinning, made my stomach turn. But I nodded anyway, pushing off the bar. Leo was right—hiding in my penthouse, drinking myself into oblivion, would only prove Hank right. And I'd be damned if I gave that bastard the satisfaction.

"Yeah," I said, draining the last of my glass in defiance before setting it down with a thunk. "Early night. Tomorrow, we fight back."

————

The locker room went dead silent when I staggered in the next morning. Conversations were replaced with side-eyes and whispers that weren't nearly as subtle as they thought. I kept my gaze forward, zeroing in on my locker in the distance like it was the promised land.

When I passed Diego's locker, the asshole deliberately raised his voice to his neighbor.

"So I told her, 'Honey, I'm always careful. No surprise babies from this guy.'"

Larson snickered, checking to see if I'd caught their little performance.

I clenched my teeth and kept moving. Don't take the bait. Don't give these dickheads what they want.

Thank god my locker was at the row's end, as far away as possible. I yanked my practice gear on, keeping my eyes glued to my shit. The entire time, I could feel eyeballs drilling into me from every angle, each packed with its own premium blend of judgment.

"Heard you're gonna be a daddy, McCrae!" Diego shouted across the now-quiet room. "Hope the kid has better aim than you do!"

Laughter exploded around him. I kept my back turned, focusing on tying my cleats.

One, two, three, four, five... breathe. Ignore the fucker.

"What's the matter, superstar?" Diego pushed, getting cocky from my silence. "No smart comeback today?"

I stood up, grabbed my water bottle, and turned to face him. Everyone went quiet again, watching for the fireworks.

"Not for you," I said, ice in my voice, then headed for the exit.

As I pushed through the door, I nearly slammed into Ben Carter. The young midfielder was just arriving with his gear bag, a compression wrap visible on his hamstring.

"Oh, hey, Xander," he said, completely missing the drama behind me. "How's it going?"

"Been better," I admitted.

Ben nodded. "Yeah, I saw the news. Rough stuff." He paused, then added quietly, "For what it's worth, I think it's all bullshit."

"Thanks, Ben."

He shrugged with a small smile. "No problem. See you out there?"

I nodded, and he continued into the lion's den. Behind him, I heard Diego start up again. But at least one person didn't think I was complete garbage. It wasn't much, but I'd take it.

The practice field felt like freedom after the suffocating locker room. I jogged some warmup laps, trying to clear my head.

As the rest of the team arrived, Coach Wilkes gathered us for instructions, outlining scrimmage exercises focused on ball control and quick transitions. When he split us into groups, I noticed he put me on the opposite side from Diego—small mercies.

"Carter," Coach called, "you're on limited participation today. Go get cleared first."

Ben nodded and jogged to the sideline where the physical therapy team waited. I looked for Tara's dark hair. She wasn't there—just two junior therapists I recognized.

"McCrae!" Coach barked. "You with us or daydreaming?"

I snapped back to reality. "Sorry, Coach."

He gave me a hard look. "Focus on the pitch, not your personal drama. I need your head in the game."

"Yes, sir," I muttered, joining my group.

Practice started okay. I threw myself into drills, channeling all my anger into physical exertion. For brief moments, I could almost forget the dumpster fire my life had become—there was just the ball, the grass under my feet, the pure joy of the game I'd loved since I was a kid.

Reality crashed back when we switched to full-field scrimmage. Diego played center forward for the opposing side, matched directly against me. From the first whistle, he was all over me—fouling just subtly enough to avoid Coach's notice, whispering shit whenever we got close.

"Saw your girlfriend on TV last night," he murmured as we waited for a corner kick. "Nice rack on her. No wonder you couldn't keep it in your pants."

I ignored him, focusing on the ball's path as it flew toward the goal.

"Though I gotta say," he continued, "the doc's more my type. All that repressed energy. Bet she's wild once you get her going."

My jaw clenched so hard my teeth nearly shattered.

Don't react. That's exactly what he wants.

The ball came our way, and I headed it clear, sending it

upfield to a teammate. Diego jogged beside me as we repositioned.

"Too bad you fucked that up too," he said casually. "Heard she won't even look at you now. Can't blame her. Who wants damaged goods?"

I missed a pass, the ball rolling past me as my concentration broke. Diego laughed, a low, satisfied sound.

"Thought so," he said, breaking away to intercept the ball.

The scrimmage continued, and so did Diego's psychological warfare. Every mistake I made—and there were plenty as my focus crumbled under his constant attacks—was met with another cutting remark about Brittany, about Tara, about my drinking, about my failures on and off the pitch.

I was ready to explode by the time Coach called a water break. My hands shook as I grabbed my bottle, gulping water like it might wash away the fury building inside me.

"You're letting him get to you," a quiet voice said beside me.

I turned to find Ben, his hamstring now free of the wrap, pulling on his practice jersey.

"Doc cleared you to play?" I asked, ignoring his comment.

He nodded. "Limited minutes. But yeah, I can join the scrimmage now."

I capped my water bottle, wiping sweat from my forehead. "Good for you."

Ben hesitated, then added, "Look, I know Diego's being a dick. He's always like that when he feels threatened. But don't let him—"

"I'm fine," I cut him off, harsher than intended.

Ben raised his hands in surrender. "Alright, man. Just trying to help."

I sighed, immediately regretting my tone. "Sorry. I appreciate it. Just... got a lot on my mind."

"No kidding," Ben said with a sympathetic grimace. "If you want to grab a beer after practice, talk it out..."

The offer was genuine, and for a moment, I considered it. But the thought of adding another person to the collateral damage of Hurricane Xander made me pause. Ben was a good kid. He didn't deserve to get sucked into my mess.

"Thanks," I said instead. "But I've got some things to take care of."

Coach's whistle ended the break. As we jogged back onto the field, I spotted Tara standing near the facility entrance, clipboard in hand, apparently watching Ben's return to practice.

My heart did a painful flip. Even from a distance, I could see how rigid her shoulders were. She didn't glance my way once, her attention locked entirely on Ben as he rejoined the scrimmage.

"Second half!" Coach called. "Same teams, full intensity. Let's go!"

The scrimmage started again, but my mind wasn't on the game. All I could think about was Tara, standing yards away, deliberately avoiding me. Was she here for Ben, or was she watching me too? Did she believe Brittany's bullshit?

"McCrae!" Coach bellowed. "Pay attention!"

Too late, I realized the ball was coming my way. I scrambled to position myself, but Diego was already there, intercepting the pass meant for me.

"Still daydreaming about the baby mama?" he taunted as he dribbled past. "Or is it the good doctor over there you can't get out of your head?"

I charged after him, all technique forgotten in a red haze of rage. Diego easily dodged my clumsy approach, laughing as he kept the ball.

"Since she's available now," he called over his shoulder, "I'll give her another shot. Show the Doc what a real man feels like."

Something inside me snapped. The guilt and self-hatred, the public humiliation, and the raw, aching loss of Tara's trust —it all exploded into one blinding moment of fury.

I don't remember deciding to hit him. Next, my fist connected with his jaw with a sickening crack that vibrated up my arm.

Diego went down hard, clutching his face. Blood leaked between his fingers from a split lip. The practice field erupted —players rushing toward us, coaches blowing whistles, everyone shouting at once.

Through the chaos, my eyes found Tara. She stood frozen at the sideline, her clipboard forgotten, her face scrunched into horror and disappointment. I'd just proven her father right. I was exactly what Hank and everyone thought I was, a violent, out-of-control disaster.

Coach Wilkes grabbed my arm, his face purple with rage. "McCrae! What the hell do you think you're doing?"

I couldn't answer, couldn't tear my gaze from Tara's stricken expression. Someone was helping Diego up. Blood stained the front of his jersey.

"You're suspended!" Coach roared right in my face. "Get off my field! NOW!"

Two assistant coaches appeared, flanking me. As they escorted me off, I finally looked away from Tara, unable to bear her judgment anymore.

The walk back to the locker room passed in a blur. My hand throbbed where it hit Diego's face, but the physical pain was nothing compared to the hollow ache in my chest. I'd lost control. Again.

I changed in the empty locker room, moving like a robot, pulling on street clothes, gathering my stuff, my mind a static buzz of self-hatred.

You've ruined everything. When will you fucking learn?

As I pushed through the door, gym bag over my shoulder, I half-expected to find Hank waiting to gloat. Instead, it was Leo, his face grim as he took in my disheveled state.

"I got a call from the team office," he said simply.

I nodded mutely, following him toward the exit.

Outside, the sun hit like a spotlight. I squinted against it, feeling exposed as Leo led me to the waiting car.

"What happens now?" I asked, voice like gravel.

Leo sighed, opening the car door. "Now we do damage control. The lawyer's still coming this afternoon. We'll figure out a statement about both the Brittany situation and... this."

I collapsed into the back seat, suddenly exhausted to my bones. "What's the point? It's over, Leo. Hank won."

Leo slid in beside me, his expression unusually fierce. "It's not over until you say it's over. Are you really going to let him win like this? After everything?"

I leaned back, closing my eyes. In my mind, I saw Tara's face—not as it had been on the field, full of disappointment, but as it had been that morning in her apartment, soft with sleep and trust, her eyes full of a future I'd barely dared to imagine.

"No," I said finally, barely audible. "No, I'm not."

But who was I kidding? I may finally have played a hand I couldn't win.

CHAPTER
Twenty-Two

TARA

THE IMAGERY PLAYED on loop in my mind—Xander's fist connecting with Diego's jaw, the sickening crack that could be heard across the practice field, the chaos that erupted afterward as Coach Wilkes's furious shouts cut through the air.

I stood on the sideline, frozen, the tablet slipping from my numb fingers to hang by its strap against my hip. I watched as two assistant coaches escorted a stone-faced Xander off the field, his eyes briefly finding mine. I saw no anger in them, only a profound, hollow emptiness that somehow hurt more than rage would have.

My father's words echoed in my head, a cold, prophetic mantra: *Men like McCrae are walking liabilities. Trouble doesn't find them, they invite it in for a drink.*

I had just watched him prove it. A violent, uncontrolled outburst that had endangered a teammate and thrown the entire organization into chaos. The professional in me was horrified. The daughter in me was terrified that my father had been right all along.

"Dr. Swanson?"

The voice pulled me from my trance. It was Jess, my junior physical therapist, her eyes wide with concern. "Are you okay?"

"I'm fine," I said, the lie tasting like ash. I forced my body to move, retreating into the one identity that still made sense. "Standard protocol. I need to check Mr. Mano for a possible concussion and treat that laceration. Then I have a follow-up with Carter on his hamstring. Get Mr. Mano into exam room one."

Diego was already on the table when I walked in, a bloody towel pressed to his mouth and a smug, victorious glint in his eyes.

"Came to check out the damage, Doc?" he smirked, lowering the towel to reveal a split, already swelling lip. "Don't worry. My face can take a punch."

"I'm more concerned about your head," I said, my voice clipped and professional as I snapped on a pair of latex gloves. "Look at me. Follow my finger."

I ran him through a basic concussion check. His eyes tracked perfectly, his answers were clear. He was fine, and he knew it. As I cleaned his split lip with an antiseptic wipe, he leaned in close, his breath hot and unwelcome.

"You know, now that you're not messing with that charity case anymore, maybe you and I could…"

"Hold still," I cut him off, dabbing the cut more forcefully than necessary. He winced.

"Feisty," he murmured, his eyes roaming over my face. "I like that. He's not man enough for you, Tara. You need someone who knows what he wants."

It took every ounce of my professional training to keep my hands steady, to ignore the greasy feeling his words left on my skin. I placed a butterfly bandage on the cut. "Ice it for twenty-four hours and take an anti-inflammatory. You're done here, Diego."

I turned my back on him before he could say another word, stripping off my gloves and tossing them in the bin with a satisfying snap.

Next was Ben Carter. He was sitting on the edge of the table in exam room two, looking less like a patient and more like a kid waiting for the principal. Guilt was rolling off him in waves.

"Hamstring feels good, Doc," he said quietly as I entered. "No tightness."

I nodded, gently manipulating his leg through its range of motion. "Good. The ultrasound showed the tear has healed completely. I'm clearing you for regular practice, but continue the strengthening exercises for another week."

"I will," he promised. He watched me make notes in his file, his knee bouncing. "Dr. Swanson?"

"Yes?" I didn't look up.

"What Xander did... it was wrong. He shouldn't have hit him." He hesitated, his voice dropping lower. "But Diego had it coming. You should know what he said."

I stopped writing. The pen froze over the page. Slowly, I lifted my head to meet his gaze. "What did he say?"

Ben's eyes dropped to the floor. "He was on him the whole scrimmage, whispering shit about the news stories. But then... he brought you into it."

A cold dread coiled in my stomach.

"He told Xander..." Ben swallowed hard, clearly hating the

words. "He said that now you were single, he was going to show you what a 'real man' feels like."

The sterile air of the exam room seemed to vanish, sucked out by the vulgarity of the threat. It wasn't just a taunt. It was a crude assertion of ownership.

The image in my head—of Xander's fist connecting with Diego's jaw—violently shifted. The lens changed. It wasn't a random, uncontrolled outburst. It was a direct and calculated response.

A raw, primal, and utterly misguided defense of my honor.

"Thank you for telling me, Ben," I said, my voice a hollow whisper.

He slid off the table and headed for the door, but paused with his hand on the frame. "For what it's worth, Doc... I think Xander's a good guy. He's just... carrying a lot."

The door clicked shut, leaving me alone in the sudden, deafening silence. The horror I'd felt watching the punch was gone, replaced by a nauseating wave of guilt. I hadn't seen an out-of-control athlete. I'd seen a man pushed too far, and I had judged him for it.

My mind a whirlwind, I walked out of the exam room on autopilot. I found Jess and told her I was leaving for the day, ignoring her concerned questions. I couldn't be a doctor right now. I couldn't be anything. I just needed to think.

The drive to my apartment was a blur. I paced the living room, unable to settle and quiet the riot in my head.

My phone buzzed on the coffee table—the third call from my father in the last hour. I let it ring, watching it vibrate against the glass surface until it finally went silent. No doubt he'd heard about what happened. No doubt he was calling to say he'd been right all along.

Maybe he was.

The fact that Xander hit Diego Mano because he was protecting my honor, doesn't change the rest.

The evidence was mounting, piece by damning piece. The tabloid photos of him stumbling drunk outside London clubs. The string of failed relationships with models and socialites. The team-member conflicts, the suspensions, the fights.

Brittany Ashworth. Pregnant with his child.

My phone vibrated again. I glanced at the screen. Xander.

My heart lurched traitorously in my chest. I picked up the phone, my thumb hovering over the answer button.

What would I even say to him?

All empty platitudes that changed nothing. The man I thought I knew—the man I'd convinced myself I loved—had never existed. He was a fantasy I'd constructed, first as a teenage obsession, then as an adult delusion.

I set the phone down without answering, watching it go dark as the call went to voicemail.

A memory surfaced—Xander's half-brother, Cory, on speakerphone in Xander's living room. His voice clear and confident: *"The Valdez Case. That's the key to getting Morrison to talk."*

The Valdez Case. The one piece of information that didn't fit into the neat, damning picture.

I stood frozen for a long moment. If I was going to walk away from Xander, I needed certainty. I needed to know beyond any doubt that I was making the right choice.

I marched into my home office with fire in my veins. This used to be command central for my Xander shrine. Now the naked wall just stood there like "Congrats, dumbass." All those years playing detective, documenting his every breath, and I still couldn't figure out who the hell he actually was.

I sat at my desk and opened my laptop. My hands hovered

over the keyboard for a moment before I typed: *Valdez Case +*
Detective Rick Morrison + Palo Alto.

The search returned several results. I clicked on the first
one, a local newspaper article from eleven years ago.

CONTROVERSIAL DRUG CASE DISMISSED AMID ALLE-
GATIONS OF POLICE MISCONDUCT

I scanned the article quickly, my heartbeat accelerating as I
absorbed the details. Isabel Valdez, a 19-year-old Stanford
student, had been arrested and charged with possession and
intent to distribute cocaine. The case against her had seemed
airtight—until her attorney uncovered inconsistencies in the
evidence log and witness statements.

The charges were eventually dropped, and the lead detective on the case, Richard Morrison, abruptly announced his
retirement shortly afterward. The article hinted at broader allegations of corruption but provided few specifics.

The case had never gone to trial, the charges quietly
dropped to avoid publicity. Morrison's retirement was
presented as unrelated, but the timing was suspicious.

With renewed urgency, I continued searching, looking for
anything more recent about Isabel Valdez. Several pages into
the results, I found what I was looking for—a human interest
piece from just six months ago.

FROM WRONGFUL ACCUSATION TO ADVOCACY:
ISABEL VALDEZ'S FIGHT FOR CRIMINAL JUSTICE REFORM

The article detailed how Isabel, now 30, had channeled her
traumatic experience into a career as an advocate for criminal
justice reform. She'd founded a small non-profit organization
in San Francisco dedicated to helping victims of police
misconduct.

At the bottom of the article was a contact number for the
foundation.

I stared at the digits, my heart racing. It was late—past 8 PM in Miami, which meant it was after 5 PM in California. The foundation's office would likely be closed.

But before I could talk myself out of it, I grabbed my phone and dialed the number. It rang four times, and I was preparing myself for voicemail when someone picked up.

"Justice Reform Initiative," a female voice answered, sounding slightly harried.

I cleared my throat. "Yes, hello. I'm... I'm trying to reach Isabel Valdez."

"This is she," the woman replied, her tone shifting from professional to cautious. "Who's calling?"

"My name is Tara Swanson," I said, my voice steady. "I'm calling from Miami. I... I believe we have something in common."

"And what would that be?" Isabel asked, the wariness in her voice unmistakable.

I took a deep breath. "Detective Richard Morrison. From Palo Alto."

There was a long pause on the other end of the line. I could hear the faint sounds of an office shutting down—a drawer closing, papers being shuffled.

"I don't discuss that case with journalists," Isabel finally said, her voice tight. "If you're working on a story—"

"I'm not a journalist," I interrupted quickly. "I'm a doctor. A physical therapist. And I think... I think Morrison's corruption affected another case. Twelve years ago. A case involving my brother's death."

Another pause, longer this time. When Isabel spoke again, her voice had lost some of its defensive edge.

"What makes you think Morrison was corrupt in your brother's case?"

I hesitated, unsure how much to reveal to a complete stranger. But something told me that if anyone would understand, it would be this woman who had faced Morrison's corruption firsthand.

"The official report on my brother's death is... incomplete," I said carefully. "Certain conclusions that should have been there are missing. And I have reason to believe my father may have influenced the investigation."

"Your father," Isabel repeated slowly. "Is he wealthy? Influential?"

"Yes," I admitted. "He is."

"That fits the pattern," Isabel said, a bitter note entering her voice. "In my case, Morrison was paid by the rich father of the actual drug dealer to pin it on me instead. The evidence against me was fabricated. Witness statements were coerced. The whole thing was a setup from the beginning."

My stomach clenched. "How did you prove it?"

"We never did, not definitively," Isabel said. "My lawyer found enough inconsistencies to get the charges dropped, but we couldn't prove Morrison took a bribe. So he was allowed to retire quietly instead of being prosecuted."

I felt a flicker of disappointment. If Isabel couldn't prove Morrison's corruption in her own case, what hope did we have of proving it in Jimmy's?

"But my lawyer was convinced Morrison kept records," Isabel continued, as if sensing my deflation. "A private ledger, a notebook of some kind, with details of all his side deals and the bribes he took. We could never find it, but he swore it existed."

My pulse quickened again. "A ledger? Are you sure?"

"My lawyer had a confidential informant in the department who insisted Morrison documented everything. Names, dates, amounts. He was paranoid about being double-crossed, apparently. Wanted insurance in case anyone ever tried to deny payment or expose him."

"So this ledger, if it exists..." I began.

"If you can find it, you can burn him to the ground," Isabel finished for me. "That's what my lawyer always said."

I leaned forward, gripping the phone tightly. "Do you think he still has it? After all these years?"

"Men like Morrison don't destroy leverage," Isabel said with certainty. "If that ledger exists, he still has it. Somewhere safe, somewhere no one would think to look."

By the time we hung up, my mind was racing with possibilities. If Morrison had documented his corruption, if there was physical evidence of a bribe from my father, it would change everything. Not just for Xander, but for me, for my understanding of what happened. But no matter what, this proves a pattern. It's more than likely that Morrison also took a bribe from my father.

I sat back in my chair, my earlier despair replaced by certainty. Xander—the man I loved, the man I'd almost given up on—wasn't a monster. He was another one of Morrison's victims, just like Isabel Valdez.

I had a choice to make—protect my father's secret, or fight for the man I love and the truth of my brother's death.

It wasn't even a choice. Not really.

I grabbed my phone again and scrolled to Xander's name, but decided against it. A call wouldn't cut it. Not for this.

Twenty minutes later, I pulled into the parking garage beneath Xander's building, a strange calm settling over me. Security recognized me and waved me through without question. The elevator ride to the penthouse floor felt endless, each floor number illuminating with painful slowness.

What would I find? The last time I'd seen him, he'd been escorted off the practice field in disgrace. The image of his hollow, defeated eyes haunted me.

Outside his door, I hesitated. My knuckles hovered inches from the sleek wood surface. What if he didn't want to see me? What if he'd already given up—on the investigation, on us, on everything?

No, I refused to believe that. The Xander I knew—the real Xander, not the one my father had painted—wouldn't give up. Not when we were so close to the truth.

I knocked firmly.

Silence stretched on the other side. I knocked again, louder this time.

"Go away, Leo," came a muffled voice. "I told you I don't want dinner."

"It's not Leo," I called, pressing my palm against the door. "It's me."

More silence. Then footsteps, slow and hesitant. The lock clicked, and the door swung open.

My heart sank at the sight of him. Hair disheveled, dark circles beneath bloodshot eyes. He wore wrinkled sweatpants and a faded t-shirt that hung loosely on his frame. The apartment behind him was in disarray—empty glasses scattered across the coffee table, throw pillows on the floor, a blanket tangled on the couch where he'd clearly been sleeping.

But it was the naked shock in his eyes that gutted me—as if my presence was the last thing in the world he'd expected. As if he'd already accepted that I was gone for good.

"Tara?" His voice was rough, disbelieving.

I took a deep breath and met his gaze steadily. "I believe you, Xander. About everything."

CHAPTER
Twenty~Three

XANDER

THE MORNING SUN blasted through the windshield as we cruised south toward Naples. Tara occupied the passenger seat, dark hair in a casual ponytail, her face locked in quiet focus while scrolling on her phone. The vibe between us buzzed with nervous purpose—completely different from the wild makeup sex that had dominated our night.

That part blindsided me. After everything—the Brittany clusterfuck, that brawl with Diego—I was sure we were done. Then Tara showed up at my door, eyes blazing, voice steady.

I believe you, Xander. About everything.

Those words cracked something inside me. A tornado of relief, shock, and raw hunger crashed through my chest, and I yanked her into my arms before she fully crossed the threshold. The door barely shut before clothes flew off and restraint went out the window. We bumped into walls, knocked some decorative crap off a table while desperately trying to reconnect.

Even now, watching her profile as she studied her phone, I remembered her hands on my skin, the taste of her neck, that little gasp when she—

"You're staring," she said without looking up, her mouth quirking at one corner.

"Can you blame me?" I squirmed in my seat, eyes back on the road. "After last night, it's a miracle I can drive at all."

She laughed, deep and throaty, shooting fresh heat through my body. "Eyes on the prize, McCrae. We've got a dirty ex-cop waiting for us."

"I'm totally focused," I lied, grinning like an idiot. "Just... handling multiple tasks."

Tara dropped her phone in her lap and turned to me. "Let's review the plan again. We need perfect coordination when we confront Morrison."

I nodded, mood shifting as our mission came back into focus.

"I still think we should throw him off guard right from the start," I said, zipping around a slow truck. "Tell him we know about the Valdez case dirt. Make it crystal clear we'll blast it everywhere if he doesn't play ball."

Tara shook her head. "Too hostile. Threaten him immediately, and he'll just wall up. We need to outsmart him."

"We tried being nice last time," I reminded her. "He basically told us to fuck off."

"I'm not suggesting 'nice,'" Tara clarified. "I'm suggesting 'smart.' The Valdez case isn't our opening move... it's our knockout punch."

I tapped the steering wheel, thinking it over. Strategy wasn't exactly my forte—I typically preferred the more direct approach of a wrecking ball. But her measured thinking made sense.

"What's your take, then?" I asked.

"I start," she said. "Professional doctor-to-detective approach. I'll point out report inconsistencies, stick to facts, keep emotions out."

"And when he blocks you? Because that's guaranteed."

Her eyes flashed with purpose. "That's your cue. That's when we drop the Isabel Valdez bomb and mention his secret ledger."

I couldn't help grinning at her fierce expression. "So, good cop, bad cop?"

"Exactly." She reached over and squeezed my hand. "I'll be the reasonable one, and you'll be the unpredictable hothead ready to torch his reputation if he stonewalls us."

"I do 'unhinged and dangerous' pretty well," I admitted, recalling the moment my knuckles connected with Diego's face. "Not exactly something I'd put on Tinder."

"Today it's a weapon," Tara said, her voice going gentle. "And just so you know, I see beyond that."

Fuck, isn't she incredible? Most people defined me by my greatest fuckups—the booze binges, the brawls, the self-destruction greatest hits collection. Having someone—having *her*—see the real me felt incredible.

"So we're locked in," I said, pushing past the lump in my throat. "You start, I lurk menacingly, and if he doesn't cooperate, I unleash hell about Valdez."

"And we don't leave without that original report," Tara added, her face hardening. "Whatever it says, we need the truth."

I nodded, my gut tightening. I'd always carried Jimmy's death on my shoulders. Believed my drunken state somehow caused that crash, even from the passenger seat. What if Morrison's notes confirmed that? Or revealed something worse?

As if she could read my thoughts, Tara placed her hand on my arm. "Whatever we discover, we handle it together. Got it?"

I swallowed hard and nodded, covering her hand with mine. "Together."

———

Our plan was simple. Morrison volunteered at the Naples Marine Conservation Society three days a week. Today was one of those days. Perfect spot to corner him—public enough he couldn't tell us to fuck off, but exposed enough he'd want to keep his shit quiet.

I pulled into the parking lot of the conservation center, a blue building with a giant sea turtle painted on it. Spotted Morrison's crappy old Buick right away.

"He's here," I said, parking a few spots over.

Tara nodded, inhaling deeply. "Ready?"

I looked at her—this brilliant badass joining me on this truth-hunting mission.

"With you? Always."

The place was cool and dark, with marine displays everywhere and families wandering around.

"Excuse me," Tara approached a teenager working the front desk, and slipped him a twenty for admission. "We're looking for Rick Morrison. He volunteers here?"

The kid barely lifted his eyes while making change. "Mr. Morrison's running the eleven o'clock turtle talk on the east boardwalk."

We followed the signage past outdoor exhibits featuring pools of fish, crabs, and sharks. The wooden walkway extended over a pool where sea turtles drifted without urgency.

And there stood Morrison, a tourist crowd gathered around him, rocking khaki shorts and a logo polo, playing kindly old nature enthusiast instead of the corrupt bastard who'd destroyed people's lives.

"...and this is Daisy," he explained, pointing to a turtle. "Found her tangled in fishing line. We'll release her next month."

A little girl with pigtails raised her hand. "Does she miss her family?"

Morrison smiled gently. "Sea turtles are loners, sweetheart. They don't have families like us. But she probably misses the open ocean."

The disconnect hit me hard—this turtle-loving volunteer was the same bastard who took bribes, falsified evidence, destroyed my life, and buried the truth about Jimmy. My blood boiled watching his wholesome act.

Tara squeezed my hand. "Easy," she whispered. "Remember the plan."

I forced myself to breathe as the tour group dispersed. When Morrison spotted us, his face transformed—grandpa vanished, replaced by a cold, hard stare.

He hustled the tourists away and stormed over.

"I told you to stay away," he hissed, eyes darting around. "This is harassment."

"We just want to talk, Detective Morrison," Tara said calmly. "About the inconsistencies in my brother's case."

His jaw clenched. "I already told you. I have nothing to say."

"I think you do," Tara continued, cool as ice. "Your final

report leaves out key conclusions. No determination of who drove, no toxicology, no witness statements. It's incomplete."

"Filed my report based on evidence," Morrison snapped. "Take it up with the department. I'm retired."

I watched him sweat despite the cool breeze. Tara's approach wasn't working.

Time for me to be the asshole.

I stepped into his bubble. "We're not here about your official report, Detective," I said, voice low and threatening. "We're here about your ledger. And Isabel Valdez."

The effect was fucking beautiful. Morrison went ghost-white, eyes bulging. He stumbled backward toward the railing.

"Don't know what you're talking about," he stammered.

"Pretty sure you do," I pressed, invading his personal space. "Isabel Valdez. Stanford student you framed for drugs ten years ago. Case tossed because you manufactured evidence. The real reason they kicked your worthless ass to the retirement curb. We just had a fascinating little chat with her. Turns out she's become a criminal justice activist. Fucking poetic for our purposes, isn't it?"

His eyes pinballed between us and the nearest tourists. "Keep your voice down," he begged.

"Why?" I asked, eyebrows raised. "Scared these nice families might learn that Mr. Turtle Talk is actually a dirty ex-cop who took cash to frame innocent people?"

"You don't know shit," Morrison insisted, voice cracking.

Tara stepped forward, radiating ice-cold authority. "She told us all about the ledger, Detective. Your little bribe diary. Including, we believe, one from my father about my brother's death."

Morrison's face twisted. "You can't prove any of this."

"Don't need to," I let a razor-edged smile curl my lips. "Just need to make noise. To the right people. How's your retirement look after that? Your reputation? Your pension?"

A family with kids wandered onto the boardwalk. Morrison grabbed my arm and yanked us to a secluded corner.

"What the fuck do you want?" he demanded, whispering harshly. "Money?"

Tara shook her head, disgusted. "We don't want your money. We don't even care about exposing the Valdez case or your other corrupt bullshit."

"Then what?" Morrison asked, confused and terrified.

"Your original notes about my brother's accident," Tara demanded. "The ones that never made the official report. The ones that detail exactly what happened."

Morrison stared, breathing fast. "And if I give you these supposed notes, you'll what? Leave me alone? Never mention Valdez again?"

"That's the deal," I confirmed. "Give us the truth about Jimmy Swanson, and we forget your name, the ledger, Valdez, everything."

He studied us, hunting for tricks. "How do I know you'll keep your word?"

"You don't," Tara said bluntly. "But what choice do you have? Take the deal or watch your cozy retirement burn."

Morrison deflated. He rubbed his face, suddenly looking ancient. "I don't have the notes here."

"Where are they?" I demanded.

After hesitating, he pulled out a key ring and removed a small, tarnished key.

"Storage unit off I-75," he said hollowly. "Unit 218. File's in a lockbox on the back shelf." He pressed the key into my hand. "Take it, and then never come back again."

I closed my fist around it, feeling its weight—both real and symbolic. This tiny piece of metal might unlock everything.

"If this is bullshit—" I started.

"It's not," he cut me off wearily. "You'll find what you want. And when you do..." He looked at Tara with something like regret. "Sorry about your brother. For whatever that's worth."

He walked away, shoulders slumped, steps heavy. We watched him disappear into the main building.

Tara turned to me, eyes wide with shock and victory. "We did it," she whispered. "He caved."

I stared at the key. So ordinary-looking for something so potentially life-changing.

"Think he's telling the truth?" I asked. "About the storage unit?"

Tara nodded. "You saw his face. He's fucking terrified. Whatever's in those notes, he wants us to have it more than he wants to protect it."

I pocketed the key. "Well, let's go find out what the truth really is."

We walked back through the center, past displays that now seemed bizarrely normal. How could everything look so ordinary when we were about to uncover the truth that had warped our entire lives?

In the parking lot, Tara checked directions. "Twenty minutes from here. Just off the interstate."

I started the engine, heart hammering. "Twelve years," I muttered. "Twelve fucking years of guilt and not knowing."

One thing was certain: after today, nothing would ever be the same again.

CHAPTER
Twenty~Four

TARA

XANDER PULLED out of the parking lot, following the GPS directions to the storage facility. We drove in silence, both lost in our own thoughts. My hand found his on the center console, our fingers intertwining without discussion. The simple contact anchored me as my mind raced ahead to what we might discover.

The storage facility appeared on our right after about twenty minutes—a sprawling complex of identical orange metal units baking under the sun. A faded sign proclaimed "SecurStore Self Storage" above a small office building. Xander pulled into a visitor spot, and we both stared at the rows of numbered doors stretching into the distance.

"Unit 218," I said, breaking the silence. "Let's find it."

The woman at the front desk barely glanced up when we entered, focused on her crossword puzzle. An oscillating fan pushed hot air around the cramped office.

"Can I help you?" she asked.

"We need to find Unit 218," Xander said. "We have the key."

She pointed a pen toward a map on the wall. "Row D, about halfway down." Her eyes flicked to us briefly. "You have until six."

Outside, we followed the lettered signs until we reached Row D. The units stretched before us, each identical to the last except for the numbers stenciled on the rolling doors. My heart hammered against my ribs as we counted down—222, 220, 218.

We stopped. The padlock hung from the latch, unremarkable and rust-spotted.

Xander held out the key. "You should do it."

I took it, surprised by how heavy it felt in my palm. My fingers trembled slightly as I slid it into the lock. It turned with a reluctant click, and the padlock sprung open.

Xander lifted the door with a metallic rattle. The smell of dust washed over us. We stood side by side, peering into the gloom.

The unit was small, maybe ten by ten feet, and surprisingly empty. No towers of cardboard boxes or old furniture like I'd expected. Just a few plastic containers stacked in one corner, a folding table against the back wall, and on it, a single metal lockbox.

Our prize.

"There it is," Xander said quietly.

We stepped inside, the concrete floor gritty beneath our shoes. The air was stifling, trapped heat making it hard to breathe. Xander pulled out his phone and switched on the flashlight, illuminating the space more clearly.

I approached the lockbox slowly, as if it might disappear if

I moved too quickly. It was military-style, olive green with a combination lock on the front.

"Shit," I breathed. "We need a combination."

Xander kneeled beside the table, shining his light across the dusty surface. "Check underneath. People always hide codes under things."

I ran my fingers along the bottom of the table and felt a piece of tape. Peeling it back revealed a small slip of paper with four numbers: 1-9-6-7.

"Birth year, maybe?" I suggested, entering the digits into the lock. It clicked open on the first try.

Inside the box lay a single manila folder, labeled in neat block letters: "SWANSON, J. - ORIGINAL NOTES - DO NOT FILE."

My throat constricted. I'd been building my entire life around finding Xander, confronting him, making him pay for what I thought he'd done to Jimmy. And now the truth was literally in my hands.

"I can't—" I started, then stopped. "Can we look at it in the car? I need air."

Xander nodded, understanding without explanation. He took the folder, and I closed the lockbox, leaving everything else untouched. We pulled the storage unit door down, replaced the padlock, and walked back to the car in silence, the folder clutched in Xander's hand like a bomb that might detonate at any moment.

Once inside, the air conditioning washed over my flushed skin. Xander placed the folder on the console between us, neither of us immediately reaching for it.

"Let's do this," he said quietly.

I nodded, steeling myself. Then I picked up the folder and opened it.

The first page was a handwritten note on police department stationery:

Case #94-7821 - Fatal MVA - Swanson, James (deceased)

My hands shook as I turned the pages—a detailed accident reconstruction report with diagrams, measurements, and photographs. Unlike the sanitized version in the official record, this one left nothing to the imagination. The car's path, the angle of impact, the position of the bodies afterward—it was all there in detail.

I forced myself to read every word, absorbing the technical language that painted a picture so different from what I'd believed:

No skid marks present for minimum 50 yards prior to impact point.

Acceleration marks indicate vehicle INCREASED speed before collision.

Driver's side sustained catastrophic impact. Passenger protected by seatbelt and airbag deployment, and deliberate positioning of seat (fully reclined, maximum distance from dashboard).

Blood alcohol level of passenger (Alexander McCrae): 0.18%

Blood alcohol level of driver (James Swanson): 0.00%

The words blurred as tears filled my eyes. I blinked them away, determined to see this through.

The next page contained Morrison's handwritten conclusion:

Based on physical evidence, witness statements, and scene analysis, the death of James Swanson was a deliberate act of suicide. The positioning of the passenger seat, the lack of braking, and the acceleration marks all indicate the driver intentionally crashed the vehicle. The passenger (A. McCrae) was unconscious at time of impact due to intoxication and was deliberately positioned by driver to minimize injury.

Final conclusion: Suicide.

The folder slipped from my fingers, papers spilling across my lap. A strangled sound escaped my throat as the truth crashed through twelve years of certainty.

Jimmy killed himself. He had deliberately ended his own life.

And my father had covered it up.

"Tara," Xander said softly, his voice breaking through the roaring in my ears. "Tara, look at me."

I turned to him, vision blurred by tears. "He did it on purpose," I whispered. "Jimmy killed himself."

Xander reached across the console and took my hands in his. They were warm and solid when everything else seemed to be dissolving around me.

"I'm so sorry," he said.

"Why?" The question tore from my throat. "Why would he do that? He wasn't depressed. He wasn't... there were no signs. I would have known. I would have seen it."

How had I missed it?

"We were so close," I said, my voice breaking. "I thought we told each other everything. But he was planning this, and I never saw it coming."

Xander squeezed my hands. "Tara, you were sixteen. You can't blame yourself for not recognizing signs that adults miss all the time."

"But I should have known. I should have..." The words dissolved into a sob that I couldn't suppress.

Xander unbuckled his seatbelt and awkwardly pulled me into his arms across the center console. I buried my face against his shoulder, finally letting the tears flow freely. He held me without speaking, one hand stroking my hair while I cried for the brother I'd lost twice—once to death, and now to the truth.

When the sobs finally subsided, I pulled back, wiping my face with shaking hands. "There's more," I said, picking up another page from the folder. "Read this."

Xander took the paper—a statement from a witness who'd arrived at the scene moments after the crash:

I heard the impact and ran over. The dark-haired kid in the passenger seat was coming to. He was dazed but conscious. The other boy—the driver—was pinned behind the wheel, bleeding badly. I heard him say something to the passenger. Then he stopped breathing.

The paper trembled in Xander's hands. "I thought I had imagined it. I was so drunk, and everything was hazy, but I remember now."

His words sparked something in me. I flipped through the remaining pages until I found what I was looking for: a receipt stapled to a handwritten note.

Arrangements made with H. Swanson - a donation for discretion regarding manner of death.

"He knew," I said, my voice hardening. "My father knew it was suicide, and he covered it up. He 'donated' to Morrison's retirement fund for him to falsify the report."

"Maybe to protect Jimmy's memory," Xander suggested. "A lot of families want to hide suicide."

I shook my head, anger building. "But that's n*ot right. Blaming you when he* knew it was a suicide."

My father hadn't just buried the truth about Jimmy's suicide—he had deliberately used my brother's death to drive away Xander.

"We're going to expose him," I said, my voice steady despite the hurricane of emotions inside me. "My father manipulated me, he manipulated you, he manipulated everyone. And he's still doing it now, with this Brittany situation."

Xander nodded, his jaw set with determination. "We take this to a lawyer first. Then we go public with it—all of it. The original police report, Morrison's ledger entry, everything."

"He'll try to discredit us," I warned, gathering the papers back into the folder with trembling hands. "He'll say we fabricated the documents."

"That's why we need to talk to Morrison's ex-partner, Miller. Get him on record corroborating that Morrison kept these kinds of records. And Valdez can verify the ledger's existence too."

We started formulating our plan as Xander pulled back onto the highway toward Miami. The truth was finally in our hands—a weapon we could use to right twelve years of wrongs.

Xander's phone rang through the car's speakers, interrupting our strategizing. Ben Carter's name flashed on the display.

"Hey, Ben, what's up?" Xander answered casually.

"Xander! Oh thank god." Ben's voice was breathless with panic. "I need help. It's Diego—they took him!"

My stomach dropped at the fear in Ben's voice.

"Whoa, slow down," Xander said, immediately alert. "Who took Diego?"

"These guys he owes money to—he's into them for like two hundred grand from gambling. They took him from the penthouse parking lot. There were three guys... they forced him into a van."

Xander's knuckles whitened on the steering wheel. "Have you called the police?"

"These guys will kill him if the cops show up." Ben's voice

cracked. "But I heard one of them mention El Santuario. It's this place in the industrial district where they run these high-stakes games. Diego wanted to take me there once. But I told him I didn't gamble."

"Text me the address," Xander said without hesitation. "I'll meet you there."

He ended the call and I stared at him in disbelief. "You're not actually thinking of going there."

"I have to." His voice was quiet but firm.

"This is crazy! These people kidnap guys over gambling debts," I said, staring at the address. "We should call the police. Let them handle it."

"The police won't get there in time," Xander said, his voice grim. "And they won't have the leverage I might have."

"What leverage?"

"I'm Xander McCrae," he said simply. "I'm famous in latin circles. You know how they love football. I'm valuable. These guys might be criminals, but they're still smart enough to know that killing or kidnapping a high-profile world-class player brings the wrong kind of attention."

I wanted to argue, wanted to point out all the ways his plan could go wrong. But I could see the determination in his eyes. He wasn't about to fail to save a teammate, no matter how much he disliked the man.

"Then I'm coming with you," I said.

"Absolutely not."

"You need backup," I insisted. "You need someone with medical training in case Diego is hurt."

Xander looked like he wanted to argue, but another glance at his phone—probably another panicked text from Ben—changed his mind.

"You stay in the car," he said finally. "No matter what happens, you stay in the car and you call 911 if things go bad."

I nodded, though we both knew that if things went bad enough to require police intervention, it would probably be too late for all of us.

Xander accelerated toward the industrial district, the precious folder secure in my lap. My father's reckoning would have to wait—but it was coming.

CHAPTER
Twenty~Five

XANDER

I FOCUSED on the road ahead, the tension from the warehouse visit coiling inside me. Ben's text with the address sent us speeding through Miami's backstreets toward the industrial district. Twelve minutes. That's how long Google Maps said it would take to reach this place called "El Santuario." Twelve minutes that could determine whether Diego lived or died.

The irony wasn't lost on me. Not long ago, I punched Diego in the face. Now I was racing to save him from God knows what.

"This is insane," Tara said, clutching the folder with Morrison's notes to her chest. "These people are dangerous enough to kidnap someone in broad daylight."

"I know." I pressed harder on the accelerator as the light ahead turned yellow.

"And your plan is to just... what? Walk in there and ask nicely for them to let him go?"

"Something like that," I said, shooting through the intersection as the light turned red, earning an angry honk from a delivery truck.

Her fingers dug into my arm. "Xander, these aren't people you can charm your way past."

"Good," I said, taking a sharp right turn that had Tara bracing herself against the door. "Because I'm not going to try and charm them. I'm going to make them an offer."

"What kind of offer? You want to pay off Diego's debt? It could be hundreds of thousands. These guys deal in cash only. You don't have immediate access to that much in cash, do you?"

"It's not about cash." I glanced at her, my mind racing, a wild idea starting to form. "Men like this, they deal in a different kind of currency. Power, respect, status... I just need to figure out what they want more than Diego's money."

She fell silent, and I knew she was calculating the odds, weighing variables like she always did.

My phone pinged with another text from Ben: *Hurry. I'm outside. Back entrance, like you said.*

We'd pulled over briefly so I could call him back, instructing him to wait at the building's rear entrance rather than going in alone. One hostage was enough.

The GPS directed us into a section of Miami most tourists never see—a labyrinth of warehouses, truck depots, and industrial parks sitting under the constant hum of the airport flight path. The buildings here were utilitarian, sun-bleached concrete boxes with minimal signage and barred windows.

"That must be it," Tara said, pointing to a nondescript building at the end of a dead-end street. No signs, just a gray box with a loading dock and a bunch of cars parked out front like vultures.

I pulled over a block away, killed the engine, and turned to face her in the sudden silence. "Okay. You stay in the car."

"Xander—"

"I mean it, Tara." I took her face in my hands, my thumbs resting on her cheekbones, forcing her to meet my eyes. "This isn't a game. If I'm not back in thirty minutes, or if you hear anything that sounds wrong, you call 911. Not your father, not the team—911. Got it?"

Her eyes flashed with that familiar fire I was coming to know so well. "Thirty minutes," she said, her voice steady and leaving no room for argument. "Then I'm calling the police, and I'm coming in after you."

"No. Absolutely not," I started to say, the words a knee-jerk reaction. "Under no circumstances are you to come in there. That's an order."

It was useless. I saw it the moment the words left my mouth. She didn't even have to say anything. The slight lift of her chin, the narrowing of her eyes—it was a look of such absolute, unshakeable defiance that I knew I'd have better luck arguing with the tide. This woman, who had meticulously plotted my downfall for twelve years, was now prepared to walk into a nest of gangsters for me without a second's hesitation.

And in that moment, staring at her stubborn, determined face, a wave of something fierce and protective crashed over me. I loved her for it. I loved that fire. I wouldn't have her any other way.

A small, humorless smile touched my lips. Of course she wouldn't just sit here. "Okay," I breathed out, the argument dying before it began. "Deal."

I leaned in and kissed her, hard and fast, trying to pour everything I couldn't say—*be safe, I love you, don't do anything stupid*—into it. When I pulled back, her eyes were wide, her lips slightly parted.

"Be careful," she whispered.

"Always am."

It was the biggest lie I'd ever told, and we both knew it.

I left the keys with her and jogged the remaining block to El Santuario. Ben was pacing nervously by a metal door at the rear of the building, his face pale in the harsh afternoon sun.

"Thank God," he breathed when he saw me. "I thought you weren't coming."

"I said I would." I clasped his shoulder. "Tell me every-thing you know about this place."

Ben swallowed hard. "It's called El Santuario, or The Sanc-tuary. High-stakes gambling, mostly. Cash only. Diego said the buy-in starts at ten grand."

"Who runs it?"

"Some guy named Torres. Vicente Torres. Diego said he's connected, you know? Like, South American mob connected."

Perfect. Just perfect.

"You don't have to come in with me," I told him. "In fact, it's probably better if you wait out here."

Ben shook his head. "No way. Diego's an asshole, but he's my teammate. I'm coming."

I studied him—this twenty-two year old kid, willing to walk into danger for a guy who probably treated him like dirt. His loyalty was admirable, if misplaced.

"Fine. But you follow my lead. Don't speak unless I tell you to. Understand?"

He nodded, and I pulled open the heavy metal door. It opened into a dimly lit hallway that smelled of cigarettes and bleach. A bulky man in a black suit stepped forward, hand moving instinctively to what I assumed was a concealed weapon.

"Private establishment," he said flatly. "Members only."

I straightened to my full height, meeting his gaze directly. "I'm Xander McCrae. I'm here to see Vicente Torres."

Recognition flickered in his eyes, but his expression remained impassive. "Regarding?"

"A business proposition. One that solves his Diego Mano problem."

The guard studied me for a moment, then touched his earpiece, murmuring something I couldn't catch. After a brief pause, he nodded.

"Follow me. Your friend stays here."

"He comes with me," I said firmly.

The guard hesitated, then shrugged. "Your funeral."

He led us down the hallway and through another door that opened into an upscale gambling den. Rows of tables where well-dressed men and women played poker, blackjack, and other games I didn't recognize. A polished bar stretched along one wall, and private booths lined another.

Our escort guided us past the main floor toward a hallway in the back. I could feel Ben's nervous energy beside me, his breathing shallow and quick. I kept my pace measured, my expression neutral. Whatever was waiting for us, showing fear wouldn't help.

The hallway led to a door marked simply "Office." The guard knocked twice before opening it.

The room beyond was surprisingly tasteful—more executive suite than mob boss lair. Leather furniture, dark wood bookshelves, and abstract art on the walls. The man behind the large desk stood as we entered, buttoning his tailored suit jacket.

The man who met us was shorter than I expected, maybe five-nine, with salt-and-pepper hair and the build of someone who still made time for the gym. He was handsome in a weathered way, with laugh lines around his eyes. This was Vicente Torres, and the moment I walked into his office, his entire demeanor changed.

A slow, appreciative smile spread across his face. "Xander McCrae," he said, his voice carrying a hint of an accent and a surprising amount of warmth. He extended a hand. "As I live and breathe. My men just told me you were here, but I didn't quite believe it. Welcome."

His handshake was firm, confident. This wasn't a man sizing me up; this was a fan meeting a legend. He completely ignored Ben Carter standing beside me.

It was only then that I saw Diego.

He was zip-tied to a chair in the corner of the room, his face a bloody, swollen mess. One eye was puffed shut, his lip was split, and his expensive shirt was torn and stained. He looked up with his one good eye, disbelief and a flicker of hope breaking through the pain. "McCrae?" he croaked.

"Quiet," snapped one of the two bulldozers flanking him.

Torres didn't even glance in Diego's direction. His focus was entirely on me. "Please, sit," he said, gesturing to the leather chairs in front of his immaculate desk. "To what do I owe the pleasure? I admit, I was surprised to hear you were interested in the affairs of this… *Colombiano.*" The way he said it made Diego sound like a piece of discount furniture.

"We're teammates," I said simply, taking a seat.

"Of course." Torres nodded, leaning back in his chair. The mask of the fan slipped slightly, revealing the businessman beneath. "A noble sentiment. But his debt is substantial. Two hundred and thirty-five thousand, to be exact. A sum I require today."

While he spoke, my eyes scanned his desk. It was minimalist, organized, but one thing stood out: a single, ornate silver photo frame, angled so he could see it. From my vantage point, I could just make out Torres with his arm around a teenage girl. A girl wearing a brand new, authentic Miami Pirates jersey.

Jackpot.

"I'm not here to pay his debt in cash," I said, leaning forward. "I have a proposition I think you'll find far more valuable."

Torres's eyes narrowed, a flicker of professional interest replacing the fanboy excitement. "I'm listening."

"You have a daughter," I said, nodding toward the photo.

His posture went rigid, his hand instinctively moving to shield the frame. "My family is not part of my business, Mr. McCrae."

"Of course not," I agreed smoothly. "But I couldn't help but notice she's a fan."

The tension in his shoulders eased. A proud, paternal smile transformed his face. "Sofia. My Sofia. She is... passionate. Plays midfielder for her high school. Thinks she's the next big thing."

"And she has a birthday soon?" I guessed, seeing the youthful glow on her face. "Big party planned?"

Surprise, then dawning understanding, flashed across his face. "Next month. Her quinceañera. Her mother has been planning it for a year. It's costing me a fortune." He paused, the pieces clicking into place. "You're offering to show up at my daughter's party?"

I leaned back, letting the idea sink in. "Not just show up.

I'll be the guest of honor. I'll take pictures, sign autographs, dance with her if that's the tradition. I will give her a night her friends will be talking about until their own kids' quinceañeras."

From the corner, Diego made a choked, disbelieving sound. Torres didn't even register it. He was lost in thought, the mob boss and the doting father at war behind his eyes.

"Mr. Torres," I pressed, going in for the kill. "You can get your pound of flesh from him," I gestured to Diego, "and it's just another Tuesday. Or... you can give your daughter something no amount of money can ever buy. You can be the dad who made her ultimate dream come true. You can be a legend to her."

He was silent for a long moment, his gaze distant. "She has been talking about your transfer for a month," he admitted softly. "Bought your jersey the day it was released, just before it sold out. Convinced me to get season tickets."

"Then you know what this is worth," I said.

He looked at Diego, then back at me. Finally, he burst out laughing, a loud, genuine sound that filled the room. He stood and extended his hand again. "Deal, Mr. McCrae. My wife will be in touch about the details for Sofia's party."

I shook it, relief washing over me so fast I felt light-headed. "Looking forward to it."

Torres nodded to his men. "Cut him loose. Get him out of here." To me, he said, "Mr. Mano is, of course, no longer welcome here. But tell him he is lucky. Loyalty like yours is rare." He gave Diego a look of pure dismissal. "He should find a way to repay it."

We made our way back through the club, Diego leaning heavily on Ben and me. The patrons barely glanced at us this time, returning to their games as if nothing unusual had happened. The same guard escorted us to the exit, his face expressionless as he held the door open.

The bright sun was blinding after the dim interior of the club. I squinted, scanning the street until I spotted our car a block away. Tara was in the driver's seat, her posture tense as she watched us approach.

She jumped out when she saw Diego's condition. "Jesus Christ," she breathed, her doctor's instincts taking over. "Get him in the back seat. I need to check those injuries."

We maneuvered Diego into the car, where Tara began examining his face with a practiced, gentle touch. "Looks worse than it is," she pronounced after a moment. "Contusions, possible hairline fracture of the cheekbone. You'll need X-rays." She paused, her fingers gently probing his mouth. "And you've split your lip. Again."

The pointed remark hung in the air. Diego flinched, but not from her touch. He wouldn't meet my eyes. "Appreciate it, Doc," he mumbled.

Ben fidgeted nervously by the car. "Should I drive him to the ER?"

"I've got him," Tara said. "Let's take him to your penthouse, Xander, and I can clean the wounds."

I nodded. "Ben, take Diego in your car, and follow us. I'll ride with Tara."

We pulled into the parking garage beneath my penthouse building. Ben parked beside us, then helped Diego out of the car. Despite Tara's assessment that his injuries weren't life-threatening, he still looked like hell—battered, exhausted, and defeated.

"Let's get him upstairs," I said.

The elevator ride to the penthouse was a study in tense silence. Diego leaned against the mirrored wall, his good eye closed, looking like a man who had just seen the end of his world. Ben stood by his side, a silent, worried guardian. When the doors finally slid open, Leo was waiting. His face shifted from relief at seeing me to controlled shock at the sight of Diego.

"What the—"

"Long story," I cut him off. "Can you get an ice pack and the first aid kit?"

Leo nodded once, disappearing toward the kitchen as Ben and I guided Diego to the large leather couch. He sank into it with a groan, his head falling back against the cushions.

Tara had already followed Leo, and she returned with the kit and a bowl of warm water. She knelt in front of the couch, her movements efficient and all business.

I stood over them, crossing my arms. "You owe me an explanation, Mano."

Diego's good eye fluttered open. The shame in it was a foreign look on him. "I know," he rasped. "First thing tomorrow, I'm withdrawing the police report. From the other day." He shook his head, a pained, self-deprecating motion. "I had it coming. I provoked you."

He then shifted his gaze to Tara, and the usual arrogance was completely gone, replaced by a raw, genuine remorse. "And Dr. Swanson... Tara... I'm sorry. For the way I've been acting. The things I said to you, to him about you... there's no excuse. It was bullshit."

Tara paused in her work, her eyes meeting his. She simply nodded. "Apology accepted, Diego."

The apology hung in the air, a fragile truce. It didn't explain nearly enough.

"It wasn't just you, was it?" Tara asked, her voice quiet but sharp as she started cleaning a cut on his cheek. "The provocations, the hostility. It felt... organized. Who was paying you, Diego?"

His eye widened slightly. He looked from her to me. "How did you know?"

"We know more than you think," I said grimly. "Start talking."

Diego let out a long, shuddering sigh of defeat. "It started when I got here. I got in deep with some bookies... sports betting. Thought I had some inside track, but it just kept going wrong. Suddenly I owed fifty grand. Then a hundred."

"And Hank found out," I guessed, the pieces clicking into place.

Diego nodded. "Don't know how, but he knew everything. Called me into his office, laid out every single one of my debts, and offered me a deal. He'd cover all my payments if I'd do him a 'favor'."

"Make my life hell," I said flatly.

"Yeah." He had the decency to look ashamed. "He wanted me to get under your skin. Provoke you in practice, talk shit to the press, make you look like the out-of-control hothead everyone already thought you were. He said he needed to show Tara what kind of man you *really* were. If I could get you to break, get her to finally dump you, he'd wipe the entire debt clean."

Tara's hands stilled for a fraction of a second, her knuckles white around the gauze. "And you agreed."

"I was desperate," Diego said, his voice pleading. "And it wasn't like I had to fake not liking you, McCrae. You came in with the big contract, taking all the attention. It was easy to hate you."

"So why did Torres's men grab you today?" Tara asked, her voice devoid of emotion as she resumed her work.

Diego's face darkened. "Hank said I wasn't delivering. That you two were getting closer instead of falling apart. He said you weren't breaking like he wanted." He shrugged, a gesture of futility. "He stopped paying my markers. Told me I was on my own."

"But your signing bonus was worth over a million," Tara pressed, voicing the question I was thinking. "Why not just pay the debt yourself?"

Diego's gaze dropped to the floor. "Back home... in Colombia... I owed some people. The kind of people you don't say no to. They took everything before I even left the country."

The room fell silent as we all processed the depth of the manipulation. Leo, who had been listening from the kitchen doorway, was the first to speak.

"So Hank orchestrated this whole thing—bringing Xander to Miami, paying off his own player to harass him—all to prove a point to Tara?"

"That's what he said," Diego confirmed. "He wanted to show her that the man she was obsessed with was nothing special. Just another self-destructive party boy who'd crash and burn."

Tara's face had gone pale, her hands trembling slightly as she finished bandaging Diego's cuts. I reached over and took the gauze from her, our fingers brushing.

"He underestimated both of us," I said quietly.

She met my eyes, and I saw the shock in them harden into pure steel. "Yes," she said. "He did."

Diego looked between us, a slow, dawning realization on his battered face. "You two are actually together, aren't you? Not just hooking up. I mean, like... real."

"Yes," Tara said simply. "We are."

Diego leaned his head back, a strange, pained laugh escaping him. "Damn. The old man really miscalculated."

"He did more than that," I said grimly. "He broke the law. Multiple laws. And now we have a witness."

"What're you going to do?" Diego asked, his voice barely a whisper.

I looked at Tara, letting her answer.

"We're going to expose him," she said, her voice steady and certain. "For everything. The bribery, the cover-up of my brother's death, the manipulation, the harassment. All of it."

Diego's eye widened. "He'll destroy you both. He has connections everywhere."

"Not after we're done," Tara said. She stood, gathering the bloody supplies. "Ben, can you take him to the hospital now? He needs those X-rays, and we have work to do."

Ben, who looked like he'd just watched a multi-car pile-up, finally moved, helping Diego to his feet. At the door, Diego paused and turned back to me.

"Why did you do it?" he asked. "Why risk your life for me when I've been nothing but an asshole to you?"

"Because I'm tired of watching people get hurt when I can do something about it," I said.

Diego nodded slowly, a flicker of true understanding in his eye. "I owe you. Whatever you need against Hank, I'll testify. I'll put it in writing. Whatever it takes."

"We'll be in touch," Tara said, holding the door open for them.

After they left, the penthouse felt suddenly quiet. Leo busied himself cleaning up while Tara and I stood in the center of the living room, the full weight of what we'd learned settling over us.

"Your father did all of this," I said finally. "Just to prove to you that I wasn't worth your... what did Diego call it? Your obsession?"

Tara's jaw tightened. "He's been controlling my life for as long as I can remember. This is just the most elaborate version of it."

"What now?" Leo asked, returning from the kitchen.

Tara's eyes met mine, and I saw in them a determination that matched my own. "Now we end this," she said. "Once and for all."

CHAPTER
Twenty-Six

TARA

I STOOD in the center of Xander's living room, the adrenaline from Diego's confession still singing in my veins. The lies were all out, a tangled, ugly mess on the floor. Now, it was time to clean them up.

"I need a drink," I announced, not to anyone in particular, and strode to the kitchen. I bypassed the whiskey and pulled a bottle of sparkling water from the fridge. I didn't need to be numb; I needed to be sharp. My hands were perfectly steady as I twisted the cap off.

The cold bite of the water grounded me. I leaned against the counter, watching Xander pace like a caged animal.

"We have him," he said, turning to me, his eyes blazing. "Morrison's notes, Diego's testimony... We can finally end this."

I took a long, deliberate swallow. "Can we?"

He stopped pacing. "What do you mean?"

"I mean, let's look at our hand, Xander," I said, setting the bottle down with a sharp click. "We have the word of a disgraced, bribe-taking cop and a gambling addict who was on my father's payroll. In a courtroom, Hank's lawyers would shred them before lunch. It's not enough."

Leo, who had been watching silently from an armchair, gave a grim nod. "She's right. It's a mess, but it's not checkmate."

"Then what the hell do we do?" Xander demanded, frustration cracking his voice.

I pushed off the counter and walked to the massive wall of windows. Miami glittered below, a city built on ambition and secrets. My father's city.

"We need something irrefutable," I said, my voice low. "Something his money can't bury and his lawyers can't spin." I turned back to face them, the plan fully formed, cold and clear in my mind. "We need him to confess."

Xander stared at me. "Confess? To who? He's not going to just offer it up."

"Not to you," I said. "To me."

He took a step toward me, his face darkening. "You're talking about going to him alone."

"Yes."

"Absolutely not. It's too dangerous."

I raised an eyebrow. "This from the man who just walked into a mob den to rescue Diego?"

"That was different."

"How?" I challenged.

"Because Torres is a businessman with a code!" he shot back, his voice rising. "Your father is a monster who has spent twelve years trying to destroy my life while pretending to protect you. There is no code. There are no rules with him."

He was right, and that was exactly the point. I reached for

his hand, my touch calming him instantly. "He won't see this coming. His blind spot has always been me. He thinks he's won. He thinks he's finally broken us apart and that I'll come running back to him." I squeezed his hand. "He'll be so high on his own victory, so desperate to justify why he was right all along, he won't be able to stop himself from talking."

Leo cleared his throat. "And how do you prove it?"

I pulled my phone from my pocket and held it up. "I record him."

Xander was already shaking his head. "Tara, no. What if he finds it? What if he realizes it's a setup?"

"He won't," I said with a certainty that left no room for argument. "He has never, not once in my life, seen me as a threat. I'm just a daughter to be managed. That arrogance is the weapon we're going to use against him."

"There has to be another way," Xander insisted, his voice pleading.

"There isn't," I said gently, but firmly. "We can't go to the cops or the league. He owns them. This is our only shot, and we have to take it now, before he finds out Diego flipped."

A heavy silence fell over the room. I could see the war in Xander's eyes—the instinct to protect me fighting against the cold logic that I was right.

"I don't like it," he said finally, his voice rough.

"You don't have to like it. You just have to trust me."

He pulled me into a fierce, desperate hug, his arms a steel cage around me. "Be careful," he murmured into my hair. "If anything happens to you…"

I held onto him, drawing on his strength. "He's played his last card, Xander. Now it's my turn."

When he let me go, I saw the terror in his eyes, but underneath it, he was letting me do this. He was trusting *me* to handle it. It was a terrifying and beautiful thing, a love that didn't seek to control, but to empower.

"I'll call you the second it's over," I promised.

Leo gave me a quick, awkward hug. "Give him hell, Tara."

I walked toward the door, my purpose a shield around me. I flashed a grim smile over my shoulder. "That's the plan."

———

In my car, I rehearsed what I would say, how I would act. The key was to make my father believe he'd won without seeming too eager or compliant. A delicate balance—defeated enough to satisfy his ego, but not so broken that he'd be suspicious.

I pulled over a few blocks from my father's mansion and called him, my heart pounding as I waited for him to answer.

"Tara." His voice was cool, controlled—as always.

I took a deep breath and let it out slowly, then made my voice small and uncertain. "Dad, I... I need to see you."

A pause. "I thought you made your position quite clear the last time we spoke."

"I know. I'm sorry." The words tasted like ash in my mouth. "I've been confused about everything, and I... I need your help sorting it all out."

Another, longer pause. I could almost hear the gears turning in his head, weighing my sincerity, calculating the odds that this was a trap. Finally, he spoke.

"Come to the house. I'm in my study."

"I'll be there in twenty minutes," I said, relief—both genuine and performed—coloring my voice.

"I'll be waiting."

The line went dead. I sat for a moment, gathering myself. *First hurdle cleared.* He was suspicious alright—he wouldn't be

Hank Swanson if he wasn't—but his confidence in his ability to read and manipulate me had won out. Now came the hard part.

I drove the rest of the way to the mansion, rehearsing my lines, adjusting my demeanor. I had fully stepped into the role of the confused, vulnerable daughter seeking her father's guidance.

The security guard waved me through without question. I parked in front of the house, but before getting out, I opened the voice recording app on my phone and started it, then slipped the phone into the outer pocket of my purse where it would have the clearest access to pick up our conversation. I checked that the screen was locked so it wouldn't accidentally stop recording, then stepped out of the car.

The front door opened before I could ring the bell. Maria, my father's longtime housekeeper, greeted me with surprise and genuine warmth.

"Miss Tara! It's been too long."

I managed a small smile. "Hi, Maria. Is my father in his study?"

"Yes, yes. He's expecting you." She stepped aside to let me in, her eyes lingering on my face with concern. "Are you alright, mi niña? You look tired."

"Just a long day," I assured her, touched by her concern.

I made my way through the sprawling mansion, each step taking me deeper into the lion's den.

When I reached the study door, I hesitated, hand raised to knock. This was it. Once I stepped inside, there would be no turning back.

I knocked.

"Come in," my father called.

I entered the same room where, just a week ago, he had

caught me searching through his files. He was seated behind his desk, reading glasses perched on his nose, a stack of papers in front of him. He looked up as I entered, his expression carefully neutral.

"Tara. Have a seat."

I moved to one of the leather chairs facing his desk, perching on the edge rather than settling in.

"Thank you for seeing me," I said, keeping my voice soft, my eyes downcast.

He removed his glasses and set them aside, studying me with the penetrating gaze that had intimidated business rivals and league officials for decades. "You said you needed my help."

I nodded, fidgeting with the strap of my purse—partly for show, partly to ensure the phone was still recording. "I've been... overwhelmed. By everything that's happened."

"With McCrae, you mean."

I looked up, allowing some genuine pain to show in my eyes. "Yes. And with what I found in your files about Jimmy. And what Diego told us today."

A flicker of surprise crossed his face. "Diego spoke to you?"

Careful. I needed to give him enough information to open up, but not so much that he realized we had him cornered.

"He came to the facility," I said, sticking close to the truth. "He was... injured. Gambling debts. He said some things about you, about arrangements you had with him."

My father's expression hardened. "And you believed him? A man who can't control his own vices, who would say anything to shift blame?"

I shook my head. "I don't know what to believe anymore. That's why I'm here." I leaned forward, injecting desperation into my voice. "I need to understand, Dad. All of it. Jimmy's death, why you brought Xander to Miami, everything."

He studied me for a long moment, assessing. I held my breath, waiting.

Finally, he stood and moved to the side of the room where a small bar was set up. "Drink?"

"Just water, please."

He poured himself two fingers of scotch and a glass of water for me, then returned, handing me the water before leaning against the desk rather than sitting behind it. A calculated move to appear more approachable, more paternal.

"What exactly do you want to know?" he asked.

I took a sip of water, gathering my thoughts. "The truth," I said simply. "Jimmy committed suicide, didn't he? You bribed Detective Morrison to cover it up. And you paid Diego Mano to destroy Xander's career."

I stated it as fact, not accusation—a technique I'd learned from watching my father in negotiations. Make the other person deny rather than explain, and they're already on the defensive.

But he didn't deny it. Instead, he took a slow sip of his scotch, his eyes never leaving mine.

"You've figured it out," he said, and there was something almost like pride in his voice. "I always knew you were smart. Like your mother."

A chill ran through me. I hadn't expected him to admit it so easily.

"Why?" I asked.

He set his glass down, the crystal clicking softly against the marble coaster. It was the only sound in the cavernous room. "You were sixteen, Tara. A child. You had just lost your brother to suicide—a brother who, by all accounts, was happy and loved. Do you have any idea what that kind of death does to a family? The questions? The shame?"

"So you buried it," I said, the words sharp and brittle. "To protect the Swanson family name."

"No." He shook his head, a look of profound disappointment on his face, as if I'd missed the entire point. "I did it to protect *you*. To save you from a lifetime of wondering why you weren't enough to make him stay. I took the burden of that truth so you wouldn't have to carry it."

I swallowed against the acid rising in my throat. This was his genius, the cruelest part of his manipulation: twisting poison into medicine, making control look like sacrifice. The tears pricking my eyes were disgustingly real.

"And Xander?" I pushed, my voice tight. "Was destroying him for my protection, too?"

"Especially him." His voice hardened, losing its paternal softness. "I saw you at the funeral, Tara. I saw the way you looked at him. A seventeen-year-old boy already drowning himself in a bottle, and you were looking at him like he was a lifeboat. I knew, right then, that he was a disease, and I had to be the cure."

"So you made him a pariah," I said, the timeline of Xander's ruined life flashing before my eyes. "You drove him out of the country to keep us apart."

"I did what was necessary," he said, his tone utterly unapologetic. "And I was right. Look at what he became. An alcoholic with a new scandal every month. Was that the life you wanted?"

Breathe. Stay in character. Let him empty the clip.

"Then why bring him to Miami?" I asked, letting a note of genuine confusion color my voice. "If he was so toxic, why bring him right to my doorstep?"

A slow, reptilian smile spread across my father's face. It was the smile of a chess master explaining a winning move. "Because you never let him go. I watched you. I saw you tracking his career, his life." He paused, letting the next words land with surgical precision. "I've been in your apartment, Tara. I saw the wall."

The air rushed out of my lungs. My entire body went cold. He had been in my home. My private space. He had walked through my rooms, seen my life, and I had never known. The violation of it was so profound, so absolute, it was all I could do not to physically recoil.

"That..." he gestured dismissively with his hand, "*obsession... was* unhealthy. You were clinging to the ghost of a boy. I brought Xander here so you could finally see the man for what he is: a disappointment. I knew if I put him under enough pressure, the real him would crack."

"With a little push from Diego," I stated, the pieces clicking into place with nauseating clarity.

"Mano was a useful tool," he conceded with a shrug. "A necessary accelerant."

I stared at him, at this man who was my father, and felt nothing but a vast, empty chasm. "The lying, the bribery, the manipulation... ruining an innocent man's life. None of this bothers you?"

"Innocent?" He laughed, a short, barking sound that held no humor. "McCrae was never innocent. He may not have been driving, but he was drunk and reckless—the reason Jimmy was in that car. He deserved every single thing that happened to him."

"That wasn't your decision to make!" The words tore from me, louder than I intended.

"No?" He leaned forward, his eyes boring into mine, dark

and intense. "Then who protects you, Tara? Who makes sure men like that don't drag you down into their chaos? I do. It has always been my job to protect you from your worst impulses."

"I protect myself," I said, my voice low and dangerous.

He smiled that patronizing, infuriating smile. "You think you do. But you are still, and always will be, my daughter. You need my guidance."

This was it. The final piece. "So that's what this was?" I asked, my voice dropping to a near-whisper. "Bribing a cop, lying to me, orchestrating this entire, insane scheme... all of it... was just to guide me?"

"I did it all for you," he said, and the sincerity in his voice was the most terrifying thing I had ever heard. "So that you could become the woman you were meant to be, without the anchor of a broken man dragging you to the bottom."

He truly believed it. In the twisted architecture of his mind, he wasn't a villain. He was a hero. A father saving his daughter from herself.

I stood up slowly, my phone a heavy, righteous weight in my pocket. I had it. I had it all. But the victory felt like ashes in my mouth.

"I have to go," I said, my voice hollow.

"Tara." He stood, a flicker of uncertainty in his eyes for the first time. "I hope you understand. Everything I did..."

"Was for me," I finished for him. My voice was flat, dead. "I understand perfectly."

I turned and walked to the door, each step a deliberate act of will. My hand was on the cool brass of the doorknob when his voice came from behind me, sharp with a sudden fear.

"Where are you going?"

I paused, but I didn't turn around. To look at him again would be to legitimize his existence in my world.

"You're not my father," I said to the door. "You're just the man who ruined my life."

Then I opened it, walked out, and closed it quietly behind me, leaving him alone with the wreckage he had made.

I walked through the mansion on legs that felt like they might give way at any moment. Maria called something to me as I passed, but I couldn't process her words through the roaring in my ears.

Somehow I made it to my car. I slid into the driver's seat and sat there, staring blankly at the imposing facade of the house, the home that had never felt like one.

With trembling fingers, I reached into my purse and pulled out my phone. The recording app was still running, the timer showing it had captured every word of our conversation. I stopped it and saved the file, then sat staring at the screen.

In my hand, I held the weapon that would destroy my father. Justice for Jimmy, vindication for Xander, freedom for myself—all contained in a simple audio file.

I should have felt triumphant. Instead, I felt hollow, scraped raw by the realization that my father's love—the one constant I had always counted on, even when I disagreed with his methods—was nothing but another form of control.

My vision blurred with unshed tears as I started the car. I had what we needed. It was time to end this, once and for all.

CHAPTER
Twenty~Seven

XANDER

MY NERVES WERE FUCKING SHOT.

For the third time in ten minutes, I paced my penthouse living room, from kitchen island to the windows. Leo perched on a barstool, pretending to care about his phone instead of my mental breakdown.

"She should've called by now," I said, checking my watch again. "It's been almost two hours."

Leo glanced up. "She said she'd call when it was done."

"What if something went wrong?" My words stuck like peanut butter. "What if Hank figured her out? What if—"

"Xander." Leo cut me off. "Tara knows her shit. She's not some helpless princess. She's a badass with a plan."

He was right, but my brain kept playing disaster movies starring Tara and her father. I'd faced Diego Mano's mobsters yesterday, but Tara alone with her dad froze my blood in ways Torres's goons couldn't touch.

"Should've gone with her," I muttered.

"And done what?" Leo dropped his phone. "Hidden in the bushes? Climbed the walls like Spiderman? Get real."

My phone buzzed. I pounced on it.

On my way. I got it.

Relief hit me, and I collapsed onto the nearest chair.

"She did it," I told Leo, my voice tiny. "She got the confession."

Leo's eyebrows jumped. "Holy shit. She actually pulled it off."

"Never doubted her," I lied, suddenly floating.

"Bullshit. You nearly wore through your shoes," Leo fired back, grinning.

The next twenty minutes dragged on like a snail race. I tried emails, social media, anything to avoid staring at the door. Failed miserably.

When the knock came, I nearly broke my neck getting there. I yanked it open to find Tara—pale but fierce-eyed.

"You did it," I said, pulling her inside and against me in one move.

She held on tight, shaking slightly. When she stepped back, her face told the real story.

"I'm okay," she said, glancing past me to Leo. "I got everything. The confession, Morrison, Brittany, Diego—all of it."

"Let's hear it," Leo said, suddenly serious.

Tara pulled out her phone. We moved to the couch while she remained standing, too wired to sit.

"Fair warning," she said, finger hovering over play, "this is fucked up."

I grabbed her hand. "We're in this together."

The recording started with background noise, then Hank's voice. As I listened to him casually admit to bribing Detective

Morrison, framing me, and orchestrating my Miami return just to destroy me, my stomach twisted.

"I did it all for you, Tara."

When it ended, we sat in shocked silence.

"Jesus Christ," Leo finally muttered.

I couldn't speak. A decade of guilt and self-destruction—all because of this twisted fuck and his warped idea of fatherly love.

"It's enough, right?" Tara asked. "To prove what he did?"

I nodded. "It's a goddamn smoking gun."

"So where do we go from here?" Leo asked. "Cops?"

Tara shook her head. "He owns half the department."

"The league then," I suggested. "MLS ethics committee?"

"Same problem," Tara countered. "Too many connections. He'd bury us in legal bullshit for years."

She was right. Hank didn't get where he was playing fair.

"Then what?" I asked, frustration bubbling up. "What good is the truth if nobody will hear it?"

Leo straightened suddenly. "We go public."

We both turned to him.

"How?" Tara asked.

"Fuck official channels. We create a media shitstorm too big to contain."

The idea terrified and excited me. "How would that even work?"

Leo's eyes lit up. "I know journalists who'd kill for this dirt. Give them everything and watch it explode. Once it's out, Hank can't control it."

"Career suicide," Tara said quietly.

"Not if we control the story," Leo argued. "You're the whistleblower who exposed daddy's corruption. That makes you the hero."

I looked at Tara. "Your call. Your father."

She thought for a moment, then met my eyes. "He stopped being my father when he chose his reputation over Jimmy's truth. Over us." Her voice hardened. "Let's burn him down."

Leo grabbed his phone. "I know exactly who to call."

———

The next twenty-four hours were a blur. Leo, in full crisis-manager mode, set up a meet with a journalist named Gabriela Reyes.

"She's the one," he said as we drove to some quiet, upscale joint in Coral Gables. "Big-time investigative reporter. Wrote a piece a few years back questioning Hank's business practices, and he got her blackballed from some local circles."

Tara was sitting beside me in the back seat, her knee pressed against mine. "So she has a grudge," she said.

"So she'll be thorough," Leo corrected. "She won't run with a story this big unless it's bulletproof. And ours is."

Tara squeezed my hand, her touch sending a jolt of electricity straight through me. "You ready for this?" she asked, her voice low, just for me. "Once this door opens, it doesn't close."

I looked at her. At this woman who had been a ghost in my past, then the architect of my present, and now… now she was the only thing that felt real for the future. The only thing I wasn't willing to lose.

"For an eternity, I've been running from that night," I said, my voice rough. "I'm done running."

The restaurant was quiet. The host led us to a private room where a woman with sharp, intelligent eyes was waiting. She looked like she could smell bullshit from a mile away.

"Ms. Reyes," Leo said.

She nodded at him, but her eyes were on us. "Dr. Swanson. Mr. McCrae. Leo says you have a story that's going to make my year."

We sat, and for the next two hours, we let it all spill out. The whole damn, ugly, fucked-up saga. Tara laid out the timeline, and I filled in the gaps with the raw, messy emotion of it. Gabriela just listened, her expression unreadable, occasionally cutting in with a question so sharp it could draw blood.

When we finally finished, the silence in the room was deafening.

"That," she said, leaning back in her chair, "is one hell of an allegation."

"It's the truth," I said, maybe a little too forcefully.

"Proof?"

Tara slid a small USB drive across the polished table. It looked tiny and insignificant, but it was a damn bomb. "It's all on there," she said, her voice pure steel. "The recording of my father's full confession. Morrison's original notes on Jimmy's death. A sworn affidavit from Diego Mano detailing the harassment campaign. And financial records proving the payments to Brittany Ashworth."

Tara had snapped a picture of a receipt before her father busted her in his study. Turned out to be the smoking gun payment to Brittany. Cory tracked the money trail perfectly.

Gabriela picked up the drive. "You understand what you're doing, right? This doesn't just burn your father. It could burn the whole team. It will definitely burn you." She looked from me to Tara. "You ready for the hurricane?"

I didn't have to think. I looked at Tara, at the unshakeable strength in her eyes, and felt my own resolve harden. We were in this together. That was the only thing that mattered.

"Let it rain," I said.

She tucked the drive into her bag. "I'll need to verify everything, of course."

"Of course," Leo said.

"If this all checks out…" She let out a low whistle. "This is the kind of story that ends careers. Plural." She held our gaze. "I'll ask you one last time. This is going to be a media tsunami. Your lives will be picked apart by strangers. Are you absolutely sure?"

"What we want," Tara said, her voice steady and clear, "is for the truth to come out. For my brother finally getting peace."

I reached for her hand under the table, our fingers lacing together. A silent promise. Whatever came next, we'd face it.

Gabriela nodded, a flicker of something like respect in her eyes. "I'll be in touch. Soon."

The call came three days later. Three days of living on a knife's edge, of every phone buzz sending a jolt through my system. Three days of Tara and me existing in our own bubble, a pocket of calm before the hurricane we had summoned.

"It's done," Gabriela told me, her voice all business. "Story goes live tomorrow morning. 6 AM sharp. It's going to be a firestorm."

I ended the call, my heart hammering against my ribs. *The point of no return.*

I called Tara immediately. "It's happening," was all I had to say.

"I'm on my way," she said.

By nightfall, the penthouse had become our command

center. Leo brought takeout, but none of us had much of an appetite. The air was thick with a strange, electric tension—the feeling of standing on a cliff, about to jump.

Around midnight, when the silence had stretched too long, Tara's voice cut through it. "I keep thinking about Jimmy," she said softly.

I found her hand in the dark. "He'd be proud of you, Tara. For fighting for the truth."

"I just wish..." Her voice broke. "I wish I'd known how much he was hurting."

I pulled her into my arms, her head fitting perfectly under my chin. "Hey. You were a kid. His sickness was never your fault." I felt her nod against my chest. "And I've been blaming myself for a choice he made. We've both been carrying ghosts that weren't ours to hold."

We didn't sleep much. We just held each other, a silent promise that whatever came with the dawn, we'd face it together.

It felt like I'd just closed my eyes when Leo was banging on the door. "It's 5:45. Time to go."

We stumbled into the living room. Leo had ESPN on, the volume low. Tara's hand found mine, her grip so tight I could feel her pulse, a frantic rhythm that matched my own. The seconds ticked by like hours. 5:58... 5:59...

And then, at 6:00 AM, the world exploded.

The morning anchor's face filled the screen, her expression grim. "We begin with a breaking story sending shockwaves through the world of professional sports. An exclusive ESPN investigation has uncovered a decade-long conspiracy of bribery and manipulation orchestrated by Miami Pirates FC owner, Hank Swanson..."

The first headline scrolled across the bottom of the screen:

ALEXANDER MCCRAE VINDICATED IN 2013 FATAL
ACCIDENT.

The words blurred. A sound escaped my throat, something between a laugh and a sob. Twelve years. Twelve years of carrying the weight of being a killer, of believing I had stolen my best friend's life. And in a single sentence, it was gone.

Tara squeezed my hand, her eyes shining with tears as she looked at me.

On screen, they showed a picture of a younger, smiling Jimmy, then cut to the recording of Hank's voice, cold and clear, filling the room. *"I covered it up to protect you. From the pain of knowing your brother chose to leave you."*

A small, wounded sound escaped Tara's lips, and I pulled her tight against my side, a white-hot rage flaring on her behalf.

The anchor continued, "The recording also contains Swanson's confession that he orchestrated McCrae's multi-million-dollar transfer to Miami not to improve the team, but as part of a cruel, elaborate scheme to destroy McCrae's reputation and permanently separate him from his daughter…"

My phone, sitting on the coffee table, began to vibrate. Then it didn't stop. It buzzed and lit up with a relentless flood of notifications, a tidal wave of texts and calls. The story was everywhere. My brother Sean. Cory. Teammates. Old friends from London.

Leo turned up the volume. "The league has announced an emergency meeting… major sponsors are releasing statements…"

He looked up from his own phone, a grim smile on his face. "It's working. It's too big to kill. Every major outlet has it. It's the number one trend worldwide."

I looked at Tara. Her face was a canvas of conflicting

emotions—grief for the father she thought she had, relief for the truth, and a fierce, undeniable strength.

"You okay?" I asked softly.

She nodded, a single tear tracing a path down her cheek. "He can't hurt us anymore."

The story kept unfolding. Gabriela had done her homework. They detailed the payments to Diego. They ran a deep dive into Brittany Ashworth's history, complete with a photo of her and the baby's actual father, exposing the paternity scheme as just another one of Hank's vicious little plots.

My phone buzzed with a text. It was from Ben Carter. *The whole team's talking. We got your back, man. Always did.*

Another came through from a number I didn't recognize, but the message was unmistakable. Diego. *I owe you. I'll make it right.*

The truth was out. All of it. The weight wasn't just lifted; it was annihilated. Hank's empire was crumbling on live television, and in its place, Tara and I were finally free to build our own future.

CHAPTER

Twenty-Eight

TARA

I WOKE to the sound of my phone having a full-blown panic attack on the nightstand.

It wasn't just a buzz. It was a relentless, percussive symphony of pings, dings, and vibrations. At 5:47 in the morning, the digital world was trying to break down my door.

I fumbled for the device, my eyes bleary. CHLOE was flashing across the screen in all caps, which was her permanent setting. I took a deep breath, braced myself, and answered.

"Before you say a word," she began, her voice a whirlwind of crackling energy, "I've already texted the gallery and told them I'm having an 'acute spiritual crisis' and can't come in. Then I went to that vegan bakery you love and got a dozen of those cinnamon things that are basically just sugar held together by hope. I'm five minutes from your place with oat milk lattes and an industrial-sized bottle of moral support. Open the damn door."

A laugh bubbled up from my chest, a weird, hysterical

sound I didn't recognize. "Have I told you lately you're my soulmate?"

"Not nearly enough," she replied breezily. "You're my muse for a new tragic heroine series I'm working on, so this is technically a business expense. Four minutes. Pants are optional but encouraged."

She hung up. I dragged myself out of bed and into the strange, quiet apartment. It felt like it belonged to someone else now—a woman whose life hadn't just been detonated and reassembled on national television.

The buzzer shrieked, and I let her in. Thirty seconds later, Chloe exploded through my door. She was a riot of color—purple hair a chaotic halo, a paint-splattered denim jacket, and arms overflowing with a bakery box, a tray of coffees, and what looked like a large, lumpy sculpture wrapped in burlap.

"Holy fucking shit, Tara," she declared, dropping everything onto my kitchen counter with a loud thud. She grabbed me and pulled me into a hug that smelled like turpentine and cinnamon. "You magnificent, terrifying bitch. You burned it all down."

I hugged her back, clinging to her solid, vibrant presence. "Yeah," I whispered into her shoulder. "I guess I did."

She pulled back, her sharp artist's eyes scanning my face. "How are you? And don't you dare say 'fine.' 'Fine' is a beige color, and you are currently a Pollock painting of rage and vindication. So, give it to me."

"I'm…" I searched for the word. Not broken. Not fine. "I'm free," I said, the truth of it landing as I spoke the words aloud. "For the first time since Jimmy died, I'm actually, completely free."

Chloe's eyes went bright. "Damn right you are." She

shoved a coffee into my hands. "Now, sit. Tell me everything the news didn't. I want the behind-the-scenes director's cut."

As I talked, she unwrapped the lumpy sculpture. It was a grotesque, vaguely man-shaped clay head with a crown falling off. Your father, she explained, gesturing with a half-eaten cinnamon roll. I'm calling it 'The Patriarchy Eats Itself.' It's cathartic. I brought you a hammer. We can smash it later.

I told her everything—the storage unit, saving Diego, the chilling final confession in my father's study.

"So what now?" she asked when I'd finished. "With the smoldering remains of your father's empire, the team, and Sir Brooding McHottie?"

I sighed. "The league is taking over the team. My father is… gone. And Xander…" I trailed off. "We went through a war together. But what happens when the war is over? What if we're just a trauma bond? What if normal, quiet, boring life is something we can't actually do?"

Chloe rolled her eyes so hard I heard them click. "Tara, honey, listen to me. 'Normal' was never in the cards for you two. You built a literal serial-killer wall to him in your office. He flew across an ocean and walked into a mob den for you. This isn't a rom-com. It's a goddamn epic. Stop trying to shrink it down to fit in some boring little box." She leaned forward, her expression fierce. "I've seen the way he looks at you. That man is a goner. So maybe, for once, stop analyzing the brushstrokes and just enjoy the damn painting?"

My phone buzzed, saving me from having to answer. It was a video link from the team's official social media. Diego's bruised but resolute face filled the screen.

"…Everything in those reports about Hank Swanson is true," he was saying. "Xander is a great player and a better man. He saved my life when he had every reason not to. I'm telling the truth to start repaying a debt I'll never be able to fully square."

The video ended.

"Well, look at that," Chloe said, grabbing the burlap-wrapped head. "The dominoes are falling, and the patriarchy is about to meet its maker." She handed me a small mallet from her tote bag. "Your turn first."

I looked at the ugly clay head, at the hammer in my hand, and for the first time all morning, I smiled. A real, genuine smile. Maybe she was right. Maybe it was time to smash a few things and let myself be happy.

———

By noon, three major sponsors had announced they were pulling out of their deals with the Miami Pirates FC, citing ethical concerns. The league had appointed an interim management team to oversee the club while Hank was under investigation. The local news was reporting that my father had been seen leaving his mansion with suitcases, destination unknown.

It was surreal, watching it all unfold from the quiet isolation of my apartment. The man who had controlled so much of my life, who had manipulated and lied and schemed to keep me under his thumb, was being systematically stripped of his power, his reputation, his empire.

And I felt... nothing. Not satisfaction or vindication or even anger. Just a profound emptiness where those emotions should have been. As if my father had become a stranger, someone whose fate no longer affected me.

My phone rang—Xander.

"Hey," I said, my voice softening automatically at the

sound of his.

"Hey yourself," he replied, and I could hear the smile in his voice. "How are you holding up?"

"Honestly? I have no idea. It's all so... overwhelming."

"I know." He paused, and I could picture him running a hand through his hair the way he did when he was gathering his thoughts. "Listen, I was thinking... do you remember that morning we met to run? When we first decided to work together?"

"Of course." How could I forget? It had been the beginning of everything—our partnership, our reconciliation, our journey toward the truth.

"Meet me there," he said simply. "At South Pointe Park. Same spot, sunrise tomorrow. Just you and me, away from all this madness. We need to talk."

My heart stuttered in my chest. *We need to talk.* Those four words that never preceded anything good in the history of relationships. But no—I was being paranoid. After everything we'd been through, Xander wouldn't bring me to a meaningful place just to end things. Would he?

"I'll be there," I promised, trying to keep the sudden anxiety from my voice.

"Good. Thank you."

The call ended, and I stood in the middle of my bedroom, phone clutched to my chest like a talisman. Tomorrow at sunrise. Our spot. Just the two of us.

———

That night, for the first time, I let myself truly grieve. Not for the abstract victim of a car crash, but for Jimmy. My brother. The boy who hid his demons behind a blinding smile. I cried until my body ached and the knot of pain I'd carried for so long finally, blessedly, began to loosen.

When my alarm went off at 5:00 AM, I was already awake, watching the sky bleed from black to bruised purple. I dressed in the dark—running clothes, a ghost of that first morning—and slipped out before Chloe, who'd insisted on sleeping on my couch like a bohemian guard dog, could wake up and offer a pep talk I didn't have the strength to hear.

The drive to South Pointe Park was a masterclass in anxiety. Every traffic light seemed to mock me. *We need to talk.* The words echoed in the silent car, a four-word death sentence. The war was over. The mission was complete. What if I was just collateral damage he no longer needed to protect? What if, after all this, he was letting me go? The thought was a shard of ice in my chest.

I parked and walked the familiar path, the air cool and thick with the smell of salt and new beginnings.

And there he was.

Standing at the water's edge, hands shoved in the pockets of his shorts, staring out at the horizon. Xander. For a dizzying second, I saw them both—the haunted ghost boy from my memories and the impossibly real man who had become the center of my universe.

He turned as I approached, a slow smile spreading across his face that was warmer than the sunrise itself.

"You came," he said.

"Did you really think I wouldn't?" My voice was tight, betraying the fear churning in my gut.

He shook his head. "No. But I was afraid you'd think..." He trailed off, gesturing vaguely.

"That you brought me to our spot at sunrise to dump me after we just burned down my father's empire?" I asked, a hint of bitter humor in my tone. "The thought might have crossed my mind."

He winced, and the tension in my shoulders eased a fraction. "Fair. That's on me." He took a step closer, his green eyes serious and searching. "That's not what this is. But I do need to talk. Walk with me?"

We fell into step, the wet sand cool beneath our feet. The silence between us wasn't comfortable; it was heavy with unspoken words, with the weight of our entire future.

"I've been thinking about Jimmy," he said finally, his voice soft. "Really thinking. Not just about the accident, but about him. The pressure he was under to be the perfect son."

"We should have seen it," I whispered, my throat tight. "How did we not see it?"

"Because he didn't want us to," Xander said gently. "He was always protecting everyone. Especially you."

"I don't know anymore. I keep thinking about my father," I said, the words tasting like poison. "About what he said. The real reason my father covered up the suicide."

Xander stopped walking, turning to face me. "Tara..."

"No, I need to say it," I insisted, the awful words tumbling out. "He said he did it to protect me. To save me from a lifetime of... of wondering why I wasn't enough to make Jimmy stay." The last part came out as a broken whisper, the deepest, most secret fear of my life laid bare in the morning light.

Xander's expression hardened, a flash of pure hatred for my father in his eyes. He took my other hand, holding me gently but firmly. "Don't you dare," he said, his voice low and fierce. "Don't you dare let him plant that poison in you. That was a lie. A cruel, calculated lie from a man who wanted to keep you broken so he could control you."

"But what if—"

"No." He cut me off, his gaze intense. "There is no 'what if.' I have proof."

I stared at him, confused. "Proof of what?"

His voice dropped, becoming soft, almost reverent. "I remember now, Tara. His last words. In the car, after the crash... he made me promise something." He took a deep breath, his eyes locked on mine. "He told me to take care of Tara-bean."

The world stopped.

The sound of the waves, the cry of a distant gull, the very air in my lungs—it all just ceased to exist. My mind snagged on the name, a relic from a life I thought was buried forever.

"How..." My voice was a strangled whisper. "How do you know that name?"

"He told me," Xander said gently, watching me, letting me process the impossibility of it.

"No one knew that name," I breathed, the realization hitting me with the force of a physical blow. "Not my parents. Not Chloe. Not you. *Only Jimmy called me that.*"

And there it was. The final, unbreakable truth. This wasn't a memory Xander could have invented or misremembered. It was a secret code between a brother and sister, a name whispered in the dark of his final moments. It was proof that Xander was there, that he held my brother, and that Jimmy's last thoughts on this earth... were of me. Not with anger, not with blame, but with love. A love so strong it transcended death itself.

A sob tore from my chest, a sound of twelve years of pain and misplaced guilt being ripped out by the roots. Tears streamed down my face, but they weren't tears of grief. They were tears of release. My father hadn't been protecting me from the truth; he had been shielding me from the one thing that could have healed me all along.

Xander's arms came around me, pulling me into a fierce, protective embrace, and I buried my face in his chest and let it all go.

When the storm finally passed, I looked up at him, my vision blurry.

"He loved me," I whispered.

"More than anything," Xander confirmed, his voice thick with emotion. But he wasn't the only one."

"What do you mean?"

"I've spent half my life running from the truth. Running from that night. Running from myself. But the one thing I could never outrun was you." His voice grew thick with an emotion that made my heart ache. "I love you, Tara. I think I've loved you since I was a stupid seventeen-year-old kid who didn't know what love was. I loved you when I hated myself for what I thought I'd done. And I loved you even when you were plotting my ruin."

The confession hung in the air, a raw and beautiful thing. The icy knot of fear in my stomach finally melted, replaced by a wave of warmth so profound it stole my breath.

I cut him off the only way I could—by surging forward and pressing my lips to his.

It wasn't a kiss of passion, but of homecoming. It was the pain and misunderstanding and anger melting away under the light of a new day. He responded instantly, his arms wrapping around me, pulling me in until there was no space left between us, as if he could absorb me into himself.

"I love you too," I whispered against his lips, the words a sob of relief. "God, Xander, I never stopped. Even when I hated you, a part of me was still that sixteen-year-old girl who was hopelessly in love with you."

He let out a laugh, a sound of pure, unadulterated joy that echoed across the empty beach. "We're a mess, aren't we?"

"The biggest," I agreed, smiling through my tears. "But we're *our* mess."

We stood there for a long time, just holding each other as the sky turned from gold to brilliant blue.

Epilogue

XANDER

THE MARIACHI BAND cranked up another tune as I scribbled my fifteenth autograph of the night, this one for a kid barely twelve who gazed at me like I'd just walked off Mount fucking Olympus.

"Could you make it out to Sofia?" she asked in careful English, her eyes huge with that hero-worship shit that still throws me off balance, even now.

"Of course, sweetheart." I grabbed the soccer ball she'd shoved at me and found a clean spot. *To Sofia—Chase your dreams with the same fire you showed tonight. Xander McCrae.* "Here you go."

She hugged that ball like it was made of pure gold, bouncing like a pogo stick. "Gracias, Señor McCrae! You're the best player in the world!"

In the world. Jesus, kids really don't bullshit, do they? But her absolute certainty lit something warm in my chest. A month ago, I was persona non grata, suspended and disgraced. Now I'm signing autographs at a quinceañera for the daughter of a guy who runs half the illegal gambling in South Florida.

Fucking bizarre how life works out.

"She's not wrong, you know," Tara whispered next to me, quiet enough for my ears only. She looked knockout gorgeous in that midnight blue dress that clung to every curve I'd traced with my hands, her dark hair pulled up to show off her neck. The same neck I'd kissed that morning when she tried sneaking out for her run.

I looked over, catching that little smile playing at her lips. "About what?"

"Being the best." Her fingers found mine with a gentle squeeze. "You scored Saturday, plus two assists. That's practically a hat trick. And Diego's been telling everyone you're the most unselfish forward he's ever played with."

Diego's name still caught me off guard. Three weeks back, he was my worst enemy on the team. Now we had this weird almost-friendship thing going, forged when I wouldn't let Torres's thugs beat him to death over those gambling debts. Nothing bonds guys like almost dying together.

"Diego's just happy to be breathing," I said, but couldn't hide my pride. What we'd built on the field was magic—his aggressive runs creating space for my technical play, my passes finding him perfectly positioned to score. We topped the league in goals, and better yet, we kept winning.

Another pack of teenagers approached, and I slipped back into the photo-and-autograph routine. The quinceañera was exactly as over-the-top as expected—Coral Gables Country Club, enough flowers to fill a botanical garden, and a seven-tier cake. Vicente Torres had gone all out for his princess.

Weird as hell being here. But a promise is a promise, and this particular one saved Diego's life. Plus, Isabella Torres was actually pretty cool, more interested in talking about her soccer team than begging for selfies.

"Mr. McCrae!" The birthday girl herself popped up beside me, rocking a pink gown straight out of Disney. "My dad wants to introduce you to some of his business associates. They're really big fans."

I shot Tara a look, and she raised an eyebrow. Vicente's "business associates" were definitely other criminals, but they were keeping their word about treating this as a legit family celebration. No shop talk, no threats, just a dad showing off to his daughter's party.

"Lead the way, birthday girl."

The guys Vicente introduced as his "business associates" looked like they'd walked straight out of central casting—thick necks, silk suits, and handshakes that were a quiet test of nerve. But they were die-hard soccer fans, and the conversation quickly turned to strategy, formations, and the Miami Pirates' real shot at the championship.

"Good thing we didn't have to *make-an-example* out of that Mano kid," a guy named Tony said with a wry grin, gesturing with his cigar. "The chemistry you two got on the field is somethin' else. We'd have been robbing ourselves."

"Tell me about it," another one chimed in. "My bookie's crying every time you guys step on the field. That pass you fed him last week? Beautiful."

"Diego makes it easy," I said honestly. "He's got an instinct for finding space. My job is just getting him the ball where he can use it."

"You look good," Tony observed, his gaze shifting to where

Tara was laughing with Isabella and her friends. "Happy to see it, after all that mess with your old boss."

He meant Hank, of course. "That's all behind us."

"Good riddance," the other guy grunted. "A man who'd use his own kid's suicide like that... there's no honor in it. It's one thing to ruin your enemy. But to do that to your own daughter? To steal her grief so you can use it as a weapon? That's a whole other kind of sickness."

No honor. Coming from them, the words landed with a different kind of weight. They weren't wrong. What Hank did —the manipulation, the lies—wasn't just about revenge. It was about a complete perversion of family, a sickness that rotted everything it touched. He hadn't just let Tara believe a lie; he had actively prevented her from mourning her brother, keeping her trapped in a cage of rage he had built just for her.

The Feds were still picking through the bones of his empire. His lawyers were angling for a deal—probation, forfeitures, a slap on the wrist that would still cost him everything that mattered. He'd dodge a cell, but he'd lose the team, his reputation, and his daughter.

"Mr. McCrae!" Isabella bounced back over, tiara slightly crooked from dancing. "Will you take a picture with the whole family? Please?"

I spent the next twenty minutes in what felt like hundreds of photos—with Isabella, her parents, every cousin and aunt and family friend who'd made the trip. The photographer, a nervous little dude constantly wiping sweat from his forehead, directed us through pose after pose until my face hurt from smiling.

It was totally worth it though, seeing Isabella's joy, watching her glow with pride at having her hero at her party.

At fifteen, she was just figuring out who she wanted to be, and if my presence helped her believe dreams come true, I'd smile until my face fell off.

"You're really good at this," Tara said when we finally escaped the photo marathon. We found a quiet corner by the dessert table, temporarily free from autograph hunters.

"At what?"

"Being someone's hero." She straightened my tie, her fingers lingering against my chest. "You've got this natural way with kids. Like you actually remember what it felt like to be their age."

I did remember, more clearly than I sometimes wanted. That desperate hunger for approval, how one word from someone you admired could make or break your entire week. I'd been lucky to have coaches who understood that power, who built kids up instead of tearing them down.

"Speaking of kids," I nodded toward the dance floor where Leo was teaching Isabella's younger cousins some complicated line dance. "How's our boy doing?"

Tara laughed, the sound cutting through the mariachi music. "He's been flirting with that server for an hour. The one with the dimples who keeps finding excuses to refill his wine glass."

I spotted Leo getting very attentive service from a young guy who looked like a romance novel cover model. Good for him. About time he found someone who appreciated what a catch he was.

"Think he'll ask for the guy's number?" I asked.

"Already did, he told me. They're going to brunch tomorrow."

"Fast worker."

"I think he's making up for lost time."

Before I could ask what she meant, a cymbal crash announced the cake's arrival, all seven tiers wheeled in on a cart requiring three people to maneuver. Isabella squealed with delight as the crowd pressed closer, Vicente grabbing the microphone for a toast.

"My beautiful daughter," he began, voice thick with emotion, "fifteen years ago, you made me the luckiest man in the world. Tonight, you become a woman, and I couldn't be prouder of the person you're becoming."

Tara took my hand, her fingers fitting perfectly between mine. I looked at her, catching her soft smile. We were both thinking of Jimmy, I realized. All the celebrations he missed. But also everything we'd survived.

Here we stood, together, having weathered the worst. That counted for something.

The cake cutting turned into organized chaos as two hundred guests lined up for their slice of tres leches with raspberry filling. I got cornered by Isabella's school friends, all wanting to know if I was dating anyone and whether they were too young for pro soccer tryouts.

"Focus on your grades first," I told them, falling back on the same advice every adult gave me at their age. "Soccer will always be there, but you can't get your education back once you've missed it."

"But you left school to play professionally," pointed out a girl with braces and enough confidence to suggest she'd be trouble soon.

"I did," I admitted. "And I got lucky. For every player who makes it, thousands don't. Having a backup plan isn't giving up—it's being smart about your dreams."

"Mr. McCrae!" Isabella appeared again, dragging a boy her

age. "This is Miguel, my boyfriend. He plays forward just like you."

Miguel looked ready to die from embarrassment, but managed a strangled, "Nice to meet you, sir. I'm your biggest fan."

"Nice to meet you," I said, shaking his sweaty hand. "So, Miguel, what do you love most about playing forward?"

The question broke the ice, and soon Miguel was explaining his team's formation. These kids knew the game inside out, studied it like scholars.

"You should come watch one of our games," Isabella said. "Miguel scored two goals last week."

"I'd like that," I said, meaning it. "Text Leo your schedule, and we'll see what works."

Miguel's jaw dropped. "You'd really come watch us play?"

"Why not? Good soccer is good soccer, no matter what level."

As they walked away, probably telling every friend about talking with a pro player, I felt something click into place. This was what mattered—not trophies or headlines or money, but how the game connected people, built communities, gave kids something to dream about.

"You're going to have to actually show up now," Tara said, appearing with two champagne glasses. "You know that, right?"

"I know. And I will." I took the champagne gratefully. "Might be good for me. Keep things in perspective."

"You don't need help with perspective anymore." She clinked her glass against mine. "You've got that figured out."

Did I? Some days I still felt like I was discovering who I was without the guilt and shame that had defined me for so long. But Tara had a point—something fundamental had changed. The anger that used to eat me alive was gone, replaced by something steadier, more focused. I played the best soccer of my career, but more importantly, I enjoyed it again.

"Ladies and gentlemen!" Vicente's voice boomed over the speakers. "If I could have your attention one more time!"

The crowd quieted, turning toward the stage where Vicente stood with his arm around Isabella. She glowed with happiness, her tiara catching light from the crystal chandeliers.

"I want to thank everyone for celebrating my daughter's quinceañera," Vicente continued. "But special thanks to our guest of honor, Mr. Xander McCrae, who kept his promise even when he had every reason not to."

Applause rippled through the room, and I felt my face heat up. I wasn't used to praise for basic decency, but in Vicente's world, keeping your word probably was rarer than it should be.

"Mr. McCrae showed my family what real character looks like," Vicente said, finding me in the crowd. "And that's a lesson worth more than all the money in the world."

More applause, with whistles and shouts of approval. I raised my glass in acknowledgment, trying not to dwell on the irony. Here I was, praised for character by a man who probably ordered hits for breakfast.

But life was full of contradictions, wasn't it? Vicente was a criminal and a devoted father. Diego had been my enemy before becoming an ally. Hank claimed to love his children while destroying them both.

Maybe what defined a person wasn't their contradictions, but how they resolved them when it mattered.

"And now," Vicente announced, "let's dance!"

The band launched into something with a driving beat that

sent younger guests flooding the dance floor. I watched Isabella spin with her friends, her dress a pink blur as she laughed with pure joy. Fifteen years old with her whole life ahead. I hoped she'd make better choices than I had at that age.

"Want to dance?" Tara asked, already pulling me toward the couples.

"Oh no, I suck at this," I protested, but let her drag me along anyway.

"You're just self-conscious. Don't worry about it."

She was right, as usual. On the field, I could read the game perfectly, anticipate movements, place the ball exactly where needed. But put me on a dance floor, and I turned into a collection of awkward limbs with zero rhythm.

Tara moved like she was born dancing. She guided me through the steps with patient amusement, her body warm against mine as we swayed.

"See?" she said, her breath tickling my ear. "You're not so bad after all."

"I'm stepping on your feet."

"Only occasionally. And I have good insurance."

I laughed despite myself, pulling her closer. This was happiness—not the wild, desperate high I'd chased in clubs, but something more sustainable. The simple pleasure of holding the woman I loved while mariachi played and fairy lights twinkled overhead.

"Penny for your thoughts," Tara said, looking up with those dark eyes that had haunted my dreams for over a decade.

"Just thinking how different everything is now."

"Different how?"

I watched over her shoulder as Leo attempted to dip his

new friend and nearly dropped him. "A month ago, I thought my career was over. Hell, I thought my life was over. Now I'm dancing at a quinceañera with the woman I love, and tomorrow I get to play the sport that made me who I am."

"And?"

"And I'm grateful. For all of it, even the painful parts. If none of that had happened, if your father hadn't brought me here, if we hadn't gone through everything... we might never have found each other again."

Tara went quiet, her fingers tracing patterns on my neck. "You really believe that? That it was all worth it?"

"Don't you?"

She smiled, transforming her face in ways that still knocked the wind out of me. "Yeah. I do. Even the obsession wall."

"*Especially* the obsession wall. That thing was a masterpiece."

"Shut up," she laughed, swatting my shoulder. "I'm never living that down, am I?"

"Not a chance. I'll still tease you about it when we're eighty."

The words slipped out unplanned. *When we're eighty.* Like our future together was inevitable, and as natural as breathing.

Tara's eyes widened slightly, and I panicked, wondering if I'd pushed too far too fast. We'd never discussed long-term, too busy surviving the present to plan for a future that seemed impossible weeks ago.

But then her smile brightened, enough to outshine the chandeliers. "Eighty, huh? That's a long time to perfect your dance moves."

"I'll need every minute of it."

The song ended, shifting to something slower and more

romantic. Around us, couples moved closer, the energy changing from celebration to intimacy. Vicente and his wife swayed near the stage, lost in each other despite the crowd. Twenty years married, according to Isabella, still looking at each other like teenagers in love.

"Want to get some air?" I asked. The ballroom was getting hot, and French doors led to what looked like a terrace.

"Thought you'd never ask."

We slipped away from the dance floor, the thrum of the party fading into a gentle pulse behind us. The terrace was a quiet haven, the air blissfully cool. Below, the golf course stretched out like a dark velvet sea under a canopy of stars.

"It's beautiful out here," Tara murmured, leaning her hips against the stone railing.

"Yeah, it is." My gaze was fixed on her—the way the moonlight caught in her hair, the gentle curve of her smile. My entire world had tilted on its axis and found its new center right here.

"Tara?" My voice was rougher than I intended.

She turned to face me fully, her eyes searching mine. "Xander?"

"I meant what I said in there. About being eighty with you, sitting on some porch complaining about our knees."

A flicker of a smile touched her lips. "Did you?"

"More than I've ever meant anything." I stepped closer, my hands finding her waist. "I know this is crazy. I know it's only been a month. But this... us... it's the only thing that's ever felt completely real."

"Xander," she breathed. "I've loved you since I was sixteen years old. I'll love you when I'm eighty. We'll figure it all out. Together."

I lowered my head and kissed her, a kiss that wasn't about

passion, but about promise. It was soft and slow and tasted of salt and absolution. In the distance, the city lights sparkled, but right here, on this terrace, we had created our own universe. This was our beginning, the first page of a story free from lies, finally written in our own words.

When we broke apart, Tara rested her forehead against mine, eyes closed and breathing uneven.

"So what happens now?" she asked.

"Now we go home," I said. "We wake up tomorrow and go to work and have dinner and watch terrible movies and fight about whose turn it is to do the dishes. We do all the boring, normal things that people in love do."

"That sounds perfect."

"It does, doesn't it?"

We stood there for a while longer, wrapped in each other's arms and the quiet peace of the night. Inside, the party continued without us—Isabella dancing with her friends, Vicente holding court with his associates, Leo charming his new conquest. The world kept spinning, life kept happening, but for this moment, it was just us.

Jimmy's final request had taken twelve years to fulfill, had cost both Tara and me more than we'd ever imagined paying. But being here now, feeling her heart beat against mine, I knew it had been worth every moment of pain.

I'd taken care of Tara-bean, just like I'd promised. And somewhere, I hoped Jimmy knew that we were going to be okay. More than okay.

We were going to be happy.

THE END

Thank you for joining Xander on his intense journey to find love and truth in Miami.

If you're new to the family, go back and discover what happens when Xander's twin brother—Sean McCrae—meets his match in *One Night in Glasgow*.

The Scottish Billionaires Series

Alec & Lumen:
When Alec mistakes a young woman's salon for a "happy ending" massage parlor, things get more complicated than he prefers. Especially when their lives become entwined in ways never imagined.

1. *Off Limits*
2. *Breaking Rules*
3. *Mending Fate*

Eoin & Aline:
After Aline Mercier, a young American teacher, is taken hostage in Iran, Eoin McCrae is tasked with getting her out at all cost. He never imagined falling for her.

1. *Strangers in Love*
2. *Dangers of Love*

Brody & Freedom:
At his distillery, Brody McCrae crafts the finest Scottish

whisky, while Freedom Mercier is finishing her Master's degree with big plans to change the world. When the two of them are brought together at a holiday party, things heat up more than anyone could predict.

1. *Single Malt*

2. *Perfect Blend*

Baylen & Harlee:

After Baylen McFann discovers that his fiancée has left him, he escapes Scotland to find advice from his friend across the pond, Alec McCrae. As Alec presents his newest statistical analyst, Harlee Sumpter, Baylen's already smitten.

Business or Pleasure

Drake & Maggie:

When Drake Mac Gilleain lays eyes on Maggie McCrae, he believes he's seeing the ghost of his late wife and decides to follow her.

At First Sight

Carson & Vix:

When Carson McCrae, the hottest designer in Manhattan, asked me to model a new bra in a fashion show, I knew it was a line. I'm anything but a runway model. I got more curves than Kim Kardashian.

It was definitely a line. So why did I say yes?

A Dress for Curves

Spencer & London

Spencer York, a dashing and distinguished British theater producer, arrives in Manhattan with the exciting prospects of bringing his production to Broadway's illustrious stages.

Destiny steers him to a cozy, intimate pub where he encounters London McCrae, a fiery and ambitious actress with dreams of conquering Broadway's greatest stages.

A Play for Love

Blaze & Trisha

Airport closed and stranded by a Christmas storm, Blaze and Trisha embark on a cross-country road trip from Chicago to San Francisco, discovering laughter, chemistry, and challenges that test their pact to remain just travel buddies.

Mistletoe Detour

Cory & Rylee

Cory McCrae, a charming hunk yet socially awkward finance guru, clashes with Rylee Palmer, a brilliant rival, sparking an intense, steamy romance amid a fierce rivalry and a scandal that threatens their passionate connection.

Rival Desires

Fury & Sienna

When a rugged billionaire meets a fierce talent coordinator, sparks fly and secrets unravel. As passion ignites, they're thrust into a dangerous game of love and survival. Can Fury and Sienna overcome their pasts to forge a sizzling future together?

A Dance with Obsession

Sean & Beth

A rebellious Scottish heiress, desperate to escape her family's gilded cage, finds an unexpected connection in a one-night stand with a charismatic American motivational speaker. But when their passion explodes into a scandal, she's thrust into a web of manipulation designed to break her. Can she shatter the chains of her past and forge her own destiny, or will the life she's fighting so hard to escape claim her for good?

One Night in Glasgow

Printed in Dunstable, United Kingdom

78900274R00211